C.M. Taylor grew up in Yorkshire and Suffolk, and has lived in India, Belgium and Spain. He now makes his home in Oxford with his wife and daughter.

PREMIERSHIP PSYCHO

C.M. Taylor

corsair

Constable & Robinson Ltd
3 The Lanchesters
162 Fulham Palace Road
London W6 9ER
www.constablerobinson.com

First published in the UK by Corsair,
an imprint of Constable & Robinson Ltd., 2011

A copy of the British Library Cataloguing in
Publication data is available from the British Library

ISBN: 978-1-84901-594-3

Printed and bound in the EU

3 5 7 9 10 8 6 4 2

To Our Lad, the Maldini of Cambourne.
And to Mum and Dad, for whom every day is Wednesday.

Part One

landmark translucent atrium

'The paps just red-handed me muffing out the Captain's wife in the Bentley.'

'Fuck. Kev. What? Calm down. From the beginning.'

It seemed pretty clear to me: paparazzi; forbidden quim; twelve-cylinder Bentley Continental GT with twin elliptical exhausts. I pull my triband Nokia 8800 Arte away from my ear and stare at it. Did this tit, my agent, not understand the Queen's?

I'm shouting now. 'The Captain's wife. The red-tops just snapped me going down on her.'

'Who was it?'

'I forget her name. Jane or something. Some girl's name.'

'No, not the girl. The pap. Who was the pap?'

'I don't know his name. Know his face. *Super Soar-Away* or something. *Mirror*. *News of the Screws*. Seen him around.'

'Where are you?'

'M4.'

'You'd better come over.'

I kill the line and accelerate. The six-speed 2F automatic transmission with Tiptronic override obeys my injured foot and the Bentley noses out towards Berkshire. *Royal* Berkshire.

I notch up the Acura ELS surround sound and flip to Radio 5 Live.

Ex-England manager Terry Venables rejects the Newcastle job. Verbal pugilist Joe Kinnear instead the surprise appointment.

Reports of Gazza's death untrue.

Merseyside derby. Steven Gerrard on ninety-nine Liverpool goals.

The multi-link air suspension sits me on a cushion. Of. Air.

Fucking foot, should be playing today, owning the 08-09 season. Should be scoring. But this foot, this dirty foot's keeping me out. I am the fucking daddy. I can play all over the park.

Off the M4 towards Maidenhead, then nail the A4130 towards Henley. Excellent local amenities. Exceptionally secluded plots.

Buzz down the window and ring the intercom. Gated residence. Ironwork swings open and the Bentley crunches the gravel. Substantial detached home, finished to exemplary standards. Stone embellishments. Six bedrooms. Five receptions. Show-home condition.

The door opens and Colly steps out and walks towards the car. He's wearing an Allesandro Dell'Acqua single-button casual jacket with checked Etro trousers and a Tim Hamilton gingham shirt. He's got taste, Colly, and he's doing very well, as this gaff attests, although handsomeness-wise, he's not a patch on me, due to his weirdly large head and the sort of clumpy, shanky hands that you might find hulking from a butcher's sleeves. Still, agenting-wise, Colly's got some of the Prem's top boys under his wing. Not that he has a wing.

I step out and dink the Bentley locked.

'Was it worth it, Kev?'

'What?'

'Was *she* worth it?'

'The skirt? Don't know yet. Depends if I get away with it. And that depends on you.'

Colly looks a bit wired. Could be the situation. Or it could be the bugle he's no doubt been hammering all morning. Because he does like the high life, the boy. Has done all the time I've been with him; all the seven years he's been looking after me. First player to sign with him, I was, and even now, when he's got more than a few internationals on his roster, we're still close, me and Colly. Thick as thieves.

'Nice house I bought you, Colly.'

He just laughs. 'Come in.'

We walk into the outstanding split-level reception area and down the marbled hallway to the architect-designed leisure complex. Sauna. Steam room. Gym space. Infinity pool. A nosed-up bimbo's giggling in the hot tub. She looks over. She recognizes me. Course she does. I *am* Kevin King…The Enforcer.

The likes of your Gerrards, your Lampards, your Kevin Kings… *The likes of your Kevin Kings.*

'Give us a minute,' Colly tells the girl and she scowls but stands and bikinis out towards the hallway.

You would. I probably will.

'Take a seat, Kev.'

Colly gestures towards the Tropitone Cabana Club modular stainless-steel armchairs and we walk over and sit down, facing each other.

'You really don't know who the pap was?'

I shrug.

'Describe him, Kev.'

'Twat with a camera.'

'C'mon, make an effort.'

'Don't know his name, do I? Told you that.'

'Look, Kev. If these snaps get splashed, you'll have to leave. The transfer window's closed. Where will you go? You can't fuck around with the Captain's holster and expect to stay at the club.'

'*I* should be the fucking Captain.'

'That's not the point, Kev. Look, describe this pap to me. Maybe we can work out who it is, get the pictures off him. Anyway, you sure he got the photos? You've got tinted windows.'

.M. TAYLOR

'Colly, I'm sure. I looked up from between her legs and saw a fucking lens.'

'You had the window open?'

'We were dogging.'

'How did he know you were there, Kev?'

'Maybe he's a dogger. Maybe he followed me from Nan's... Give a shit. He's got the snaps.'

'What did he look like?'

'Tall. Dark hair. Scruffy cunt.'

'Sounds like Taff. Was it Taffy?'

'You deaf?'

'I'm gonna call Taff, see if he knows anything.'

Colly pulls out his T-Mobile G-1 Android phone and pisses about with his menus. He finds Taff's number, calls it, and flips the phone on to speaker, holding it out so I can hear. The ringing stops and a voice climbs out from the Android.

'Colly. Thought I might hear from you.'

'It *was* you then.'

'Was me what?'

'You know, Taff. Anyway, can I buy you lunch?'

'Yeah, Colly, you can buy me lunch. The Fat Duck?'

'Cheeky cunt. That's two hundred quid a throw.'

'Thought you might want to treat me, in the circumstances.'

'All right, Taffy. See you in an hour?'

'Fine.'

'And Taffy, don't forget your camera.'

'And Colly, don't forget your chequebook.'

Colly thumbs the call closed and we look at each other.

'Wanker,' we both say.

'Can you really get a table at the Duck?' I ask Colly.

'No problem. Know Heston.'

He *knows* Heston Blumenthal. TV chef. Three Michelin stars. Colly knows him, the flash bastard. Wouldn't have done, a while back, no way. But now Colly's virtually a sleb in his own right. They get him on sport radio, now and again, to give his opinion.

6

Been on the goggle, also. Talking head. State of the game. That kind of shit. Building an empire, Colly is. Like the Romans. Except without the viaducts. Presumably.

Colly's already speed-dialling the Duck. He don't hang about.

'Hi. Table for today…Yeah, yeah, I know. You're full. As always. Tell Heston it's Colly, right. He'll find me a spot.'

Cocky fucker. There's a wait and Colly leans down and rubs a mark from his black Cesare Paciotti shoes. I listen to the hum of the infinity pool and then the phone monkey must be back on because Colly says, 'Good. Thought so. One hour. Table for two.'

The call ends and Colly tosses the G-1 Android phone on to the low Tropitone modular table.

'Table for *two*, Colly?'

'Yeah. Me, one. Taff, two.'

'And what about me?'

'You come, Kev, and your mouth'll double the cost of the pictures.'

'It'll be worth it.'

'Last year, the year before, Kev, when you were on proper Premiership cash, maybe it'd be worth it to you. But not on Championship wages.'

Championship wages. Listen to him, the wanker. I may be on Champs cash now, but I know – and every fucker who's seen me knows, every fucker who really understands the game, that is – that I'm Prem quality.

Made for the Premiership, I am. Made *of* it, almost. If you like. Yet now I am exiled, adrift in the Bermuda Triangle of the lower leagues. But one day I will return triumphant, passing adored once more through the gates of the Prem, riding an enormous footballing horse, or somesuch. And when I do return, I will win everything. I simply will.

I, Kev King, will merely amass silverware. That is a given. It is my goal, my driving ambition. Though I do have other goals, such as upholding consumer rights, which is crucial. And getting my nuts in, clearly. Obviously.

'Look, go home, Kev. I'll call you when it's a done deal with Taffy. Go back to the flat. Watch some games. Put that knacked foot up and relax. I'll get you out of this.'

Colly stands and walks out from the leisure complex and I follow. His Paciottis squeak across the hallway's marble and he bellows, 'Off out,' up the stairs, then we head through the door.

I slide into my four-seater coupé and watch the nearest door of Colly's quadruple garage hum open. He emerges in a 4.2 litre super-charged V8 Jaguar XKR-S. Not a bad little motor. But if Colly had done a proper spec reccy he'd have seen that his 420 bhp is dwarfed by the Bentley's 552.

I watch Colly back out, spin round and turn left out of his drive and I nestle within the Bents for a while, musing on returning inside and bopping his playmate. But I don't. Not the right time. I turn the coupé over then hang right out of the drive, heading back to the flat.

There's some countryside or something and then I hit the outskirts of town. Not London. The gaffer won't let me live in the proper city. Part of the deal when I signed with this tinpot and recently relegated club was that I had to live near the stadium, near the training ground. Could have taken a spanking, out-of-town exec ranch like Colly, but I've been nailed drink driving too many times to risk the ride home from the town's bars. So I took a flat in town.

Sophisticated living in a secure location. Concierge and lifestyle management services. Enviable and privileged settings.

The coupé dips into the underground parking and snugs into my parking spot, 'King. Penthouse', painted on the concrete in its centre. Up to the flat. Superb specifications. Generous living space. Elegant and stunning.

I toss the car keys and hunt the remote and the BeoVision 7 forty-inch LCD TV with tilt and turn functionality hums alive. I twist the Venetians open and the BeoVision's VisionClear technology adjusts to the new light levels, altering the screen's abundant light output and contrast levels.

I press play on the built-in DVD and last night's porn churns through the advanced digital surround sound processors and climbs from the speech-optimized optional BeoLab 7-4 vertical central speaker with acoustic lens technology. A variety of women are displayed in frame-by-frame dynamic contrast. From a variety of positions they climb variously to a variety of climaxes and I relax. I scan to 5 Live on the Nokia 8800.

Merseyside derby. Early kick-off.

Liverpool two up. Torres double.

Fucking Torres. He's nothing. A nothing player. Like to see him dazzle once I've been through the back of him, raked my studs down his fucking calves.

I flip to the Championship scores. My muppets aren't playing yet.

Three o'clock kick-off. Half an hour to go.

I sit down and do some porn then I call Colly to see how he's doing with the pap but he doesn't take me. The afternoon stretches out like a fucker in front of me. Pop over and see Nan?

No, not yet. I've got a test to do.

In the bathroom I take out an eyeliner pencil and look at myself in the mirror. I draw a black line from the centre of the bottom of my nose downwards to touch my top lip, then I pick that line up underneath my bottom lip and continue it down, over my chin, then under it and down over my Adam's apple.

I have split my face in two halves. It is a face of two halves.

I take out my scientifically formulated Elemis ice-cool foaming shave gel and lather up. Having applied the software of shaving, I reach for the hardware.

From the bathroom cabinet I take out the King of Shaves Azor hybrid synergy system razor and place it on the left-hand side of the sink. Then from the same cabinet, I take out a Wilkinson Sword Quattro Titanium Precision razor, placing it on the right-hand side of the sink.

I begin with the Azor, weighing its ecoptimized body in my palm. I peer at the product, enjoying the tuning-fork-shaped polypropylene twin-shot blade holder. I place the Endurium-coated blade to my skin, high up on my cheek, and move the razor slowly down towards my jaw.

The touch skin technology snugs pleasantly to my face. The product handles well. The lo-fi aesthetic of the razor's componentry synergizes with the Endurium glide of the blade, and as I remove the scrub from my chin, I muse that the razor combines the unfussiness of the disposable with the high-end technique of the multi-use.

The King of Shaves Azor, I feel sure, will establish itself in a difficult market, dominated, at this particular moment in consumer history, by the Gillette/Wilkinson duopoly.

The Azor has pleased me. But let's see how it goes head-to-head with the Quattro's quadruple titanium-coated blades. Again, I start from high up on my cheek and move down towards my jaw. The aloe vera, vitamin E and Pro B5-impregnated lubricating strip offers a glide, which, in the opinion of this consumer, is at least equal to that of the Azor's touch skin technology. The skin comfort, if anything, is marginally better.

The single, AAA battery, enclosed in the body of the Quattro, offers a surprisingly powerful motor for the multi-length trim functionality, and the pulse it gives seems – from memory at least – distinctly less vicious than that of the Mach 3 Turbo.

I rinse the Quattro under the tap and feel no anxiety about the battery coming into contact with water. Wilkinson have long been known for the quality of their product seals.

I flip the Quattro and guide the back-mounted edging blade towards the smaller hairs in the difficult-to-reach area beneath my nose. I come away pleased with the well-positioned nimbleness of the edging system. I undo my fly and withdraw my almost-full erection, resting it on the curved front ledge of the sink.

The low friction technology of the Quattro Titanium Precision has moved me, and that, combined with compact motor, edging

blade and multiple trim levels, puts it perhaps even slightly ahead
of the elegant and dextrous Azor.

I lean forward and wash the remnants of the Elemis ice-cool
foaming shave gel from my face, then curl my finger and glide it
down each of my cheeks.

Nice. And. Smooth.

The Azor? The Quattro? It's very close.

I have some real thinking to do. I pull an Elemis recovery mask
from the bathroom cabinet and apply. Which is it to be?

The differences are minute at this level.

A single mistake can turn a game.

I lift the Azor and it rinses easily beneath the running tap.
Good. But as I lift the Quattro, I spy a darkness pinned beneath
the blades, which on closer inspection reveals itself as a residue
of facial hair. The tap water struggles to run behind the closely
packed blade head and some tenacious beard clog holds on.

The Azor edges by the Quattro.

The King of Shaves brand has a future, providing it continues
to innovate its product design while keeping it tight at the back.

The Azor's qualified for the next round. Quattro's limped out
on pens.

I wash the recovery mask from my face and slip into a Tisseron
après bath robe and leave the bathroom. In the split-level leisure
area, the porn's still porning. I call Colly but he does not take
me.

A text comes in from my Wag in Dubai, but I do not reply.

The Nokia tells me that the three o'clocks have kicked off.

Should be out there.

Box-to-box player. Terrific engine.

Technique. Power. Pace. The full package.

I walk over to the penthouse's window and look down across
the river towards the award-winning retail and leisure complex
on the far side of the water. I peer out to the retro-modern
storefronts, the granite, stadium-style external seating, the
landmark translucent atrium.

It's not a bad place. For the sticks, that is. A reasonable combination of big-name retailers, and a higher end of merchandise mix than you might expect: Hobbs, H&M, French Connection.

It's all right. Don't get me wrong. Vital consumer needs are addressed.

But it's not boutique. It's not *me*.

I am Premiership quality and this retail and leisure complex is Championship. I mean, they've got a Zara in there. They've got a fucking *Burtons*.

I'm better than this place. I want truly high end. But right now I'm stuck. Frozen within the lower leagues.

Radio 5 Live tells me we're already one down.

Missing that bit of quality in the centre of the park.

boutique atmosphere

I'm dressed in a light blue Viktor and Rolf two-button suit with a white sleeveless Raf Simons dress shirt and a pair of brown velvet Dirk Bikkembergs shoes. I'm listening to Kid Rock on the Acura ELS surround sound. I am fucking brilliant.

The Bentley's gliding down Charing Cross Road, the street lights striping the hefty bonnet. Civilians make their way into theatres: *Blood Brothers* at the Phoenix, some Monty Python student shit at the Palace. Outside the Ambassadors, there's a poster of some pov cunt smashing bin lids together.

Stomp or something.

Tramp, more like.

I turn right into Shaftsbury Avenue.

Les Mis. Rain Man. Eddie Izzard. *Grease.*

Queues of punters snake in through the doors, but queues are for jumping, that's what the civilians don't know, that's what all these zone four fuckwits haven't figured.

But that's what you learn in the Prem, day one, that the point of a queue is not so that civvies can file in, in some kind of orderly-fucking-manner. No, the point of a queue is for the muppets in it to see you jump it.

Shafts Ave becomes Piccadilly and I still the Bents outside the Athenaeum. Some door monkey dressed in a camelish rag eyes the tinteds. He waits for movement, waits for

13

someone to step out. But I don't.

I watch the door monkey. He flicks his head towards the car, showing me I should drive on. But I don't, I watch him through the glass. I can see him. He can't see me. I'm better than him. I am much. Much. Better. Than. Him.

The door monkey steps over and rat-a-tats the Bents.

Twat. He waits for an answer, but there is none.

He taps the window again, and I wait again.

I move over into the passenger seat and wait until he's about to tap a third time, then I dink the Bents open and shove the door out, so that its window smacks his approaching hand.

He steps back, looking at his fingers. As though looking at the fuckers will stop them stinging. I'm out on the pavement. 'Park this. Luggage in the boot. Bring it in.'

His mouth flaps open. And because he has a beard with full tache, his lips are all muffishly framed with hair, so I think of the Captain's wife again, and about Colly's meeting with Taff. Still haven't heard from him. Fifteen per cent he makes. Fifteens for what?

The doorman still stands there, mingey mouth still open. 'Do you have a room booked, sir?' he manages to say.

'What do you think?'

'I don't know, sir. I presume so.'

'Rightio then.'

'Very good, sir.'

I step inside. Sumptuous decor. Stylish renovation. Discreet glamour.

Travel and Leisure magazine-listed top 500 world hotel.

I approach the desk and all that.

The, 'Hello, sir,' happens.

The receptionist is fit. She processes quick and well. You would.

I take the stairs. I enter the room.

Hypnos bed. Egyptian cotton. English elegance combined with twenty-first century technology. My luggage arrives. The twat that brings it in smells of fags.

'Cancer, cancer, cancer,' I chant under my breath as he puts the bag down.

'What was that, sir?'

'Nothing.'

Then, 'Cancer, cancer, cancer,' I continue as he stands there waiting for the tip that doesn't come. He leaves.

I sprawl on the Hypnos and do some goggle then I go to the bathroom and have a good look in the mirror. I look the absolute fucking shit.

The Wag texts and I do not reply. I call Colly and he does not answer. It's a kind of doze I take and then I'm downstairs in the lobby. I hand in the key.

'Call me a cab.' And because she's fit I add, 'Please.'

She peers forward through the street doors to see a cab dropping off at the kerb. 'Hold that,' she bellows to the door monkey and then, 'Have a good night, sir,' she says.

I will. Obviously. The likes of your Kevin Kings.

Through the door to the street then into the cab. Which is clean. This knowledger must have vac'd it recently. Good. Kev'll tip him for that.

'Where to?'

'St Martin's Lane.'

He looks a bit disappointed, a bit, 'That's only round the corner, hardly worth my while, is it?' But in fairness, he bites his tongue and just pops the cab into gear, then swings it round and we move back up the Dilly.

I look at the back of the cabbie's bald head. He's a young lad to be looking as chemo'd up as that. But he's all right. I'm trying to work out what zone he's from. One and two will be out of his league, far too pricey. Even zone three will be a stretch for this boy. The cab's all tidy and clean and for some reason that makes me think he's from the 'burbs. Zone five maybe, maybe even further. Sunbury or something. Barely even London. Virtually the Midlands.

He's all right, though. The cab doesn't reek of takeaways.

There's one of those perfume trees hanging from the rear-view and, as I say, it's freshly vac'd.

He eyes me in the mirror. 'Whereabouts on the Lane?'

'Bungalow Eight.'

'Right you are.'

Right down St James's Street, then down Pall Mall and all that shit.

Baldy eyes me in the rear-view again. 'Don't I know you, mate? I recognize you from somewhere.'

'Yeah, you probably do recognize me.'

'Right. You been on that *Big Brother* or something?'

Fucker. No. *No*. I'm an athlete. A fucking fucking athlete.

'No.'

'Must be from somewhere else then. Were you in the 'Lympics? Cyclist or something? Rowing?'

'No.'

'Right.'

We pull up on St Martin's and I note the knowledger and step outside. Then, before I walk off, I turn back towards the cab and tap his window. He winds it down and peers out, his eyebrows raised in question.

'Football. I'm a footballer.'

I pull another note out and flight it in through the window.

'Kevin King. Remember the name. Have a good night.'

He may reply but I do not hear because I am already Keving forward towards the Bungalow. Civilians line up to the right, but there, left side of the velvet rope, there's a bunch of jumpers. Proper jumpers.

Actor Rhys Ifans. Designer Jade Jagger. TV's Calum Best.

The door brute unhooks the velvet and the slebs sleb in.

Boutique atmosphere. BoConcept furniture.

Model Sophie Dahl. TV's David Furnish.

Specialized services. Reliable discretion.

The zone fourers eye me as I make towards the rope and the door brute eyes me too. He's fucking massive. An old-fashioned centre half. On 'roids though, you can see that. He's juiced himself right up.

'Sir?' he says, but pronounces it so that what he actually means is, 'Twat.'

'Evening.'

He looks at me. He can sense the quality of the schmutter and he knows I'm an HNWI. But he can't place me. He's waiting for me to offer him my credentials. I pause, I'll let him work it out.

'Sir?' he says again.

I smile at him. He's bound to clock soon. Kevin King, see. Kev King.

'Members only,' he says.

I smile again.

'You don't recognize me?'

'Should I?'

'You like the football?'

'Yeah, I like the football. Millwall through and through.'

'Right. You like the football and you don't recognize me?'

'That's right. You fucking Pelé or something?'

'Not quite.' I pause. 'I'm Kev King.'

He breaks out laughing. 'Kev King. You missed that sitter last season against ManU.'

Anger anger anger inside me.

'Your lot went down,' the bouncer adds.

Anger is now fury. Exclusive nightspot. Exclusive nightspot.

'You going to let me in?'

'No, Kev King, I am not going to let you in. Last year maybe, when you were top flight. Not tonight though. Not this season. Fuck off down to Stringfellows or something, you Championship tosser.'

I look over to the queue on my right. The civvies are laughing. They are laughing at me, at the likes of your Kevin Kings.

Fucking civvy fuckers. Zone eighteen wankers.

Toilets. Fucking toilets. Each and every one is a fucking toilet.

I look at the door brute and he raises his eyebrows in, 'You

want to try something on then, pal?' And I don't, not with him
being all Millwall and juiced up. Not my way. Not like this.

'What's your name?' I ask him.

'You gonna tell my mum?'

'What's your name?' I ask again.

He ignores me and turns his attention to the queue. 'You two.
Ladies. Come here. Come in.' Then he turns to me, 'Fuck off
back to your Barratt mansion, King.'

I look at him one more time and I will always remember his
face, his big shit head and his big shit hands and his juiced-up
fucking neck. I will always remember him. I turn round and walk
back towards the kerb and my arm jumps up to stop a cab.

Inside and the cabby says, 'Where to, mate?'

And I do not know the answer. I do not know the answer.

'Drive around for a bit.'

Where to? Maya? Tamarai? Detroit? The Kingly Club?

It was not a sitter against ManU.

Tricky angle, defensive pressure. It was not a sitter.

I'm back in the Athenaeum room, lying on the Hypnos,
watching *Match of the Day*. Ex-England strikers Lineker and
Shearer are in the studio. And relaxed defensive curmudgeon
Alan Hansen. These three are the holy trinity of football
presentation, the very blades on football's punditry trident, if you
will. How many goals, how many assists, how many goal-line
clearances between them? Thousands. And thousands. And
thousands. The day's Prem games come on.

The Arsenal go one up against Hull, then blow it. At home.
Unbelievable. Hull went up last year as we went down, and now
they've done the Arse. At home.

Shocked, gutted. Shocked and gutted. No easy games at this
level. The Gunners don't like it up 'em.

Get amongst them.

Let them know you're there.

Win all the 50/50s, all the second balls.

Against Bolton, ManU get their usual dodgy pen, which Ronaldo slots, then Rooney doubles the lead. I played against these two last season. Same grass, same park. Me and them. Now I'm like all the other monkeys, watching them on the goggle. I am so far away from where I want to be. I am a refugee from the Prem. Turned away from the Bungalow. Got turned away from the Bungalow. Like I'm some retard civvy on twenty grand a year. And that hurts. I mean, I may be much better than everyone, but I am still human. Cut me and I bleed. Actual blood. The next game.

Merseyside derby. Torres double.

Everton look shit. I'm better than every man in that blue shirt.

Disgrace. Fucking disgrace. How must the Everton consumers feel?

The 8800 trills. Colly.

''Bout time, Colly. You been earning your fifteens?'

'Did you see Torres, Kev? What a player.'

'He's all right. Anyway, talk to me.'

'Got the snaps.'

'Good. Nice. How much?'

'Twenty thousand, I'm afraid, Kev.'

'Twenty thousand? *Twenty?*'

'Yeah, I know.'

'That's fucking disgusting, Colly.'

'I know, Kev, I know. What the *fuck* is Lineker wearing?'

'*Twenty* thousand? Is that *all?*'

Rooney would have been triple that. Quads even. Even some lame twat like Jenas would have been more than that. Twenty thousand. Fucking peanuts. Is that really all I'm worth?

'Jesus, Kev, Shearer is such a dull fucker. Hard, though.'

Colly could have paid more. He *should* have paid more...And what if it gets out? What if people find out that Colly only paid the twenty? What if the tabs find out?

Fear, fear, fear moves through me as a voice whispers somewhere near the back of Kev's mind: maybe I am kidding myself, maybe I *am* only worth the twenties. Maybe I've found my level in the Champs...

But no. Not true. Can't have it. Stay positive, stay sharp, Kev.

'You there, Kev? You seen Hansen's tan? Mr fucking Tango or what?'

'I've got to go, Colly.'

I climb off the bed and slip the Bikkembergs and the Viktor and Rolf back on, then I fling the rest of my shit into a bag and go downstairs, pay the bill, and they bring up the Bentley.

I drive to Nan's and let myself in, tiptoe upstairs and climb into bed in her spare room.

I need the Prem. I am bereft.

snakewood front splice

Sunday.

Gravesy's Aston DBS is already there, parked right next to Boves' Audi Q7 V12 TDI. I snug in next to the Aston and dink the Bentley locked, then I step through the front doors, up the stairs and into the club.

Gravesy and Boves are in the corner, on the far table. I walk over.

'Gravesy, you convict.'

'Kev-o. How you doing, mate?'

Gravesy's an Aussie. He does actually put an 'o' on the end of words. I am not making this up. He's a tough blond runt of a man, Gravesy. His eyes seem too close together, like he's trying to look at his own nose, and he's got that tripey skin that all the Aussies have since they decided that the sun's a ball of cancer. Gravesy is wearing a Hublot Big Bang timepiece, Chip & Pepper Tuck jeans with a stone-coloured Morphine Generation Deer Hunter T and woven Cole Haan Air Court.

Always casual for the snooker.

'You really are not the same team without me,' I say.

'Oh yeah, Kev-o. It's all about you.'

'It is.' Then, 'Bonjour, Boves,' I say and nod over to Boves.

'Bonjour, Kev.'

Boves had a stinker yesterday, much worse than Gravesy, but

21

I won't take the piss out of Boves. I can't. He's won the World Cup. Youngest player on the field when France beat Brazil 3–0 in Paris and lifted the actual World Cup. Not the player he was, mind. That's why he's playing for us, that's why he's in this provincial snooker club. But still, the World fucking Cup.

He's wearing 7 for all Mankind Blade jeans, a Drifter Knuckle polo shirt and navy blue Munich Acropol trainers. He's holding a PowerGlide Control cue with a snakewood front splice and eight-point blue veneer inlay. He slides the cue over his bridge and pots the blue.

Florent Bovary is the only Frog I've ever met who likes the snooker. He's also the only black guy I've ever seen on the baize. Excluding, naturally, Rory McLeod, the English cuesman of Jamaican heritage, currently ranked forty-four in the world professional game. And he can play, Boves can. Lost a plumber's annual wage to him last week. Not that I noticed.

'Where's our ginger friend?' I ask, not that I care. 'Where's Tone?'

'On his way.'

'Right. Let's hear it then.'

They know what I mean; which is, let's hear about the game. They (we) got panelled. Some two-bit Champs side cut us a new arsehole.

'Four fucking one, Gravesy? Four fucking one?'

'I got the one, mate,' says Gravesy and nods over to Boves who is lining up a red. The nod says, 'Talk to him', the nod says, 'Defensive weakness', the nod says, 'Beyond his sell-by date'. But I can't grill Boves...World Cup. Actual World Cup in his actual hands, in the very hands that ping the red down into the top left bag.

Boves looks up from the table. 'It was defensive errors that cost us, Kev,' he offers. 'We were not at the correct level.'

Too honest for his own good, that lad. A gent. Some kind of D'Ar-fucking-tagnan.

'I did not play well,' he continues. 'Gravesy had a good

game. We miss you, Kev.'

'Course you do. Course you do. How did Ginge do?'

'Tone-o's got a lot of heart,' Gravesy says.

'And pretty good technique,' adds Boves. 'Which is unusual for an English player.'

Shit. Do I not like that. Heart *and* technique. Sounds like Tone, the cocksure ginger wanksman who's standing in for me during this period of foot fuck, had another good game. Which is a royal bastard, because with the flame-hair in form, reclaiming my rightful berth's going to take longer than hoped.

Boves misses his yellow and Gravesy takes the table.

I walk over to the window and place my cue case on the sill. I open the case and assemble the Paeradon King 3/4 Split with selected ash shaft, hand-spliced ebony butt and sycamore and plum veneers.

Boves glances at the new wand.

'Very nice.'

'Course.'

Ginger Tone walks in. The local hero. He's wearing DKNY Eboy 718 trainers, Jaxx boot-cut Hudson jeans and a vanilla-coloured momimomi circle face T. He's got a Tag Heuer Aquaracer Digiana timepiece and he's carrying a BCE Grand Master 3 cue in bird's-eye maple. For a ginger cunt he's a handsome cunt.

'Boves. Gravesy.'

'Tone,' they both say.

'Kev. How's the foot?'

'Getting there. Enjoy your place while you can, Tone. Gonna have splinters in your arse in a couple of weeks.'

Tone stares straight at me, a goofy, punchable smile on his lips. 'You wish, Kev,' he says. 'What's the score with the snooker?'

'What do you think, mate?' Gravesy asks Tone.

'Boves is fucking you.'

'Yep.'

Gravesy clips a red into the right middle. 'Signed yet, Tone-o?' he asks.

'No. Lawyers and that.'

Tone's been offered a new contract. Improved deal. Excellent recent form. Progression from the academy.

'You going to sign?' presses Gravesy, strolling round the table to line up the brown.

'Maybe. Depends on other offers.'

Other offers. Other fucking offers.

'What other offers, Tone?' I ask.

'This and that.'

This and *twat,* more like.

'Oh yeah, from who? Barça, is it? The fucking Chels or something?'

'Can't really talk about it, Kev. One or two things have come in.'

Tone changes the chat. 'You been re-signed with Nike yet, Boves? They still gonna pay you now you play for a pub team?'

You Can Not Talk To Boves Like That.

You Can Never Talk To Boves Like That.

'You ever lifted the World Cup, Tone?' I ask. 'Ever lifted the Cup in front of a capacity home crowd?'

'Not yet, Kev. Not yet.'

'But you will?' asks Gravesy.

'Probably,' answers Tone, then he inhales a pretend wince as Gravesy pings a red miles wide. Boves approaches the table.

'What we doing later?' asks Tone. 'Bit of the old Wii? Round of the golf?'

Gravesy sits down by the ginger Pelé. 'I'm up for a few holes, Tone-o.'

'You always are, Gravesy, but do you fancy a game of golf?' Tone replies and the two of them five.

'You up for a round, Kev-o?' Gravesy asks.

'Better not. Got to rest this foot. Big sesh with the physio in the morning.'

Boves clips a red into the lower left bag and lines up the pink.

'Always after the pink, eh, Boves?' quips Tone.

Gravesy laughs. Even Boves does a kind of chuckle.

I do not laugh. Tone's taken my place on the park. I look out of the window and see his Mercedes CL63 AMG slotted home next to the Bentley. This time last year he was in a Ford Focus.

The twat was in a Focus.

training ground incident

The gym's empty. The rest of the lads are out on the pitch. I'm
lonely. I'm fuming. But I'm keeping the cardio together on the
Excite 700iE gym bike.

The iPod gives out some Leona Lewis and the Excite's
twelve-inch LCD touch screen with active wellness TV
interface is displaying high-contrast real-time performance
graphics.

Jimbo, the club physio, comes in. He's got a big round head,
like a big sweaty cheese. He walks towards me then leans over
the LCD and eyes the graphics and nods. He says something
which I don't catch.

'What?'

Jimbo tugs a headphone out from my ear and the lead
tumbles down so that Leona's voice lays across my thigh.
She'll be there again, for real, sooner or later. Bound to be.
Girl like that. Boy like me. Bound to happen. One time or
another.

'Cardio's looking good, Kev. How's the foot?'

'Foot's good.'

'You been following the RICE?'

Rest. Ice. Compress. Elevate. Jimbo's mantra.

'Course, Jimbo.'

'Good lad, Kev. Right, let's get you stretching the gastrocnemius and soleus on the trainer.'

I dismount the Excite and walk over to the strength area, snugging into a physiologically correct position thanks to the calf trainer's bio-mechanical design. Jimbo's followed me over. 'Off you go then,' he says.

And off I go. Jimbo watches as I lift and lower. 'Any reaction, Kev?'

'No reaction, Jimbo.'

'Stop a minute.'

I stop and Jimbo reaches down and grips my mid-foot, squeezing lightly to test the troublesome extensor, the muscle that's been giving me all this grief. He unlaces my Nike Air Tiempo Rival Premium iD trainer and pops it off. He grips the foot again and squeezes. 'What about that?'

It twinges but it doesn't hurt.

'Feels fine.'

'Any twinges?'

'No twinges, Jimbo.'

'Well, well, well, Kev. You are the bionic fucking man. Tendonitis seems to have gone. Some recovery. I'll have a word with the gaffer, but I think you might be ready for a bit of light running.'

I'm ready for more than that. I know I am. I'm desperate to get out there. But unusually, weirdly, it's not all about me, because at the end of the day, and even in the morning, Jimbo's got the whistle on this one.

'Keep on with the calves, Kev, I'll go find the boss.'

Cheese-head Jimbo toddles off. I pop the phones back in and Leona is hitting a high note, R&Bing upwards, moving to a climax. I work the calves. You would. I work the calves. I no doubt will. I work the calves.

It's nearly over. The weeks on the sidelines. The weeks of following the humpty on the Sky and the 5 Live instead of being on the fucking park, the weeks with no fucker talking about me. Nearly done.

I'm in stoppage time of my wasted time.

Then Jimbo's back. 'Get your outdoor kit on. Gaffer wants to see you jog round the training pitch.'

I dismount the calf trainer, walk into the changing rooms and slip on the club Umbros, then I jog through the gym and out the door. I can smell the turf. It smells like home. I look out across the training ground, the two full-size pitches, the five-a-side ground, and behind them the leccy pylon and the barbed wire fence. Light drizzle falls on the rows of top, top motors in the car park by the ground's far corner.

All the boys are out. The gaffer's got them set up for an eleven-a-side. A proper game. First team versus reserves. Unusual move, a full-scale match in training, but the 4-1 beating last week has forced his hand.

Match practice. No substitute for that.

I jog out to the white line but I do not cross it. I do not touch it.

Not yet. Can't. Superstitious.

'Right, if the reserves beat you numpties,' the gaffer shouts, 'that's a grand off your wages and into their pockets. If you beat them, I'll let you off with a five hundred fine for your fucking dismal show on Saturday.'

He blows the whistle and the reserves kick off.

It's fair enough. He's a character, the gaffer. Last of his breed. Should be wearing a sheepskin. He sees me and nods and sticks his hand in the air and twirls it, showing me he wants to see me do some laps. As I jog up towards the far goal I look at the shape of the first team.

Gravesy and Benji up front. Then two flat banks of four. Orthodox 4-4-2. With me in the middle of it all, next to the Captain, pulling the strings. Or so it should be. Tone'll be there instead. But I can't see his ginger helmet. The Captain's there, Darren, carrying the water, but no Tone. Not in my place, not even on the park.

Where is the ginger muppet? Late maybe? That'd be nice. A

bollocking and a week's fine. Injured maybe? Even better. Either way, the little thief's not about.

I jog towards the goal and the big new Polish keeper nods at me. Now'd be the time for a bit of banter with the keeper, a dig about the four goals, a gag about his slippery hands. The normal shit. But I don't do that.

Boy's only been here five weeks. Barely a word of the Queen's has passed his lips. He's learning, he's trying, he's all right, I'll give him that. As a bloke. Not as a keeper. He's a shit keeper. And we don't understand a word the other one says. So I just keep nodding at him and he just keeps nodding back.

I jog behind the goal and the wind slaps me round the face.

Boves is in at left back. 'Morning, Boves.'

'Kev. You're jogging. Great news.'

'Thanks, Boves, yeah. Where's Tone?'

'No idea, Kev.'

'The gaffer know where he is?'

'No, Kev. He was asking. The boss is fuming.'

Day's getting better. Great cardio. Gastrocnemius and soleus nice and tidy. Jimbo won over. And now Tone's fucked up. Bingo.

I jog by Boves towards midfield. Captain Darren tidies up a loose ball and slots a decent enough pass through to Gravesy who drills it wide. The gaffer claps.

'Better, Darren. *Better.*'

Darren looks over and sees me jogging. He gives me a wave. He's a functional player, a touch agricultural, but he's reliable. He's not a patch on me in terms of quality, and he shouldn't be wearing that armband while I'm in the squad, but as I say, you know what you're going to get with Darren. Carved out of Yorkshire granite. Apart from his dick, it seems, which perhaps is not as hard as often as it might be. Otherwise, why would his missus be playing away?

I'm level with the halfway line and Gravesy drops back to pick up a short pass and winks at me as he releases the winger and then turns and heads towards the box. Good old Gravesy. Nifty little player. Gutsy too.

I'm jogging round the reserves' half by now, the new boys, the stringy youngsters forcing their way out of the academy, and the old pros beside them, on their way down. The old heads trying to keep the cash coming in, and the young legs trying to break into the first team. There'll be a few tasty challenges today, no doubt.

The ball dribbles through to the reserve keeper and he picks it up and punts it deep up field, deep into the first team's half. I jog round the back of the reserves' goal and then come back round to the halfway line. Done one lap. I look over to the gaffer but he's whining at someone and he doesn't see, so I start a second.

I'm looking over to the car park and I see a car pull in. It's a Mercedes CL63 AMG. It's Ginger Tone. I clap my hands together. I'm going to enjoy this.

Jimbo must have seen Tone pull up too, because the old cheese-head is over to the Merc like a shot, and before Tone turns the engine off, the fat physio's standing at the end of his bonnet, waiting, no doubt, to tear a strip off him.

I'm jogging and I'm watching, not the match, I'm watching the scene between Jimbo and Tone. Jimbo's at the car and Tone must've buzzed down a window because the top of Jimbo's head disappears into the car, in through the passenger window.

After a moment, old cheese-head is standing by the car again, except now he's moving – jogging even, the fat knacker seems to be jogging – towards the training ground. Tone's still in his car.

What's this? What's going on?

Jimbo makes the turf and then stands by the side of the pitch. 'Gaffer,' he shouts, all wheezy and horrible.

'Fuck off, Jimbo, I'm busy,' the gaffer replies, still watching the game.

'Gaffer, Tone's here.'

'Right. Good. About fucking time. Take him indoors. Make

him sweat. Tell him I'm going to hang his ginger balls on my Christmas tree.'

'No, boss,' Jimbo shouts. 'I think you'd better come over.'

The gaffer turns round at this one, takes his eye off the game. 'What?'

'I think you'd better come over.'

'You joking, Jimbo?'

But Jimbo's face says he's not joking, and the gaffer decides to do as the cheese-head asks.

'Right, carry on. No slacking,' bellows the gaffer to the players, then he jogs towards Jimbo, looking an absolute muppet in his tracky bums. I've stopped running now and I stand still by the white line on the far side, looking across the practice match towards the opposite touchline.

The gaffer reaches Jimbo and they have a chat. Then they both walk over to Tone's car, and when they get there, the gaffer, like Jimbo before him, tucks his head inside the open passenger window of the Merc.

This is fucking odd.

Then the gaffer pulls his head out from the CL63 and stands next to Jimbo in the car park. They both stare over at the training ground. Are they looking at me? Am I being para, or are they looking at me?

Then, 'Darren,' the gaffer shouts over towards the pitch. 'Here. Now.'

And the Captain shoots the lads a 'what the?' look then jogs off the park over to Jimbo and the gaffer. Darren has a quick chat with the two of them and then he, too, sticks his head inside Tone's Merc.

What's Ginge got in there? Lovely ickle puppies? Girls Aloud or something?

And then Darren is walking – no, he's jogging, no, actually he's sprinting – away from the Merc back towards the training ground, back towards the lads, and Jimbo and the gaffer are both shouting his name. He's got something white in his hand as he runs, and this is getting weird and the game has sort of stopped. And then Darren is on the field and he sprints straight by some of the lads on the far side and he sprints by some of the lads in the middle and he sprints by the rest of the lads on my side of the park and then he's quite close to me, and it's all weird because even though it's happening quick, even though Darren is approaching at full pelt, it seems all slow-mo'd up, like it is with Hansen, or Townsend maybe, exploring defensive errors on TV, using state-of-the-art technology.

And Darren's face is all ugly and red and there's spit running down his chin and he's still got the white thing – a paper – in his hand and then he's right by me with the white thing – the paper – still in his hand, and he absolutely fucking larrups me on the side of the face and says, 'Cunt,' and I'm dizzy and down and my face is on the grass and there's a football boot – the classic Copa Mundial, still an excellent boot despite a conspicuous lack of recent design innovation – cracking into my ribs and the paper falls down from above me and lands right by my eyes and there she is, a photo of her anyway, of Darren's wife, and me, wearing her thighs as ear muffs in the Bentley, on page one of the fucking red-top.

Kevylingus, that's the headline above the snap. *Kevylingus*.

I'm bleeding on the floor now but I look all right in the snap. I look all right. Looks like I've got good quim technique and the hair looks good and you can tell the shirt's a Cerruti. She looks fit as well, and the Bentley's upholst looks pure quality and it's all right. Taff's double-crossed me, but it's alright, because I'm on page one.

Page fucking one.

Then the Copa Mundial cracks into my jaw and before I black out I hear Gravesy. 'That's enough, Dar-o,' he says. 'That's enough, mate.'

queasy yellow formica

I open my eyes. Well, I open one of them, the other stays shut, bloated from where Darren lumped me. My head hurts, my ribs hurt, my jaw fucking kills.

I reach over and palm the Nokia 8800 Arte from the Calliagris Bridge bedside table. Message from Colly. Message from the Wag. Another from Colly. Four more from the Wag.

The Arte rings. Nan. The only caller I'd take right now.

'Kevin, what have you been doing?'

Nan's a red-top fiend. 'You know what I've been doing, Nan.'

'What does Saskia think about it?'

'Haven't spoken to her.'

'No. Not surprised you haven't.'

'She's called, a few times. But I've been. Well, I'm a bit.'

'I bet you are, Kevin. What you going to do now?'

'Play football.'

'For who?'

'What do you mean, for who?'

'It's all over the radio.'

'What?'

'Oh Kevin, why did you have to?'

'Look, Nan. I've got to go. I'll call you later. I'll come round later.'

'You be careful, Kevin.'

I ease out of the Cattelan Italia Patrick bed and walk to the kitchen, opening the Gorenje Premium Touch fridge freezer and hoiking out some OJ, which I glug.

Don't remember too much about yesterday. The red-top on the floor, coming round in A&E with the old cheese-head and then being driven back here and passing out. I walk to the bathroom and look at my face. I'm claret and blue, like the Villa kit, or the Hammers. My face is like a Hammers' shirt.

I feel like utter shit. Got to make an effort.

I lather with the Elemis, shave with the Azor, and dab on some Pinaud Clubman Vanilla aftershave lotion. I pop on some grey Yigal Azrouel trousers, a white Michael Bastian shirt and a light blue Perry Ellis cardigan, then I slide on my black leather Hogan trainers, sit down in the Gino Lemson Kubos armchair and look at myself in the bevelled, Rocco Verre Sorocco mirror, hung on the far wall.

I look the don.

Apart from the head, from my big purple face, I look the shit.

My Andrew Marc Marshall sports bag's on the floor by the Kubos. Jimbo must've brought it here from the training ground. I rummage through the Marshall and pull out the Bentley keys, then I look out through the Venetians to the landmark translucent atrium of the retail and leisure complex.

I need to get hold of this. I need to go into the club, show my (purple) face, find out what's going on.

I head out of the flat, into the lift, and descend to the underground car park. The Bentley's not there. Of course, it'll still be at the training ground, so I pull out the Arte and speed-dial a cab, walking out of the underground parking to wait for it on the street.

I check my Franck Muller Long Island timepiece. One in the arvo. Training'll be done for the day. I'll go straight to the stadium and try and catch the gaffer in his office.

The cab arrives and I tell the driver where we're heading. He has a look at me in the rear-view. He has another look, then a snigger. 'You're that Kev King.'

'Not now, mate, all right, just not now,' I say and, to his credit, to be fair – with all fairness and credit – the cabby shuts up and just drives. Good lad. I'll note him for that.

And so I do when we pull up outside the ground, with the sweep of the ramshackle North stand in front of us and the plate glass of the club shop blinging in the afternoon sun.

I leave the cab and walk towards the staff entrance, keeping my head down. I push through the outer swing doors and I'm in a corridor, queasy yellow Formica on the floor and battered grey paint on the walls. It's lunch, must be, because there's no one around, nobody sees me, and I walk towards the gaffer's room with his plastic nameplate glued to the door, just below the square window that peers through the cheap, beige wood.

He's in there. I can see him. His back to the door, his back to his desk, looking out the office window, feet up on a low table, phone to his left ear, mug in his right hand.

My Villa head throbs, my eye Hammers away. I am bricking myself. The gaffer puts down the phone and through the door I hear him take a long, dirty slurp of his cuppa.

I knock and he does not turn, but shouts, 'Come.'

I open the door and step inside. 'Gaffer.'

He hears my voice, knows it's me, and he swivels quickly in his crumby chair to face me, a little tea sloshing on to the crotch of his M&S strides.

'Kev,' he says. 'Sit down.'

He sees my bruised head and winces.

I wheel out the chair in front of his desk and sit down on its fuzzed-up fabric.

'So,' the gaffer says. 'So. So. So.'

He looks at the breeze-blocked wall, its bobbly surface daubed a washed-out red. There's a team photo on the wall from four seasons ago, the season we went up to the Prem, the year I took us up to the promised land. Fifteen goals from midfield, twelve assists. Crucial tackles. Goal line clearances. The lot.

He sees me looking at the promotion photo. 'Good year that, Kev. You had a good season.'

'Didn't miss a game, gaffer.'

'No, Kev, you didn't.'

I look at him. He looks at me.

'So,' he says. 'So. So. So.'

He looks at me. I look at him.

'You spoken to Darren, Kev?'

'No.'

'You spoken to Colly?'

'No.'

'The police?'

'No.'

'Your lawyer?'

'No.'

'You've spoken to your nan, though?'

'Yeah. I've spoken to Nan. Look, gaffer…'

But he cuts me off. 'It's no good. If it'd been a fringe player, an academy boy, or one of the lags on their way down, but it wasn't, was it? The Captain's wife, Kev. The Captain's wife. You do not play with the Cappo's wife's fun bags. You do not go down on the Captain's wife.'

'Gaffer, I…'

'Team meeting yesterday, after Jimbo took you to hospital. We spoke about it. The lads are on Darren's side.'

'The lads are on Darren's side?'

'Yeah.'

'Boves is, is he? Gravesy as well?'

'They are.'

'They aren't. They *can't be*, gaffer.'

'Look, if they want to carry on playing for this football club, then they are. The *Captain's wife*, Kev.'

36

'But he's a nothing player.'

'A nothing player, is he? He may not have your class, Kev, he may not have your guile, but he's a grafter. He loves the shirt, Kev, never goes into his shell. The fans love him.'

'You know I'm a better player.'

'Football-wise, you are, Kev. No contest. Temperament-wise, you're not. You've put me in a situation, Kev, and I've had to choose and the lads are all behind me.'

'So what does that mean?'

'You're out.'

'*Out?*'

'Gross misconduct.'

'What?'

I stand up and lean forward over the desk, pointing at my face. 'And what about this?'

'What about it, Kev?'

'Fucking assault. He beat the shit out of me.'

'Look, Kev, we talked about it at the training ground and we all agreed that Darren shouldn't have said those things to you. But it was you that swung for him, Kev, and it was you that tripped and landed on a bollard.'

'I landed on a bollard?'

'You landed on a bollard.'

'I landed on a bollard?'

'Yes, Kev, you landed, face first, on a training bollard.'

'And everyone saw that, did they, gaffer?'

'Everyone saw that, yeah.'

'Gravesy saw me fall on to a bollard and smash my eye and jaw and ribs in, did he?'

'He did, Kev.'

'And Boves saw it?'

'Boves saw the unlucky tumble on to the training bollard, yes.'

'You are a cunt, gaffer.'

'Now now, Kevylingus.'

'Cunt.'

C.M. TAYLOR

'*Kev.*'

'Cunt.'

'Do you want me to call security?'

'So I can fall on another bollard?'

'Look, Kev. I don't want to let you go. You cost me two million quid. And it means I'll have to play Ginge all season, and in form he may be but he's not a patch on you. You are a very good player. But if you stay, I lose the dressing room. Simple. As. That. You're out, my son.'

'Compensation, then. Contract termination. What about compensation? A pay-off or something?'

'No, Kev, nothing like that. I am well within my rights to sack you. And sack you I have. No pay-off. Nothing.'

'Nothing?'

'Not a bean, Kev.'

'My fucking lawyer'll skin you.'

'*Your* fucking lawyer, Kevin, happens to be *my* fucking lawyer as well, and I had a nice long chat with him yesterday afternoon while you were having a little lay-down after colliding with that bollard.'

'But we came up together, gaffer.'

'And then we went down together as well, Kev, and you've been doing a bit of freelance going down yourself, which is *the root of this fucking problem.*'

'There nothing I can do?'

'There's nothing you can do.'

The gaffer opens his desk drawer and pulls out a whisky bottle and a couple of tumblers. It's shit whisky and he fills the tumblers and pushes one over to me, then he stands and he walks over to the breeze-block wall and hitches the promotion photo off its hook.

He steps over to me and nods at my glass. 'Drink that,' he says, and I do, then he hands me the team photo. 'And take this,' he says, and I do.

'Now fuck off,' he says and he leans down and puts his hands on my shoulders and pulls me to my feet and I stand and he turns me round and walks me towards the door which he opens and then steers me out into the corridor.

'Send my regards to your nan,' he says, then closes the door.

gift concierge consultant

Call from Gravesy. Call from Boves.

I do not take them.

Call from Colly. Call from the Wag.

I do not take them.

Lifestyle. Fucking lifestyle.

I leave the flat, jump in the Bents and tank it down to London. On the Westway I whip out the Arte and speed-dial the Harrods By Appointment service.

'Yeah, hi, Kev King. Coming down now. Be there in half an hour. I need a personal shopper.'

'I'm afraid all the personal shoppers in the By Appointment section are with clients today, Mr King.'

'Yeah?'

'So perhaps sir would like to call the Gift Concierge Consultants in the Luxury Gift and Objet Room? They may be able to help you.'

'No. No. Not at all. Perhaps *you* would like to call them, let them know I'll be in soon, and then call me back.'

'Very good, sir.'

I panel the Westway. Long strips of concrete shit on the left of me, new gleaming blocks being craned together on my right. Deeper in. The Wembley arch sleeking over the skyline behind me.

Paddington. Edgware. The Arte trills.

'Mr King, Duncan in the Luxury Gift and Objet Room on the second floor will be pleased to help you.'

'Nice.'

Marylebone. Marble Arch. Hyde Park. Brompton Road.

I'm ready for this. I *need* this. I still the Bents outside Harrods and hop out, lobbing the keys to the door monkey.

'Park that. No scratches.'

'Very good, sir.'

'Valet it,' I add.

Through the doors and yes, this is better.

Indulgence. Exclusivity. Prestige.

Through the Egyptian Room (scenes from the life of Ramses II), up the escalator to the first floor.

Sleek and unrivalled. Theatre of retail.

Up again. Second floor.

Towards the Luxury Gift and Objet Room. Unprecedented access to a world of convenience. Fit bird behind the desk in green livery. Little name badge. Christine. You would.

'I've got an appointment with a Gift Concierge Consultant.'

'Yes. Please, come in. Sit down.'

She's good. She does not second-glance my bust-up Villa head. I walk in and plonk down on a huge green Harrods own-brand three-seater and look at the back of Christine's head. It's a good, fit head. A quality little head.

They've got *her* here and they give me this *Duncan* shit.

Duncan walks up. Rubbish hair and bad teeth, name badge pinning a red carnation to his lapel. He's wearing a suit so mid-range that I don't even know what brand it is.

'Mr King?'

'Duncan.'

'Yes. Welcome to Harrods, Mr King.'

He sits down on a green chair next to the sofa. He tries not to but he winces a little at my big, squashed head.

'Right, how can we help you today?'

41

'Shopping.'

'Right. Any idea where you want to start? Are you after something for yourself? Or a gift?'

'For Kev. For me.'

'Right. Good. That's a start. What kind of items are you after?'

'Quality items.'

'Er, OK, sir. Menswear? Leisure? Watches and Jewellery? Tableware? Furniture? Grooming? Where shall we start?'

'I. I...What's that posh game?'

'Polo?'

'No.'

Do I look like I'm into horses? Do I look like I wear the jodhpurs?

I'm getting angry.

'No horses. No Dobbin.'

'Er, bridge? Bridge can be exclusive.'

He is getting on my nerves. He is getting on my nerves.

'Not cards. They play it with a hammer. You twat the opposition's ball.'

'Ah. Croquet. We have an excellent John Jaques Olympic croquet set which I can have brought over for you to have a look at.' He turns his head. 'Christine, could you call...'

I cut across him. 'Don't bother bringing it up. I'll have it. I want this stuff delivered, yeah?'

'No problem, sir. Is that all?'

'No.'

'Right. What else can I help you with then?'

Christ.

'Duncan, what do you think I do for a living?'

'I don't know, sir.'

'Football. I'm a footballer.'

'Right.'

'And Duncan, what do you do for a living?'

'I'm a Gift Consultant.'

'Right, so would I ask you for advice on the football, Duncan?'

'No, sir, you would not.'

'So why are you asking me for advice on the shopping? You are here to help me. I am here to relax.'

'Very good, sir.'

'No, not very good, Duncan. Not so far. You are here to *serve* me, to bring me exclusive things.'

'Might you give me a clue as to the sort of thing that you might like, sir? We have several thousand items in stock.'

'I want the sort of thing I want.'

Not effortless shopping.

Not enjoying unlimited access to prestige labels.

Not truly bespoke.

Angry. Getting angry. Eye throbbing. Jaw hurting. Ribs stinging. Angry.

'Duncan, you sit here claiming to be a highly skilled professional shopper. When in fact, in fact, Duncs, you are beginning to strike me as a muppet.'

I don't need this. Not today.

I am supposed to be relaxing, after the dismissal from the club. A dismissal, incidentally, I could take if it were for footballing reasons. If I'd been let go for not producing quality on the park, then I'd just have to hold up my hands – all of them – and say, 'Fair enoughski, gaffer,' and move on, become a potter or a whale surgeon or what have you, and admit it was not to be, humpty-wise.

But it wasn't like that. I was sacked, fired, slung, whatever, for non-footballing reasons. I was sacked, in fact, for minge reasons. And while that may mark me out from the footballing pack – for who among them has been sacked for quim misdemeanours? – and while it may secure a front-page red-top splash for the likes of your KKs, it's just not right. I mean, if you're good enough to play, you should play, right, irrespective of who you tongue. I mean, I bet some excellent porn stud, a master of the lingus, say, has never been chucked off set for not being able to ping a pinpoint thirty-yard ball over to the wing. No. He has not been treated so. Because football reasons would not come into it for the porn star. So why do quim considerations intrude for the footballer?

Unfathomable, it is. Really.

And so, after the beating and the sacking – the rupturing of the Kevish dreams, so to say – it is fucking imperative that I relax today. Because I need to address the feeling I have, this swirly, soggy feeling that I am being flushed – swiftly and unfairly – down football's U-bend.

I say that – and I *do* say that – but how can I relax when right now, at this time, there is only one team out here shopping today, and that team is me. Duncan's having a 'mare. We need to freshen it up. I look over to the concierge desk. *There's* the solution.

Christine. Get warmed up, love, you're coming on.

'Christine? Is there any way you might take over from our friend Duncan here? I don't think we are on the same wavelength, shopping-wise.'

Christine looks puzzled. She exchanges a glance with Duncan.

'Not a problem, Mr King,' she says and walks out from behind the desk.

Duncan stands and walks off, looking shithouse. And so he should. Boy done bad. Did not deserve his starting place. Disgrace to the Harrods shirt.

Christine takes Duncan's position on the chair. She looks a little nervous. Needs to get the pace of the game. But she will. Raw talent. You can see that. Top shopper.

'Right, Mr King, how can I help you?'

'The thing is, Christine, I'm not sure what I want. Why don't you bring me some *exclusive* items?'

She looks confused, still a bit off the pace.

But she'll get there. We can salvage this.

'*Look* at me. Take a good look at me. At *who* I am. Picture my lifestyle.'

She smiles. She gets it. She oozes shopping.

She has a good look and she can see behind the busted eye to the very lifestyle beneath. She makes a few notes, she makes a few calls and then bingo, kick-off.

Quality comes at me from all angles. She sees me. She knows. She can feel my lifestyle. I choose a personalized Daniel Hanson cashmere robe and get measured up for some bespoke Nick Tentis shoes.

I am into it. Oh Christine, there is a pulse in my cock now, quickened by the customized Valextra suitcase, and the Etro crocodile belt. And quickened again by the limited edition Caithness Punk Rocker paperweight and the pair of Duchamp silver cube crystal cufflinks, and by your little ponytail that wags around on the back of your fit, round head.

Oh Christine. Getting hard. Getting harder. This is better. The sacking recedes as the lifestyle confidence begins to flow. Grooming-wise there's the Acqua Di Parma Colonia Intensa deo spray and some L'occitane Code organic shaving oil.

'What about kitchenware?' she says. 'I see you as a man who worked hard, very hard, in his younger years but is now keen to find time to spend in his beautiful kitchen.'

She's right. Not really, but she is.

'Very much so,' I reply. 'Very much so.'

Haviland porcelain with customized colours and bespoke KK monogram to be added at the workshop.

Customized Volga linen and a Wusthot nine-piece knife block set.

I'm upright, solid as a goalpost, twitchy as the crowd on derby day.

I commission a contemporary chandelier from Windfall Lighting.

Oh yes. Oh yes. I'm definitely getting closer.

I'm going to…

'And you drive yourself hard, I know you do,' Christine says. 'And you play hard. That comes through when I look at you.'

There's a little seeping of pre-cum.

'But there's a lot of fun about you. The real you is a playful you.'

'Very much so.'

'With a personalized, leather-bound Monopoly set you can choose your own street names for the board.'

'Excellent. Excellent.'

I'm about to…

'Right then.' Her pen is paused above some paper. Her eyebrows are raised in anticipation.

'What?'

'Your street names sir. Make them personal to you.'

'Right.' I have a think. 'Kev Street.'

She writes it down. 'OK?'

'King Street.'

She writes that down too.

'Kev King Street.'

'Go on.'

'Kev Road. King Road. Kev King Road.'

'OK?'

'Er. Nan Street. Nan Road.'

'Right?'

'Football Road. Football Street.'

'OK?'

'Lifestyle Street. Lifestyle Road.'

'OK?'

I am not relaxed. I am not relaxed.

'Look, how many more of these do we have to do?'

'There's quite a few more, Mr King.'

'Can't you finish them off? All what I've said, but with Cul-de-sac and Close and Avenue as well. Kev King Avenue. Nan Close. You know. And Bentley Street. Hat Trick Road. Premiership Street. Use your imagination.'

'I'm sure that I can, sir. I'm sure I can choose names congruent with your lifestyle.'

The L word. Nice. Good. Better.

She pulls her weight. She tracks back.

The blood starts pumping. We can still win this.

There's a Brioni leather weekend bag and some Fonseca Giumeraeans 1998 port with accompanying funnel. I am pumped up. I can convert this.

A Dal Negro dark elm chess and draughts set, a sweet cross, a cushion header, a Lorenzini herringbone shirt, an Aquascutum Hockney cashmere jacket and it's there, it's in. I cum, shoot into my Zimmerli boxer shorts and then seep down inside my Duckie Brown trousers.

Take that, gaffer, you cheating fuck, take that, Darren, Captain Twat.

Take that, Ginger Pelé, Bungalow doorman.

I shudder a little, twitch my head about.

…Even Gravesy…Even Boves.

'Are you cold, sir?'

'Not cold, no. I'm done. I'm finished. Thank you, Christine. You were great. That was. Great. But you can't stay the night. I'll call you a cab.'

'Sorry?'

'Nothing. Nothing.' I stand up. 'Get this shit, I mean this stuff, these goods, sent over, will you?'

There's a bead of runny cum nuzzling at the top seam of my Pantherella cashmere sock. 'Where's the toilet, Christine? Need to get cleaned up. You were great. Really. It's not you, it's me.'

'It's that way, sir.' She points, and as she points she frowns.

twice stuntman of the year

I'm lying in bed. I can't sleep.

I am lost in the football wilderness, wandering alone on a pitch with no markings, a pitch with no goalposts. The Prem is a million miles away now, its silverware as distant as the grail.

Images. Images of Gerrard in my mind, bossing the midfield, dragging his team forward. Exhilarating form. And Lamps, images of Lamps, tidily combining with little Joey Cole and slamming one home.

The world record for being dragged along the pavement by a speeding car is held by Reno Jaton, who reached 236 mph, subjecting himself to more than six times the force of gravity in the process.

Even Gravesy.

Carrick. Breaking up the play, snuffing out the danger. Pinging them forward. Landing them on the winger's toe.

German daredevil Karl Traber steered a 250cc motorbike along a 300-metre-long tightrope, reaching a top speed of 97 kmh. He made it unharmed to the other side.

Fabregas. Box to box. Tracking back, bursting forward. One two with Walcott and then shaving the inside of the woodwork from the edge of the area.

Even Boves.

Paddy Doyle of Birmingham completed 1,500,230 press-ups

in a single calendar year. He is considered by many to be the world's fittest athlete.

Back into the past. Keane and Vieira. Squaring up. Going in hard. Winning the mental battles. Picking it up in the deep, driving on, drawing the man, laying it off.

Ricky D, twice stuntman of the year, jumped through a 900°F wall of fire, wearing a Pierre Cardin tuxedo. He is the holder of eight world records.

The bed feels empty. The penthouse feels empty.

The Prem is so far away, its silverware a dream.

Exile, exile, exile.

Even Gravesy. Even Boves.

But Colly, Colly. I've still got Colly.

6.175kg

I'm in the Resort Spa 830L hot tub round at Colly's. Air bubbles lick up around the crotch of my Bjorn Borg Everglades surf shorts and tickle my bollocks. I'm drowning my sorrows with Dres Ribaud's Hommage au Temps fifty-year-old cognac, drunk from twenty-two-ounce Madison glasses.

'Thing is, Kev, it's not *all* bad.'

He's wrong. It is all bad. But I'll hear him out.

'How do you mean, Colly?'

'The bugle. You can nose up now that you won't be tested.'

I give it some. 'Career's not over, Colly. I'll be back.'

'Know you will, player like you. But not for a while and this stuff doesn't stay in the system too long.'

'How long?'

'Not very.'

'Not sure, Colly.'

'Come on, Kev, it'll cheer you up. You'll have shit it all out by lunch tomorrow.'

Colly slides out of the hot tub, he looks toned and his Vivienne Westwood Union Jack swim shorts are top notch. He slips on his silk GrigioPerla leopard robe and black Just Cavalli flip-flops and walks towards the Tropitone Cabana Club modular poolside furniture. I follow him and we sit down.

He reaches into his robe pocket and pulls out a small,

transparent plastic bag. 'Got to keep the bugle in here. Humidity in the complex'd kill it otherwise.'

Colly lays it down, chops it out and noses it up. He dips his head towards me, encouraging me to go on. Fuck it. I do go on, snort the bugle right up.

It's a while – it's years – since I've hoovered up the old chang and I don't like the feel of it. Powders getting wet and turning to snot and seeping backwards up the nose, like a cold in reverse, a cold climbing into your head rather than running out. Still. That'll be gone soon and the buzz'll come on, which is welcome, given my current predicament.

Colly heads back to the tub, loses the robe and flip-flops and climbs in. I follow. He reclines and flaps a hand out from the tub, grabbing for and finding the plastic-wrapped remote. He does some buttons. Michael Bublé starts to croon out of the multiple hidden speakers. I look at Colly, remote in one hand, Madison glass in the other, staring ahead. He looks far away, concentrated and slightly tense. The layman might think he was summoning a tremendous fart, but I know Colly, I know he's thinking.

'Now, Kev,' he suddenly says. 'The transfer window's closed. Slammed shut till Jans. That we know. But I've been doing a bit of chat on your behalf. Few calls to the PFA.'

'Oh. Right.'

'Thing is, Kev, because you've got no club, you're a free agent. If you were to move on, it wouldn't be a transfer. So you don't need to wait for the window. Plus, you're not tied for the FA Cup.'

'Or the Champs League.'

'No, Kev. Now listen, what do managers always complain about?'

'Losing. Internationals. Everything.'

'Yeah. But two other things.'

'Chalfonts…Stud fees.'

'No, Kev. One, injuries. Two, fixture pile-up.'

'Right.'

'And when is the worst time for fixture snarl-up?'

'Christmas.'

'And the transfer window only opens *after* Christmas.'

'So?'

'So, you've been injured, but you've kept yourself in good nick. You're fresh as a daisy. Which is good. You've got Prem experience and you're not signed.'

I'm getting it, I'm beginning to get it.

'What we need is a club that's hit by injuries and shitting it about fixtures. A club like that'll be looking at the closed transfer window, willing it open. But it's not going to open yet, is it? So, rather than wait and get their number-one target in Jans, a club like that might take a chance on a lesser player...'

'A *what*, Colly?'

'Sorry, Kev. I mean a player who's had some recent troubles. A player who might not, as a consequence of recent media coverage, be considered by everyone in the country to be the best bet. A club might swoop for a player like that if they can have him for free and exactly *when* they need him...So, I'm going to keep an eye out for midfield injuries in the Prem, study the fixtures and work the phones. More bugle?'

I sniff. I'm feeling better.

'Yeah.'

We return to the Tropitone seats and nose up. Colly's T-Mobile G-1 Android phone rings and he plucks it from his leopard robe's pocket and glances at it. 'One more thing, Kev.'

'What?'

'I've invited Boves and Gravesy over.'

'You've *what*?'

'They're outside.'

'Fucking...'

'They want to talk to you, Kev.'

I stand up, water drips down from the Borgs on to the Tropitone seating.

'Fucking…'

'Kev, stay here.'

Colly stands up and walks out of the leisure area.

Ambushed. I walk back over to the two-pump, thirty-jet, six-seater hot tub and sit down. I am not into this, I am not into this at all.

Gravesy comes in. He's wearing Prada Mirror Wave trainers, a Unified Last Chance T in navy and 575 jeans. He's holding a pair of HOM Palace swim shorts.

'Kev-o.'

I glance at his tripey head but say nothing. Boves is behind him. He's holding a box, about a foot and a half high, wrapped in Jung Design pearlized gift paper. In his other hand Boves holds a pair of hibiscus D&G Fever shorts. He's wearing Lanvin navy and plum suede trainers, a grey Ermenegildo Zegna shirt and black Kilgour trousers.

He looks the bollocks.

'Kev.'

I say nothing. Colly follows them in and walks over to the hot tub. He gives me a warning look. The bugle's beginning to dig into me. I am not into this. Boves and Gravesy whip off the schmutter and step into their shorts and soon enough they're in the tub, cognacs in hand, the box Boves brought in resting on the tub's ledge next to the stereo remote.

'Kev,' says Boves again.

'Kev-o,' repeats Gravesy.

I say nothing. Bublé's the only voice for the moment.

Then, 'The boys here have got something to say to you, Kev.'

'I bet they have.'

'Colly's told us what the gaffer said to you, Kev,' Boves says, his eyes looking all sad and serious. 'But it wasn't like that.'

'What *was* it like then?'

'Well, come on, Boves-o, it was *a bit* like that.'

This is Gravesy's idea of a joke.

Boves gives him a look. 'Not for me it wasn't, Gravesy.

And you stuck up for Kev as well.'

'Look, Kev-o,' Gravesy says, 'there was a major row after Jimbo drove you off. You took a right pasting. It wasn't fair. But everyone's on Dar-o's side, because he's so "I'm from the north and I'm so fucking hard and...".'

'So limited as a player.' That was Boves. I can't help it. I like Boves.

'Yeah, Boves-o, and such a fucking bludgey player.'

'But Kev,' Boves says, 'the gaffer told us to tow the line or we'd rot in the reserves.'

'And I can't do that, Kev-o,' says Gravesy. 'World Cup qualifiers are on. I need to play. I'm getting old.'

'Same with me, Kev,' adds Boves. 'Maybe I was selfish. Maybe I should have said, "Kev goes and I go".'

'But you didn't.' I try to sound narky, but I'm melting. I can't help it. 'What's that?' I ask, nodding at the box.

'A present,' Boves says and reaches over and picks up the box. 'It's to say sorry.'

'Yeah, sorry, Kev-o.'

No one's apologized to me before. No one has. I don't think. Apart from Nan. The bugle's weirding me, stranging me. They said sorry. I tear off the wrapping and open the box. I look inside. A golden metal globe, held up by four golden hands.

'Is this?...Is this?'

'We had a copy made.'

I take it out of the box. Twin layers of malachite at the base; lines, becoming arms, rising up from that base, to cup the globe above. I hold it up. It's the World Cup. Designed by Silvio Gazzaniga, 36 centimetres tall, 6.175kg in weight.

'I'm. I'm...'

'Turn her over, Kev-o. Look at her arse, mate.'

On the bottom are the names of the previous winners. Uruguay, Argentina, Germany, Italy, Brazil, France. And England. Obviously. At the end of the engraving it says, '2010 England. Captain, Kevin King.'

'It was hard, Kev-o, as an Aussie, getting that last bit done.'

'It was hard for me too,' adds Boves.

'I'm. I'm…'

I stand up, holding the trophy, water swooshing off the Borgs. I step out of the hot tub, holding the cup aloft. I don't know what to do. I bring it down and kiss it, then hold it up again. Maradona. Zidane. Pelé. Fucking Pelé's held this, one like this anyway.

Moore. Hursty. Charlton. Little Nobby Stiles. The World Cup.

I stagger about on the poolside tiles. Colly starts a commentary.

'After a hard-fought match against five times winners Brazil, it was Kev King's last-minute goal that won the cup for England.'

Boves and Gravesy are laughing. I start to run. I pelt up along the poolside, holding the cup. I take the corner and run round the deep end. I run back down the other side.

'And with that strike,' Colly continues, holding his hand over his mouth to sound like a radio pundit, 'King becomes the tournament's leading scorer, beating David Villa by a single goal.'

I am running round and round the pool, showing the cup to the leisure complex, showing the cup also to the ecstatic crowd, the thousands of English fans – good honest patriots – who have made the long journey to South Africa, hoping, dreaming of this moment.

The hurt is over. The pain is over.

The bugle and the Cup are lifting me up. They believe in me. The boys believe in me. I have won the Cup. I am England Captain. I have scored the goal that won it.

But what's that?

I hear a sound above Bublé's croon. It's the trill of the Arte, left by the side of the tub. I look over. Too late, Gravesy's answered it.

'Hi. No, it's Gravesy. Yeah, he's here. He's just won the World Cup. Kev-o,' he shouts over. 'It's Saskia.'

knife-edge love summit

I am walking up the Tottenham Court Road.

Walking's not right but it does happen. The Bents is in for a service and the courtesy car they offered me was a piece of shit, was discourteous in fact.

Left into Hanway Street, civilians all around me. Bad clothes, bad teeth. Some of them stink, but some, surprisingly, are fuckable. I keep a tally: definitely would, wouldn't, wouldn't, wouldn't, wouldn't, wouldn't, would (at a push), wouldn't, wouldn't, wouldn't, have.

Maybe. Have I? Could have. Looks familiar. Anyway.

I'm walking among the civilians but we're not the same. Not at all. I am much better than them. Despite now being clubless, and despite my nerves since hearing that cold tone in Sas' voice, the civvies know that. They must do. They can see I'm better. I am wearing a single-button Dsquared2 suit, a yellow Jil Sander shirt and Ann Demeulemeester lace-up boots.

Right into Hanway Place. There's a monster outside the door, a huge bloke, two blokes really, but sort of moulded into one bloke.

'Good evening, sir.'

'Park that,' I say. 'No scratches.'

'Park what?'

'Oh. Nothing, nothing.'

I step quickly through the door into the subway-style entrance and take the stairs. Down by slate-lined walls studded with lights, down into the restaurant proper, a large cellar space chopped by latticed screens.

Sultry ambience. Distinctive blue lighting strategy. Oriental chic.

Voted nineteenth in the San Pellegrino world's fifty best restaurants.

Some kind of greeter. 'Do you have a reservation, sir?'

'Yeah. Kev King. She here yet?'

'No, sir, nobody has arrived for you.'

Weird. Not like Sas to be late. Too much of a career girl for that, she is. Too much of a professional. Worried. Might lose Sas over this whole lingus thing. My toppest remaining lifestyle asset could be in jeops here. And what if she gives me the elbow, casting me clubless and Wagless into the very actual lifestyle wilderness?

'Would you like to wait at the bar, Mr King, or go straight to your table?'

I need a fucking drink. 'Bar.'

I Kev over to the bar, which does not double as a tropical fish tank as it does at Yauatcha. There's a barmaid, who you would. There's cocktails and all that, but I'm thirsty and take a lager, which I neck. There's a menu on the bar and I take a look, then glance at the maid. Because shitting it Sas-wise I may be, but I'm still Kev King, with all that implies in terms of sheer fucking quality. And you've got to pass the time. So, let's have a little dabble with the maid then, see if she's biting.

'What do you think, steamed crab in Shao-Hsing wine or stir-fried lobster tail in XO sauce?'

She's pissing about with some glasses or something but she stops and looks thoughtful; then, 'I'd go for both,' she says and smiles.

It's good. It's a good answer. It's greedy.

'Both. You think so?'

'Everything on the menu is excellent, sir.'

Bollocks, I thought she was playing a bit, having a tease, but she's just toeing the line, pushing the PR message. Still, she does have a tremendous rack. So it's right you are then, let's cast her another line.

'You like the sport?'

'Sorry, sir?'

'You like the sport? Acts of athletic prowess, you know.'

'Not really. Pilates. Yoga. A bit of ice skating from time to time.'

'Ice skating, right. But not the football?'

'No, sir, not really.'

'Cars then, you like the cars?'

'No, sir.'

'The fashion. Designer gear?'

'Not really, sir. I like vintage clothes.'

'Vintage. Right. Vintage cars then?'

'No.'

'What about gadgets?'

'Not really, bit of a technophobe, I'm afraid.'

'Cash though? You must like the cash, right? Let's talk about cash.'

'OK.'

'Right. How much does the *average* person make in a year, do you think?'

The barmaid steps forward and eyes me squarely. 'Well, that's an interesting question. Do you mean in this country, which has one of the highest per capita incomes in the world, or do you mean globally, where more than three billion people scrape by on the slenderest of resources?'

'The latter, that one, the last one.'

'Well, that's hard to say. A huge amount of the products and services in the developing world are obtained via the informal economy. When resources are scarce, barter comes to the fore. They might only have a few pennies a day to spend, but their social capital earnings will be much higher than that.'

'Yeah, good, but why do you think these poor folk are so into the Premiership?'

She exhales. 'Do you want me to ask you then?'

'What?'

'*You know.*'

'What?'

'So. Are. You. A. Footballer?'

'I am, yeah.'

'Right. Do you want me to ask you the next question?'

'What?'

'Oh, come on.'

'What?'

'How much do you earn?'

'Well, that depends if you include barter and social capital as well, love.'

She laughs.

'You surprised or something? Thought I was thick just because I look so fucking good? Sexist, are you?'

'That's funny,' she says. 'Get your phone out.'

I whip out the Arte and she whispers her number to me and then, 'He really is an excellent chiropodist, sir,' she says, weirdly and loudly, before adding, 'And what can I get you, madam?' And I turn round and see Sas stood behind me at the bar.

Sas is glowering, but she is also looking very fit. She is wearing a Collette Dinnigan feathered mini dress and heel-less Antonio Beradi PVC boots. She's holding an Anouk Biker clutch bag in buffalo leather and and and what's that? I have a little sniff – she's dabbed with Miller Harris Le Petit Grain eau de parfum.

My oh never. You absolutely would. Whenever you could.

Irrespective of injury, loss of form, or post-match fatigue.

Sas levels a hard glare at the barmaid and then looks down coldly towards where I sit on the bar stool. 'Come on, let's eat.'

Hardly the passionate embrace of long-parted lovers, is it? Hardly shimmering with the promise of shag. We walk over and sit, our table surrounded by latticed screens, a lamp hanging low between us, lighting up the bottoms of our faces, shading their tops.

Sas' lips look, she looks so, all of her, all over she looks so.

Doesn't just look it though, she is.

A waitress steps into the booth, she's bathed in some weird electric-blue glow. *Bladerunner* or something. But with fit people, and better food. And no crazed androids. As yet.

Sas doesn't say anything to me. Total composure, she is. She takes the stir-fried asparagus with lotus roots, and the lily bulb with black pepper. I order the jasmine tea-soaked organic pork ribs, the Sanpei chicken claypot, the salt and pepper squid, and the abalone with goose web. Still she's quiet. We take a 2004 Egidio Shiraz.

I'm nervous. I crack first.

'So, Sas, how was Dubai? You're looking very good.'

'Dubai was good.'

'Right, and how's being back? Got any work on?'

'Lots, Kev.'

She's a model, Agent Provocateur. Kinky undies.

I am getting a lob on, which is weird because I'm nervous and I usually need to relax to summon the emperor, so to say. It's odd, this whole nervy erection thing, but, 'Do you have anything to say to me, Kev?'

'Lots of things, as always. Chatty old Kev.'

'Anything specific?'

'Dress is nice.'

'Nothing you want to mention? Like getting splashed all over the papers fucking another woman.'

'You saw that then?'

'Of course I fucking saw it, you dick. They do get the papers in Dubai.'

'Right. Course they do. Was it on the TV over there?'

'No.'

'Shame.'

'What?'

'Nothing.'

'It wasn't very fucking nice, you know, for me to see that stuff.'

'I bet. I'm sorry.'

And I am sorry. Because this could be big trouble for me. Clubless already. And now about to be cast out of the world of sleb minge; ostracized potentially from both club and cuntry, if you will. I stare at her. I'm scared. I'm waiting.

I want Nan. I want to see Nan.

'Why didn't you *clear it* with me, Kev?'

'It wasn't planned. Pap just papped me. I lost my bloody club.'

'I heard.'

'And I got my head kicked in.'

'I can see. Something I want you to have a look at.'

She reaches into the clutch bag, pulls out a Polaroid and hands it over. Jesus. There she is, in the Provocateur kecks, just about anyway, though hanging out of them rather than wearing them would be more specific. And what's that? She is bending over some geezer, some absolutely gymed-up, buff geezer. She's got a whip in one hand.

'What do you think?'

What does she think I think? I mean, she's getting it on with some other bloke. 'Fuck's...'

'That's just a test shot. We're going to do the shoot proper next week.'

'What?'

'*The Revenge Shoot*. Min reckons she can place the pics worldwide.'

Min is Sas' publicist.

'What do you mean, Sas?'

'Look, me and Min have worked it out. If I do nothing about this, about you playing away, I'm weak, in the eyes of the public. And you're a rat. Nobody wins. So we get someone to leak these shots, say that I went on some kind of sexual rampage in revenge.'

'A sexual rampage, Sas?'

'Yes. Then I'm seen as strong and hot and it's your turn to get a bit of sympathy.'

'Right.'

'All this assumes, of course, that you get another club, that you can keep your profile up.' She tosses me a stern glance. 'You need to do that, Kev. I'm not pulling all the media weight on my own.'

I am affronted. 'My profile's pretty fucking good, Sas. Front-page news, I am.'

'You *were*,' she says, then pauses and looks suddenly grave. 'You could have damaged my *career*, Kev.'

'I got papped.'

'You should have been more careful. What have we agreed, Kev?'

'Lots of things.'

'About the media, Kev, come on.'

I recite the rules. 'Colly can handle my football stories, alone. Min can handle your modelling stories, alone.'

'Yes? And?'

'Relationship stories we do together.'

'Yes Kev, relationship stories we manage *together*.'

The wine arrives. The *Bladerunner* waitress knifes the seal and screws and pulls the cork and glugs some into my glass. I sip and then nod to her and she fills us both up and moves off.

I can't help it. I've got to know.

'Did you fuck that bloke then, Sas?'

'Which one?'

'The one in the photo.'

'No. He's gay. He asked for your autograph.'

Right. Fine. That's fine then. I think. But that model didn't look too gay to me, and I wonder, I mean, if that matters. If a gay guy fondles your Wag, is that somehow better than if he were straight? I mean, does his heart have to be in it for it to count as cheating? I don't know, and this sex rampage test shot has weirded me right over. But still. The crisis has passed. Sas has calmed it. Looks like I won't be Wagless after all. I look at her tits – well, the tits she's packing right now anyway – and they are fucking brilliant. I'm going to give it a go. I am. I can't help myself.

'Really, good to see you, Sas. You look gorgeous.'

She says nothing.

'You do, you look stunning. Absolutely *stunning*.'

'You look like shit.'

I rub my eye. 'Should have seen it a few days ago. Come on, Sas, let's fuck off to yours, you look gorgeous. Bit of the old squeaky.'

'Kev, I've told you I want us to wait.'

'But Sas, my balls are big as...'

'Anyway, we can't.'

'Why?'

'They'll be here in a few minutes.'

'Who will?'

'Min and the snapper.'

'What for, Sas?'

'To get some shots.'

'Of us *eating*?'

'No, Kev, exclusive images of our knife-edge love summit.'

optimum wellness

At the spa I monster the rotary torso exerciser.

Most players would fold without a club, but not me, not Kev. I can't think like that. Got no fallback, see. Haven't exactly saved a lot of my wages; not too many prudent investment properties. And didn't exactly rack up a shitload of quals. But tell myself I'm fucked and I am. Whereas, think there's a chance and there is.

Adversity is an opportunity, in the right ears.

Concentrate on the silverware, Kev, picture yourself in the Prem. Keep yourself in shape.

I breathe in. PMA. I am at the top of my game, both physically and emotionally. I am experiencing a level of fitness and wellbeing that is just not possible in a civilian's gym. I breathe out.

I work the internal obliques. I work the external obliques.

I breathe in. PMA. I am achieving optimum health, I am achieving optimum wellness. I am cocooned in an exclusive health setting. I breathe out.

I work the abs, I work the waist.

The silhouette must stay sleek.

I leave the spa's wellness area and walk to the changing room where I do some mirror. World-class physique. They would. But not all of them can.

I shower and change into a black Armand Bossi single-button jacket with Gilded Age jeans and an orange Missoni floral print shirt. I slip on my black nappa Bruno Bordene zip boots and leave the changing room. I catch sight of Kev in the spa's plate glass and smile all the way to the Bents.

Athlete, fucking athlete.

I am replacing lost fluids with an isotonic sports drink. PMA. I am zinging with overall health. In every way, at every level, I am peaking.

I check the Arte. There's a message. Billy Four Chins.

The Chins is Captain of the Stepney Strollers, a team I used to play for years ago, before I spiralled upwards through the leagues and graced the Prem turf. I listen to the message. Because while he's not the sort of bloke I'd like to be snapped standing next to in *Hello!*, old Four Chins has certainly had his uses in the past.

Because the truth is, Billy's well known across the capital, known for his skills in location, shall we say. You never ask how, but the Chins can source pretty much any illegal, wrong or unpleasant item that any deviant, of whatever leaning, could need. And he can do it fast. Could lay his hands on eight k of plutonium within the hour, that lad, could bag fucking Nessie with a crab line. Given the correct cash incentive. Clearly.

'Kev, know you're "between clubs" as they say. We're a man short for this afternoon. Thought you might want to keep your hand in…Let me know.'

I drum on the steering wheel, I pop some Il Divo on the surround sound. I have a think. Don't want to slum it, don't want to take the chance of falling down to their level. Because you play with shit players and their shitness rubs off; they make you as bad as them. That's one law of the football jungle. Not that there are jungles in football, for many reasons, most of which should be obvious.

I should ignore Billy Four Chins. But then again, there's the match fitness angle. No substitute for a game. It might be shrewd to integrate actual match practice into my bespoke fitness programme. Need to keep that half a yard.

Maybe a shit game's better than no game. I speed-dial the Chins.

'Billy. Kev. What time's kick-off?'

'Three.'

'Three on a Saturday? Been a while since I've had a proper start time.'

'Yeah, Kev. You in?'

'Where's the game?'

'Away. South London.'

'I'll come and get you in the Bents, Billy. Pick you up about half one?'

'Nice.'

'Text the address.'

'One thing, Kev. You're not registered to play. But I know the ref. Done him the odd favour. I'll call him and swing it.'

I end the call, nip back to the flat and wolf half a kilo of fresh pasta, then I pick up my kit and the Nike Vapours and descend to the lair of the Bents. I feel better, feel galvanized. I stick Billy's postcode in the GPS and rev her up. I tonk it into town, Il Divo giving it some.

Westway, Edgware, Euston, all that, I do all that. I barrel ever on.

Finsbury. Old Street. Stepney. The Mile End Road.

Round here somewhere. The GPS gives out the lefts and rights and I take them. Here we go. Pull up outside some shit-awful block of flats. White trash, faces greasy as fried eggs, mull about, disrespecting themselves with cheap weed, doing their 'shopping'. Fuck's sake, Billy, what a place.

I bell Billy and then relax, leaning back in the optimum seating. Street rats eye the Bents. Billy rounds a corner and I toot the horn and he jogs over. But what Billy's wearing is not right, not right at all. He looks like shit, and as he moves, his chins jostle amongst themselves and ooze down around his neck, falling, eventually, on to the top of his chest, where he keeps his uppermost tit fat. What Billy has done to himself is not right and I am chilled. Without the rigour of the professional game, am I looking into the future here with Billy? A future where my body resembles a lard sculpture of a dipso manatee?

No. No. PMA. Athlete. Fucking athlete. Billy climbs in.

'Wehey, Kev, long time.'

I spark the engine. 'Long time, Billy.'

'Looking good, Kev. Upmarket.'

'Where we heading?'

'Eltham. Some pony club.'

'Pony as the Strollers?'

'Not quite, Kev. Seen you in the papers.'

'Course.'

'Using that bird's legs as a scarf.'

'I'd better be in the centre of the park today.'

'She was tasty, Kev, she looked all right. Bet you've got that on tap these days.'

'Centre mid, yeah?'

'Do you, do you get a lot of snatch, Kev?'

'I'll play on the right of centre mid. Who's on my left?'

'Bet you're beating them off with a shitty stick.'

Now I am shouting. 'Who's on my left, Billy?'

'Jesus, Kev, chill. I am. The old firm. Me and you.'

'Christ. You? *You're* bossing the centre of the park?'

'Eye still looks a bit tender, Kev. Read that in the tabs too. Did he really twat you?'

Muppet. I whack up the stereo.

Poplar. Blackwall. Over the river. Greenwich. Blackheath. Eltham.

Turn off the Sidcup Road and here we are.

'Christ.'

'Not exactly the Theatre of Dreams, is it, Kev?'

It is not the Theatre of Dreams, no, it is certainly not that. It's a grubby open field with a grubby little shed at one end, for a changing room, presumably. I park the Bents near the shed and we step out. The sky is grey and shit and the air seems grey too. Fuck's sake.

Cars begin to arrive – Toyotas, Fords, other types of shit – and podgy lads with gelled hair and hangovers climb out. Primark. Next. Fucking Topman. Jesus. Some of our lads – the Stepney Strollers – walk towards us and say hello to Four Chins, while their lot – the Eltham team, the Eltham All-Stars or something – walk over to cluster around a Fiat now parked on the far side of the shed and start to pass round a joint.

I do not belong here. This is not my level. I ache for the Prem.

'Lads,' says Billy, 'this is Kev King. Our ringer. Marts,' he says to one burly lad, 'you're dropped.'

Marts looks pissed off but he does not complain.

The lads say all right to me, some shake my hand, some mutter about me being a pro, some are too shy – too intimidated by the King brand presence – and they hang back and give me the doe eyes. They all know who I am, they've seen me on the goggle… The likes of your Kevin Kings.

I look at the lads, still gormless with last night's beer, tripe building up already around their middles. I am furious that I have to be here, that I have to play with these appalling, cholesteroly cunts. But given that I *am* here, I will punish the fuck out of this game.

I decide to be Captain and consider a team talk. Some tactics maybe? A 4-1-4-1 formation? A 3-5-2? No, tactics won't work with these jokers.

'Get the ball, give it to me. We're going to fuck this lot.'

That'll do.

The Eltham lads make their way into the shed and come out a little later, dressed in their kit. All white. They think they're fucking Real Madrid or something. We go in next and don the crimson of the Strollers. The ref pitches up and pops his head inside the shed. 'Good clean game,' he says, as he winks at Billy.

Yeah. Right.

We step outside and I make my way to the centre circle, facing off with the Eltham Cap, bloke called Andy or something. He glances at me and then away, but then he quickly glances back.

He rumples his brow. He sees Kev. He knows me.

'Er, ref?' this Andy fucker says. 'This is an amateur league, yeah?'

Listen to him.

'That's right.'

'Well, how come they got a pro playing?'

The ref turns to me. 'You don't play for any pro club, do you?'

'Not at the moment.'

But I fucking will.

'He *is* registered,' says the ref, blushing slightly. 'It is legit.'

This Andy mutters, 'Fuck,' to himself. Then, 'They've got a fucking ringer,' he bellows over his shoulder to the rest of his team, who are too busy talking civvy bollocks to pay much attention.

The ref flips the coin. I win the toss and kick into the breeze. Everyone'll be fucked in the second and the wind'll be more useful then. We change ends and I spot the dropped Marts, looking sad in his minging tracky on the sidelines.

The Eltham lot are still chatting, but the man in black blows and Four Chins nudges it off the spot towards me and I push forward, out of the circle, and I'm very much on the front foot, I am taking the game to them. And I want to punish and humiliate this Eltham shower for their pony clobber, their shit cars and shit hair and huge guts, for their miserable wages and their shitty birds. After this game I want these fucking Eltham space-wastes to feel shocked and humiliated. That's what I want.

I carve through the midfield, who are not expecting it. I nutmeg a skinny lad ('Megs,' shouts a gleeful Billy) and push up on to their defence, who are still caning the keeper about some shit he pulled last night. I unleash one.

The tubby keeper doesn't even dive for it, just sort of looks at the ball.

Bottom left. Get in. One nil, as early as the sixth second. Christ.

'Kev.'

'Nice.'

'Quality, Kev.'

The Eltham lot don't know what's happening.

But I'll tell them. Ability. Strength. Pace. Technique. Character.

That's what's happening.

I am happening to them; a top, top player is happening all over them.

These Eltham fuckers will be punished for what the gaffer did to me, for me being clubless. These are the fuckers I will take it out on. Ninety minutes of sheer hell coming up for these lads.

We're 5-0 up by half time. The game finishes 13-2.

I get nine of them. And these boys, the opposition, this fucking Eltham lot, do have a bit of a whine about the inclusion of your Kings in the Strollers starting eleven. But really, what can they do? Given that the Chins has pocketed the ref.

Afterwards we convoy back across the river, Billy shotgun, a couple of little Herberts in the back of the Bents, soiling the upholst with their Wranglers and Reeboks, or whatever muck they've got on.

'What's it like to play against Rooney?' they give it.

'What's the most you've got out of the Bentley, Kev?'

'Who's the hardest defender you've ever come up against?'

I'm not answering these bullshit civvy questions. I crank up the Divo. You can tell they don't like the tunes, too classy for them. But they don't say anything. How could they? I mean, nine goals. *Three* hat tricks. Shame I got sent off.

Still.

The Strollers are going for a few drinks in the Albion. I pull up outside.

'Coming in, Kev?'

'No.'

'Come on. There'll be a late kick-off on the Sky.'

I eye the pub, scruffy as fuck outside, and sticky as hell no doubt inside. A man could soil his schmutter in a pub like that. A couple of the Strollers' cars pull up behind me.

'No, Billy.'

'Come on, Kev,' one of the Herberts pipes up from the back. 'I'll buy you a pint.'

'No, lads.'

Billy and the Herberts climb out of the Bents and Billy gives me a sad little nod and they're off, deflated by my refusal, walking slowly to the Albion's front door. I watch the Strollers file into the pub and see the orange fug of the bar room through the streaky window. There'll be tales of Kev told in that pub tonight, tales told aplenty, of the hero Kev and his many, many goals. Of his class and spirit. Of his quality.

I tune the Acura ELS surround sound to 5 Live.

ManU v West Brom, late kick-off. Half time, still 0-0.

Fucking ManU. A nothing team.

They give out the earlier results, my old lot got fucked again. Gravesy got one, though. Boves got stretchered off.

I look again through the pub window, see some of the Strollers clustered at the bar, the pints being bought and poured and drunk, the lads laughing and joking, some eyes on the flat screen, tuned to Sky no doubt, on the far wall. I see Billy's face, still red with the run-around and now with the laughter. He's chatting to some Herbert. Then Billy looks out of the window and spots the Bents, still resting by the kerb. Billy sees me and smiles and waves at me, beckoning me into the pub.

No. Fuck them. Not getting sucked in. Not getting pulled back on to civvy street. I turn the Bents over and pop her in gear. I swing the car around and drive home, get cleaned up and go back to the spa.

I work the abs, I work the glutes, I work the obliques.

Need to stay sharp, keep the Prem dream alive. Keep that half a yard.

turf-resistant v-shaped sole

'What the fuck am I supposed to do with all that?'

'Don't know, mate, I'm just delivering it.'

'There's no room. Where's it all going to go?'

'I don't know, mate, not my problem.'

The gear from my Harrods splurge is being delivered. There are boxes and bags all over the flat. The delivery man gives me the 'make us a cup of tea' eyes. Fucking joker.

'What's your name?' I ask.

'John.'

'John what?'

'John Wallace.'

I step towards him. 'Right then, John Wallace...'

But the Arte trills. It's Colly. I take it.

'Kev. Kev. You're not going to believe it.'

'What?'

'Guess.'

'No.'

'Henk Neeskins wants to meet you.'

'Yeah, right, and I've just smashed Beyoncé's back doors in.'

'Kev. I'm serious. His secretary just called me.'

'You are fucking joking.'

'No, Kev.'

It's amazing. Neeskins. Colly's done well, Colly's played a blinder.

'What? When?'

'Today. Wants to play a round with you.'

'Fucking *nice!*'

'Three o'clock, at the Riverside Golf Club.'

'Never heard of it.'

'They've told me the address, town somewhere. I'll text you it.'

'Christ, Colly. Neeskins. Jesus.'

'I know, Kev. I know.'

'Does he want me to play for them?'

'Don't know, Kev, maybe. They've got nobody injured centre mid for the first team. But they're still in Europe, and the Carling. The FA's about to start, and they're going well in the Prem. Maybe, Kev, maybe.'

'Christ, Colly. Henk Neeskins.'

'Total football, Kev.'

'Total Kev, Colly.'

The call ends and I look over to the lounge to see the delivery man staring at me. 'Henk Neeskins, eh? Two European cups as a player, two as a manager, and five league titles in three different countries. Some record,' he says.

'You done, Motson?'

'Yeah.'

'Then fuck off.'

I walk to the door, swerving the Harrods swag. I open the door and the delivery man picks his way towards me and heads out.

Neeskins. Christ. Right. Neeskins. Too good to be true, this is. Go from facing the Eltham All-Stars to eighteen holes with one of the football world's tacticalmost gurus. Colly's turned things right round, done right by his eldest – and best – client. Nice.

I lather with the Elemis, shave with the Azor and dab on the Pinaud Clubman Vanilla aftershave lotion. In the bedroom I slide into the Ashworth X-static golf socks, the Oscar Jacobson tour performance trousers and the Ian Poulter Pin Tuck long-sleeve shirt with split side hem. Then I pop on the Stuburt Darren

Clarke Collection golf shoes with leading underfoot support technology, suede inner heel grip lining and rubber outsole directional tracking lugs.

I slip on the Galvin Green Spiro cap, pull out the Mizuno cart bag and fix it to the Motocaddy s3 digital trolley. Ready.

I cart the stuff to the Bents, whack some Craig David on the Acura and stick the address from Colly's text into the GPS. I head off, into town.

The Riverside's south of the Thames and it takes me a while, but I cross the river in good time, gun through Charlton and Greenwich, swerve Woolwich and make Thamesmead, home of the Riverside.

Why don't I know this course? Got to be the bomb if Neeskins plays here, got to be the shit. Why don't I know it?

I soon find out why. I pull off Fairway Drive and up towards the Riverside. It's a municipal course. What? A civvy fucking course. One of the greatest managers in the history of the game's meeting me at a public course. What style of wank is this? I think about throwing a U-turn, but I don't. A place in the Prem's at stake here. Calm it, Kev.

I swing into the parking, climb out the Bents and sniff the air… Human shit. The course is next to the South London sewage works. There's a notice on the outside of the clubhouse – *Drugs Are Not Tolerated On Site*. Junky golf course. Is this some kind of joke? Neeskins is known to be an oddball, this some kind of test? He taking the piss? Is Neeskins taking the piss out of Kev?

A kaput old Saab pulls up next to the Bents and a tall, wiry figure gets out. It's the man. I walk over, my hand extended to shake and I feel his fingers grip the King palm. He looks me in the eyes before he releases my hand. His eyes are blue and clear and shining. He's fit as a butcher's dog. He is wearing rumpled cords and a blue polo shirt and a shitty wool cardy.

'Kevin.'

'An honour, Mr Neeskins.'

He shrugs, unimpressed. 'Come on.'

Neeskins walks round the back of the Saab and dinks the boot open. It's crammed with papers and weird bits of rubber pipe and everything's coated in dog hairs. There's a crumby old leather golf bag in there with some shit old clubs poking out the top of it. The kit looks about fifty years old, not fit for a charity shop. Neeskins leans into the boot, picks up his old golf bag and slings it across his shoulder.

We go into the clubhouse and he does not speak. Where is the Prem chat? The contract offer? We pay up for a round and he does not speak. The course is just nine holes and it only costs six quid for a punt. It's a joke. Any fucking civvy can afford that, any civvy could walk on to this links, in fact I can see some kids legging it across a fairway over to my left. What's Neeskins doing? Blokes minted, bound to be, and he's coming here.

He is taking the piss out of me. He is.

We walk up to the first hole, a 254-yard par 4, and I reach into the Mizuno and pull out a Bruch Pyramid tee and a Titleist Pro VI X ball with drop and stop accuracy control and staggered wave parting. I place the ball on the tee and return to the bag, lifting out a Footjoy Sta-sof golf glove with Coolmax Lycra knuckle inset, angled ComforTab closure and patent satin cuff reinforcement.

I look at Neeskins. He's not got a glove on. He's wearing Dunlop trainers and he's clutching some piss poor wood in his hand, its face all chipped and battered, the club shaft splattered with paint, a few dog hairs still clinging to it. He pulls a golf ball out and shows it to me. It's got a little Homer Simpson logo on it and he does a weird little laugh.

This is not Prem behaviour. More like Conference North. At best.

I am furious. Maybe Colly's stitched me up, hired some Neeskins impersonator, some Henk-alike, to wind me up. Maybe he's filming the lot on his mobes from behind those minging bushes. It might be so. Because really, there has to be an explanation for all this shit.

This Neeskins bloke pulls a coin out of his pocket and eyes me. I want to hurt him, but I've got to keep a lid on it. I've got to play it straight. It could be for real. This weird round could somehow seal Kev's return to Prem paradise.

'Heads,' I say as he flips and catches the coin.

'It's tails,' he says, careful not to let me see it.

'I'll play first,' he says and walks forward. He plants a tee and his Homer ball and then waggles his club horizontally in front of him, like a baseball bat. A little wind rises and an empty Frazzles packet blows in front of us, followed by the stench of half of London's shite. The Neeskins-like person addresses the ball, swings a perfect swing and absolutely twats Homer down the fairway. It's a good shot, a Kevishly good shot in fact. It's the shot of somebody who's spent years on the golf because he only works three hours a day. It's definitely the shot of a football man.

It is him. It's Neeskins. No doubt. This is for real.

I select my TaylorMade R7 TP wood with launch control technology, Fujikura shaft and turf-resistant V-shaped sole. I approach the Titleist Pro VI X.

Neeskins stands back and I try a few practice swings. I zone in. I visualize the ball pinging off the sweet spot. I believe in the R7 TP with its low, penetrating ball flight, soft responsive control and extra forgiveness. It is tour quality, and so am I.

I believe in Kevin King.

I shuffle forward and wind up for my swing. I begin to unleash the R7 TP, then, 'How is your fitness?' Neeskins asks just as I'm about to swat the Titleist.

I lose the arc of my swing and fluff it, top-edging the ball so that it dribbles about thirty metres forward. You do not talk as the opponent addresses the ball. You do not do that. Not happy. Not happy at all. I look at Neeskins. Is he smiling? I start to loom forward, weighing the club in my hand, then I remember who he is, remember this oddball holds my Prem dreams in his hands. I swallow hard.

'I was back to full fitness before the…incident…I'm fit as fucking fuck.'

He shoulders his bag and walks forward on to the fairway. I activate the digital trolley and follow. We come, obviously, to my ball first and I shape with the R7 TP and slog the ball forward. This time Neeskins keeps it buttoned and I make a fairly decent contact. We walk down the fairway together.

'A lot of people at my club think you are a liability, Kevin,' he says, looking off into the sky, eyes fixed on a filthy pigeon as it creaks over us.

'And?'

'And I was wondering if they are right. Or I was wondering if you might have something to prove instead.'

'To who?'

'To yourself.'

What is this, golfing with Freud? 'I've got nothing to prove to myself.'

'So you think you are as good as you can be, as a player?'

'I didn't say that. I know I'm the bollocks. But I also know I can get better. Right coach. Right team around me. Right club.'

Are these the right answers? Am I giving him the right answers?

We reach my ball. Two shots I've had and he's still ahead of me. I take out a limited edition Mizuna MP-100 iron with True Temper Dynamic Gold S300 steel shaft, double nickel chrome plating and Tour velvet cord grips.

I approach the ball and assess the lay, then I address the Titleist. I am about to swing.

'Would you say you were an arrogant man, Kevin?'

Anger, fury, anger. He's done it again, but I will keep cool.

'I am realistic about the high level of my own talent,' I say.

Is that the right thing to say?

I swing and hit and just make the near side of the green and we walk towards his ball. Neeskins is about fifty metres from the green. He pulls a shitty old club from his shitty old bag and walks straight up to his Homer ball, takes one practice swing and then dinks it to within about ten feet of the pin. Fucker.

We approach the green and I look across the course. There's some kids smoking reefers in a bush just off the fairway, and there's a bloke actually fishing in a water hazard further on.

I look across the green. Terrible condition, bare soil in places. I whip out the Titleist Scotty Cameron Studio Select putter with precision milled 303 stainless steel shaft and heel and toe weighting, and I address the Pro VI ball.

I take a few practice swings and then I'm ready. This is going in.

'Will you sleep with a teammate's wife again, Kevin?'

I fluff the putt and the ball wobbles forward. I turn to Neeskins, my club raised up, pointing at him.

'Look. That's the third fucking time you've done that.'

'I like to win too, Kevin,' Neeskins says, eyes raised in 'you don't want to do that' at my pointing club, a little self-contained smile on his face.

Calm it, Kev, calm it.

I lower the club.

I approach the ball and breathe deeply. Neeskins keeps quiet. My putt's not that bad, stopping four feet or so the other side of the pin.

We walk towards the flag and Neeskins pulls out his ramshackle putter. He addresses the ball. He's about to swing. I can't help myself. Bit of his own medicine. 'Can I ask you something, Mr Neeskins?'

He stops his swing and turns and smiles at me. 'Of course.'

'How did you feel when you lifted the European Cup?'

'I felt nothing.'

He turns and quickly dinks the ball with his crappy putter and it bobbles towards and then into the hole. Birdy.

I walk over, slide mine in and bogey the first. We walk to the second tee. It's surrounded by dog shit. Neeskins says nothing to me about playing for him. There's a bloke asleep next to an empty six-pack of beer on the fourth. Still Neeskins says nothing. A kid steals my ball on the seventh. We're offered crack cocaine on the ninth, but I'm offered nothing from Neeskins.

I get round the nine in forty-three, eight over. Neeskins hits par. He cuts me a new one. We walk back to the car park. Neeskins opens his boot, drops his crumby golf bag inside and turns to face me.

Is this it? This the 'five-year deal' conversation, the 'we are desperate for a player of your stature' moment? Come on, Neeskins, speak. Open the gates to the Prem.

'You know where we train, Kevin?'

'Yeah.'

'Be there at ten on Monday.'

And that's it. He says no more. He climbs in the front seat, turns the Saab around and drives off. I stand there watching the car move off, wondering what just happened. What does it mean, this 'see you at ten' bollocks?

A contract maybe? A trial? Or nothing at all? I mean, this guy's so whacked out that he might be asking me to come in and do the fucking laundry. But other hand, it might turn out to be something: a light at the end of the door, a foot in the tunnel. And I'm not exactly inundated right now, am I? Not exactly fielding calls from a host of top clubs.

I see Neeskins' car disappear and I guide my Mizuno cart bag so it stands directly behind the Bents. I climb in the motor, wake her up, and whack the Craig David right up.

I reverse slowly over my fucking kit, crunching the shit out of it.

Beaten at the golf by some bloke in Dunlops and a cardy, some bloke with a Homer Simpson golf ball. Not just any bloke, though. Henk Neeskins. Dripping with cups, that bloke, they're coming out of his arse.

I drive over the kit one more time then gun the Bents over to Colly's.

nābha sparsham dīptam

Sunday night, down at the flat.

What does it mean, 'See you at ten'? My career's on the line and he's feeding me riddles...But I'm heating myself up. I need to calm it, regain Kev's composure. I need to zone right in for tomorrow, whatever the challenge may be. Need to big myself up, spend some proper Kev time with the ink.

First, I wake up the BeoVision 7 forty-inch LCD TV, whack the vol right up and stick on my *Kev's Goals* DVD compilation. Then I strip off my white Allesandro Dell'Acqua shirt and drop to the floor, pumping out the press-ups so the muscles are nice and pingy. I stand in front of the bevelled Rocco Verre mirror and have a look. The tats are looking good, very good indeed.

Normally I'm the shit, but today I'm the absolute fucking shit.

Feeling better already.

The ink is a massive part of the Kev King package; of who I am, of what I stand for, of what I fight and shop for.

I hold my left arm up towards the mirror.

Bellum omnium contra omnes.

It's Latin. The war of all against all. That's what it says on the inside of my left forearm in spanking great gothic letters. It fucks the opposition right up, shows them I'm a warrior. They may not understand the words, may not be able to read the tat, but to

80

them it's an ominous sign of my footballing potency. At the highest level, an athlete's aura can give him a very real edge.

Nābha sparsham dīptam.

That's Sanskrit. Touch the sky with glory. Got that inked on my right forearm. It was the first tat I ever got done, apart from a Nike swoosh, but that's long gone.

Useful tool, the Nike brand, now and again, mainly for trainers and boots, but for me there's no mystique to it any more. Saw Jimmy Tarbuck at a Pro-Am in a Nike StormFit Paclite Gor-Tex jacket with competitive internal climate. Got my swoosh lasered off the next day.

I spin round and peer over my shoulder towards the Sorocco.

I look down towards the bottom of my back where the King arse begins. *Aut Caesar aut nihil*: Either Caesar or nothing.

The biggest tat I've got, and I often think the best, runs right across my back, at shoulder-blade level. Massive letters. It's a quote from *The Terminator*, Arnold Schwarzenegger: The meaning of life is not simply to exist, to survive, but to move ahead, to go up, to achieve, to conquer.

Achieving. Conquering. Essence of life.

Says it all, really. Arnie nailed it there.

Lovely bit of inkmanship as well.

The BeoVision's playing the peach I slammed in against Bolton. The Bolton game was one of the few we won in our unfortunate relegation season.

I turn from the mirror and watch the goal, seeing it zing off my left and fly in, rippling the onion bag – quality, Kev – then I spin back round to face the Sorocco mirror. I lift my arm.

Running down from beneath my armpit to my waist on the left is a fucking belter from Mr T: I believe in the golden rules…The man with the gold makes the rules.

An enduring truth. One to aspire to.

I lift my right arm: A Jedi's strength flows from the Force.

That's inked on the right of my torso, also running down from the armpit to the waist. It's a quote from Yoda. No comment needed.

I Kev forwards, closer to the mirror. In small, ornate lettering on my chest, snug between the nipples, it reads: What good is money if it can't inspire terror in your fellow man?

What good indeed?

There's a lot of wisdom in my tats. They push me on, remind me of my worth, what I'm about. As I say, the ink is a keystone of the whole Kev package.

Feeling better now, feeling Kevish.

I'm ready for you, Neeskins. I'll see *you* at fucking ten, mate.

freakish, almost

The GPS is telling me I'm here, but all I can see is a high, curving wall, a long bastard topped with razor wire, like the outside of some huge borstal. The Bents purrs around the wall, and then there it is, the entrance to the football fortress. A small, brown double gate. No sign. Unassuming.

There's a little intercom thing on a pole and I nose the Bents forward so that I'm level with it, buzz down the tinteds and jab a button. There's no answer, and there's no answer, and then there is one. 'Good morning. Corlham Wood Training Complex.'

'Hi. Yeah. It's Kev King...Neeskins, Mr Neeskins told me to come in.'

'Yes, Mr King, you're expected.'

I'm expected. Promising. Nice. The gates zzzz open and the Bents hums forward and I'm in. Long drive. Tree-lined. Then a fuck off great bib of tarmac for the parking and then there it is, Corlham training pavilion.

Split face blockwork. Iroko timber cladding. Glazed facades.

Exuding quality to attract high-calibre users.

I still the Bents and step outside and have a good look.

The promised land. This is your chance, Kev.

I Kev towards the doorway which is rimmed with silver-grey zinc-effect cladding and as I reach the entrance I wait for the sliding doors to part. But they're still, the doors do not slide. Not *manual*, are they?

I peer inside. Yellow ochre rendering. Modern and top entrance hall.

I see a receptionist behind a long, sleek desk and she sees me. She leans forward and I hear a voice, emitting from a discreet speaker somewhere near the door.

'Mr King?'

'Yes.'

Now the doors slide open and I step into Eden. Ten strides and I'm at the desk. The receptionist has a name badge: Carol. Chubby. Bad hair. Very zone six. You wouldn't. Not unless…No, you just wouldn't.

'Hello, Mr King. Pleasant journey?'

'Yeah.' I peer around. Pure Prem quality, everywhere.

I feel awe rising, but I crush it.

I am equal. I am equal. I am more than equal.

'First things, Mr King. Can you sign these, please?'

She lifts a bundle of forms and wafts them up on to the ridge of the desk.

'What are these?'

'Consent forms.'

'For what?'

'A medical.'

'A medical!'

Bingo. It's a done deal then, a quick lark on the treadmill and Kev's banged straight in the first team. The gods of football lark and sway above me, wearing my new shirt with the King moniker scribed across their backs.

'Don't worry, though, it's not the full one, the one we do before signings.'

Shit. Shit. 'What's it for then?'

'Afraid I don't know, Mr King. I wasn't told that. Please sign the forms.'

I start to have a read, but I've gone all peevish. 'Look, do I need to read all this?'

'Not really, Mr King. It's all pretty standard. You're not signing your soul away or anything.'

'Right.'

But then when I do sign, I feel my soul leave my body and disappear upwards into the award-winning vaulted roof space.

Not really.

'Right,' this Carol monster says and lifts a beige plastic object, about the size of a shitty old mid-nineties mobile, from behind the desk. 'Put your finger on the screen here.'

I do, but, 'What is this?' I ask.

'Biometric fingerprint recognition technology,' Carol says, and these exclusive words seem odd coming out of her zone six mouth. It makes me angry that someone like her can say something like that, it makes me feel dirty.

'Allows full access to the players' area,' she adds.

That's better, promising. Full access.

A small light pulses beneath my fingertip on the screen, like a halo round my finger. Carol makes a call. 'Mr Babel, Kevin King's here.' And I am. At Corlham Wood, Neeskins' famous football fortress.

A door opens and a tall bloke in poor chainstore schmutter walks out and heads towards me. Who's this wank patch? He's taller and thinner and weirder than Neeskins. He holds out his hand and I hold out mine and we shake.

He does all the 'Hello, I'm Claus Babel' stuff and then he gives me the 'Follow me', which I do and we step through another door and he's giving me the 'Latest in training, rehabilitation, medical, pitch and media technology' chat, which is all right, and I notice they've got top art on the wall, work by Banksy, the notorious anonymous graffiti artist, and so I'm looking at that and wondering how much, and then before I know it we're in the split-level isokinetic gym with hypoxic chamber and adjacent physio suite.

He's giving me the chat. Seventeen showers. Fifty-seat press lounge. Fifteen pitches.

Relaxation facilities. Signing area. Tactics room.

We walk round, he tells me all about it. 'Nice. Nice. Nice,' I say. But what is he getting at? Where is Kev's fucking contract?

A pool with tiled team crest and jet streams for resistance training.

A highly regarded football-in-the-community department.

New standards in facilities.

'Yes. Yes. Yes. Nice. Nice. Nice.'

'What do you think, Mr King? Footballistically, of course.'

'Football-wise, it's top, top stuff.'

And it is. I may be fuming because I still don't actually know what I'm here for, but I'm not lying either. It's a top, top place. I'm not just giving them the job interview shit, the 'In five years I'm going to have climbed Everest, moved it into the back garden and be making a mint flogging donkey rides up it' cobblers. I am not doing that at all. I am impressed. The whole place is Kevishly good. Football-wise I could thrive here.

'One thing though.'

'Yes, Mr King?'

'Where are the, you know, footballers?'

For an answer we walk towards a huge floor-to-ceiling window and he points out across the flat apron of green behind the pavilion. On one of the far pitches I can see thirty or so figures, some in yellow bibs, some in red, some jogging, others passing the ball, others swerving through chicanes of bollards, balls presumably at their feet. Three other figures watch the activity, hands behind their backs, heads observantly tilted. Neeskins presumably, and his coaches.

Why aren't I out there? I want to be among the lads.

Going in hard. Going in fast. Ball skills. Intelligent running. Commitment. Total fucking commitment. Worth little without technique, though, which is fine because that's what I've got, technique, falling out of my arse, got bundles of it all over the house, got it stashed at Nan's, hidden in lock-ups, got so much of it that I don't even use that I stick it in carrier bags and leave it

86

outside charity shops for lesser players to pick up.

'Can I go out there? Say hello to the boys?'

'Mr Neeskins was very specific about your tasks for the day.'

'And what are my tasks?'

'This way, Mr King.'

Fucker.

We go into the changing room, and Babel gives it the 'Our changing room is split into friendship groups according to languages' chat, and then he hands over some club Umbros and walks out, saying, 'This way when you're ready,' as he leaves.

I'm alone in the changing room.

I look at the kit Babel gave me. There's some blue tracky bums and a blue sweat top with the club crest on the front.

I take off the black suede Voile Blanche shoes, the white Victor Glemaud trousers and the grey Neil Barrett short-sleeved shirt and climb into the club Umbs. I slip on my Nike Air Tiempo Rival Premium iDs and have a pad around the changing room.

Some of the lads are tidy, all their clobber is packed away in their named and numbered lockers. Nice. But some of the lads are filth, their clothes chucked down on the bench or the floor. Still: Armand Basi, Claiborne, Number (N)ine. There's some top, top brands.

I look at the names on the lockers and find Dukey's. Number fourteen. Like me he's a midfield marauder. Second choice for the squad right now, after Rantanen, and a very good player.

Silverware galore. Current international. Illustrious career.

But I can't give a fuck about that. Because the Jock's my competition, Dukey's got what I want. A place in the squad. And it's my job to take it from him. If I get the chance, that is. If I manage to cut through this weird Neeskins bullshit, then Dukey'll find I'm a direct competitor, that me and him are at war.

I look down at his Maison Martin Margiela trousers, tossed carelessly on the floor. Good strides. Really. Dukey's got some taste. But so sloppy, leaving them on the floor like that.

I eye his locker. 'You've just met your fucking match, mate.'

I put the hex on the Duke.

I walk over to number eight, Rantanen's locker. Ahti Rantanen, the Finnish maestro. Current first choice for the Kev King position. The guy I have to deal with after I've faced down the Duke. And that'll be tough, I admit, because the Rant is a top, top player. Really. The best his country's ever produced, and how quality like he's got came up through the primeval Moomin forests of Finland will remain an eternal footballing mystery. But however it happened, happen it did, and Rantanen has been a stalwart of the Neeskins' tenure since day one. He's been the first name on the sheet. Undroppable, almost, he is. And it's up to me – to Kev – to reverse that, to nip in front of the whey-faced maestro and snaffle his midfield berth. It's a tall order, I know. But then I am a tall orderer. Especially for a man of medium height.

I stand in front of Rantanen's locker. And for a moment I feel nervy and daunted, out of my league almost. But then I conjure the ink to the Kevish mind's eye and summon the power of the Prem.

'You're about to get found out, mate,' I say to Rantanen's locker.

I close my eyes, picturing myself in the number eight shirt, his number eight shirt, saluting the faithful, taking the plaudits, hoisting the cups. Then I picture Rantanen and his shitty flyaway hair, his scrubby blond mutton chops. I picture him injured, losing form, slipping down the leagues.

Here he is, I can see him in my mind, playing for Scunthorpe or Brentford or some muck like that, grunting it out in lower leagues. I give him the full voodoo…Losing his international place, losing his model wife, enduring the qualifying rounds of the FA Cup on a piss wet November night. Remembering the day he first saw Kev, the day it all started to unravel for the Finnish fucking maestro.

Yeah. That's right.

I open my eyes and take the door Babel left by. I spot him in a corner of the gym, next to a treadmill and some monitors. I'm on it now. I'm galvanized. You can only take the test that's put in front of you.

I walk over and Babel sits me down and takes my heart rate, then looks at me all baffled. Always the same with these fucking tests, I always stroll them: weirdly low resting heart rate, supremely low lactate levels, huge aerobic capacity.

Huge numbers. Physically unusual. Blah blah blah.

What do they expect? I mean, they know who I am.

I take off my top and he wires me up to an ECG and I pop on an oxygen mask. The treadmill starts and gradually the speed and incline increase.

Jogging jogging, la la la.

Babel is looking at the monitors as I wind up the run. I know what'll happen when I'm done. And it does.

'You've got a VO2 max of seventy-six, Kevin.'

'Yeah.'

'That's very, very good.'

'I know.'

'Freakish, almost. The next best at the club is sixty-seven. It's really very unusual.'

'Yeah.'

Babel is scratching his head, bald twat. I pop my top back on.

vast ragged testes

'No, Colly, it was utter dog shit. Not a sniff of a deal. Met no one apart from some gym monkey who measured me up.'

'No practice at all, Kev?'

'I was only there an hour.'

'What about Dukey and Rantanen? You hear anything about them, Kev?'

'Nothing.'

'Weird. A couple of their *reserve* centre mids are out, but if Neeskins has got those two, that should be enough.'

'Hang on, Colly, Sas's on the other line.'

I flip the Arte from Colly to Sas. 'Babe.'

'Kev, you'll never guess what.'

'You're right, Sas, I won't. Colly's waiting. Tell me.'

'I've been chosen.'

'What?'

'I've been asked to do *I'm A Celebrity…Get Me Out of Here*. It'll be the highest profile work I've ever done.'

'Who else is on it?'

'They won't say.'

'Hang on, Sas, the landline's ringing.'

I walk over and pick it up.

'Kev. It's Colly.'

'Thought you were on hold on the mobes?'

'I am. I'm on here as well. You'll never guess what, Kev?'

'You're right, I won't.'

I'm holding the Arte in my left hand and I can hear Sas screaming over the line.

'Hang on, Colly...Hi, Sas.'

'Kev, you were talking to me.'

'I was, but I was talking to Colly before that.'

'Who was that on the landline?'

'Colly.'

'I thought he was on the mobes?'

'He is. Listen, Sas, Colly's got some news for me. Can I call you back?'

'Not really, I'm about to go into a shoot.'

'Oh yeah, for what? Got anything nice on?'

'I'll have nothing on. It's my revenge shoot.'

'The sexual rampage stuff?'

'Yeah, that's right. Sweet you remembered, Kev.'

Sweet? Not the word I'd use. Not exactly going to forget about my Wag's plans to be snapped in a naked, erotic tussle with some Adonis, am I? No matter how gay that Adonis claims to be. But at least now she'll be jetting off afterwards, deep into the Aussie sticks, where he won't be able to touch her. But anyway, I can't deal with this now, can't think about it. I need to talk to Colly.

'Yeah. Listen, Sas, well done about the jungle. Talk to you later.'

I close the call to Sas and flip to the other line on the mobile, but Colly's not there any more. I flip to his number and speed-dial, but then he might still be on the landline, which I put back to my ear.

'Kev. It's all over Sky News. You'll never guess what.'

'Just fucking tell me, Colly.'

'It's Dukey. He's got ball rot.'

'What?'

'The Duke, his nuts are fucked.'

'Colly, come on.'

'Testicular cancer, Kev. That's why they want you. The Duke's out. You're second in line to Rantanen.'

I look out of the Venetians towards the award-winning retail and leisure complex on the far side of the river, the landmark atrium like a huge misshaped translucent bollock, the clouds above it like vast ragged testes.

Neeskins must've known about the ball rot.

Nice. It's between me and Finnish maestro now.

in the box

I leave the Bents in the car park and walk towards the crematorium, a red-brick box with some crumby stained-glass windows depicting spindly spaz people walking towards some big purple sun. The walk towards death, I suppose. Modern you'd call it.

There's a crowd round the doors of the building, waiting to go in. I spot Gravesy and Boves and walk over. Gravesy's wearing a black three-button Bottega Venetia suit, a white Miharayasuhiro shirt and John Varvatos brogues.

'Kev-o.'

'Scored again, Gravesy,' I say, keeping my voice respectfully low.

'Yeah, mate. On a bit of a run. That's five in six.'

I shake with Gravesy and turn to Boves.

'Kev.'

'Boves.'

He is wearing a charcoal-grey single-button Wintle suit with a white Richard Chai shirt and five-eye Gibson lace-ups.

'Any word from Neeskins?' Boves asks.

'Fuck all.'

'Dar-o's over there,' says Gravesy and he nods towards a gaggle of old pros stood closer to the crematorium door. I look over and spot Darren. He's alone, not brought his missus. Wise, Darren, very wise. I thought I might be angry when I saw him, but I'm not.

Darren did what he had to. He lumped me because I fucked his wife.

Fair play. Understandable transaction.

What does make me angry, though, is seeing Darren chatting with ex-England playmaker Paul Gascoigne. Gascoigne may be a muppet, but he was the most naturally gifted player of his generation. He should be over here, talking to me, his natural heir, not making small talk with a journeyman player.

Still.

I look at Boves and at Gravesy. There's some jokes to tell, no doubt, and some new quim to chat about, I suspect, but we can't, not really. Not the place for gags, a funeral. We know that. Instead we just stand around looking fucking excellent.

My old gaffer's widow is here, standing near the door, a hem of crying family surrounding her, most of them dressed in mince clobber.

Shame. Important day. Should have made the effort.

We file inside, into the wide, cold hall. The gaffer's in his coffin on the right-hand side, brass handles shining in the strip lights.

Gaffer's in the box. First time for everything. Defensive midfielder, the gaffer, in his playing days. Seem to remember that he didn't score a single goal his entire senior career, barely got out of the centre circle.

Now he's loitering in the box for good.

He's dead, the gaffer. Gone. It's sad. Not really, but it is. The gaffer was a servant to the game. And a character, an individual.

But there's more important things than individuals. Customer service for instance, without which we are no better than the animals – we might as well be grubbing about in the shit, scoffing berries and fingering squirrels or whatever the cave-fuckers did… No, customer service, consumer quality, these things are the cornerstones of civilization. Take that away and we are barbarians, giving and receiving no respect. Da Vinci understood that. Keegan does as well, no doubt.

And I'll tell you what else is crucial, is more important than individuals. And that's contracts. They are the glue that holds consumers together; shopper to shopper, customer to customer, man to man. And if you start to break them, if you treat a contract as though it were nothing...Well, do that, and as I say, we're grubbing about with the beasts.

There's some vicar lad, some priest or something, and he wheels out the god cobblers. I look down. The black Gucci brogues with russet and platinum leather trim are excellent.

God god god. Yeah yeah yeah.

We've all been there. Not possible, these days, to use the photogenic real estate of the church – for a wedding say, or just a simple get-together like today – without having to listen to the god blurb.

Opportunity cost, I suppose. Entrance fee.

Shame, because God may have worked wonders in the early days. I'm not joking, he may well have done, I keep an open mind. But he's not the player he was, and you've got to move with the times, update the squad.

Entrepreneur Richard Branson. Technology guru Alan Sugar. Retail overlord Philip Green.

These are the people who make the world today.

Genesis. Exodus. Paphitis.

That's how the world evolves.

There's a reading. Gaffer's daughter, Denise. Memories, or something, that's what she's talking about.

Denise, Denise, Denise – black Balenciaga dress, Lanvin overcoat, Fendi suede boots visible occasionally from the side of the lectern as you move about and give it the 'Dad was the best' chat that we all wheel out when someone carks it. She's the only one of their lot that's dressed, though, give her that, the only one that's not chucked a sack on over her head.

Shag-wise, Denise-wise, you certainly would have done a few years ago, but the dough's going a bit stale now, the sag has come upon her. Still. Maybe. I wonder. I put my hands behind my back and look all solemn. I give it a bit of the dignity. I scrutinize the gaffer's daughter.

I wonder if I would, now, this afternoon, say, after we torch the gaffer. Or tomorrow maybe, that'd be better; after all, she's a bit tearful right now and I wouldn't want the mascara staining my Egyptian cotton.

Yeah. Maybe. Yeah. Good jays. And yeah, I think, all things considered – I clear my throat – I probably would do her. I mean it would take a dull, wet afternoon. But I probably would.

Because firstly, as select teammates both past and present know – and I seem to remember that Gravesy once had a pop at her – Denise has experience, she's got a lot in her fuck locker.

And secondly, as she is now on the turn, entering the autumn of her years so to say, I'd bet she'd seek to compensate sexually. It's standard practice in all realms, football, commerce or shagging: if the competition's hotter, you've got to put the graft in.

You've got to track back.

So yeah, I would. It's decided. Weight off my mind. She's finished her reading. They're playing a song. Gaffer's favourite – 'Islands In The Stream'.

Rogers and Parton. Kenny and Dolly. Very nice.

Is that Ron Atkinson, ex-Wednesday, Villa and ManU manager in the second row? It is. Certainly. He's got a square head, and as he moves that square head to one side I see his tanned cheek, orange as the Dutch kit.

Glutton for the sunbed, that boy.

The gaffer's widow takes the stand.

And she finds it hard. I mean, she is upset. Him passing in such nasty circumstances, and out of the blue like that. One day he's giving out to the players on the training ground and then coming back to the house for his nightly bottle of Rioja and an appointment with Blackburn vs Stoke on the goggle. And then it all stops. One night they're still going at it maybe, her squeezing her blubber into a push-up Ann Summers bra, him braying like a shot zebra as he unleashes, and the next night he's gone. Dead by the patio doors, cold as a witch's tit. No more gaffer.

Sure she misses him. Sure she does.

Forty years in the saddle. Bound to. She's crying and Denise steps forward and puts us all out of our misery. She takes the gaffer's widow's hand. Denise puts her arm around her and walks her slowly back to the pews.

There's another song now. 'Hotel California' by the Eagles. Enjoyed his music, the gaffer. We stand and once again we look like we mean it, we look like we are feeling the Eagles (which I am) and this suit – by Kris Van Assche – is very, very comfortable. Or maybe it's the Patrick Ervill shirt that is providing the wonderful sense of comfort I am feeling.

Either way, I feel like the daddy.

I can see the back of Denise's head. Gascoigne's. Atkinson's. Welcome to the Hotel California. I am getting a lob on. The vicar comes back. Never satisfied, this lad. He says the gaffer's gone to a better place.

'What, the Emirates?' I shout out.

Not really.

The coffin rolls towards the heavy curtains which open and the foot of the box moves beyond the fabric, as the gaffer slides towards the furnace beyond.

I look over to the boys and Gravesy has a little tear, a proud Aussie tear that has escaped from the 'roo pouch of his eye and is gambling and hopping down his boss-eyed little Aussie face. And I look beyond Gravesy to Boves and Boves is crying too, the tears on his cheek looking so silver and wet against his black skin, and then I feel all horrible.

I should be crying too, I suppose. I should be upset. And I am. I mean I'm not, but I am.

The gaffer's gone, the curtains close. We file outside. It's pissing down.

The gaffer's smoke is rising out the chimney.

Part Two

enigmatic, the dutchman

Training. Training with the first team at Corlham Wood.

Been out here for two hours; shuttle runs, passing, running with the ball. Boy Scout stuff.

Third time I've been back to Corlham. Member of the squad, by now, you might think. But no. Not a word. No noise on a contract, no noise on the cash. Not a fucking squeak. Just keep getting asked to come back in. And you know, despite my pissed-right-off-ometer being about to blow, of course come back in I do. Got no other opps, see; no other offers. And I need to return to the Prem. It's my destiny. And then when I get there, after I have re-pitched my tent on firm Premish soil, then I will clearly need some silverware.

So, I put up with this silence, this 'come back in' cobblers, because this is a top, top side, fighting for pots and pans on all fronts, and what would I do otherwise? Bang in two hundred goals a season for the Stepney Strollers? Give me a fucking break.

The lads – internationals, Premiership stalwarts, winners to a man – jink and dribble. Neeskins is not around. 'Paperwork' or something, hasn't actually spoken one word to me as yet.

Morales, the Spanish coach, is giving us the training drills and he can barely speak the Queen's, waves his arms around like he's landing a fucking plane. Whistles and tuts and grumbles.

He's a twat, Morales, but then again he's a twat with a lot of silverware under his belt, or in his locker, or wherever the lad likes to stash his cups. Wouldn't like to be his cleaning lady, put it that way. Tennis elbow in a week from gleaming all them trophies.

He's won what I want, and a top-class midfield schemer in his day, Morales was. Received the ball nice, gave the ball nice. Made himself time. Won the Champs League with Real. Played with Zidane at Juve. He's a prick, though.

Dresses like a civvy. Dresses even worse than Neeskins. What is it with these backroom boys? Don't they want to make the best of themselves? If you can look like the don, then look like the don. This lad, though, Morales, el Primark Kid, he's not interested.

'OK, OK,' says Morales, clapping his Umbro mittens together like some hungry seal, 'Enough. Enough. Warm down. Warm down.'

You buddy up with someone for the warm-down, that's Morales' way.

Ashley Hughes walks over.

'Kev,' he says and puts his hand on my shoulder and raises his leg behind him to stretch the thigh. Terrific centre half, Ash, built like a heavyweight, but with pace to burn. We use each other for balance as we warm down the legs.

Ash is all right, a bit mopey, a bit of a worrier. But he's all right.

I am warming down, I am stretching out the calf and, hang on, what's that? A figure stood at the window of the training pavilion. Far away, just a stickman really in the big window. That Neeskins? Checking out the likes of your Kev Kings? Is that Neeskins, making up his mind to sign me or not? Better fucking be.

I must have shifted a bit while I'm looking, because, 'Concentrate, Kev.'

'Sorry, Ash.'

Warming down next to me and Ash are Boro Danzo, the

Gambian target man, and Rantanen, our Finnish friend. Rantanen's been a bit off with me, a bit sullen. I don't mind that. He is my enemy, and I am his.

We're in competition. There's no 'team' in the letter I.

Was thinking of going into him in practice a couple of times. Wouldn't be unheard of, a player gliding into the first team because he nailed a rival deliberately. Wouldn't take much, a stud to the ankle, a boot to the calf, and the boy'd be out for a while, the boy'd be out for our visit to St James's Park next week. Then hey presto, look what we have here, a ready-made replacement in the shape of your Kev King.

Like to play there again, in Geordie land, at the temple of doom. Disarray, that's what the Geordies do best, disarray. Scored last visit. Toe poked in a corner when the ball came loose. Lost 3–1 though, the season we went down.

I haven't gone into Rantanen though. Or poisoned his pasta, or paid Four Chins to cut his breaks, or any of the shall we say less orthodox ways a player might be caused to miss a game or two. Not done any of that. Because I rate Kev, I do. I back myself and I can take the Rant's place – I know I can – through sheer, undiluted footballness. I can fend off the mutton-chopped Moomin using the power of my football quality, or the quality of my football power. Either way round, don't matter to me, either way's fine. I'm a better player than him. I know I am. And why indeed nobble when you can outclass?

'I'm done, Kev.'

'Me too, Ash.'

'Kev?'

'Yeah?'

'This stuff in the papers? The stuff with your girlfriend and the sexual rampage?'

Oi oi. Here we fucking go then. Wondered how long it'd be. I look over and see Boro Danzo and Rantanen, both earwigging, both smiling, as though they've put Ash up to this line of questioning. Which they no doubt have; dumb Ash being a stooge

103

in all this. And I'd love right now to tell Rantanen to stick it, or to see off Danzo with a fucking bollard even. But the reality is that I'm the new guy here. Or not even that. Reality is, I *hope* to be the new guy here. Meaning I'm low, totem pole-wise. And despite, in Kev's view, having been the best player out here today on this training ground, I am still – eerily – without contract, and therefore not in a situation to provoke full rumpus by slapping down key squad members. I control Kev's anger and instead give it a go with the old humility.

'Yes, Ashley?'

'What do you make of it?'

'How do you mean?' I ask, in fact knowing exactly what he means.

'I mean, you were caught with someone and she was caught with someone and you're still together, yeah?'

'Yeah, Ash, we are.'

'But...She mind you seeing other women? She mind you playing away?'

'She weren't too happy about it, Ash.'

'You mind her playing away, Kev?'

I hear Rantanen chuckle to my left, but I keep my Kevposure.

'She didn't. She never touched that bloke.'

'What?'

'They did it with angles.'

'Right. Photoshop or something?'

'Yeah, that. Angles. Photoshop. Yeah.'

'But Kev, she did touch him, she had his...'

'She *did* touch him, but she never *really* touched him. Bloke was gay, wanted my autograph. It was a set-up.'

I've had enough now. Before Ash can reply, I turn abruptly away, feeling the Finman's eyes rubbing into my back as I walk towards the pavilion to get changed up. Slightly ahead of me there's French striker Leon Bédard, the 2006 World Cup finalist, chatting web porn with Alvar, the great Brazilian left back and 2002 World Cup winner. Those two men, pinnacle of the game.

That's why I'm here. Ride the jibes, Kev. That's the way.

And there's big Simmy, the third choice striker, or is it fourth? Got a good touch for a big man, Simmy, I'll give him that. Thick as pig shit, though. We stroll back towards the pavilion.

Two hundred and sixty-seven million quid, if you add it all up, which I did. That's what this full first team squad cost. That's a lot of cash, especially considering a couple of the boys came on frees, and three were brought through the academy.

Two hundred and sixty-seven million quid. That is a Kevish amount of cash. It's a top, top squad.

The lads sit around in the changing room. I look around. Anselmo, the Uruguayan keeper, is talking *Top Gear* with Daaf Bakker, his Dutch deputy. Three Champions Leagues between them, those two. Our Egyptian winger, Ali el-Masri, who made such a mark for himself in Milan, is chatting PS3 with the Greek Euro 2004-winning right back Ilias Pappas.

I'm next to the English lads, Simmy and Ash.

'Come on, Kev, cough up.'

Simmy is holding a cash-filled baseball cap out towards me.

'What?'

'Whip-round for the Duke. Buy him something.'

'Come on, Kingy,' Simmy adds. 'Double the money from you, seeing as you're the one gaining from his fucked ball.'

No problems.

I reach into my locker – a spare berth on the far side of the changing room, no name on it as yet, no number added – and pull the Aspinall of London cognac EBL and espresso suede breast wallet from my beige Belstaff strides. I pull two crisp fifties from the wallet and flick them into the cap.

'That a purse you got there, Kev?' Simmy asks.

I'm not even going to bother.

'What you going to buy the Duke then, Simmy?'

'A new bollock.'

'You can get them, actually,' Ash chimes in, all strangely in-the-know.

'Like a boob job or something, Ash?' asks Simmy.

'Bit like that, yeah.'

'What *are* you going to buy him, though?' I ask, because for some reason I do actually want to know.

'Don't know. Might just give him the cash. Then he can get what he wants.'

'Simmy?'

'Yes, Kev?'

'You're going to give a multimillionaire a hat full of notes as a present?' I ask. 'Very fucking thoughtful.'

'What would you get him then, Kev?'

'What about an orchid?' Ash pipes up.

'Twat,' Simmy says.

But I like it, it's a good idea. The orchid is a very minge-like flower, and you could imagine doing it, really. Having an orchid by your sickbed would be like having a sweet, small vag nearby as you recovered. A minge on a stalk. On a stick, even.

'I think that's a good idea, Ash.'

Ash looks at me. He thinks I'm taking the piss, which I'm not. I like the boy, despite the grilling earlier. But he's not used to support. What with his dozy questions and his queer medical knowledge and now this orchid suggestion, the lad's used to getting it in the neck, questions being asked about his lifestyle, his sexuality even.

As though that matters.

The gay man has every right to play the humpty, same as your Eskimo. Football is a global democracy. There's only one consideration on the pitch and that's quality.

And if you've got quality, well…

The lads change up. I pop on the Borg swimmers and fuck about in the pool. I'm in no hurry. Truth is, I've got nowhere I want to go. This lack of offer situ means I've got the hump, the arse. The humped arse.

I'll kill some time here.

I zone out in the hot tub. Then there's a slow shower and I slip on the Unified Last Chance T-shirt and the beige Belstaffs. The changing room's empty. I stroll over to Rantanen's locker and give it the eyes. I unleash the Kev voodoo on to the Finn's locker. He'll feel that.

The door opens. It's Neeskins. He walks straight over.

'Kevin. I saw your car still here. Come with me.'

Aye aye. Here we go. Here we fucking go.

If you'd just like to step this way into the Premiership, Mr King…

Neeskins turns and walks away from me and I follow. Out the door and through the isokinetic gym space, then up the stairs, passing the investment street art, and on to the top floor of the pavilion. Then there it is, at the end of a long, light corridor. The lair of fucking Neeskins.

He walks in and I follow.

Interesting space.

Next to me by the door is a simple collaboration area with twin KnollStudio tabular Brno chairs in black spinnybeck leather. Deeper into Neeskin's lair, where he now paces, there is a carefully considered smoked walnut TechWood desk. It is immediately clear to me that the colours of Neeskin's furniture have been diligently edited and that a palette has been applied across product lines, using an optimum surface finish library.

This really is excellent furniture and the monochromatic panel fabrics both define the space and complement the architecture. But looking at Neeskins where he stands, his back now to me, peering out across the seventeen training pitches, and knowing him as I do, as a man who drives a fucked Saab and dresses like he's on probation – knowing him as a man who uses a Homer Simpson golf ball – I can't help being surprised by the quality of his workspace, and the unquivering commitment to the power of modern design which it embodies. He has both perplexed and interested me.

Neeskins turns from the window and walks back towards me, rounding the office system in his battered corduroy strides, and joining me in the collaborative space. He gestures for me to sit on one of the Brno chairs.

Enigmatic, the Dutchman; scarecrow clothes and yet low-emission, Ludwig Mies van der Rohe-designed furniture. I sit.

'Kevin.'

'Mr Neeskins.'

'Footballistically, Kevin…'

'Yeah, football-wise…'

The Dutchman eyes me. I have interrupted him. Why did I do that? Nerves, that's why. Nerves. Neeskins is the St Peter of the Premiership gates, if you'll allow.

'Sorry, Mr Neeskins. Gaffer.'

'Footballistically, you can play. And I think in many ways you are near optimum levels. Pass-wise you are sometimes blinkered, but fitness, desire to win and technique – yes, Kevin even your technique – are good.'

'Thanks yeah.'

It's good. It's not exactly news to Kev, but it is a compliment.

Still, where's the offer? Where is it, you mystifying twat?

I look at the Dutchman, with his thin head and his slightly droopy lower jaw which falls open, and I want him, great man – footballistically of course – though he may be, I want him to just spit it out. I want to know if I'm in or out. Am I chasing the proper silverware, or am I frozen out with the Stepney Strollers? Because Kev is in the balance here.

Neeskins looks at me. 'Kevin, turn your phone off.'

Turn off the Arte, mate? What crazed horseshit is this? He's a wacko, this boy, three players short of a cup run. But I pull out the Arte and dink it to sleep.

'For me, Kevin, it is very simple. I want you to play for me for the rest of the season.'

'I…'

'But I will not speak to your agent. Not today, or ever. If you wish to pay him out of the money we pay you, then do so. But that is none of my business. He represents two other players at this club, Anselmo and Paul Whelan, and today I have said the same to them. This football club will no longer be dealing with Mr Collingwood.'

What? Why? Why freeze out Colly? What's going on? He's not done anything. He's my mate.

But 'No Colly, no deal' I don't in fact state, instead being seized by a feeling of total Premiership and, 'Right,' I merely say, because, you know, there's a hierarchy at work here, with Kev naturally being higher up it than Kev's mates.

And I've got no time to think about Neeskins' weird Colly move, because, 'Your Premiership experience,' he continues, 'rates you in the mid range of our pay scale. But you have not played as a senior international. And also, your merchandise value is demonstrably low.'

Low merchandise value? Bollocks. This just gets weirder. But keep it zipped, Kev. Shut it until you get the offer.

'I will use you as a squad player. You will play while I rest Ahti against lesser Premiership teams. There will be games in the Carling and in the FA Cups. Possibly even as an impact sub in Europe.'

Good. Nice. Quality. But how much, mate? Spit it out.

'You will be paid sixty-three thousand pounds a week.'

Fuck off. It's unfairly low. Verging on insulting. But then again, it's my route back to the Prem.

'Done.'

keegan

Away fixture. We're on the team bus. I am back where I belong. My whole body – my very hair and ball bag – zings with irreducible Premiershipness. Elated does not cover it.

I am relieved and exhilarated. I am vindicated.

We are driving up to Geordieland. I was named after Kevin Keegan, who has twice managed the Newcastle club.

A lot of shit has been written about Keegan, so let's get back to basics and have a look at his pots and pans. Three First Division titles. Two UEFAs, a European cup. Two FA Cups. All with Liverpool. Sixty-three caps. Twice European Footballer of the Year, even while playing for little-fancied Hamburger SV, a club whom he helped to their first Bundesliege title in almost twenty years.

Forty-eight goals in seventy-eight games for Newcastle United.

Five hundred and ninety-two career appearances.

Trophies. Application. Achievement.

That's what we talk about when we talk about Joseph Kevin Keegan, the player – Mighty Mouse, King Kev, the Messiah – a Yorkshireman idolized by the Kopite, the Toon Army, and on the banks of the Elbe.

I admire Keegan, yes, but I am not blind. I know his management record is patchy. Plus-wise, he gave Newcastle fleeting title hopes, and at the first time of asking returned a beleaguered Man City side to the top flight. Even management-wise there have been trademark swashbuckling moments. But what is inescapable is that Keegan has also been a cavalier and touchy gaffer. He has shown a tendency towards whimsical resignation.

I will be the first to admit that.

And as a respecter of the contract, as a consumer rights idealist, I cannot sanction that aspect of Keegan the man. Not at all. But Keegan is an idealist too, football-wise. I think about Keegan as we travel north on the bus. I sometimes feel that my life is intertwined with his.

sumatran blue ling tong

The game's already kicked off when I walk with Simmy into the executive space of the Platinum Club, high up in the Jackie Milburn Stand of St James' Park; which means we've missed the minute's silence held for my old gaffer. Still. Not going to kill him, is it?

Simmy tweaked his hammer in training, my paperwork hasn't quite gone through. Neither of us made the squad. Disappointed, yes, definitely, I am, not to at least have graced the bench. But this Prem return is early doors as yet. The gilded gates have been scaled, if you will, and now I'll be calm and await my chance.

Studious, in fact; behaving with none of the rashness which some claim marked my earlier career. New leaf, see. A calmer Kev King, the Prem'll see now, a student of the game. A scholar.

We are wearing the club schmutter, me and the Sim: brown, two-button Hermès suits. Simmy's teamed his with a white Prada shirt and distressed leather Paul Smith brogues. Which, frankly, looks shit. I am wearing Yohjiyamoto black leather baseball boots and a Junya Watanabe shirt.

St James' is hosting a capacity 52,000 crowd.

I look around the executive box – giving an excellent view of the pitch actually – to see if our Indian Chairman's here. There was talk he might make it. There's some upper-mid-range

112

schmuttter in here – and there's Colly, far side of the box, who breaks off his schmoozy chat with Geordie legend Super Mac to toss me a furtive little look – but I can't see the Chairman anywhere.

Simmy and I walk towards the catering facilities of the Platinum Club. There's some little Herbert, finned hair, maybe a student or something, serving the drinks.

'What brands of coffee do you have?' I ask.

He purses his lips as though he is thinking about it, as though he reckons he knows, but then, 'Lavazza. We have the Pienaroma and the Tierra,' he says, assuredly. Which is a surprise.

He doesn't have a Geordie accent, though. Definite student, working the match days to pay the fees. Which is good, got to pull your weight with the cash. I like that, but then at the same time he's being all Mr Coffee, being all 'I know the coffee' about things.

'Right,' I say in actually-mate-you-know-fuck-all. 'Don't you stock anything else bar the Lavazza, son? Maybe an Old Brown Java or an Australian Skybury?'

'Sadly, sir, we only stock the Lavazza. But the Lavazza Tierra is made with excellent beans, picked from medium to high altitude areas in Colombia, Peru and Honduras.'

Oh. Oh. Oh, I see. Coffee war, is it? Fucking let's parade our fucking coffee knowledge, is it? Get our coffee cocks out, is it, measure them up?

'Honduras and Peru,' I say, 'are certainly emergent coffee nations, but Lavazza-wise, I'm traditional, preferring the premium Brazilian plantation beans of the Pienaroma.'

'Fuck's sake,' says Simmy. 'Give us a tea, mate.'

'One tea for you, sir,' says the coffeeish Herbert, and turning to me says, 'The Pienaroma for you, sir?'

I nod. 'Americano. Milky. Fat Free.'

'Very good, sir, I'll bring them over. Where are you sitting?'

I gesture, quite naturally, towards the best seats, at the front of the Platinum Club box, and Simmy and I turn away from the

Herbert, walk towards them and sit down.

The Magpies are kicking towards the Leazes End and we're attacking the Gallowgate. The game's being played at full tilt.

Deep in their half our Gambian hitman Boro Danzo runs the channel and receives the ball nice from el-Masri, our Egyptian right winger, but their keeper Given comes out quick and gathers and punts up to Nicky Butt who lays it in to Obefemi Martins, before our Greek right back Pappas thunders in and dispossesses, pinging it off Martins for a throw-in.

Pappas takes it and throws back to the feet of Anselmo, our keeper, who clips a long one off the floor over to the left of midfield where it's gathered by Dutchman Wally de Groot who plays a one two with Eyodema, our ex-Barça Togolese, and – keeping chalk on his boots – heads for the by-line, jostling with Beye, the Newcastle left back.

We've got good width.

Definitely having the best of these exchanges.

We're battering them nil nil.

Beye prods it out and it's our throw which Pappas lumbers up to take, before dropping a short one in to Bédard, our languid French striker, who plays Pappas back in and watches the Greek knock one into the mixer where leggy Danzo rises and glances in a little near-post header, which is easy for their keeper Given to take and boot, looping the ball up to the centre circle where their unsettled strike dwarf Michael Owen is easily dispossessed by Ash Hughes, our dozy, colossal centre half.

And so we build again. This time with Baki Ozan, the ball-playing German-Turkish centre half charged with bringing it out from the back.

Rantanen's been quiet so far, which is good. Still, that's the boy's style. Anonymous for periods of the game, before stumbling trollishly out of the ancient Finnish woodland, or the midfield, or wherever the tit's been hiding his stringy little head, to drop a couple of killer passers on to a striker's toe and change the game. It kills me to say it – though actually in fact I admit that it does not really kill me to say it – but he's a very good player. Football-wise.

Their team-wise, Owen's not the striker he was. Not going to force himself back into the England reckoning on this sort of form. Like the look of their Nigerian Obefemi Martins, though. The lad's an athlete. Inconsistent, but athletically so. Other players, their side-wise, Shay Given's an instinctual shot-stopper who's been a fantastic servant to the Newcastle club, in the Shearer Era and now beyond. While Nicky Butt still has a range of passing and Damien Duff – while not being as direct as he once was – is an intermittently threat-wielding player.

They've got just about enough in the locker to do you some damage.

But that said, we've got the edge all over the park.

Any of their players get in our team? I'll be frank. Would they fuck.

Different league. We are. Basically.

I want a shit. I don't but I do.

I ordered coffee. Where's the coffee?

I look quickly behind me for the Herbert, but hang on, is that retired Newcastle and England striker Peter Beardsley sat behind us? It is. Class act, Beardsley, elegant player, for both club and country. A gentleman.

Eyes back to the game and we must have sprung an offside on them because Anselmo's taking a free kick just outside our box, the big Uruguayan herding our team up the park then unleashing a long, ambitious ball into the left corner for de Groot to chase down, which he does, knocking it inside to the advancing Rantanen who guides an angled ball into the path of Bédard, who slices it ineffectually behind for a goal kick.

Carving them open. They've got no midfield. Only a matter of time.

And here's the coffee. The Herbert's hand reaches low to my side and pops the cup down on the ugly but ingenious match-day tray which pivots out from the arm of my executive seat. I glance down. Chunky raw sugar cubes and twin almond Cantuccini biscuits. Nice. The rich South American blend strikes upwards to the King nose.

Simmy picks up his tea.

Their kick's looped high and long by Given but Alvar's on it, gliding out of our left back position to nod it forwards on to the chest of Gilchrist Eyodema who then taps one into the path of Rantanen who looks up, looks down, opening his legs, their midfield melting away, heading through the centre circle, el-Masri as a runner to his right, de Groot to his left, Danzo and Bédard in support as well, trying to stay onside. And we're in a five man attack suddenly and they are in disarray and Rantanen keeps nudging it in front of him, and he's pushing up towards their box, runners everywhere, runners and channels swirling everywhere for the Finn, and now at this time, at this level, it is all about choice.

As in the consumer realm at the highest level, so at this, the highest level of sport, quality is about the choices you make.

One two with de Groot, or play Bédard in?

Fade towards the line, using el-Masri as cover to draw the man, then clip one in to the tall head of the Gambian?

These are the choices that the tricksy Finn is faced with and these are the choices of life.

The Tierra or the Pienaroma? To pass or shoot?

And Rantanen chooses, he plays in de Groot who...

This is not the Pienaroma. I can smell that. This coffee *is* Lavazza, true, but surely the Herbert has served me the Tierra instead. He has. I can smell that. I went to the trouble of instructing the young Barrista, clearly stating my preference for the Brazilian Arabica bean, and yet when the coffee is made and served, the lad forgets. He neglects the choices which the customer has made.

It is shoddy and insulting. It is not acceptable.

I stand and gormless Simmy looks up at me, wanting an explanation which I do not give him. I turn away from the game, and walk by the watching Beardsley, making my way back towards the Platinum Club's catering facilities. I spot the Herbert walking out of the club, wearing his little silver match-day waistcoat, and I follow.

The coffee Herbert steps out into a corridor which runs half the length of the Milburn Stand. I follow the Herbert down the corridor into the Staff Only area where he pauses at a door and whips a fob out of his pocket, jangling through its keys to find the right one, which he inserts.

I look beyond him. I glance behind me. We are alone.

I run towards the Herbert as he steps forward and I use his moving weight to dink him through the doorway into a small dark room, a store cupboard, in which he turns towards me as I pull a Case Trapper pocket knife with mother-of-pearl handle and grooved nickel silver bolsters from the inner pocket of the Hermès suit, splay the blades then jab him just the once, ever so nicely and Premiershiply, in the throat, puncturing his windpipe so quickly that he just looks baffled still. Rather than in any way terrorized, as yet.

I take the key fob from his hand, pop the light on in the cupboard and turn and lock the door behind us.

So. Coffee, then. Coffee, coffee, coffee.

Store cupboards are great for this kind of work. One side, comestibles, including – sweetly enough – large tubs of Lavazza Pienaroma. Other side: cleaning and small-scale handyman items.

Simple simple job.

He is staggering backwards and let's not fuck about now. I push him on so that he collapses, dobber-eyed, back on to a stool and I select some tape from the stock and find its end and step forward, spinning the tape from the back of his head, and round, firmly wrapping his mouth and nose. Round and round it goes and there is blood now on his natty waistcoat and I select *the correct* tub of coffee, ping the lid up with a key end, jab the key though the foil seal and take the tub towards him. I waft it near his face.

'*This* is the Pienaroma. This is what I ordered.'

I toss the tub aside and look at him on his stool, all taped up, flinching a bit now as he looks up at me.

'Yemeni Matari,' I say. 'That's an excellent fucking coffee.'

He doesn't respond.

'You tried the Kenyan Peaberry?'

Bemused is the word. He just looks bemused. And well he might because my coffee knowledge is the bomb. Really. And, 'Maybe you prefer the Ethiopian Harrar Longberry, or the prestigious Guatemalan Huehuetenango bean?' I say, goading him. But it doesn't work. He just wheezes and sweats.

Christ. Maybe he doesn't even know these coffees?

This is not even a contest. It's a waste of my time.

'How's about the Celebes Kalossi Toraja roast?' I ask, hopefully.

But nothing. No reply. There is no credible response. He just sits there.

He's not worth it, not worth it, Kev. Fucking amateur.

I tape his feet. I slit his wrists. I tape his hands. I turn off the light, step outside and lock the store-cupboard door. I go to the nearest bogs, flush the keys, take a piss, wash my hands and straighten out the Hermès.

When I return to the Platinum Club, it's one nil. Rantanen having laid on the assist for de Groot.

Do I not like that.

the av coal face

Colly's lounge. Empty cardboard boxes all over.

I am wearing BBP Regimental Ivy jeans with a Vael Deckard mid shoe and a white Sean Paul T-shirt. Gravesy's here. He's waving a Wii nunchuk in front of Colly's box-fresh, wall-mounted sixty-inch Pioneer Kuro plasma.

'Nice TV, Coll-o,' says Gravesy. 'Excellent black levels,' he adds, turning round to face me where I sit, next to Colly on the brown leather Cerak modular sofa.

'How are your new teammates, Kev-o?'

'A changing room's a changing room, Gravesy,' I reply, with casual, off-hand brilliance.

'Apart from your lot are on a hundred grand a week, mate.'

'Not quite that, Gravesy,' I parry.

Colly shoots me a nasty little look.

Weird times, must be, for Colly, a humpty agent, now ostracized by one of the world's toppest clubs and not knowing why. Or else perhaps knowing exactly why. Myself, I don't get Neeskins' grief with Colly, haven't asked about it. Just told Colly about the offer and said my new club wouldn't deal with him, a fact he'd gleaned already, through Whelan or Anselmo.

Colly said nothing when I told him, and I didn't want to discuss it too much myself, because then Colly might start taxing me with questions – about what they're really paying me, and what I might or might not have said to defend him. So we fell into a kind of stand-off, Colly and I, acting normal but feeling all weird.

And either way, if Colly knows why they black-balled him, or even if he doesn't, one sure thing is that he'll want to keep it schtum; keep the vote of no confidence quiet. Because mud sticks, and if this shit gets out, then all his clients and all the clubs are going to want to know the full story. Must be tough for the lad. And because we're mates, because we've been together so long, I'm not going to stick my oar in. I might have a chat to the inner circle, to Boves and Gravesy, if needs be, but beyond that I'm going to tell no one about Neeskins' refusal. I owe Colly that.

But what I don't owe him – and this is the way I see it – is a full fifteen per cent of my new wage. Mates we are, but I told him I was only on forty grand. A little white lie, because I fronted the twenty grand for Taffy, which was wasted, and I also did the deal with Neeskins on my own. So, as far as Colly need know, I'm only on the forty, which is still not too bad, given that if I were a major fucker I could have cut him out completely, him naturally not wanting a high-profile court battle on the subject right now.

And what also makes me feel quite generous is that Colly's fifteen per cent of the forty has just fronted this gadget splurge, a splurge which Colly may well come to regret should this Neeskins situ get out of hand and really start to mess with his income streams.

Anyway. I look at Colly, then over to Gravesy, who is again working the nunchuk in front of the plasma. Gravesy is playing *Disaster: Day of Crisis*.

He is taking the part of former Special Forces Marine Raymond Bryce, charged with rescuing seismologist Lisa Hewitt from a rogue elite government unit named Surge, themselves under the command of maverick Colonel Hayes. Gravesy is doing all right. Previously he has driven at breakneck speed, now he is defusing a bomb.

Gravesy is wearing an Akademics distressed T-shirt, Rocksmith

Mixtape jeans and Creative Recreation Dicoco trainers.

I turn to Colly on the Cerak modular, trying to be all chirpy. 'So you got the Pioneer LX01 home cinema with omni-directional speakers to go with this then, Colly?'

'Think so, Kev.'

'What? You didn't get too involved in the purchase spec then?'

'No time, Kev. Can't pour over the gadget mags like I used to.'

No time. Listen to that. And it's odd, it's weird. It's vexing that a bloke like Colly, formerly so spec'd up AV-wise, would prove to be so hands-off with such a key lifestyle purchase.

'So how did you arrive at your system choice?'

'There's an expert I trust. He knows I've got good ears, he knows I've got good eyes, so he won't fuck me about. I call him, tell him what the rent is. He finds me the best kit for the best price, brings it over and sets it up.'

'Doesn't take his boxes away with him though,' pipes up Gravesy.

What Colly has said about his purchase has confused me. It is true, we are time-poor individuals, and I admire Colly's method of leaving ultimate choice to a designated AV specialist who can invest the purchase with research hours unavailable to in-demand HNWIs like ourselves. I see that. From this angle, Colly's approach has an imperial sense to it which is congruent with his aspirant lifestyle.

But on the other hand, being structurally laissez-faire about your market information moves you far away from the consumer nitty gritty, the actual AV coal face, if you will, leaving gaps where unscrupulous traders might prosper. And so overall, I think I would prefer to keep abreast of the market than to delegate to a potentially rogue expert, as Colly has done.

'Which wire do I cut now?' asks Gravesy.

'The green one,' says Colly.

Colly is wearing a Crooks & Castles Revolt Bandido T with

Triumvir Castor Raw Selvedge jeans and Jhung Yuro JY crepe mid sneakers. On the sofa next to him are his Jag keys, a Christian Audigier hoody, a Von Dutch mechanic beanie and his T-mobile G-1 Android phone.

'Anyway, Kev,' asks Colly, 'why d'you not want Ginge to come tonight?'

'Couldn't be doing with him letching over Sas.'

'Nothing to do with him showing Darren that paper then, Kev?'

'Darren would've found out anyway. Thing is, Sas is gonna be in the shower and that probably, showing off her work. And if I had to sit here and think that Ginge's fucking soldier was getting angry...'

'What, and you don't think I'll be checking her out, Kev-o?'

'That's different, Gravesy.'

'How so, mate?'

'Because you, and Colly, are my mates...Where's Boves tonight?'

'Out with Fabretta.'

'Right. Anyway...Gravesy. Bovesy. Colly. Three mates.' I am making the effort with Colly here. I am laying it right on. 'Good mates. Fine. But Ginge is different.'

'What time's it on?' asks Colly.

I check the Franck Muller Long Island timepiece. 'Three minutes.'

'First show, is it, Kev-o?'

'First show, Gravesy.'

'Reality TV, is it?'

'Yeah, ten slebs dropped in the jungle. Tasks and that. Phone votes.'

'Pause this Wii shit then, Coll-o. Let's get the box on.'

Colly finds some remotes and points them at the plasma and presses some shit and he loses the picture, once or twice, then the sound goes off, and then there's sound but no picture. And while he does all this I chat with Gravesy.

'Jimbo still your caretaker for next week, is he?'

'Seems so, Kev-o.'

'They can't want old cheese-head in post for too much longer – who they looking at?'

'Allardyce is the board's choice, I'd say, but there's talk of Curbs of course and Jimmy Jewell. Pards, they say, may well be looking. Staunton. Poyet. McClaren, even. These are the names floating around, Kev-o.'

'You might end up with Jimbo. He'll be cheap.'

'We might, especially since we got no transfer fee from you.'

'Things still a bit shaky, cash-wise, at the club?'

'There's talk about it, Kev-o, but nothing official said yet.'

'Weird what happened to the gaffer, isn't it, Gravesy?'

Although I don't know why I say that – nerves maybe? – because it wasn't weird at all. It was an understandable demise, given that the gaffer violated a contract. But what is weird – what is galling – is the police viewing it as a botched robbery, when it was so very clearly…

'Fucking weird, Kev-o. '

Not a great one for the chat, your Gravesy. Still. I try again. 'What's your dressing room make of that fan at St James', Gravesy? They going for this red-top chat about the so-called football murder?'

I peer at Gravesy as I ask this, but the Aussie isn't listening, 'Kev-o, you know when you bopped Dar-o's wife and then Sas popped up with her sexual rampage shoot?'

Fuck's sake. Here we go. Got to take it, though. Show annoyance, show weakness and they'll be on this till the 14-15 season. 'Yeah, Gravesy?'

'Well, Kev-o, you know how you told us that she never touched that bloke, and the contact was faked with angles.'

'Angles. Yeah. And Photoshop. And the bloke was gay.'

'Yes, because of the angles, and him being gay, that meant that actually, Sas hadn't cheated on you.'

'That's right.'

'Well, Kev. There won't be that many angles in the jungle.'

'How do you mean, Gravesy?'

'Well, not all of these blokes are gay…Who are they, Kev-o?'

'Some sleb copper. Singers. Soaps. That kind of shit.'

'I'm just saying that in the jungle, some things might happen that the angles can't explain.'

'Gravesy, you toilet. She's a Wag. Untouchable, shag-wise. She'll tell the soap cunt and what have you that she's a Wag. No pony Wag either. Premiership, these days. She said she'd do a piece about me to camera.'

'What about?'

'Our lifestyle together.'

'Do you think,' says Colly, who returns to the chat now, having synched the Kuro plasma with the LXO1 home cinema audio, 'she'll tell us all how much you're really earning?'

doing a leeds

One all, twenty-three minutes to go, Elland Road.

Floodlights on, quarter-final of the Carling. The Leeds fans are frisky, sensing a major mid-week scalp.

I'm on the bench. Rantanen is rested, probably kicking back in the forest in a gingerbread castle, or fishing for seals through ice holes, or whatever these Finnish monkeys do when they're not out on the field. And in the Moomin's absence, Neeskins has drafted in the Croatian playmaker Janko Lasich as a not-like-for-like replacement.

Not happy. Told me I'd be playing, Neeskins did, in the Carling. He said that. But he's brought in the dainty Lasich for Rantanen, neglecting the power of your Kevin Kings. It's not right. How am I going to depose the Rant, making myself first choice for the big Prem games and the glamorous European nights, if Neeskins is not even trotting me out for tinpot Carling games?

I feel let down. Misled. Angry.

We're in the dugouts in front of the John Charles Stand, our fans to our right, the Leeds Kop baying to our left in the Revie Stand. Opposite us is the cantilevered East Stand. It's pissing down.

Intimidating ground, Elland Road; can be.

Forty thousand capacity. They've been getting a few less than that since dropping down into League One, but they've got us, one of the so-called big five, for visitors tonight, so I'd put the ground at more than three-quarters full. Poor old Yorkshire muppets.

If I was a civilian following dirty old Leeds, I'd be miffed. No, livid.

Seven years ago, Champs League semi against Valencia, squad packed with internationals – Keane, Viduka, Dacourt, Kewell, Ferdinand, Woodgate. Two relegations later, got Captain Birdseye – fucking Ken Bates – at the helm and you're losing to Hartlepool on a Tuesday night in the Johnson's Paint Trophy.

My oh my.

Would test the loyalty of even the diehard rank and file. Still, the upside for fans of Leeds-based club Leeds is that they've made a contribution to the Queen's English: *Doing a Leeds.*

Meaning financial meltdown and multiple relegation.

Yes, doing a Leeds. Sadly, though, Leeds are not doing a Leeds tonight. In fact, they're having most of the ball. They actually look the better side. A few shakes at the back for them with their agricultural centre halves, but they genuinely have quality going forward with the local lad Delph, the silky Beckford, and Argentinian targetman Becchio, all combining well together.

'Fabian Delph, not for sale,' comes the chant from the Leeds Kop down the old Gelderd End.

Not true, Leeds. Not in fact true, men of Leeds.

We could have him if we wanted. It's just that we don't.

Either way, Gary McCallister, the Whites' young Scottish manager, has got them playing on the deck, and they're a threat. True, we are not operating with our strongest hand. Neeskins has shuffled our pack, fielding English Sri Lankan striker Dilip Ranga in the stead of top scorer Leon Bédard, and bringing second-string keeper Daaf Bakker in for the resting Anselmo. The tight calf of Ilias Pappas sees Spaniard Estervan Vargas replace him at right back, while Irish international Paul Whelan covers the left wing for hamstrung Wally de Groot.

Four change.. And as I say, Lasich for Rantanen.

Five changes in all for us from the Newcastle game. Five of the first-choice squad out. Still. We've got eleven internationals out there. We've got a World Cup winner. We've got players who've won top leagues in top footballing countries. We've got Neeskins pulling strings in the dugout and we've got Kevin King itching to come on.

We should be bettering Leeds.

But as I say, McCallister's got the Whites playing on the ground.

I'm sat with Simmy on the bench.

Ali el Masri, our goalscorer, is having a good game and Ozan and the boy Hughes have held strongish in central defence. But a lot of our team just aren't firing after back-to-back away games. Janko Lasich is getting passed around, and even Eyodema is lacking his usual incision.

Tap tap, my shoulder goes, and I look right to see Claus Babel, all wrapped up in club raincoat, comb-over wilting across his wet head.

'Kevin. Mr Neeskins wants to talk to you. Take my seat.'

Babel gestures along the dugout to the empty seat he's just vacated next to the manager.

Oh yeah, here we go.

I stand and step past Babel and he takes my seat next to Simmy and I trot down the bench and sit between the gaffer and head coach, Morales. Both of them say nothing, just staring at the game.

Then, 'Kevin.'

'Mr Neeskins?'

'Mr Morales has a question for you.'

The ball goes out of play on the far side and our left back Alvar chucks it forward to Gilchrist Eyodema who nods one down towards Whelan who sets off on a mazy.

'Mr Morales?' I say.

'Kevin.'

'Yes?'

'What do you think?'

'He means about the game,' clarifies Neeskins, watching Leeds prodigy Fabian Delph take the ball off Whelan's toe.

'What do I think about the game?'

'Yes,' says Morales. 'Footballistically.'

Right. OK.

'Footballistically they're playing the fucking football. We've turned up here thinking we can out-pass them, which is normal, considering we're forty-four places above them in the league and we've got class all over the field.'

'Go on, Kevin,' says Neeskins.

'But you've got to play the game that's in front of you, not the one you had in your head before the whistle, and actually, weirdly, what's hurting us is trying to play football. Tonight they're on their game and we're leggy. Simple as. We've got twenty minutes left. We don't want a replay.'

'So?'

'You might think, "Fuck football." You might think, "Let's go route one. Let's chuck Simmy on and hope to win the nod down".'

'But?'

'But. Look at their centre halves. Huntington. Six foot three. Michalik. Six foot four. Big lads. Is Simmy really going to win it going route one against those two? Maybe he is. Maybe he isn't.'

'So?'

'Direct running. They've looked sketchy when we've gone vertical on them. Chuck me on now and I'll run at the Leeds, direct. Exploit the turning circles of those big defenders. Nothing fancy. No real football. But no route one either.'

'What is he saying?' Morales asks Neeskins.

'He agrees with me. Get warmed up, Kevin.'

'Aye aye.'

That's better. About to make my debut, begin the run of form and quality which will see me sodomize Rantanen – in a purely footballing sense – right back to the Arctic, and then inch the King fingers around every major piece of silverware that the club game has to offer. That's what is about to happen, starting now, with my first run out, because remember, a journey of a thousand miles starts with a single Kev.

I walk back down the length of the bench and then walk towards the touchline and start my warm-up. I go down on to my right knee and put my left foot out, keeping an eye on the unfolding game, and I lean over the left, stretching my hammy by easing back my toe.

'Kingy, you twat,' someone shouts from the crowd behind me.

'King, you fucking twat.'

'Kingy, you fucking reject.'

'King, you missed that sitter against the scum.'

He means ManU, that's Leeds talk.

I have a quick look over my shoulder. And I see him. Stood up. A furious, red-faced Herbert, woolly Leeds hat on, Topman clobber.

About twenty years old.

'Kingy, you Cockney wanker. You pointless wanker.'

Got you, mate. Spotted you. No problem.

Row L, three seats in from the gangway.

I do some shuttle runs down towards the flag.

I have another glance at him. Row L, three seats in.

Swearing like that might have been acceptable on the terraces in the past. We do all enjoy strong language. Nothing the matter with the swearing, it's as legitimate a part of the Queen's as the word dodecahedron, for example. But, as the Herbert of Row L should know, there's a time and a place for language. And if I'm not mistaken, he is sat in a family enclosure.

And when you are in a family enclosure, Row L Herbert, you are pressed up against football's changing demographic – the prawn sandwichers, the mum with her kids, some kind of graphic designer, even. So when you curse me so loudly, ask yourself this:

Ask yourself if you think these fan consumers, who have coughed up, despite ticket inflation and the vagaries of the civilian job market, want to hear your language in their carefully chosen season ticket seats? Do you think that your 'Kingy, you wanker' talk is contributing towards the quality of the mid-week leisure outing of the customers in your vicinity?

Because I fucking don't. And neither, I suspect, would top broadcaster and tireless consumer rights champion Nicky Campbell. What Nicky would say, I think, if he were here, was that by your abuse, Row L Herbert, you are degrading the wider entertainment experience. I think Nicky would say that you are displaying unacceptable anti-consumer tendencies.

That you are infringing consumer rights.

Now, Row L Herbert, some of the traditional enemies of the consumer affairs work of Nicky Campbell might make the argument that it is the match-day steward that is really at fault here. That it is the Leeds-based club Leeds that are failing the consumer by not policing the entertainment experience sufficiently well. And I do have some sympathy with that. Certainly the Leeds-based club are obliged to protect their consumers. Certainly. They are obliged to show vigilance. That's a given.

But for me, and I strongly suspect for customer advocate Nicky Campbell also, ultimate responsibility always rests with the individual. Which is you, Herbert. And while it is lax of Leeds' stewards not to quash your filthy soapbox in Row L, it is not their fault that you are a consumer foe. That fault lies with you. And what I think Nicky would suggest is that you should be met with tough measures.

A clampdown, if you will. Some draconian, pro-consumer activity.

But all that is for the future because I'm ready to be brought on.

I go over to speak to the officials. They check my name, they check other shit, and the ball goes out and the ref waves me on. I'm replacing Gilchrist Eyodema and he ambles over and shakes my hand. Hasn't had the best of games, the Togolese.

I jog on past their bugger-gripped ex-Forest player David Prutton and I give him the voodoo eyes. I jog on towards Leeds players Delph and Douglas and I stop by them in midfield, right between them. Just near enough for them to read the ink.

The ref blows. The exile is over. I'm going to own this game.

'We've all fucked your Wag,' the Leeds Kop start singing.

vintage ericcson t28

Jesus, what's that?

Christ, there's something on my dick, on the end of my dick. What is it?

Oh, it's Denise.

Here we are then, over at mine, clambering all over each other.

First time I've seen her since we popped her dad in the furnace.

Lovely girl. Energetic. Very well dressed.

Not at the moment, but usually. Usually.

I'm giving it the old in out. The old fucking squeaky. You've been there.

Gravesy's been there as well. And currently he's walking around my Cattelan Italia Patrick bed, taking some snaps of me and Denise on his RIM Blackberry Storm. Which is nice, because loyal Gravesy won't sell these to the red-tops, and there's always room in the King archives for more erotic art. And what is also nice is that far from going stale, Denise has had some good recent work done. Not so recently that she retains bruising mind, but recently enough that her fun bags don't need upgrading. It is a happy medium and I enjoy tucking in to the whole enhanced Denise package.

Gravesy's wearing a white Armand Basi shirt, a grey two-button

Dsquared2 suit and Bluedy intersia effect shoes.

'What time we got to be at the Kingly, Gravesy?'

'Nine, Kev-o.'

'Time is it now?'

'Seven, mate. You should start getting ready in a bit,' says Gravesy, working the 3.2 megapixel camera.

So in a bit I do start getting ready. I see Denise out, employ the King of Shaves Azor, and dab on the Pinaud Clubman Vanilla aftershave lotion. I don a collarless Robert Geller shirt, a CP Company two-button suit and Paparo monk shoes, finishing the garb with a five-button Comme des Garçons Homme Plus mac.

I come out of the bedroom and from the way Gravesy eyes the schmutter I can tell it's a good look. A Kevishly good look.

Right. Out the door, take the lift, make the Bents, dink her open, fire her up and pop on the new Lemar album.

We tank into town.

'So what's this party then?'

'Football fashion.'

'Not some pony sportswear launch, Gravesy? Some fucking Diadora-type low-end utility wear?'

'Not sportswear, Kev-o. More football-inspired urbanwear, mate.'

The Westway. The sweep of the Wembley Arch back to our left.

'Fanny, yeah?'

'Yeah, mate. Bound to be.'

'I am irresistible, Gravesy. Tonight I'm on fire.'

Edgware. Marylebone. Down on to Baker Street.

Turn into Wigmore. Regent Street. Left on to Great Marlborough.

Here we are.

The Bents purrs up to Soho Square, the HQ of the FA right in front of us. Office of the England manager. One time home of the Swede, but currently the lair of thrust-chinned Italian disciplinarian Fabio Capello. Makes me wistful, seeing it, the office. Because while there's been under 17, 19 and 21 caps for the likes of your Kevin Kings, as yet there's been no senior call-up. Thorn in my side. Wound in my heart.

But then, Kev. Kev mate. Cheer it. Cheer up. Back yourself. All will come right, all is in hand, because like it or not, men of the Football Association – oh, you suits of Soho Square – I am about to start playing the best humpty of my life.

I feel that. I do. I feel it. The football sap is rising.

I'm about to go on a streak of form that will make me undroppable, that will make me the first name on the team sheet for both club and country.

I just am.

I park the Bents and we climb out into the neon-splattered darkness of Soho. Right you fucking are then.

We leave the square and head across Soho, towards Beak Street.

'Right, Kev-o, see you inside in about half an hour.'

I nod. Gravesy tonks off to see a Mexican hooker he favours and I approach the Kingly Club alone. Door host looks nice. Sinewy. Serene. She's into her Thai boxing, would be my guess.

She must recognize me, she must, or maybe it's just this HNWI clobber because she nods me straight in with no ticket or guest list bollocks and I enter.

Intimate and chic environment. Dramatic aquariums. Stunning glass bar.

Fifty people or so. Maybe fifty-five. Three of them you would.

Good clothes, on the whole, good clothes. Apart from one group, young crowd, maybe the models for tonight? But I'd hope not. Or maybe the weed-melted brains behind this football-inspired urbanwear we're here to launch?

I don't know.

But what I do know is that they've all fucked up, wear-wise.

Now, right off, let's be clear about this. I do enjoy urban street style. I've got skinny and ultra-baggy denims, and everything in between. I've got various designer mechanic beanies and WeSC

Stretch Oboe headphones. I respond effervescently to the majority of R&B-influenced fashion collections which I view. I do.

But you have to pick your moment. You have to dress for the venue. So.

Night on the PS3 at Gravesy's in an LRG Bigby Bustle track jacket? Perfect. But parade that item through a members' bar voted Most Stylish Venue at 2007's prestigious London Club and Bar Awards? No. Fucking obviously.

I could go on. This may be a night to launch streetwear, homeboys. And homegirls. But then again, you're not exactly launching it on the street are you?

No, you are launching amidst Terryaki Maki and Tobiko Maki canapés. You are launching over a bar selling Henriot Cuvée des Enchanteleurs 1990 and Cohiba cognac. You are launching within Barbarella-esque plastic and leather combination booths. That's where. Not in zone fucking five. Not outside KFC or while you're smoking fat ones under a rusted railway bridge.

It's simple. Make the effort. Brush up or fuck off.

I spread my hands out on the bar.

'Kevin King.'

There's a bloke to my right. He has flat, custardy hair in a sort of inadvertent Caesar style. He has a whopping fat head beneath it, bigger than Jimbo's cheese head. Bigger even than Billy Four Chins' head. He is wearing some House of Fraser shit or something and some type of Hush Puppy-type footwear.

More than anything, I want him to go away. I do not want him near me. What if someone snaps him stood there? What if I get papped talking to this twat? How's that going to look?

I scowl at him but he just stands there.

'Do I know you?'

'Not really. Although I did write a piece about you a few years ago for the *Mail*. Possible new England crop coming through, that sort of thing. Just before you came up into the Premiership. I'm Don Caxton.'

'Right.' OK. Journo. Fine. I can deal with him now. He may

look like a fucking special needs blancmange, but he could be useful.

'Sorry to hear about your old gaffer, Kevin.'

'Yeah. Yeah. You want a drink?'

Caxton scrunches his lips up towards his nose, which appears to be his way of making a decision. He mistrustfully eyes his comp glass of Veuve Clicquot Yellow Label.

'Beer?'

'Doubt they serve it.'

But, 'We do serve beer, sir,' chirps up the barman, all fucking-about-with-cocktails as he says it. 'But only Cobra.'

'One of them then,' says Caxton.

'Classic lime daiquiri,' I say.

The barman gets to work.

'You, er, a fan of football-inspired urbanwear then?' I ask, turning to Caxton.

'Hardly, Kev. Been over at the FA this afternoon and thought I'd stay on, see who might be here.'

'And who is here, Don?'

'Well, you are, Kevin. What about an interview? English player, down to the Championship, now signed to a big club. That angle. Sent off in his debut at Elland Road, but otherwise things are looking rosy.'

'You'd write that?'

'Yeah. Easy. One-time England fringe player, been on a difficult journey…'

'But now redeemed by the Premiership, Don?'

'Easy, Kevin, you ain't played a league game yet.'

Cunt.

'But I will, Don. I'll be first name on the sheet soon enough.'

'OK, Kevin.'

He doesn't believe me. He doesn't rate me.

'And then, Don, I'll be looking to burst my way into the England reckoning.'

Caxton does a sort of shrug-chuckle. 'We can talk about your ambitions. Give us your mobile, Kevin, I'll see what I can do.'

Caxton whips out his phone. His 'phone'.

It's an Ericcson T28 flip phone, circa 1999. He has got to be joking.

'Fucking hell, Don, I give you my number, will it all fit in that? What's the memory on that?'

'It's a just a phone, Kev. I don't run NASA from it.'

'Let me have a look at that.'

He hands it over. I can't believe it. No colour screen. No camera. No internet. Not even a fucking ringtone facility. Christ. He's not putting my number, the number of my s-o-t-a Arte 8800, into that shit phone. He is not soiling my digits with his museum-piece mobile.

Made in 1999. Look at it. Fucking hell. The sky was all purple when you bought that, Don? Were there people running everywhere? Were there? Just before the millennium, was it, when you bought the Ericcson T28? Time of the Dome, was it, the river of fire? Get caught out by the millennium bug, did you, Caxton, whilst buying this Ericcson?

I can't believe it's here, in my hand, this relic. It grieves me that a grown man can let himself go in such a way, can keep a phone for so long, going to seed in his House of Fraser jacket pocket. It angers me.

'Kev?'

Caxton is looking at me looking at his phone. He seems a little confused. Maybe a little scared. The drinks have arrived.

'So can we do an interview then, Kev? Next week maybe?'

I hand him back the T28. I'm appalled. I have to go.

'I don't know, Don, I don't know.'

I walk away from Caxton, clutching my daiquiri as I head towards the urban Herberts. But I do not make them because Gravesy arrives.

'You were quick.'

'She wasn't there, mate, got her sister to whack me off instead.'

'Drink?'

'Yeah. What should I have?'

'JL Martini. Or Bellinis are supposed to be good here.'

'A Bellini. But let's sit down, Kev-o.'

'Yeah.'

We sit and a booze monkey quickly swoops, reassuring us that client service is paramount at the Kingly.

I take a Ruinart Blanc des Blancs and watch Caxton fuck off home.

I take a Perrier Jouet Grand Brut and Gravesy shows me the Sure Touch interface of the genuinely innovative RIM Blackberry Storm.

I take a 2005 St Veran 'Merloix' Pierre Jany burgundy and the zone five streetwear girls are getting fitter.

I take another Perrier Jouet Grand Brut and stand up.

'Where you heading, Kev?'

'Come on, soldier, got some recon to do.'

Gravesy stands and we walk over towards the urbanwear clique, bathing in the fucking Giro-day mystique they've brought to the Kingly.

I walk up to them, but they sense me and sort of shuffle in closer together, closing their little ranks, rounding up their wagons of inappropriate streetwear within the prestigious Kingly. A couple of them sort of scowl at me, seeing me off, they think, but a fit one, the fittest one, the only one that you would really, sort of bobs her eyes across my clobber and then smiles.

So I stop right by them, lolling against a vibrantly clean aquarium wall and Gravesy joins me. I peer into their group and I try to catch the fit one's eye. Which is not so hard, seeing as she is staring right at me with her Skull Candy Full Metal Jacket iPhone earbud headphones hanging over the neck of her Freshjive Resurgence retro Varsity jacket.

She nods her head a little and then steps out of the group towards me. She is wearing a WeSC Marwin jean, a Schmack EU JP shirt and Gravis Lowdown HC trainers. She's posh. She steps right over.

'Your launch tonight, is it?' I ask.

'No. My friends'.'

'Right. You in fashion though, yeah?'

'Yeah. Fashion expert.'

'Oh yeah. I've seen you. You model as well, yeah?'

'I have.'

Know who she is now. 'Aren't you mates with Louise? Jamie Redknapp's missus.'

'Yeah! I am. Do you know Louise?'

'No, but I played against Jamie a couple of times. Not really, but I did. I mean we're not. Of the same era. But I played against his side. Liverpool. A few times.'

'You're a footballer!'

'Yeah. Premiership. And a football expert. Like you. An expert.'

'Right! My name's Cat.'

Gravesy gives me a wink and fucks off to shark the room.

I let the patter roll on. 'What type of fashion you into then?'

'Sports-influenced. R&B-influenced. Workwear-influenced.'

'Right. Same as me.'

'But you're dressed in a ZZegna suit!'

It's not a ZZegna. It's a CP Company suit. It's clearly a CP Company suit.

'I really like ZZegna though,' she adds. 'I'm not a complete heathen.'

'Like my Ann Demeulemeester shoes?' I say, flipping out my left for her to view.

'Very nice,' she says.

But they are not Ann Demeulemeester. They are Raparo. I have tested her and she has failed. An expert would easily distinguish the Raparo shoe.

Still, she said she experted towards the more street end of the fashion spectrum, so hold your horses, Kev. I nod towards the legs of one of her fashion gaggle.

'The KR3W Jim Greco Acid Wash denim is really something,' I say.

139

'Oh, really it is.'

But he's wearing a KR3W Chad Muska dirty grey jean. It is not even from the Acid Wash range. And it's not as though the Kingly is a dark venue. Quite the opposite. This is ridiculous.

This Cat is sold in the media as a fashion expert. I have seen that. But she does not know the Chad Muska jean. She cannot tell the Chad Muska jean. It is not right.

The King hand inside the King jacket around the King knife.

But no. Not yet. Because she's fit. And you don't want to turn a nice rack into a dead rack, do you? Not unless you have to. One. More. Chance.

'What's this then, Cat?' I say, nodding down towards my belt.

'Er.' She's frowning towards my cock. She thinks I mean my cock.

'The belt.'

'Oh.' She tilts her head to the right, then to the left. The King hand tightens around the Case Trapper handle. 'It's a Nixon Phantom. Many people prefer the Nixon Mainline, but I'm with you on the quality of the Phantom.'

It *is* a Nixon Phantom. She was close.

I release the knife and pull my hand out from inside the CP Company jacket, dropping it down to brush lightly against her arse in a did-he-mean-to-do-that-or-not motion. Then I give her a Premiership wink.

bush tucker

Sas has been imprisoned in a pitch-black cave which is teaming with jungle creatures.

The Arte trills. It's Nan.

'You watching, Kevin?'

'Yeah.'

'How many do you think she'll get?'

Sas has to negotiate the Cavern of Calamity, searching for twelve wooden stars, each of which secures a meal for a sleb in the jungle camp.

'All of them.'

'You're very confident.'

'New doctor I found you any good then, Nan?'

'Yes, Kevin.'

'Well. What did you think?'

'A very clean man.'

'Service any good? You feeling any better?'

'Much.'

She's not, though, I can hear that in her voice. She sounds worse to me.

'You make sure you go back and see him again, Nan.'

'She's got another one, Kevin.'

I look at the B&O forty-inch.

Sas is screeching a bit, but she's doing quite well. She makes alarmed contact with a moving carpet of rats, she plunges her little fingers into knots of snakes to find the stars. It's dark in there too. Pitch. I'm quite proud of her.

Sometimes I think she is the best thing in my lifestyle.

'That actor's very handsome.'

'Yes, but he's not in Sas' camp, Nan.'

The jungle slebs are divided into red and yellow camps.

'For the moment, Kevin. They're going to merge the camps tonight.'

Shit. Viewer-wise, that may well be an interesting tactic from the production team, but Kev could well do without the beefcake actor being in such proximity to the Wag. Because Sas is...well, she can be very, you know, impressionable. And if she, well, if she, you know, well, it'll be a gross and public flouting of our rigorous publicity pact. But not just that.

Because, from a purely Kev perspective, it's also the banter in the changing room, the abuse from the terraces, the snide red-top chatter, the whole George Foreman grill set, so to say. And after Sas' sexual rampage – which, if pressed, I'll admit to having handled with riveting humility – I could well do without some Wag jungle fumble. Really.

Anyway. Time's nearly up on the test. Sas has secured seven stars. Not great. She's missed five others. But it's not a disaster either. It's a solid, mid-table finish. She steps out of the cave and is greeted by dwarven presenting hydra Ant and Dec, who wave mics at her and ask her about the insects and rats.

'She looks very pretty, Kevin.'

Her tits do, but she doesn't. Not really. She is covered in cobwebs and her clobber is not ideal and she has not got her face on. It is the first time I have ever seen Sas without the war paint.

'Sort of healthy, Kevin. Rosy-cheeked. She's naturally very pretty.'

The Geordie frontmen have quizzed Sas about the bush tucker trial. They move on to a more generalized discussion of the sleb camp experience.

'I'm enjoying myself. But I'm missing my Kev,' she says.

'She's missing you, Kevin.'

'He's my soul mate.'

'You're her soul mate.'

'He's a Taurus,' says Sas.

'Same as your mum,' says Nan. 'What star sign is Sas?'

I don't know

'And I'm a Libra,' says Sas.

'She's a Libra,' says Nan. 'She's very pretty.'

She's very titty.

'Ant and Dec have got a villa in Barbados, on the same estate as Gary Lineker and Joe Calzaghe,' says Nan.

'Oh yeah.'

'Wayne and Coleen have just approved architect drawings for one in the same area.'

'Right.'

Fucking Rooney. Me and him. Once again. Soon enough. On the turf. Then we'll see who's got the better fucking villa. His in Barbados, or my villa in...I haven't got a villa, but we'll see soon enough who's got the better fucking villa. Fucking Barbados. Fucking villa.

'Have you been following the mind games in the jungle, Kevin?'

'The what, Nan?'

'The celebrity mind games.'

'Not really, Nan.'

'Sas is very good at them. She's ever so manipulative, ever so clever.'

'Yeah.'

'Is she really a G cup, Kevin?'

'They change. Fluctuate, according to the job she's doing. But they are very, very big tits, Nan.'

'I'm just really missing my boyfriend.'

'She's still missing you, Kevin.'

'We do have an enviable lifestyle but we are not cut off from the vibrant local community,' says Sas.

Cat walks out of the bathroom.

'I've got to go, Nan. I'll come and see you tomorrow after training.'

I dink the line closed but leave the TV on.

Cat walks over to the Cattelan Italia Patrick bed and lies across it in the buff. I can still hear Sas' voice. 'I have plunged into the celebrity unknown,' she says.

Ditto.

spotted the croc

Fabregas, you toilet.

Their tricksy Spaniard shimmies me in midfield and makes half a yard which he exploits by dinking one forward to Dutch teammate Van Persie on the edge of the box, who thinks about playing in their winger Nasri, but instead pivots and chips in a cross to the far post, which Adebayor nods wide.

Not got his heading boots on today, the leggy Arsenal striker.

The Emirates Stadium. Five minutes into the second half. We're two one down. Neeskins brought me on at half time, replacing Rantanen who did his knee in a challenge with Sagna. Straight swap, then. Me for the Finn. Don't mind that I only got on due to his injury. No rupture to the King pride. Only way I was going to get a chance in this game. Realistically. But one man's knee fuck is another man's Prem debut, as the sages of yore no doubt said, and this is my chance. My time. Kev's got to seize this jersey with both feet and turn this game around. Because the tide is definitely in the Arsenal's court at the moment. They are passing us literally to death.

They win and go above us. We win and move into second.

Draw and it's as you were.

Tactics-wise, us-wise, it's paramount that we keep the back door shut then seek to ask questions when we're shown a sniff of it. Anselmo punts the goal kick wide and long and our boy de Groot is up to meet it.

'Heads, Wally!' I shout, hailing the Dutchman's effort, being a talker on the pitch.

'Win the seconds!' I shout again, clapping my hands and spitting.

But the ball's picked up by Silvestre and the Arsenal funnel it left and build again through Clichy, feeding Denilson who has dropped wide. And who clips one inside to Fabregas who first looks to zing one down the channel back to the Brazilian, but then declines, swivelling instead for more central options.

I am on their Spaniard.

I Kev forwards. Fabregas is facing me, ball at his feet, and I lunge in hard and one-footed and crunch the ball away, barrelling through into the Arsenal man and taking his standing foot.

Fabregas goes down and the whistle stays in the pocket. Ball then man. No foul. Getting away with knobbling an opposition playmaker can be a matter of succession, of which one you take first. Ball then man can be fine. Man then ball usually gets blown. One then the other. Timing.

The ball cannons out to Gilchrist Eyodema and we are on the march.

I look across the turf to Fabregas. He's not hurt but he's reluctant to get up, aggrieved as he is about the silence of the whistle. I look up into the Emirates seating and my eyes find the exclusive Diamond Club area. Colly'll be up there, watching the game. He's a Gooner. He's still pissed off about my forty grand wages. He'll be even more pissed off now I've just tonked their inspirational young Captain.

Captain for only about a week mind, after William Gallas was stripped of the armband following a misguided interview given to the French press. But Captain nonetheless, and what I remember of the challenge – as I jump to my toes, click my knees, stand and move back into an open position – is that as I went into Fabregas I saw myself reflected in his eyes. Actually the opponent's eyeball reflecting the King physique itself as I Kev'd in towards him. I could see the King barnet, the King head.

My ink was visible as a blurred darkness in their Captain's eye.

He saw and felt Kevin King.

Eyodema feeds our pacy Dutch winger.

And as I now burst towards their box, tracking the penetrative wing play of de Groot, but also holding back to find space in front of their defenders Gallas and Silvestre, I am visited by a very strong sense of football. The ball-winning challenge has catapulted me into the zone. Suddenly I am oozing football.

We can win this!

De Groot cuts back to my feet, but with Silvestre already moving terrific on to me, I open my body, shaping to shoot with my right, but actually cushioning one through to myself beyond their advancing Frenchman. I swerve on to meet the disguised ball and get behind the Arsenal back four and I open my legs towards their line and cut back with my left into the mixer where languid Bédard slaps one – high and rising – into the home side's net.

Bingo.

Kev, mate, Kev! Assist, Kev!

Two all.

It's not like they hadn't been warned first half about the counter.

Half an hour to go.

Bédard's straight over to me and he points to show I made it, and I did make it, and I look up to the Diamond Club and give Colly the eyes, not that I can see him, but I give that bit of the ground the eyes. I give general eyes to the Diamond Club, and so know that I have done Colly in with that. And Bédard's got his arm around me and our Gambian hitman Danzo is over and the dainty Janko Lasich comes over with his fucking weird little Fu Manchu tache.

I'm over to the bench and I move towards Neeskins, who is on his feet in the technical area.

'Low fucking merchandise value, is it?' I say to him.

But he doesn't hear me.

The capacity Emirates crowd has got the hump. And as we mosey back into shape before the Arsenal kick-off I know that I am on my way, know I've just gained a toehold back in the Prem. Maybe not enough, as yet, to repudiate the Moomin, if you'll allow, but certainly it's an eye-catching debut, so far, for the likes of your Kevin Kings; and my head is swimming with silverware, shimmering, it is, with fucking great trophies, with goals and games and adulation, and this is why I do this: the foot fuck, the beating from Darren, the gaffer shit, the waiting for a deal, the waiting for a game, all that is behind me now, and I am getting, I think, an erection, yes, a great big Premiership lob on, which feels so tremendous, so very, very mighty that I could use it to score from the pen spot, or from forty yards out, even. Yes. Right now I could rasp in long shots with my cock, my confidence is that high.

I'm here. I'm Kev. I'm back.

Changing rooms after the game and two massive geezers in what they think is discreet Gucci come in and look around. They patrol really, earpieces in, shaved heads. They look like men in the employ of rogue elite commando Colonel Hayes from the Wii. Then Neeskins comes in behind them. Then Abtum Bahta, the Chairman, comes in behind Neeskins. He doesn't make a lot of the aways apparently, the Chairman, but pulls his billionaire finger out for the prestige games when we face one of the other so-called big five.

The Chairman is wearing, I don't even know what he's wearing. A suit. Some kind of so-high-end-there-was-only-one-made-then-they-cut-the-tailor's-fingers-off-so-he-couldn't-make-another type suit. Bespoke. Although, as I say, bespoke doesn't really cover it.

The injured Rantanen comes in behind the Chairman. Very close, they say, the Chairman and the Finn, very close indeed. If reports are to be believed, then the wives of the billionaire Indian and the iconic Finn have shopped together; while Rantanen has also been papped holidaying on the Chairman's yacht.

The Chairman has a word here, a word there, for the lung-busted players who have just secured his club three points, coming back as they did from 2-1 down to triumph at the Emirates. He walks the room, and naturally, soon enough, he spots the man of the match. He comes towards me, his shaven-headed Wii hulks close behind him, ensuring safety, cradling him in his UHNWI status.

'Mr King,' says the Chairman.

'Kevin,' I reply.

'Kevin, then.'

'Abtum,' I say.

'Mr Bahta,' says one of the Wii boys.

'Mr Bahta,' I say

'You played well, Kevin,' says the Chairman.

'Thanks, yeah,' I say, looking around the changing room at the other players. 'You bought well.'

'Thank you. But not with you.'

'How do you mean?'

'You were a gift.'

He looks at me, where I sit on the bench, top off, sweating like a shoplifter, 'You are coming to lunch with me, Kevin,' he says, eyeing the ink. 'A secretary will arrange it.'

'Right,' I say, looking over towards Rantanen who is eavesdropping on this little chat, and who looks more than quite fucked off about it.

'Yes, Mr Bahta,' I say, smiling. 'I do really enjoy a spot of the lunch.'

'Good.'

The Chairman moves off.

Washed and changed. Message from Gravesy on the Arte. He says 'nice', 'mate' and 'Kev-o' a lot. Message from Boves, he compliments me on my levels. Message from Nan, she liked our away kit. No message from Colly. Which is sad. But you know, it's my day and I'll not let it tarnish things.

Team bus back to our stadium and I pick up the Bents and pop on the Acura ELS surround sound and track to 5 Live. Bound to be some King chat on the radio, bound to be. Man of the match. On debut. Against the Arse. At theirs. Who's not going to call in about that? I mean, the dead will be phoning in, with their little dead guy phones. And what a relief it'll be to hear it, after so long with so little King humpty chat in the media.

I listen in. There's some newish Herbert presenting 606, the 5 Live football phone-in. Seen him on the box before, on Sky I think, or maybe the Beeb, wearing mid-range retro sports brands – Fila, Tacchini, a touch of eighties Nike, even.

Seen him in a Pringle jumper, I think, a Lyle and Scott.

He's made it on to 606 now, deposing the cantankerous veteran broadcaster Alan Green for the night. I point the Bents west and move towards the King flat.

The 606 Herbert takes a call.

'Hi. Yeah. Love your show,' the caller says. 'I'm an Arsenal fan, yeah, and I was at the Emirates today and I know that a lot of callers so far have come on to say that we didn't actually *deserve* to win, and I think that's right. I mean at the most maybe we deserved a point. But the reason I'm calling up is because I want to talk about Kev King.'

Right. Nice. Yeah. Course. I whack up the vol.

'I mean I know that he's just come back into the Premiership, but already he's got to be the dirtiest player in the league. The way he went into Fabregas just before their second goal.'

Which I set up.

'The way he went into Cesc was clinical. He was trying to take the man, you could see that. To me there was genuine intent there from King.'

Ball then man, oh 606 caller. Ball then man.

Oh, this is great.

'And they went straight up the other end and equalized. Goals do change games and their belief was up and after that I thought our body language wasn't quite right. I just think that King set out to hurt our Captain and I think it was the turning point in the match.'

150

One of the turning points, oh 606 caller, *one* of them.

Another being the goal I set up for Bédard.

It really is all about me.

'I disagree,' replies the mid-range sportswear-wielding 606 presenter, happily correcting the civilian caller on his libellous tirade. 'For me, he did seem to take the ball.'

Thank you.

'But I do know what you mean about Kevin King,' the host adds.

'Scuse?

'I've been following his career since he was at Wycombe.'

And?

'Football-wise he's got the full package.'

Certainly.

'But there is something suspect about the King temperament. The cards do add up. And then the business with Darren Perkins' wife. The profile. I just think King needs to tone down his lifestyle a little bit.'

Do what? I need to *do what*?

To what down my whatstyle? To do what?

For living fuck's Christ. Did I just hear that? And on this day, of all days. On the day of redemption and return, on the day that Kev marched out from his forty days in the humpty wilderness, on a day which may well – though I'm not one ten on this – be celebrated by future, football-centred societies as Kev's Day. Misguided doesn't cover it. Misguided's not a fifth of the way there.

I check the Bents' rear-view, scan ahead, then fling the Continental round and head back into town, towards Langham Street, where this muck is broadcasting from.

Tone down my fucking what?

I mean, he sits there in his fucking Leo Gamelli polo shirt, or whatever he's got on. His fucking Gino Gabbici tank top, or what have you, and he gives out to me. He gives out to me about lifestyle. In his sports casual wear, his 'let's all dress like we're hooligans from the 1980s and Pierre Cardin and Fila and Lacoste are in' clobber.

Actually, scrap Lacoste. Lacoste is an interesting brand. So he sits there in his fucking Adidas Ivan Lendl V-neck tennis pullover and his Ellesse eighties fucking towelling sweatbands and he gives out to me about the L word.

The fucking L word.

The muppet, the fucker. The muppet fucker.

Right.

Back on to the Marylebone and into Park Crescent and down on to Portland Place. Then dink into Langham Street and still the Bents.

There's a clock on the dash but I do not want to look at it. I want instead to learn the exact time from my Panerai Radiomir Black Seal timepiece. Which I do. Six forty-seven. Thirteen minutes of this shit left to air before the Herbert takes his fucking Adidas Forest Hills or whatever off the desk and calls it a night.

Give him ten minutes to piss about. A couple to reach the door.

Reckon I've got about half an hour to wait.

Half an hour. A long time in an HNWI's life. I pull out the Arte. Still no call from Colly, which is harsh, I mean, me and him once being so close and now things being so cold between us. I'll call him then. Yeah, be magnanimous. I'll reach through the briars of weirdness to proffer the Kevish hand of friendship. I dial.

'Kev.'

'What you up to, Colly?'

'Home alone. Tired.'

He sounds it. 'You were at the Emirates today, Colly.'

'Yeah.'

'Right. Good game?'

'No, Kev, Arsenal lost.'

'Any stand-out players?'

'Van Persie had a good game.'

'And what about me, Colly? What did you think…'

'Look, Kev, I'm tired. Speak later, yeah.'

Colly hangs up. It's weird. It's sad. I start to get angry, but no, it's my day, I want to relax. I check the Panerai again and have an idea. I'll call Gravesy's Mexican friend, or her sister, she'll only be a five-minute drive away, other side of Oxford Street. I can get there, get noshed off, and be back here in a half, easy.

But what if the 606 Herbert tanks down straight after the show? Could be out of here in fifteens, that boy, with his speedy Reebok Classics on. Could easy nip down the back stairs quick in his crushed raspberry Converse All-Stars and be out the door before the Hispanic has even warmed up.

It would be risky to visit the hooker. But then again, half an hour I could be sat here. Lot of time for a high-profile sportsman to waste. So...Maybe she should come here? Could get the girl to cab over, then she could nosh me while I keep an eye on the studio door.

Better, Kev. *Better.*

I call, she cabs. I move to the passenger seat and she climbs in and hunkers down in the generous leg space. Which becomes the cockpit, if you will. She unzips the strides and we begin to enjoy the full Hugh Grant, me keeping my left eye on the studio, my Jap's eye in her mouth.

Why is it called the Jap's eye? I mean I know why. The urethra slit is held to resemble the Japanese eye shape. But I wonder if the Japs themselves know of this expression?

I wonder if the Japanese international at Celtic, say, Shunsuke Nakamura, the left-footed midfield free-kick specialist, has ever come across the term? Overheard a Hoops teammate in the changing rooms away at Tannadice, for example, referring to his own Jap's eye?

Chances are, he has. Which makes me further wonder if Nakamura, who did ever so well in the Bhoys 2006-7 Champions League campaign, enquired about this reference to his countrymen's facial features, only to be told by his Jock teammates that it was slang for cock end.

I wonder if knowing that his elegant peepers are compared, shape-wise at least, to a prick nozzle is disturbing to the lad. As a player and a man. Or if he takes a level-headed attitude to an argot which is at least offensive, and at worst potentially racist. Perhaps I'll never know.

But, 'Thanks for all your calls. The FA Cup's been up to its old tricks today and it's a great day to be a Histon fan. Good night,' says the 606 radio host, his shabby Adidas Stan Smiths lifting no doubt from the corporation desk as he imagines the journey home, the takeaway, the potential bunk-up with the rising TV actress fiancée.

I pay off the Mexican and rethrone the member, smiling at my Jap's as it snuggles back into the Zimmerli boxers. I watch the Central American professional walk off down Portland Place and turn my eyes back to the door. I glance at the Panerai Radiomir Black Seal and wait.

There's a flash of plate glass and the host is on the street.

Just as I thought, as I remembered him off the goggle.

Deliberately retro mid-range sportswear. He is wearing 1985 Puma G Villas trainers, an unforgivable Ellesse tracksuit bottom, and a mauve Le Coq Sportif windcheater. He's got the big sideburns on the go, the boy.

It is a carefully assembled look, nodding downmarket as it ironizes that which it nods to. The look says: 'Yes, I do wear second-hand G Villas, but I get them shipped by online used-sneaker specialists operating in the Bay area. And yes, they were shit the first time around.' The look says: 'The flannel inner hood of my 1982 Sportif cheater may have previously sheltered a striking miner's head, but I have launched the garment's ironic renaissance since discovery in a sports offshoot of West Ken vintage boutique Elustrian.'

That's what he thinks it says. And other denizens of these not so McTellish streets might agree with him, valuing his trash sports retro chic as much as he does.

But I am not one of those people.

To me his look says: 'I buy manky shit.'

It says: 'Lifestyle-wise I am not fit to comment on my style betters.'

Right.

I'm out of the Bents and I dink her locked and stride over Langham Street, following the radio host as he moves west, towards the Titchfield area.

On I go. Follow follow.

Cross over Titchfield into Foley Street. Keeping near. Near enough.

And oh, I forgot. I am wearing a Dries Van Noten two-button suit and a yellow Evisu jumper. I am sporting a Salvatore Ferragamo shoe. Not that it is a sports shoe, because in a trick of the Queen's English, you can in fact sport a non-sports shoe.

Foley Street becomes Mortimer. Right out of Mortimer, follow Herbert down the Wells and then fuck this, one firm hand on the Le Coq hood yanks the radio host backwards, and I jitter him quickly down into dark little Mary Lane and dump him, terrified, on his arse.

The Case Trapper pocket knife is smoothly out and I'm looming all Kevly over, his mouth all open and agog, forming the shape of a black egg, and easy peasy. This will be. But then a minute later I'm sitting on the ground in the alley, slicked with the Herbert's blood, cradling his dying body to the King chest, saying, 'Sorry, sorry, sorry.'

Because what happened was that I'd gone at him, naturally, with the Trapper, and done him, true to form, with a tidy one, up under the rib cage, up towards the lung. Business as usual.

But then fucking hell, had he not liked that. And he was off. Shouting, about to shout anyway, and I hate a scene, so before he did that, I'd flipped him over, his chest on the floor, my knee in his back, and I'd lifted up his head, running the Trapper all gently across his throat. To which he sort of died, or nearly died anyway, because he was flopping about a bit still, body popping sort of, as he twitched on to his side.

And I'd looked down at him then and his tatty Sportif cheater had sort of flapped open in the commotion and beneath it, clear as Kev, was a silver, cable-stitched Lacoste Gites cardigan in Merino wool.

Nightmare.

Seven years' bad luck.

Because the Lacoste brand is puzzling to Kevin King. One hand, it *does* seem on a level with shit civilian brands like Le Coq and Puma that the Herbert here is also flaunting. The croc *is* discovered – and in my opinion, to its own detriment – in many a mid-range zone eight wardrobe. That is inescapable brand baggage. But on the other hand, I do not want to just write off seventy-five years of sport and elegance so easily. Because Lacoste can actually pull on authentic sporting heritage, authentic de luxe lifestyle, with the family golf course at Chantaco for example, being a genuine beacon of exclusive chic.

I have visited that golf course. I have played there with Boves. And what I know is that despite Lacoste's queasy popularity with civilians, there still remains some quality – some leisurely mystique, if you will – to the brand that somehow puts it, lifestyle-wise, way above rival design houses.

And I bent down to the Herbert then, his throat and body all greased with the leakage, the Lacoste cardy itself stained all poignantly now with his blood.

'I didn't know about the croc, mate.'

And really dying, he was, by then, must have been, but he opened his eyes and sort of stared at me, no doubt at this point recognizing the high-profile King face.

And, 'Sorry, sorry, sorry,' I kept saying. 'I hadn't spotted the croc.'

Because I wanted him to know it was a mistake. That I'd never do a bloke in a Gites cardy, not if I knew about it.

But then his throat made this kind of creaky sound, as though he was trying to speak, and I put my ear close to his lips and slowly he said it, slowly he did.

'I fucked your Wag. King.'

properly cantona

The menus are out, the 2004 Meursault Domaine Michelot is open on the table, and the 'tress is coming back in five to take our food orders.

I'm having a meal out with Nan, Denise, Cat, Sas and the Mexican hooker. Not really, that'd be tricky, socially I mean, that particular get-together.

No. Instead I am out with Boves, catching up at Foxtrot Oscar, fucking Ramsay's new Brit-style Chelsea bistro. Boves' choice to eat here. I wanted to go round the corner to the eponymous mothership, Restaurant Gordon Ramsay, for some three-starred classical French tucker. But Boves was feeling a bit sniffly and preferred the comfort food of the Foxtrot.

Boves is wearing a Filippa K Tweed crewneck knit with a Hope Dogtooth trouser and Officine Creative Wing-Cap Derby shoes. The bomb, as always.

'So Bahta's car is waiting to take you after training today?' he asks.

'Yeah. Mercedes. CL63 AMG.'

'Like Ginge has got?'

'Yeah, but better, Boves. Stretched. Upgrades. Anyway, the Merc picks me up at Corlham Wood, yeah. And we drive into town. To eat. For lunch, the Chairman said. And I'm thinking Mayfair or something, I'm thinking Murano maybe. But then the

Merc's not going that way and we're at King's Cross, then going down the Pentonville, heading east, and then the penny drops.

'St John's I'm thinking, near Smithfield. Voted sixteenth in the St Pellegrino World's Fifty Best Restaurants. That's where the Chairman's taking me. Nice, I think.'

Boves is staring at the Foxtrot's striped wall design and wondering, perhaps, about the wisdom of the restaurant's cream and black central colour scheme.

'So?' Boves says, dragging his eyes from the wall to the menu, via a quick glance at me.

'So, as I say, uncompromising British cooking at St John's, I am thinking, but the Merc turns off St John Street on to the Compton Road and towards Finsbury.'

'Right.'

'So we get on Seward Street and the car just stops. By the kerb. But there's nothing there. Newsagents. Bookies. A chipper. That kind of shit. But nothing Premiership. And I'm thinking, "what the fuck?" and then the old chauff gets out and walks round and opens the King door and I step out and follow him towards the chipper. Mr fucking Chips, the place is called, and I'm stepping inside it and sat there on one of four little Formica tables is fucking billionaire Chairman Abtum Bahta.'

'No!'

'Yeah. And he's eating fish, chips and mushy peas. And he's got two slices of white bread, all margarined up, and a mug of dirty old tea on the go. Bloke could eat anywhere in the world, and he's tucking in to a filthy fish supper on Seward Street.'

'Strange.'

'Boves, it is properly fucking Cantona.'

Boves gives me the look, thinking I am maligning his country-man. But I'm not. And besides, there's a story on the go here.

'So I sit down and he makes me order and I'm not happy because I'm wearing a Steve Allan Micro Puppytooth shirt and Edun Odyssey solid slim leg trousers with a Narrative Class Micro Zeppa Wedge shoe, and naturally this clobber is catching the smell of the chip fat. But he's sitting there and he's wearing. Well, I don't know what it is. A jumper, but nothing like I've ever seen before. So soft it was, that jumper, like it was yarned from fucking cherub fluff or something. So he's wearing that and the chip smell is all on us, but he doesn't seem to mind. And then do you know what he does?'

'What?'

'He does a bit of the prelim. The old "how are you settling in, Kevin" bullshit.'

'Right.'

'And he drops a few names. Puskas he lobs in there, and Beckenbauer. Going to the geegees with Ferguson and fucking art auctions with Capello and all that.'

'Right.'

'And then one of his Wii goons walks in from somewhere and hands him this sheet of paper. And Bahta puts it on the table, my way round. And I'm thinking, "Hold your fucking horses, mate. Came to eat, not to read." But anyway I look at the paper.'

'And?'

'And it's got Colly's name on it.'

'So?'

'With details of his fraud convictions.'

'*Colly?!*'

'Boves, I know. It did me in.'

And it did. Right well in. To think that for seasons all my zeros had been vulnerable to the wiles of a crim was shocking. I mean, Colly never actually did anything, he played straight with me always, but the impact it *might* have made on the King lifestyle is unthinkable. And not only that. There's Colly to think of too. Because while I know that he and I are somewhat estranged these days, are not exactly Romeo and the Sundance Kid, still, still, I care about him. I do. I'm no monster.

To think of Colly in the clink is not nice. And to think of him keeping it secret from the likes of your Gravesys and your Boveses and your Kevs, all that time: at the golf; round at the snooker;

down Ayia Napa. Keeping schtum all that time, the lad. And now for it all to be raked up again, just like that.

'So *that's* why your club cut him out, Kev.'

'Yeah. Bahta says he had Colly checked out, before they signed me. Says he's started checking all his associates.'

And when Bahta had told me that earlier on, when he said he checked out all his associates – not that I'm giving this particular bit of chat out at the Ramsay resto to my old friend Boves – I felt crazed suddenly. I shuddered. Because a comment like that, like the one that Bahta made about checking people out, could make a brick wall and two short planks paranoid, let alone a high-performance sportsman with, shall we say, the odd little secret.

And when Bahta said it – not, as I say, that I'm mentioning this bit to Florent – I had this wild fear flash within me, rampant mental visions of Bahta's people, ex-Mosad agents or what have you, pursuing Kev twenty-four seven, relentlessly, through tunnels and streams and exclusive spas, and I thought, 'That's no way to live. I can't be having that.' So then, Bahta-wise, I did what I always do when I'm pressured, I got on the front foot, I took the game to the opposition.

'So,' I said to Bahta, all controlled like, but with a tone in my voice, as though I might be offended. 'Do you investigate *everyone* you do business with? Including your players?'

And, *'Especially* my players,' Bahta said. 'Much more than business associates, Kevin. You see, for me, business people are expendable. They can lose me some money, or they can make me some money. Which little concerns me these days. But a player is different, because a player might win or lose me a game. And that game might win or lose me the league. Which is far more precious to me than money. You see, Kevin, I have assembled a squad to win the treble, and anything jeopardizing that will not be tolerated.'

Fuckity ho. Well, Christ. Bit less confident now, I am. Bit less bullish.

'So, er, do you, for example, have your players followed and stuff? For example, Mr Bahta?' I somehow manage to ask.

'If I need to. If they need a friendly nudge to make them concentrate on their game,' he replies, his tremendously pearly gnashers gleaming from his small, rich head.

And now I'm really shitting myself. More than that though. I'm so nervous that I actually seem to be shitting other people. Because hasn't the old Mr Chips-loving Parsi Stalin here just told me, in a roundabout sort of way, that he knows the lot and I'd better stop right now because pots and pans are everything? Isn't that what's just happened?

Hasn't Bahta just let on that topping people is not exactly good for racking up Premiership points? And that he's not really going to confuse my vigilante killings with assists and goal-line clearances?

But then calm it, Kev. Calm it. Think. Because what has he actually said, details-wise? Has he actually said anything about the gaffer, or the coffee Herbert, or the radio host? No, he has not. Not exactly set out a water-clad case, an iron-tight argument proving that he knows I did it, has he?

And does he really know anything? Isn't this just the 'I piss big' chatter that he gives every new player so they think he's got them in his pocket. A few vague phrases, a few vague threats, and they're like footballing lambs to the Premiership slaughter, if you will.

Either way, clever cunt, he is. Give him that. Because now I could second-guess him until Euro 2016 and I'd still never be sure if he knows a thing. And so compelled me, he has, into a maelstrom of unknowing.

And then I sort of come to and Boves is staring at me, looking all puzzled and sad, and he's about to say something to me, about Colly no doubt, when the 'tress arrives, and Boves orders the wild boar and pistachio terrine, and the Casterbridge 9oz rib-eye in Béarnaise sauce, while I take the baby squid with chilli and parsley, then the beer battered hake with thick-cut Maris Piper fries and pureed peas.

'And one fish and chips,' says the 'tress and walks off.

I watch her go. You wouldn't.

'Fish and chips, Kev? Like at Mr Chips.'

'No. No. She's wrong. Beer battered hake. Thick-cut fries. Pureed peas. Not fish and chips.'

'Fish and chips, Kev.'

'This is a fucking Ramsay restaurant, Boves.'

'Fish. And. Chips. Kev.'

'So. Anyway. Bahta starts on about Colly, telling me he's neither fit nor proper. And then he starts going on about introducing me to some super agent.'

'Colly's not going to like that.'

'I haven't done anything yet, Boves. Unlike Colly.'

'There's bound to be some explanation, Kev.'

'Yeah. Maybe. Probably involving an urgent need for other people's cash.'

'Kev.' Boves is all serious now. 'Don't let this new move go to your head. When I won the World Cup…'

Which he did.

'…people were offering me everything.'

'Yeah. And?'

'I'm just saying, Kev. Don't let your head get turned. Talk to Colly about it. He's really in trouble. People don't know the facts, but it's getting round that your club won't deal with him. People aren't taking his calls. Some of his clients are talking about leaving. But not me, Kev. I'm staying with Colly. And so should you. Remember your friends.'

'I do remember my friends. Saw Gravesy yesterday. He was a bit down.'

'It's not surprising, Kev. You got out just in time.'

He's right. I did. But Boves is still there and he'll be all right. There'll be no probs for Boves if his club goes bust. He's near the end of his career. Played two seasons at PSG, four with Roma, three at Deportivo, and two in the Premiership with us before demotion.

Eleven top-flight campaigns.

That kind of shit is going to feather your nest. Add in the sponsorship deals that came his way after the World Cup, and Boves is sitting pretty fucking pretty. He won't want if my old club goes under. He won't want at all. Not like old Jimbo, old fucking cheese head, who's been grunting it out in the lower leagues all his cheese-headed life.

And not like Gravesy who turned pro in the Aussie fucking Boomerang League or whatever it is; Gravesy who has never tasted the bounty of the Prem. Gravesy with his gambling problems. And his fondness for the call girls. Could really sting the boy.

But now Boves' mind must have drifted too because, 'What do you make of these killings, Kev?' he asks. 'That radio host was murdered the other day. The tabloids say it's related to that one at St James'. They say there's a football killer on the loose.'

For fuck's sake. I'm not a football killer. I'm a vigilante. And I'm getting indigestion. I slam down my glass. Let's change the record.

'Boves?'

'Yeah?' he says, eyeing me weirdly.

'Johan Cruyff and Michel Platini are both three times European Players of the Year, yeah?'

He frowns at me. 'Er…Yes, Kev.'

'But who would win in a fight?'

'Michel. Obviously.'

'Boves.' I appeal to the Frenchman to put his patriotic goggles aside. 'At least think about it.'

He shrugs. 'What kind of fight?'

'Well. They're both in their pomp, at the height of their powers. That'd be the eighty-four/eighty-five season for Platini, right?'

'Certainly.'

'And seventy-three/seventy-four with Cruyff.'

'Right.'

'Let's say they're marooned. Alone. The two of them, in a rowing boat.'

'Where's the boat?'

163

'I don't know. Doesn't matter. Gulf of Bothnia.'

'Right. Are they wearing their kit?'

'Yeah. Cruyff has got his Barça kit on, and Platini's in the bar codes of the Old Lady. Long sleeves, though, it'll be cold out in the Gulf.'

'What time of year is it?'

'It's now. Today. And all they have are two oars. One oar each, and they're stood up, waving them about at each other in this rowing boat.'

'How big's the boat, Kev?'

'Twelve foot.'

'Anything else?'

'Yeah. Cruyff's got a jar of herring in his pocket which he could feasibly hurl at Platini.'

'That's not fair.'

'But Platini's got some Dijon mustard.'

'Right.'

'So what happens, Boves? Who wins?'

'To the death?'

'Naturally.'

'Balance would be important, and Cruyff had that.'

'Certainly, Boves, nimble, the man from the Netherlands. But then Platini himself had a sort of barrelesque, Maradona-like centre of gravity.'

'Michel is *not* fat,' protests Boves.

'I'm not saying that.'

But he fucking will be soon enough. Head of UEFA now. All those lunches.

'In all honesty, Kev, I think Cruyff would be the survivor.'

'Why's that, Boves?'

'Platini can't swim.'

'Ah. Right. You see the oar fight – or the mustard and herring fight, however it happened – progressing, devolving even, out of the boat, leaving the footballers manfully wrestling in the drink itself?'

164

'I do.'

'Where Cruyff's buoyancy would come into its own?'

'Exactly, Kev.'

'Interesting…Boves?'

'Yeah?'

'You ever fucked Sas?'

puce finn

Getting ready.

The Azor King of Shaves. Bahta knows everything.

The Pinaud Clubman aftershave. Bahta knows fuck all.

The Hermès club suit. The Arfango Firenze midnight-blue tassel loafers.

A packed Andrew Marc Marshall sports bag.

The lift, the Bents, the private Hertfordshire airfield.

Bahta's jet (one of them) flying us out.

Does he know about Kev?

European away game. My first. Champions League.

Playing in Rantanen's slot. Still not recovered, fully, the Moomin, from his bout of knee fuckaroo, but he's nearly there. Ninety per cent fit, they say. And on the bench, he'll be. In case we need him. Which we won't, because Kev'll be Keving tonight. Proved I can do it in the Prem. Proved it so well that we'll have no need for the Rant, even when he's back to one ten fitness. And tonight I'll prove I can cut it in Europe. I know I will.

Because I will make the pitch my refuge. When I cross that white line I'll forget about Bahta and all that 'does he, doesn't he' shit that has been pinging precise little five-a-side balls of total fear around my brain since dinner at Mr Chips. I will forget it all and merely play out of my skin.

Out. Of. My. Skin. Out of it.

The pitch is my sanctuary now, like Notre Dame was for that hunchback. Not that Kev and old Hunchy are alike in any other way. It is merely a handy, one-off comparison I am making.

We touch down in Valencia.

Spain-wise, La Liga-wise, you think straight off of the big two – Real and Barça. And Villarreal have made great European strides football-wise in European football over recent European football seasons. But there was a time – late nineties, early noughties – when Valencia, under Héctor Cúper and then Rafa Benitez, were arguably the toughest club side in the world.

Two domestic titles. Back to back Champs League finals.

Mendieta. Ayala. Aimar. Not negligible players.

The Mestella, not a negligible ground –

55,000 capacity, 50,000 season ticket holders.

A cauldron. *Yes*, a cauldron.

Overused word, stadium-wise, the cauldron word, but aptly apt for the steep terracing and intimidating atmos of the Mestella.

An actual footballing cauldron.

Di Stefano's managed here. Mario Kempes has graced the turf.

They lay currently second in the Spanish league.

And I'm on the team sheet. In fact, I'm on the ball.

I Kev towards their box, but their Captain Marchena is out of defence and slips his leg across so that he toes the ball then clatters me, which is excellent and professional play, and I'm down and it hurts and I rate Marchena because ball then man he took. Did his job, ball-wise, then had his cake by knobbling me all nicely in front of the ref, who could in fairness and honesty do nothing but stick his hands up and wave it off, turning to follow the Valencia side who build now down our right with Edu, their diminutive Brazilian.

Edu feeds Joaquin who finds Villa, with his funny little soul-patch beard, and they are slicing through us and Villa wrong-foots our centre back Baki Ozan and rasps one high, forcing an exceptional save from our Uruguayan keeper, who gets just enough strong hands to tip it on to the bar and behind for a corner. Their sixth of the game.

Nil nil. Forty minutes into the first half.

They've been battering us, to be fair. Eleven shots to our two. Six of theirs on target. Still, our Gambian striker Boro Danzo had arguably the best chance of the match. The sort you've got to take at this level, the sort he'd have buried nine times out of ten.

I go back for the corner and they've brought their big men up from the back and I'm on their Italian, Moretti, on the edge of our six-yard box when the ball swings in, dipping, left-footed to the far post where the Greek Pappas leaps and clears for us, finding el-Masri who is lightning with the ball at his feet and he mazys one and shimmies another and I'm making the ground, pumping forward, down the middle, de Groot far side keeping up with me, Bédard, our striker, just in front, and el-Masri dinks it, side-footed, between two of theirs to the feet of Bédard, who touches it cleanly, nicely, quickly, straight on to me and I dink it straight to de Groot and push towards their pen spot.

And de Groot makes to go outside and their left back stumbles and goes to ground as our Dutchman cuts in and side-foots the simplest of balls, the very simplest, towards me, slide-ruling it in so that I have the ball in the heart of Los Che's box.

And time seems to slow down. We move into football time, as I call it.

Bédard just right of me. Danzo leftish.

Our Egyptian and Dutchman also potentially open.

Choices.

It's all about the choices.

Lay it off? Have a go?

The Pienaroma, or the Tierra? Wii or PS3? Hilton or Lohan? Shoot or pass?

It opens up a little bit in front of me.

I twat the ball.

I hurt the ball forward, bruising de Groot's sweet lay-off actually into the actual Valencia net itself. No whistle.

Champions League debut. Champions League goal.

Champions League Kev.

Maaaaaaaaaaate!

Goooooooooooaaaaaaaaaaaal!

Get in.

It's not like they hadn't been warned about the counter. And what's this?

A sort of lull, a quiet in the Mestella.

Their fans have hushed. It's almost as though their side's just conceded against the run of the play, conceded a goal, in fact, that could see them put out of the Champs and see us progress to the knockout stages.

As group winners. With a game to spare.

That's the sort of hush that's descended as the cauldron goes off the boil.

I Kev behind the goal and give some to our fans in the away end.

I pump the fist. I kiss the badge.

I assume a rictus of total fucking triumph.

The lads are all on me, Gilchrist Eyodema's got me in some kind of half-Nelson and other lads are leaping on him and I sort of tumble over and lie there on the Spanish turf, Ash Hughes' kneecap against my mouth, Alvar's thigh pressing against my chest, lads all in a heap, in a heap of pure goal and the Mestella crowd all silent still.

Then the boys are off me and I, because I'm such an instinctive diplomat, I run over to Neeskins and give him the point, give him the 'that's for you' eyes, the 'you backed me' eyes. I see Rantanen all trackied up on the bench.

Pasty, aren't they, Finns? Never seen a puce one.

Till now. Does the Moomin not like that goal?

But happy days. Goal, Kev, goal.

One nil it stays. And for the moment I don't even remember Bahta's name.

Plane home and we've landed and we're taxiing towards the

disem and all the lads have popped the mobiles back on and there's fucking gabble going off in all languages. Fucking Boeing of Babel. This is.

And Morales is over and he's giving it the 'well done, Kev', as best he can, in his partial Queen's, and he's banging on, as best he can, about the defensive qualities of the Valencia side, especially in their own back yard, and he is complimenting Kevin King on threading the needle through the eye of the camel, so to say, picking a way through Los Che's defence.

And yes, of course, I say. But it's a team game, I add, repeatedly acclaiming de Groot's pinpoint ball in. And then Neeskins is over and he's all fucking angular and weird and all 'thinking of the next game' already, although you can see that he's fired up about the win. Because he was an unpopular appointment at our place, the Dutchman, when he came in only eight months ago.

His demeanour was thought too Spartan, his training methods esoteric. The fans were unsure. The pundits had their little fucking agendas too. But he's done well, Neeskins. Second in the league. Through to the European knockouts tonight, as we've seen. The board's left-field appointment is dividending, short-term-wise, so far, at least.

And do you know what? It just occurs.

Neeskins hasn't had a chance to fully build his team, to make his stamp; hasn't had the time to buy in the sort of players he fancies, as yet. He's inherited this squad. He brought me in – not as his first choice, I admit – because of the Jock's ball fuck and because I was on a free.

That's why he brought me in. I know that.

But because I'm here, now, before he starts buying in all the Rolls-Royce Continental players from his previous clubs, I've got a head start. I've got a better chance. I've got a real crack at becoming a keystone – a Kevstone – of the whole Neeskins' tenure.

And given – as we know, and as has been proved tonight – that the Kev King football sap is rising, that I, Kev, am about to go on an unplayable run, I can surely cement my place in Neeskins' thoughts.

Become his Captain even, his confidant, the anointed one of the Neeskins era, if you will. Yes. I can feel the Captain's band already round the King arm, wrapping the ink, augmenting the aura.

I can feel it.

The Arte trills and I pluck it from the Hermès pocket.

Text message. Gravesy.

Goal mate! it says. *But check out these angles.*

There's an embedded link through to some website and I take it and see a photo of Sas in the jungle, her bushman's hat on, her kecks nearly off, giving it some rub-down with the handsome sleb actor.

distinctive schnabel fore-end

I'm sitting in the Bents.

I am wearing a Pro-Logic Max 4 cap with Advantage Invisible Camouflage Technology. I am wearing a Deerhunter Smallville jacket with Deer-Tex membrane, Hitena-reinforced wear surfaces, and neoprene cuffs.

I am wearing Harkila Pro Hunter trousers.

Gravesy's screwing some posh bird, so he's got me out on this pheasant shoot with her and her mates. I came because I can't stay on my own these days. Soon as I'm solo, the King brain turns to Bahta. Because he could blow the King L-style away any time he chose. He could cast me from the Prem seemingly moments after my glorious return. Or maybe he couldn't, maybe he's got nothing. But I don't know, and round and round and round it all goes.

We're up at Ashcombe Park in Wiltshire, home of the Ritchies – Guy and Madonna. Or it was until their highly publicized recent quickie divorce. The house probably just belongs to the hardman *Lock, Stock* director now, not that he's around. Off filming somewhere, the girls say.

Gravesy reckons they'll be easy game, these posh girls, come nightfall, all horned up on hunting blood lust and therefore receptive to the King advances. He might be right, but to be honest, to be fair and frank and honest about it, I'm not so much into gunning down the pheasants as such.

I mean, I have splurged on the Bulldog Boa boot with revolutionary 'no laces' fastening system and Vibram outer sole. And I have sprung for a Beretta 687 EELL Diamond Pigeon multi shotgun with Mobilchoke tubes, low-profile closed receiver and distinctive Schnabel fore-end.

I have made the effort.

But get out there, among the flying and dying birds, and I just don't feel it. It's *not me*. Weapons-wise, I'm a traditionalist. Not that I'm insinuating that the gun itself doesn't have a centuries-long pedigree. It has. I mean, I've seen fucking *Zulu*. It's just that when it comes to the big V, the violence, I prefer the hands-on approach.

It all comes back to the football, I suppose. Killing up close with the knife – or a sword, I don't mind a good sword, or a halberd even, an honest yeoman's weapon – well, it's like making a tackle, going in close and hard, engaging the opponent. It's an intimate thing. You hear the sweat, you smell the heartbeat of your foe. You taste the hunt in your nostrils.

The hunt for ball. The hunt for man.

You are stripped back and elemental. It is a test.

Whereas your gun violence can be perped from far away. In that way, sports-wise, it's more like your tennis, in that you stand at a distance and twat some shit really hard at your opponent. Whether that be a bullet or a Slazenger Midi Championship tennis ball. To me it's the same. The shooting, the tennis, they lack the intimacy of the humpty, or the up-close violence.

They are not for me.

The Arte trills. Some unknown number.

Unusually, I take it.

'Kevin, it's Don Caxton here.'

Caxton? Don Caxton? Oh yeah, fatso from the Kingly Club with the custardy hair. How did he get this number?

'I got your number from Abtum Bahta's office,' says Caxton, answering the question before I ask it.

'You're not calling me on that fucking Ericcson T28, are you, Don? That pony old phone?'

'I am.'

'Do you mind calling me back from another line?' I say, because the Arte's not going to like fraternizing with his prehistoric mobile.

'Er,' says Caxton.

'I'm only joking,' I say. But I'm not. Not really. I do not like the idea of the Arte hooking up with Caxton's ancient T28. It seems obscene really, for us to be talking in this mismatched way.

'Anyway, Don?'

'Kevin. I want to see you.'

'You're not alone.'

'I have a proposal for you, Kevin.'

'Cash?'

'Yeah, there's cash involved.'

'A lot of cash?'

'A lot, Kevin.'

'I could come back into town, as it happens. Fucking sick of these pheasants.'

'What?'

'Nothing. Couple of hours, Don?'

'Where?'

'You tell me. You're calling this fucking meeting.'

'What about Le Beaujolais wine bar?'

'Off the Charing Cross Road?'

'Yeah.'

'Civilian's bar. What about Soho House? See you there in two.'

I end the call and peer out of the Bents towards the line of guns, as they call them. They call them guns, the people, even though they are people and not guns. It's the vocab of the shoot, that people are called guns. I learned that today. So I look over at the guns. Making a racket. I mean I would like to get in some posh kecks, don't get me wrong. But as I say, I'm not feeling this whole death from a distance thing.

The guns are stood about ten metres away. They stop for elevenses, and stand around some silver tray giving it the cognac and the sloe gin and the bratwurst, or what have you. There are some nice arses out there, there really are, and I would like to stay and get Kevvy on one of Ritchie's seventeenth-century walnut four-posters, but the deal's now done. I'm meeting Caxton.

I should tell Gravesy. I pop my finger into the Bents' door handle and make to open it, but then, you know what? I can't be arsed. I pick up the Arte and call him. I watch Gravesy through the window as he takes the genuinely innovative RIM Blackberry Storm out from his Musto carbon-coloured shooting jerkin. He sees the screen and frowns.

He looks over to the Bents and sees me inside, Arte to my ear. I give him the 'answer it then, you Aussie wanker' eyes, but Gravesy dinks the line closed and thumbs around with his Blackberry.

I get a text: *Get out of the car, you twat.*

I send one back: *Come here, you fucking convict.*

I like our little chats.

The Arte rings. 'Kev-o, what are you doing?'

'I was phoning you.'

'You are in the car, ten metres away.'

'And?'

'And, mate. Why not get out and come and talk to me? Then you can chat with these fine ladies as well.'

There's some generalized posh bird noises in the background.

'No, Gravesy. I'm off back to London.'

I close the line and peer through the window at Gravesy. He stares at the Bents. Does he have the hump? I think he might. Do I care? I do a bit actually. I like Gravesy. Very much so. He puts the effort in. On and off the pitch. Can't go like this. I make to open the Bents door handle but then, do you know what? I can't be arsed. I send Gravesy a text: *Call you tomorrow. Happy shagging.*

And off I go. Off the Ashcombe estate and back towards town

to meet old custard head about some cash. Fields, yeah, fields and that, and roads and houses and shit, and hasn't that car been behind me since leaving Ritchie's? Hasn't that Hyundai, or whatever piss-mottled chunk of landfill-in-waiting it is, been tailing Kev for fucking miles? Because I think it has, you know… But now the Arte is ringing and it's showing Sas' number.

Well I never. Fuck a goat. Sas on the phone. After all this time mobile-less out in the jungle, professing her love for the Kev Kings of this world, then dabbling with some low-rent actor.

She was voted off the show last night.

I'm glad she's called. I've had a long, hard, excellent think and I've made a decision. Because really, this Bahta stuff's got to me. And I've got to clean Kev up. On all sides. I can't take it any more, no matter how fatally excellent her tits might be. I can't handle the crowd chants, the locker-room sniping, the tabloid columnist's sly asides, the worries if Boves or Gravesy, or Everton's David Moyes, have been at her. Or Allardyce, even. Imagine that. Big Sam, doing his jiggy hippo love dance.

Anyway. It has got to stop. It will stop. Now. I take the call.

'Relationship stories we manage together, Sas,' I open with, quoting her from the night of our knife-edge love summit, quoting the rule that she caned me for flouting.

'Kev, it wasn't like it looked.'

'But he had his…'

'It may have seemed that way but, you know, things are very different out in the jungle. I did it for our profile together.'

'Sas. What you may not have noticed is that *my* profile has rocketed since you've been doing the old Crusoe.'

'I know. I've just heard.'

'My profile is so massive now, so clearly in the ascendant that I need to reassess. I really do. For many years I have resourced our lifestyle. But now. Well. Let's say it wasn't how it looked. Even then, appearing to hump an actor in a clearly agreed media set-up is one thing. Appearing to hump him without prior arrangement with Kev in some rogue stunt is another.'

'Kev, I…' she says as I close the line.

That's it then. The end of the Wag. And how do I feel? Well, all sorts of things are boiling up in Kev at once, like those pony old student lava lamps, but with my feelings as the bubbles, if you will. But no, that's not right. I don't feel like that at all. I feel weirder than that.

Because how I feel is like a plucked goose, somehow cut off from the flock and marooned on a sort of barrel, a floating origami barrel, which is in the middle of a lake, except the lake itself is filled with spunk and what's that noise? A tearing honk as a car screeches close by the Bents and eyes back on the road, to see that I've swerved somehow into the opposite lane. Christ, Kev, dangerous.

Concentrate. Concentrate. Concentrate.

More roads and shit, and then – thank fuck – the Westway. Town.

Marylebone. Euston. The Tottenham Court Road. Still the Hyundai.

Bahta? That Bahta's tail? Or that just some pointless civvy driving into town for a Pizza Express and a checked Zara short-sleeve? Fuck knows.

Charing Cross. Shafts Ave. Right into Greek Street.

There's some dirty Toyota parked outside Soho House and I drive alongside and peer in. I get a good look at Caxton, belly resting on the steering wheel, yellow Caesar barnet in full shabby effect. What's he doing there, sitting in his crumpled motor on the kerb?

Of course, Soho House wouldn't let him in.

Members only.

In-house air-con cinema. Retractable terrace roof. Circular marble bar.

Caxton'd never have made it through the doors.

Terrible shame for the tubby sports writer.

I pull up beside Caxton's motor and toot the fucker and he looks over, through his condensation-beaded glass, and he spots me. He makes to get out of the car.

177

But I have a thought. A two-hour lunch with Caxton amongst the dignified furnishing scheme of Soho House, him boring me to injury with his hack drivel, me worrying all along about the Parsi, and feeling weird about Sas, before no doubt having to cough for the bill. That's one way to spend the arvo.

Or else, get him in the Bents, a five-minute chat, find out the story, then kick him out and spend some man time scratching my itches with Denise. Or Cat. Or the Mexican.

Yep, let's get Caxton in the Bents.

I buzz the window and beckon him. He wobbles over.

'Change of plans, Don. Got to be somewhere. Get in. You've got five minutes.'

Don toddles round the Bents' nose and climbs in the passenger door, his threadbare trousers soiling the upholst.

'Shouldn't take too long, Kevin,' he says, looking over to me, all wheezy and rubbish.

'Yeah?' I say. 'Well?'

'Fancy me writing your autobiography?'

'How come?'

'I pitched the idea to a publisher, couple of weeks ago after we ran into each other at the Kingly. On the lines we talked about for an article. Thought it wouldn't do any harm. Young English talent coming back to the good. Thought it might sell OK.'

'And?'

'They weren't too into it.'

'*What?*'

'Until the game at Arsenal. And then you scored the winner in Valencia.'

'Then they were biting your fucking hand off, Don, yeah?'

'No, Kev. They were coming round a bit. But they still weren't sure.'

'So?'

'What swung the deal was Sas on *I'm A Celebrity*…That's what got them really going. High-profile couple. Open relationship. That's why they've offered you the money they have.'

'What?'

'Definitely. Your open relationship with Sas is a major plus in the publisher's offices. You're seen as the cutting edge of a new, non-possessive masculinity.'

'Oh yeah…How much then, Don?'

'One point two million quid.'

'Fuck.'

'Much more than a player without the celebrity fringe would've got.'

Celebrity fringe, Don? Celebrity minge, Don.

'What do you get out of that?'

'The figure's *after* my writing fees.'

'What about Colly?'

'Colly doesn't know anything about this. It's a lot of money, Kev.'

'Don, I think we should maybe go inside after all. Talk about this a little more.'

'Sure. But first you might want to check all this with Sas?'

'Yeah, Don.'

'So if I could just step out of the Bentley and wait in the street while you do that?'

'Or the Toyota even, Don. You could have a little kip in the Toyota.'

'Fine, Kev. And by the way,' Don winches himself out of the Bents, 'how was the hunting?'

I snatch off the Pro-Logic Max 4 cap with Advantage Invisible Camouflage Technology and pop it into the glovey. Then I call Sas.

'Kev?'

'Sas, this open relationship we're having…'

keegan, again

I am renouncing Kev's secret quest.

I am.

This Bahta stuff has got to me. And these days I've got too much to lose.

Because, remove the whole vigilante killing aspect and it's certainly happy days, Kev-wise: there's this massive new lifestyle book deal, there's cash, fanny de luxe, and looming silverware, right?

And yet I am tense; unhappy. I live in fear of Bahta unmasking Kev.

But I am a mature, self-aware Kev and I see now that perhaps I cannot eat every toy in the sweet shop without jeopardizing what I hold now. To keep the Prem dream alive, to keep the muff tap dripping, perhaps I need to renounce the vigilante work. Because you cannot burn the jack of all trades at both ends.

But there's something else. A tiredness I have been feeling. Yes. It's the perilous weight of responsibility. Because perhaps I – Kev – have been a lonesome upholder of customer service quality for too long? Perhaps I have too long been an uncaped crusader, if you will, without an Alfred the butler, or a Robin the sex wallah, to treat like shit? And now perhaps I have grown tired of my lonely – if excellent – burden?

The Parsi has made me reflect, and in that reflection I have faltered and grown cautious. Am I still able to put the consumer cause above my own personal safety, as I once was? Am I able to act mercilessly in the interests of customers, without the dark shadow of apprehension falling across my mind, like a grim troll's phallus?

I do not know.

So perhaps it is goodbye to Kev the customer vigilante.

And hello then to a life of pure lifestyle. Because humpty and media-wise I am massive, and my career and profile need some serious consideration. And a gifted young player – a player with a growing brand presence, a celebrated model girlfriend, and now a fucking great book advance on the table – might do well to scan the annals of history to learn from previous sleb sportsmen.

The B word obviously springs to mind. Beckham. The epitome, if you'll allow, of metrosexual footballing sleb lifestyle.

A top, top player like Kevin King, a top player with an extravagantly rising profile, might well study the life of ex-England Captain David Beckham, the deals and endorsements he has made, the brands he has aligned himself with. A player such as King might make use of the Beckham Experience as a template for his own sleb career pathway.

Many in my position – not that there are many – would do this. They might look to Beckham – the soccer schools, the fashion, the film star allegiances – and seek to emulate his stellar career progress. But then again, not everyone is the likes of your Kevin Kings, and for me – speaking as a serious student of footballing history – my sleb football crossover pioneer is simply Keegan. It is Keegan and not Beckham who offers me the brand paddle with which to navigate the perilous streams of sleb footballing authenticity.

Keegan's late-seventies endorsement – along with South London boxing legend Henry Cooper – of Brut 33, the lighter spin-off brand of the classic Fabergé fragrance, may lack the sleek aspirational sell of David Beckham's initial fragrance,

Instinct, rolled out so successfully on the Côte d'Azur to an audience of fifty hand-sourced journalists.

I will admit that. But remember this.

Beckham was launching Instinct from scratch. Image-wise, Beckham's brand hand was freer than Keegan's not free brand hand. What Keegan, and of course likeable pugilist Cooper, were doing in the Brut 33 ads was more arduous. They were repositioning an existing brand.

Launching your own football fragrance *is* hard to do. And let's be fair, Beckham – who recently ensnared more market share with the release of Signature, a further scent, this one oozing sensual white amber and marine notes – launched Instinct with a convincing and exclusive panache. Instinct *is* an example of a perfectly well-run sleb endorsement crossover. But for me it does not have the audacity of Keegan's repositioning of the Brut brand. Taking the exclusive Fabergé aftershave radically downmarket, and yet retaining its authentic masculine potency, was the work of a product endorsement colossus.

And let us also remember this. While Beckham's music industry kudos flows solely from the work of ex-Spice Girl wife Victoria, Keegan's knowledge of the wiles and majesty of the charts is definitively first hand.

Yes.

Keegan's EMI-released 1979 solo single, 'Head Over Heels', a ballad of rekindled love, beautifully penned by ex-Smokie duo Norman and Spencer, reached a convincing 31 in the British charts. While that same summer, the plaintive single rocketed also to an alarming 10 in the German parade.

And Keegan achieved this, not from within the chorus of a terrace-type team sing-along, as with most sports hits, but as a solo performer in his own right. Sans team. Sans ball. As a singer he charted. As an *entertainer*. And with a non-football song. Take a moment to consider that.

'Head Over Heels' offers the listener a heartrending meditation on distance and reconciliation: 'You made me a stranger. That's what time can do', being the opening couplet of verse one. That's what Keegan gave the world of music. But what's Beckham got, music locker-wise?

The wife. That's all. And not, as I say, the solid gold cross-genre performance charisma of Keegan.

isolation protocol

I researched this secluded private clinic. I researched it very well.

Integrated overview of health.

Offering continuous valuable relationships with healthcare specialists.

Patient-centred service.

They said all that. They *claimed* it.

And yet what is this? What have I just seen?

The doctor, the specialist or what have you, just touched Nan on the shoulder as she walked by him to enter the consultation space.

He did. I saw it.

And that could be all right. Could be polite perhaps, or reassuring. A gentle pat from a specialist can endow the patient with confidence and a sense of ease. I *know* that. It would have been fine, the pat on Nan's shoulder, if he hadn't just shaken the hand of his previous patient. Stood there at the door of the s-o-t-a clinic, offering individually tailored therapies, and shook the previous patient's hand. Then touched Nan. Without first using an antibacterial cleanser with persistent killing action, a cleanser such as Polysan, say, or else Chlorhexidine.

It's as though the government's huge 2004 'Now Wash Your Hands' campaign hadn't happened.

What is the point in me painstakingly researching a clinic,

assuring myself of its lack of susceptibility to hospital superbug MRSA, if he goes and does that? What is the point in me phoning the clinic to see if they sanitize their surfaces with a mixture of alcohol and quaternary ammonium in order to see off the methicillin-resistant *Staphylococcus aureus* menace? Phoning them to see if they have a policy of NAV-CO2 sanitizing, and if they use Polyson with TEFLEX to defeat the antibiotic-resistant bacteria which takes – figures be believed – around three thousand lives per year on this sceptred isle?

What is the point me doing all that, checking for Nan, assuring the quality of her healthcare provision in this renowned lakeside clinic, if the fucking doctor rubs his dirty hands all over her? If he does not follow isolation protocol?

And us being so relatively close to the Kettering area as well, where the vicious EMRSA16 strain of the superbug first originated. It is a disgrace that the medic touched the Nan shoulder in the near-Kettering area.

Good man he may be, medicine-wise, but lax with it. So very lax.

I am wearing a beige Cerutti two-button suit with a white Kilgour jumper and black, six-lace, Fendi Zucca Jacquard Selleria shoes. I walk over to the receptionist, who you would.

'How long's Nan going to be in there?' I ask, because later on I am taking her to the hairdressers. Then on to the cinema.

Taking Nan to see *Mamma Mia!*

Not really my thing, but I keep an open mind. Because actor Pierce Brosnan has done some really excellent past work. Playing James Bond, obviously. And some other things. Here and there.

'Should be around an hour, Mr King.'

I eye the Franck Muller Long Island timepiece. That's fine.

'How many sessions do you think Nan'll have to have?'

'Six is usual.'

'And how long will that take?'

'We usually do one a week, if the patient is feeling up to it. So, if your nan feels OK, it's a six-week treatment course.'

Six weeks, then, doctor. Best you make use of them. Because straight after that you'll be meeting the Case Trapper. Just got to ID the fucker now and it'll be all set up, all booked in to Kev's appointment book.

'What's the name of the specialist with Nan, then?' I ask.

'Doctor Roger Ha...' she starts to say, but then something clicks inside me. I realize that this is the old Kev at work here, the vigilante Kev. And that now I am a new Kev, a different Kev, content with being a mega-millionaire sports legend and minge titan, and not needing the customer service killing trimmings to complete his life.

And I sort of come out of Kev and loom above him – brilliantly – seeing him standing there at the desk, looking remarkably handsome to be fair, but preparing also to avenge, planning a return to the ways he – I, Kev – have just renounced. And I hear in my bones that this is a crucial moment in Kev's development, a chance to wrench Kev from the old ways, and decisively to the new.

I interrupt the receptionist.

'No. Stop. Don't tell me the doctor's name.'

'Er, OK, Mr King.' She flings me a furtive glance.

'We want him to be safe, don't we?'

She looks scared. I check her name badge. I change the subject.

'Do you, er, like the football, Sara?'

club crest topiary

Oh Kev. Kev Kev Kev.

You've gone and done it now.

You really are the don.

I turn away from the Shed End of Stamford Bridge and look up. I can see Colly in a not-top-whack-but-still-slightly-better-than-a-civvy-twat seat; his great big glum head ballooning no doubt with worries, as his players leave him, and clubs shun him, and gossip swirls all around.

But fuck that. Because all our team's on top of Bédard, writhing in a multimillion-quid heap by the corner flag. Fair enough. He scored it. But we know who did the real work.

And to be fair to Frenchman Bédard, when he escapes from the smothering celebrations of Ash Hughes and the rest, he is straight over. He runs to me and he gives me the point, he gives me the eyes, the 'without you, nothing' eyes. He gives me my respect.

And I do deserve it, although there was nothing fancy about the play. Strength and nerve, that's all it was. And a little bit of footballing faith. I took it off the toe of their Nigerian defensive shield Mikel, round about the halfway line, feigned to put Wally de Groot in and so shimmied Ballack, and then just went at the defence. Went right at them.

That's all. Direct, free running.

Not the most technical of footballing pastimes. But often effective.

And because I'm going straight at them, they've got to commit one of their centre halves to me, which they do in the shape of the Brazilian Alex, and now that the Alex lad is out of position, coming terrific at me, they're stretched at the back. Simple. And now – and this is the difference having top, top players around you makes – although I do not *see* Bédard making his run, I am aware of the space behind Alex and I know that one of ours will be aware of it too, and will be getting into it.

Because we have quality on the park, I can trust that quality, and so in an act of astonishing footballing faith, I just tap a cushioned ball behind Alex, knowing – yes, knowing – that one of ours will get on it.

And so it is.

Bédard runs their line, keeping himself just on, evades the trap and finds the ball in space. He swivels and slaps it across the keeper's legs into the bag, just by the far stick. He gives the keeper zero chance.

Clinical.

Simple, simple goal.

'Nice, Leon. Nice,' I say to Bédard as we mosey back to the centre circle for the restart. I look over to our bench and there sits Rantanen. One ten per cent fit these days – at least – and still not in the starting line-up. Displaced by the likes of your Kevs, see. Officially Neeskins' first choice marauding mid, I am. King of the fucking Prem. I feel amazing, my entire body feels like a vast nipple being nuzzled erect by a zestful St Bernard.

And I see their coach, Brazilian World Cup winner Luiz Felipe Scolari, doing his nut in the technical area, waving his big grumpy bear arms about, bellowing Portuguese unmentionables at his Chelsea side. And next to him, their assistant coach Ray 'Butch' Wilkins – an underrated asset for the England national squad in his day, and a Chelsea man through and through – is doing his best to look dignified. Which is hard, considering he's a bald gnome, and also considering he'll be fuming at the way I just fucked his team over.

Denting their title hopes like that. How could I?

Must be stressful right now for Big Phil and Sideways Ray.

And somewhere or other, billionaire Chelsea owner Roman Abramovich must be doing his cake as well. Although I can't at this time actually lay eyes on him, I'm sure that the Russian – once, before the arrival of our Chairman Bahta, the Prem's richest man – is having kittens in his cushioned seat somewhere. Astonished at the ease with which the hot Kev knife cut though the soft blue butter of the Chelsea defence, if you will. And maybe the Russian – wherever he is sitting – will be wondering how he can spunk almost six hundred million quid on a club in five years and still have them susceptible to simple, direct running.

Either way, we're one up. Against the Chels, at theirs. Oh yes.

Win this and we go top. Which is nice. Seeing as we *are* going to win it. There may be more than an hour left but we will win. We simply will. The indomitable King spirit will accept no other outcome. The King football sap is rising still. I will impose myself on the game. I will be instrumental.

And fuck, who's that in the Chopper Harris Millennium Suite of the Bridge's West Stand? Is that? I think it is. The England coach. Jut-jawed Italian disciplinarian Fabio Capello.

Here to see his Captain, Chelsea's John Terry? Or his attacking midfield choice Frank Lampard? Or perhaps Capello's got his peepers on their cheetahish left-back Ashley Cole, hoping he might consistently recover his old Arsenal form. Or maybe Capello's running the rule over our boy, young Ash Hughes?

It could be those things. It could be.

But then again…And what's that sound?

A sort of knocking sound? Like a knuckle on wood?

Oh yeah, I know what it is. The sound of Kevin King knocking on the door of the England team. That's what it is.

Knock knock knock, Mr Capello, open the fucking door. The King sap is rising. Unplayable, unplayable. I am. Open the door.

A matter of time. Simply a matter of time.

Oh yes. Washed and changed. Feeling good. Mind is clear. I'm a brand new Kev, free of consumer agony. Double-breasted Bottega Veneta suit, blue gingham Claiborne by John Bartlett shirt. Smart Voile Blanche five-eye lace-up trainers. Utterly desirable clothing. Utterly desirable Kev.

'Later,' to the lads, because I'm not driving back with them to Corlham Wood, I'm meeting up with Sas. She's booked us into some new Marco Pierre White place somewhere, apparently. Her treat, she says. Got me a present as well. Back from the jungle, she is. Actually, in my capacity as the avatar of a new non-possessive masculinity, I am really looking forward to trying to fuck her.

The Bridge crowd has all gone and I walk straight out of the Chelsea Village development and stand on the Fulham Road, waiting for her to black cab over to get me. I check the Panerai Radiomir Black Seal timepiece. I'm early.

Two Herberts walk down the Fulham Road towards me, big lads, both in Chelsea replica kit with some unacceptable trainers and tracky Bs on. One of them, the bigger of the two big lads, his round head all shaven and moonish under the sodium lights, says something to the smaller big lad and the smaller big one glances at me and then says something back to the bigger big lad.

They've spotted Kev. They know who I am.

Oh well. Calmly calm, I'll be. Uninvolved.

'King, you cunt,' the smaller big one says, as they pass.

'King, you fucking wanker,' the bigger big lad adds.

That's fine, say that, it means nothing to me. I am not interested.

I will not act. Because fine, I may well believe that you are degrading the standards of public life, swearing like that on the street where a small child or a visiting dignitary might easily hear them. That may be my strong opinion. But that does not mean I will act. Because my days and nights of upholding civic standards and customer quality are over. I have renounced.

And as the lads pass on, I calmly watch them, and I see that they are both. Yes, both. Both of them are wearing Lampard shirts. Both have them, have 'Lamps' written on the back of their Chelsea replica shirts. Not Lampard, the full name, but 'Lamps', like that. As though they know him and he is their mate or something. Which he is not.

I watch the Lampards stroll on down the Fulham, down past the Stamford Gardens and by the Billing Road.

And then it starts. Seemingly from nowhere. A little voice in my mind; far off for starters, and just sort of trying to get my attention really, by saying, 'Kev, Kev, mate,' and shit like that. But then getting louder and stronger, the voice is, this inner voice which is not my own and which I know so well yet somehow cannot place. And having caught my ear, so to say, this well-known yet unnamed voice begins to coax and persuade Kev with earnest, gallant tones, saying that if I stop my consumer war, then these Lampish barbarians will triumph, and retail standards will droop and die.

Yes, droop and die.

Exclusivity itself will crumble, the ardent, imploring voice expands, warming now quite brilliantly to its theme. Products and services will turn to dust as the bandits swamp the citadel. Harrods itself will fall and the vandals of Primark and Lidl will tear down the gates. And you, Kev, are all that stands between civilization and consumer anarchy.

Then abruptly the voice stops and I am alone, standing between civilization and anarchy. But who was that? Speaking just now into the Kevish inner mind? Who was it?

A tightening in my chest.

I look up to the sky, failing to see the Kevish twinkle of the stars beyond the sodium mask of the night. What should I do?

Because am I not betraying my true nature by turning a blind cheek to this assault on standards? But then if I act on this and jeopardize my place in the Prem, am I not betraying my true self also? Because is not my deepest nature to amass silverware? Or is it to protect commerce?

Silverware? Consumers?

Consumers? Silverware?

I don't know.

Aaaaaaaahhhhhhhhhh.

I clutch my head.

Uuuuuuugggggghhhh.

I fall to my knees.

Oooooooofffffffffffff.

I thought I had decided, but I am torn asunder.

Then it comes, a glorious relief, a dip in the pressure, a monsoon falling down down down on to the drought of Kevish indecision. Because the stalemate breaks. The struggle is over. I cannot choose. I need both. And fanny as well, clearly. Obviously. And right. I'm not having this.

I pelt after the Lampards, catching up with them as they near St Mark's Grove. I stand Grove-side of the Fulham Road and bounce up and down on my toes.

'In here, you two,' I say to the Lampards, who have stopped now and are staring at me, a demented grin breaking on to the face of the bigger big Lampard, a cautious smile cracking the mouth of the smaller big Lampard.

'Come on, Lampards. I'm giving you a chance. Two of you. One Kev King. One alleyway.'

I run off into St Mark's Grove and I hear them decide to follow. I bob behind a car. God, so easy. This will be. I've been pitting my wits against quicksilver Portuguese playmaker Anderson Luis de Souza, or Deco as these Lampards will more likely know him, all day. I've been duelling with Nicolas Anelka, the current top scorer in the world's toppest league, not one hour ago.

Do these blubber-bellied, shaven-headed Lampards think they can have Kev? I think they do. How little they know of the physical and mental perfection that a top, top athlete, an athlete like the likes of your Kevin Kings, has to attain – and then sustain, week in, week out. I find it quaint that these run-of-the-mill civilian Lampards feel confident about this West London tussle.

And right. Here we go. The old razzle dazzle.

This'll be easier than playing against the Stepney Strollers.

They're level with this shitty Citreon's bonnet and I just Kev out all panther-like towards the smaller big Lampard, and naturally I've retained the blade for self-defence, and so the Case Trapper with mother-of-pearl handle and grooved nickel silver bolsters is out of the double-breasted Bottega Veneta jacket and I do the near Lampard quickly through his ribs, in towards the glob of saturated fat he uses as a heart, then I pull a length of Marlow low-stretch Kernmantel climbing rope – also, clearly, carried for self-defence – from a Veneta pocket, and straight away I'm behind the bigger Lampard, cord over his head, dragging it over his hanging chins, back towards his throat.

I leave the smaller big Lampard down in the road and drag the bigger big Lampard off by the 9mm dri-treated static rope, strangling him all cleanly as I pull him into a small, dark front garden, its hedge all neatly clipped, and sporting, at the far end, a topiary sculpture of the Chelsea lion emblem.

I further strangle the bigger Lampard and he slumps, unconscious or dead, on to the lawn and I Kev back into St Mark's Grove and find the smaller Lampard rolling on the ground by the pony Citreon, moaning on and on about the puncture that the Case Trapper's left him with.

I drag the smaller Lampard into the garden as well, and chuck him across his twin, then I stand above them all Kevishly, a far-off street light casting a faint shadow of the Chelsea topiary lion across the Veneta jacket.

'You called me a cunt,' I say to the big Lampard, admonishing him with a wag of the Case Trapper blade.

'And you called me a wanker,' I address the smaller Lampard.

Or was it the other way round? Can't remember now.

Either way, they both contributed to the lowering of the

standards of public life. I do them further with the Case Trapper, and as I stand above them now I feel rejoined, feel that the two sides of Kev have been reunited. And I understand that it was in vain that I rejected my vigilante side. I understand now that I can no more do that than turn my back on my own back. For example.

And further, I feel the need to hunt and kill the row L Herbert of Leeds leave me. I see the harsh but fair death of these two Lampards as somehow assuaging my need to kill the Elland Road Herbert. These twin Lampards committed a similar crime to that Herbert. And they have been punished for it.

Thing is, much as my renewed consumer idealism compels it, I cannot physically seek out each offender and visit them with Kevish retribution. I do not have the time to do every fucker. I do not have the manpower. I *am* Kev, yes, with all that connotes in terms of achievement and excellence, but even I would be hard-pressed to log and follow up every instance of anti-social behaviour.

I admit that. I am realistic about the effect that even a skilled, recommitted vigilante such as Kevin King can have. That is reality.

Let these Lampards then stand as an example for the Herbert and his ilk, a warning to those who seek to cheapen our culture, to violate contracts, to impinge customer rights and to any other way fuck over consumer satisfaction. The death of these Lampards sends out a strong message.

It is a clear deterrent. But a deterrent, truth be told, that I did not completely enjoy deploying, because, while I took the usual pride in the excellent knife work inflicted on these lacerated Lampards, the reality is that I did not take so duck-to-waterly to the rope tasks. I mean, I was, naturally, brilliant at strangling, but – for some reason – it did not gel with my character. And I have learned something there. I have gone back to vigilante school and learned that rope strangling is not really for me, and at heart I am a knife man.

Know thyself, I think it was ex-Villa boss John Gregory that said. And now I know myself a little better. Thanks to this vigilante workshop with the Lampards.

Anyway. I am feeling excellent. Reborn.

I step forward and tap the nearest Lampard on the head with my knuckle.

'What's that sound?' I ask, but they're both too dead by now to answer.

So I do it for them, 'That's me knocking on Capello's door.'

I check the Panerai Radiomir Black Seal timepiece and leave the garden, walking back on to the Fulham Road and up towards the Chelsea Village where I see Sas, just stepping out of a black cab. She is wearing a Hervé Léger bandage dress with seven-inch Guiseppe Zanotti stilettos. She is holding an Aksouna black leather bloom-woven clutch bag.

First time I've seen her since she got back from Oz, from the jungle. Lost a bit of weight, got a nice tan. Looking good, actually. Right, let's see about trying to get these progressive, non-possessive nuts of mine in.

But hang on. Why's she got out of the cab? Why's she not waiting in it for Kev? Aren't we going on to Marco Pierre White's new place or something?

I approach. 'Sas.'

'Hi, Kev.'

She bestows a small kiss. She looks a little nervous.

Have I got any blood on me? On the Veneta sleeve or something? I have a check. No. No blood. Must be something else. And I think I know what it is, the cause of Sas' nerves. It's my sky-rocketing media profile.

Last time she saw me, pre-reality show, pre-jungle, I wasn't in the first team. I hadn't set up the equalizer at the Emirates, scored the winner at the Mestella, laid on our opener at Stamford Bridge. This is a different Kev she is looking at, a more profileistic Kev.

That said, let us not forget that her profile has come on too, in the jungle. The flaunting of the G cup, the professions of love for

Premiership ace Kevin King, the seeming bunk-up with the soap actor – and seeming it was, I have sought reassurances on this, and she clearly – clearly – did not touch him – all have added extra layers to the Sas brand.

Because apart, our media visibility is high. Taken together, we are wall-to-wall. The coming golden couple. Hence the million quid plus book deal for the secrets of the L-style, chez King.

'Come on, Kev,' Sas says and walks back towards the ground.

'I thought...'

'We're eating here.'

'What?' But I follow her in.

'Yeah, Kev, restaurant's a collaborative effort between Marco and Roman Abramovich, located within the Chelsea Football Club complex itself.'

'Within the very complex itself?'

'Yeah. It's called Marco. Used to be a Harry Ramsden's.'

I feel anxious suddenly. I didn't know that.

Why didn't I know that White had opened here? What's the matter with me? I should have known. Because in one way, it's obvious. It's staring you in the face. In the post-prawn sandwich era, with the fan base increasingly discerning grub-wise, the oligarch and the one time terrible infant of British cooking would naturally seek a flagship partnership within the Chelsea Village itself. You can see the sense of it. But what does me in, what is making me anxious, is that Kev hadn't heard about it, that my eatery antenna had not picked up the rumblings of the joint venture. And what gets me more is that it was Sas who had to tell me.

I hate her telling me things. I hate her seeing me not knowing things.

I follow Sas and we approach a brushed metal frontage flanked by columns of subdued blue light. I follow Sas through the revolving door and we're in. Right, let's have a look, see what decor the oligarch/chef helmsmen have settled on.

Tara Bernerd-designed retro luxurious feel.

Golden Swarovski crystal-studded central column.

Velvet mink-effect seating.

Nice, actually. Nice nice nice.

Oligar-chic, think I'll call it.

Maître d' greets and we elect to drink first at the marble bar. I want, and this is weird for me, a *white* wine. But the 2005 Pouilly Fuisse La Roche Domaine Manciat Poncet looks cheapy at around forty, and I am still feeling anxious regarding the lack of Marco knowledge, so I spend my way to happiness with the 1998 Chateau Suduiraut Sauternes, a cheeky red, priced at more than double the Fuissee. Shame, because, as I say, I *did* want the white. But I'm not spending only forty quid on a bottle of wine.

I feel better. I open the menu. Classic MPW.

Refined French cuisine, fused with modern British flair. The foie gras signature dish, so extravagantly gelatinous, is of course on the starter list. The panaché of sea scallops with black pudding. The brandade of salted cod. The oysters prunier. Oh, I *am* feeling good.

'Got you something,' says Sas, leaning sideways from her yellow bar stool, a Verneuil gift wrap-covered box held in her manicureds.

She pops the box on top of my menu and I turn and look at her.

I have a little sniff. 'New perfume?' I say.

'Yeah. Lily Moon bespoke fragrance.'

'What's it called?'

'It's called *Sas*. Had it mixed up for myself. One off.'

'Beautiful.'

And it is. And so is she. Really. The Cats, the Denises, the many many others, none – I understand in this moment – can be as strong a part of my lifestyle as Sas. Not even that little Mexican friend of Gravesy's, who really has been seeing a lot of me recently. None can match Sas' profile. I was a fool to try and end it, over something that never really happened as well, over a mere ghost fuck, if you will. And I will wear the jibes I receive from humpty crowds and players and so-called friends even. Because they don't know Sas like I do. Nobody does. Not even me. I will rise above their tittle-tattle, the baseless lies.

'Thanks for this,' I say, and get to work on the Verneuil wrapping.

'It comes with a free international concierge service,' she says, all excited as I open, unable to stop herself from blurting out some of the lifestyle features of the gift.

'Each handset has a dedicated button, auto-connecting to twenty-four seven assistance,' she adds.

I'm through the paper now. I have a proper look.

It's a Vertu mobile. An Ascent Racetrack Legends limited edition with laser-etched Silverstone circuit map, bezel-nosed radiator grille inset, and liquidmetal chassis. It's got racing grade rubber, ruby bearings and sapphire crystal componentry. Sas has accessorized with a tangerine ostrich-skin carry case and an Aerius Bluetooth headset.

I look at her.

'I hope you don't think I'm being too pushy, Kev,' she says. 'I know you love your Nokia Arte.'

'I do.'

'But you've had it for weeks now, Kev, and I just thought it was time to move on.'

'Sas?'

'Yes, Kev?'

'This is a peerless phone. Painstakingly crafted. It is a pinnacle of global mobile excellence.'

'Thanks, Kev.'

Sas is right. My sentimental attachment to the Arte 8800 needed to be challenged. And with the incomparable Vertu she has done just that. It is a truly Premiership phone.

I lean over to kiss her, but she ducks away, indicating her make-up with a waft of the manicureds. Doesn't want me to smudge her up. We'll see about that.

'Kev?'

Here we go.

'Min's brokered a deal for an intimate lifestyle shoot for us.'

'Me and you?'

'Yeah, Kev. But we don't have the right back drop.'

'I see.'

'So…'

I get it. 'Sas, are you asking if we could acquire a property together to form the intimate lifestyle shoot's backdrop?'

'I am, Kev.'

'I think that's an excellent idea. Got a few irons in the fire that way myself. But there's one thing, profile-wise, book deal-wise. When we move in, you have to, you know, maybe see other people. Not just see me, I mean.'

'OK, Kev.'

'I mean, you need to be seen to be seeing them. You don't have to see them as such, just *appear* to be doing so. I mean, I don't *want* you seeing other people, just being seen seeing other people. Unless they're other birds. You can bring birds home and do them. We can. Do them, I mean. Together.'

'Course, Kev. The angle for the lifestyle shoot is "Cosy home but open legs". Shall I instruct my PA to liaise with likely estate agents?'

'Certainly, Sas.'

She checks her Movado Amorosa timepiece.

'Min'll be here in ten,' she says. 'Just got to get you to sign a few release forms.'

the australian greetings cards sector

I am pacing St Martin's Lane. I am owning it.

Actually, no, I don't feel too good. I am not exactly owning it. I am renting it, then. I am renting St Martin's Lane.

I'm not happy about this, about where we are going, but mates is mates. Not that this particular mate, Gravesy, has done me the fucking courtesy of being on time.

Late Gravesy. But now he's here, little Aussie hand clutching a red-top and waving already from the black cab window as he approaches the kerb outside the London Coliseum. I walk over. He steps out as he notes the knowledger and continues to talk on the RIM Blackberry Storm.

'Look, mate, I know I owe you it. You'll get it,' he says, and ends the call, stepping towards me. 'Fucking bookies, Kev-o.'

Gravesy is wearing an orange, single-button Missoni suit with a white Wintle scarf T-shirt and Alberto Guardiani suede shrainers. He's looked better, truth be told.

'How's tricks, Gravesy?'

He wafts the tabloid at me with a pasty hand.

'Two more killings last night, Kev-o. Outside the Bridge.'

'Yeah, Gravesy, I saw.'

'They say the football murderer is moving into a higher gear.'

'They do, do they? A higher fucking gear? What is he, this so-called football murderer, a mountain bike? And what's more, all the red-tops and TV may be calling them the football murders, but they're not, are they?'

'How do you mean, Kev-o?'

'Well, it's just that if you bother to look, if you use a bit of nouse, then they are clearly – *clearly* – pro-consumer vigilante killings. And I know that's a mouthful, I know that "pro-consumer vigilante killing" is not the pithiest phrase in the Queen's, is not a headline writer's dream. But still, that doesn't mean it's not true. What's the point in this vigilante killing offenders so fucking diligently for the consumer cause if he remains so misunderstood?'

'I just thought they were football killings, mate. Everyone thinks that. The police are linking the gaffer to it now. They're interviewing our players.'

Shit.

'Gravesy, I thought we were mates, but to you they're just normal, weedy little football murders.'

The Aussie looks baffled, his eyes climb closer together.

'We *are* mates, Kev-o, but…'

I don't want to hear it. I change the subject.

'Look, Gravesy, you sure about this?'

'About what, mate?'

'The opera. Isn't this the famous one, the one all the fucking zone twelvers come and see? Isn't this a bit like going to Madame Tussaud's or the Hard Rock Café or something?'

'Mate. Tchaikovsky's *Sleeping Beauty* is a popular opera. It does pull in the casual goer, I admit that. But at the Coliseum, with Ken-o Macmillan's classic choreography, it is not a cut-price date.'

'Not going to be full of turds then?'

'Mate, there will be turds. Always are. But there'll be some fit posh girls in there as well.'

Loves his posh, Gravesy. Loves it. The colonial is bunking up the class system. But then he's a man of breadth as well. Loves his Mexican hooker too. Ambidextrous, Gravesy is, sexually I mean. Fuck a duchess or a wench. A man of wide tastes, refined sensibilities, hence this opera visit.

And now we're inside. Heavy carpets and scurrying civilians and drinks and programmes and all that. Some decent enough clobber. Most you wouldn't, but some you would.

'Any news on a buyer, Gravesy?' I ask, winding up some idle chat to take my mind off the news about the gaffer and the cops; and off the thoughts I'm having that after last night I have exposed myself anew to losing it all, to being flung from the Prem, my spiritual home. No matter how pure and virtuous and justified, if I am discovered, then last night's actions will cost me everything. I am playing a high-risk game.

'No news, mate. Lots of news, mate. You hear things all the time, Kev-o. But no one's put the cash down.'

My old club, and Gravesy's current, is in admin. Looking at possible extinction. At the very least a punitive points deduction.

'Perilous, is it?'

'Perilous, mate.'

'You seen Colly?'

'Saw him yesterday. He's in bad shape, Kev-o. You, me and Boves are the only clients he's got left. FA are looking into stripping him of his licence. The playmate's walked. The Jag's gone. The house is next. He's fucked.'

It's a shame. Really. But then there's some kind of bell and the posh kind of herd off towards a variety of doorways and Gravesy gives me the 'you got the tickets?' eyes and I pull them out of the grey, two-button Marni suit and hand them over.

'Dress circle, Kev-o. Front row. Very nice.'

'My treat, Gravesy.'

And he looks at me wearing his 'I believe in the power of matemanship' face, and he seems pleased that me, I, Kev, his mate, is standing close by him in his hour of need. In his hour of possible club admin. And not only standing solidly next to him in full-blown mateship, but standing next to him in a white Veronique Branquinho shirt and brown suede Santoni boots, which complement the aforementioned Marni suit.

'Right, let's go in, Kev-o.'

And so we do. In we go.

Right then. Opera. Let's see if it can calm Kev down, take his mind off this fucking jeopardy that is foisting itself everywhere. Never simple, is it? Following your heart. I mean, being true to yourself.

Three hours, it takes. Three hours. And I follow the plot easily. The plot I follow fine. The Princess Aurora blessed by the good fairies, cursed by a bad one, re-blessed by another. The sleep. The Prince. The tongue and the awakening. I get all that. Child's play.

It is not the plot that is alarming. What's alarming is the way the cast overdo it. They really do overdo it. Singing *and* acting. Dancing as well. These things sometimes at the same time. That's what gets me, the overkill of it. Sing, if you like to sing, act if you like to act, but doing both at the same time? No, thank you.

I mean, to draw a parallel from the King experience, I am into the football, yeah? And then I am into the shagging. But would I seek to do both at the same time, as these opera Herberts are doing with their singing *and* dancing?

No. I would not.

Penetrative run down the left wing? Fine. But while I'm enjoying Cat in the doggy style? No. Crucial match-saving tackle followed by a tidy lay-off? Without question. But accomplish that while I've got Denise clamouring for the best of me? I don't think so.

I like both these things, the football and the shagging, but I would never, never seek to do them at the same time.

Admittedly I have made certain girls wear certain kits at certain erotic moments, and admittedly I have felt strong sexual impulses after netting particular goals. I *can* see that the two things bleed into each other. But I have not done them at the same time, as such. Not so publicly. Not as brazenly as these singing and acting Herberts are doing out here on the Coliseum stage, tonight.

If I did try and double them up – the football and the shagging, I mean – it is clear to me what would happen. Both endeavours would suffer. My performance as a footballer would be inhibited by on-field sexual grapplings, while my Lover Lover technique would be compromised by the constant need to burst into the box. It would not work.

So too, here tonight. The singing is shit because they're acting. The acting is shit because they're singing. Settle on one, and one alone, and it might work. But to do both is pure, pure greed.

I am angry with these cake-and-eat-it operaists. And I am saddened that such artistic confusion and greed is tolerated on the London stage. It really is an eye-opener.

And what opens the King eyes further is that right near the end, well, nearish the end anyway, long after the first interval at least, and just before the second, Gravesy strikes up – *tries* to strike up – a little chat with the likes of your Kevin Kings. He wants to talk about the Mexican.

'She's really getting to me, Kev-o.'

'What?'

It is hard to hear Gravesy over the singish acting that is so shamelessly going on. But he goes further, this time louder.

'I've even stopped fucking her sister. I can't get enough of her.'

I heard that. I know what he means as well, there is something about the Mexican. Not that I'm going to tell Gravesy that. Break his little heart, it would, if he knew I'd been visiting. Discover that, and his Antipodean heart would swoon and fall out of its little pouch, to be lost forever in the outback. The outback of love, if we may. Which is actually a profound thought, a profound image, and one that would do well to be picked up by enterprising firms who could go on to market both the words and sentiment in the Australian greetings cards sector.

'She does this thing with her little finger.'

'What?' I say, although this time I did hear him over the actish singing being perpetrated on the nearby stage, it's just that I want him to say it again. I know exactly the little finger thing he means and I have shelled out for it on a number of occasions myself. I would like to hear his version of it.

'What?' I say again.

'I said, she does this thing with her little finger. It really gets to me.'

Titillation aside, his tone sounds ominous.

'You're not? Are you? Gravesy?'

'I think I might be, Kev-o.'

'Didn't catch that,' I say, because now there's some almighty act-sing going on, some climax being reached or something, because they really seem to be belting it out...

'I was just saying, Kev-o...'

It's so loud I can barely hear my dinner.

'What, Gravesy?'

That's better. A bit better anyway. They seem to be coming to an end.

And, 'I'm in love with the Mexican hooker,' he says, well, shouts really, just as the voices and the orchestra die, so in fact bellowing his declaration in favour of the Central American professional right across the now-silent auditorium, as such, causing many audience heads to swivel our way, and causing even some cast members to peer from the stage towards the source of the unlikely proclamation.

Gravesy rolls his eyes. Everyone looks at him. Even that quite tasty brunette over to our left in the burnt-orange Temperley London gown has a little scan.

It's not good for Gravesy right now. The admin horror looming, being twisted, it seems, around the Mexican's little finger, and now all this 'let's all stare at Gravesy because he bellows about hookers at the opera' stuff that has just, this very minute, come his way.

Tough times at Gravesy Grange. And not a very forgiving

clientele, the operaists, with all this overt peering that they're laying on to Gravesy.

I look over to him. He looks deflated and mental. Let's lend a hand.

'Quick drink while the interval's on?' I ask Gravesy and I stand him and we walk. Well, *I* walk, he shuffles, head down, out of the dress circle – or the seats as some prefer – and over towards the bar.

a ramsden's man

Team bus.

Third game in eight days. ManU away.

The Vertu Ascent Racing Legends limited edition is ringing its tits off. This time it's Sas.

'A compliment to any prestigious lifestyle,' she says, reading from the estate agent's brochure.

'Promising,' I say. 'Very strong. Book a viewing.'

Text from Gravesy: *Fuck them Kev-o.*

Stirring pre-match words from the Aussie marksman.

Text from Nan: *Do your best love.*

Bless. But no text from Boves, and nothing from Colly.

When was the last time I saw Colly? God knows. Weeks or something. Not since the Arsenal game, I don't think. Used to be my second home, Colly's. And now? Well, I don't know. It's a kind of Mexican stand-off I'm into with Colly. As with Gravesy. Although that's more of a Mexican kit off. If you will.

Colly's got the hump because he suspects – strongly and accurately as it turns out – that I'm holding back on the cash. And I've got the hump with him, though then again it's not exactly the hump, or if it is the hump it's the hump of caution rather than of disgruntlement. Yes. I've got the hump of caution with Colly.

Retain a convicted fraudster as my Mr Fifteens? At a time when my endorsement ops are so rocketish? Difficult to see how

I'd do that. But then, otherhandishly, mates is mates and Colly is Colly. And so far friendship – what remains of it – and the urgings of loyal Boves, have won out over caution. So far I have kept the Colly faith.

Anyway. We're at Old Trafford. We're changing up, the lads and I.

Our striker Bédard's out with cruciate fuck, so young British Sri Lankan Dilip Ranga is given the responsibility up front, partnering our rangy Gambian Boro Danzo. Dainty Croat Janko Lasich comes in for the dead-legged Ali el-Masri on the right wing, and Spanish defender Estovan Varagos moves into central defence following Baki Ozan's alarming mid-week attack of double vision. Other than that, it's as you were.

Is Rantanen in the side? To be honest, these days I don't even look. He is of no consequence to me. Is he injured still? On the bench? Doing a fucking bricklaying course at night school? Doesn't matter. This is my position now. I have brushed the mutton-chopped Finn aside with sheer Kevish humpty prowess. We are not even rivals now, Rantanen and Kev.

Performance-wise, the only way he'd get a sniff was if I got injured. And that's not going to happen, is it? I am uninjurable. Drop a breeze block on my foot if you want. Won't do a thing. Twat my hamstring with a fucking crowbar should you wish. Mr Football here would not notice.

The football sap is rising still, rising up and up, and it won't stop rising till they hand out the gongs in May. I will win some of those gongs, I can feel it. I have strong apprehensions of silverware. And an architect-designed trophy room will be appended to the new King mansion, the massive new property into which I will soon move with super-fit model sleb partner Sas. Unless, of course, Kev is exposed as the consumer avenger and it all goes to shit…

But these thoughts cannot plague me now because it's out the changing room and into the tunnel, and all queuing up now to be led by the man in black on to the sanctuary of the pitch. We're stood by their lot. Rooney's there with his Mr Potato Head stylings, next to winking Ronaldo with his sunbed skin, so fucking orange that he looks like he's just been quarried from the sun. And there's moody Bulgarian, Berbatov, with his alarmingly angled forehead. Temples you could cut your elbow on, that boy.

Carrick. Anderson. Ferdinand. Vidić. They're all in the ManU line-up. Their manager Fergie's got his strongest team out. And well he might, because we're top and they sit in a lowly fourth. Anyway.

Some bibbed-up Herbert is in the tunnel too. Some reserve team assistant to the assistant coach type Herbert. Or else he runs the MUFC 'website' or something, and he's come down for a cheeky mingle with the talent. Out of his depth, either way. Standing there with his cretinous red bib on. Can see he's not a football man, can see he's not proper football.

Maybe it's the look of sheer hatred I am aiming towards this bibby Herbert, or else maybe he just does not know how to conduct himself here in the players' tunnel, so close to the Old Trafford pitch. Because he looks at me, returns my stare, and then what he does is he mouths something at me.

'King, you twat,' I can see him say. All silently and distinctly, mouthing it to me clearly without raising any volume, so to say.

I give him the 'you fucking what?' eyes and he does it again.

'King, you twat,' he mouths, giving it the big man.

Oh dear. Twat I indeed may be, in his eyes perhaps, but to mouth off like that in the players' tunnel, right before a match? To do that? It seems…Well, there are many things it seems, and consumer champion Nicky Campbell would no doubt be outraged by this employee of the club demonstrating such piratical disdain for pre-game norms, such ungraciousness to the visiting team. Still. There's nothing to be done right now because we're moving out on the pitch, Stretford End to our left, dugouts away to our right in front of the South Stand; 76,000 prawn sandwichers fucking bellowing for the red machine.

The United fan base, they say, is over 300 million strong. Making five per cent of the world their supporters. Roughly. Or one in twenty people. Every twentieth civvy who walks by you in the road is a ManU fan. More or less. Unless you're in Manchester, of course, where the figure will naturally be considerably lower. But still, one in twenty people, they reckon, in the world.

A lot of people are going to be watching this game. A lot of people are going to smell a piece of Kev today. But then I actually find it hard, early doors, to get into the game, I will admit that. Because there is, I further admit, some inventive distribution from their boy Carrick, displaying in the opening exchanges the range of passing for which ManU coughed so heavily to his previous club, Spurs.

There is that. And their young Brazilian Anderson, acquired from Porto in 2007, is all snarl in the tackle. They are a good side. A goodish side, anyway. Senegalese-born Frenchman Patrice Evra is a danger down our right flank, that has to be said, and the tenacious movement of their South Korean Park Ji-sung is a credit to the profession of athleticism.

All that is given. But we have some players too, and the opposition are just going to have to accept that. Either after half time, or before. Personally, I don't mind which.

One thing's for sure. I will cover each blade of the pitch before this ninety ends, I will coat each blade in pure Kev football sap. If you will.

Aye aye. We're on.

I pick the ball up, our Togolese defensive shield Gilchrist Eyodema instepping one accurately into my path as I run and I've got sunbed Ron tracking back on to me, well, his version of tracking back anyway, which is to run for a bit then leave it to their right back Rafael to mop up, which he does, coming on to me, and to be fair to the young Brazilian, he makes a good fist of it, neither diving in and going to ground nor backing off too much either, but I manage to show myself inside, now towards Nemanja Vidić, their Serbian number fifteen, who is hammering out of central defence into me, and I let him come all close and then what I do – and it's so simple – is side-foot the ball, a metre or so, two at most, into the path of Wally de Groot who's cut in from our right mid, and what he does is merely twat it excellently, left side of the advancing Vidić, right side of the duck-mouthed Ferdinand, so that it flings itself, slightly uppishly, towards the van der Sar net, beating their veteran Dutchman who just stands, wrong-footed, head agonizingly swivelled, watching de Groot's shot rifle past him into the ManU bag.

One nil.

The Stretford End is hushed, and what's that sound?

A sort of tapping sound. Tap tap tap, it goes. Can you hear it, Mr Capello? Is that another little rattle of the England door?

It is, you know.

Get in. *Get in.*

Two one it ends. To us. We're changing up and the Wii henchmen come in, and naturally and unwelcomely there follows the Chairman himself and he is over to our Uruguayan keeper, who did ever so well today, shutting up shop completely, apart from the goal he conceded. And then Chairman Bahta – who is wearing some type of jumper, some kind of crafted-from-the-hair-of-a-unicorn-or-some-other-famously-luxurious-mythical-creature type jumper – and he's over to goalscorer de Groot, and he's shaking the hand of the man from the Netherlands, and then he's over to me, Bahta is, and he's standing right there as I sit, top off, ink out, sweating like a dinner lady after my dynamic man of the match performance. The third such performance of recent weeks.

First time I've seen him since Mr Chips. And to be frank – to be be fair and frank about it – I could really do without this, because having so recently recommitted myself to the way of the vigilante, this little meet is, shall we say, fraught with anxiety.

Anyway.

'You cost nothing, Kevin, and yet you give so much,' he says.

'To the team,' I add.

'To the club,' he furthers.

'Hopefully to the whole footballing community. As a whole,' I finish, knowing by now that I'm spouting utter fuck.

Bahta pops his little billionaire hand out, silky palm upwards, and a Wii goon places a white business card on there, and Bahta swivels his hand forward, towards me, and raises his eyebrows in 'take the card'. Which I do.

Aram Shishakli, the card says, *Football Agent.*

'Yeah. I was meaning to talk agents with you, Mr, er, Bahta. After the, er, revelations of the other day…Lovely meal, by the way.'

'You enjoyed our visit to Mr Chips?'

'Yeah. It was, you know, chippy,' I affirm, hoping above all that he will just fuck off.

'But did you like the mushies, Kevin?'

Christ. Just go.

But, 'The peas?' I say. 'Oh yes. Very much so.'

'Bachelor's or Harry Ramsden's?' he asks now, being all weirdly specific, being all 'I may well be a billionaire Parsi from Gujarat, but I'm also a down-to-earth, fish supper-eating, football-loving Englishman as well'.

'Oh, very much the Ramsden's,' I nervously ad-lib, in fact knowing less than fuck all about these pony foodstuffs and wanting desperately to climb right off this freakish billionaire food chat escalator.

'I also favour Ramsden's, Kevin. A darker, more reassuring colour when counterpoised with the livid Bachelor pea.'

'Very much so, Mr Bahta.'

'Good…You really should phone Mr Shishakli, Kevin. I strongly advise it…A man in your position, a Ramsden's man, needs intelligent representation.'

And with that final spin in the bollocks copter, Bahta – thank fuck – turns and walks across the changing rooms, leaving me shaking, but none the wiser as to what he actually knows. I glance again at the agent's card then pop it into the side pocket of the Andrew Marc Marshall sports bag.

But then, 'Gentlemen,' Bahta now says from the far side of the changing rooms, addressing, it would seem, the whole squad. 'The police have been in touch with the club. They wish to interview every member of our staff who travelled to the Newcastle and Chelsea games. They want everyone to account for their whereabouts at certain times. You will of course all understand why that is. And you will, of course, all comply.'

It's over, it's curtains. It's fucking curtains.

'Interview times,' Bahta continues, not that I can hear him too well now above the panicked techno whumf of blood in my own ears, 'will be posted on the noticeboard at Corlham Wood.'

Bahta looks down, seeming to scrutinize his loafers, and I think he's done, but then, 'One more thing,' he says. 'This investigation has come at an inconvenient time. But it is not going to affect our performance. We are professionals and will stay on course for the treble. Understood?'

'Yes, boss,' or gaffer, or Chairman, or Sir, or Mr Bahta, all of the lads say, although all I manage is a kind of 'Uuuuhhhhh' as the Parsi exits.

It's over. The charcoal-grey Duckie Brown two-button suit. I'm fucked. A floral print Iceberg shirt. I've had it. A leather Dirk Bikkembergs Velcro-fastened shoe.

The team bus. Corlham Wood. The Bentley.

It's a nightmare. Except it's in the day.

A call from Nan. I do not take it.

Now what? Think, Kev. Think. Because I can't just sit around shitting them, waiting for Kev's Prem idyll to end, can I?

And what did he say, back then, when he gave me that agent's card?

'You really should phone Mr Shishakli, Kevin. I strongly advise it...A man in your position, a Ramsden's man, needs intelligent representation.'

'A man in my position', that's what he said. Which could mean, if Bahta does know, a man about to have the cops snaffling at his gonads. Or which might merely mean, if he doesn't know, a man going places, football-wise.

And either way, whatever he meant, 'I strongly advise it' was a pretty clear steer from Bahta, and it's always handy to do what a billionaire wants, to have a billionaire onside, so to speak, especially when the filth have just strode questioningly into view.

I remove the Vertu Ascent Racetrack Legends limited edition from its tangerine ostrich-skin carry case and dink in the digits from Shishakli's card.

'Mr Shishakli?'

'Yes?'

'Kevin King.'

'Ah, Mr King. When shall we meet?'

'Well...'

'Business hours, you will find me at Les A.'

'Les what?'

'Les Ambassadeurs in Mayfair. You know it?'

'Course.' But I don't. Not really. I've heard of it: private club, high rollers casino. As such. Apparently. But I've never actually been there.

'Come here any day. The staff will bring you to me.'

'You there in an hour?'

'I'd be delighted to see you, Mr King.'

Right you are then. Within easy reach, the Syrian super agent, the intercontinental sports Svengali, who's been implicated in so much tapping up that... Well, let's just say that he's been involved in a lot of tapping up. Or the evidence seems to point that way. But given that he's registered in Syria, the FA can't touch him, so the evidence can do what it likes. The evidence can indicate. It can mount up. It can pull out a fucking Samurai sword and make towards him with an evident menace. Shishakli won't care.

So. Town. Edgware. Marble Arch and on to the Park Lane.

Mayfair. Hyde Park on the left, right into Hamilton Place and there it is, Georgian townhouse, looking over the park. Stop outside, peep the Bents and the door monkey skips down the stairs to do the parking and I'm out on the street and making towards the doors of Les A, as I've just discovered it's known.

There's some door quizzing, but I drop the Shish name and I'm through easy. Right you are then, let's have a look.

Bastion of exclusivity. Superior gaming. Extraordinary quality of service.

And is that the silver screen's Jude Law? I think it is.

Into the bar, and some fat bloke stands and smiles, all dimply and dessert-loving his cheeks are, and he raises a sausagey hand towards me.

'Mr King.'

I walk over. He is wearing the full Savile Row. Black Jaspar Littleman suit, a 1940s Omega Cosmic timepiece with croc-skin strap showing from the right cuff of his white, Reuben Alexander shirt. He's sporting Anello and Davide bespoke brogues.

Proper English, the Syrian, just like Bahta. Except Bahta is working the down-to-earth English authenticity with his Mr Chips love, while Shishakli here is giving it the full Eton. And what is it about these super-rich foreign boys and their English thing? I mean, I know what it is...

The Queen. The humpty. Eric Clapton. Etc.

But they are so up front about it. Still. As much as I love the England, as much as it thrills me to be a subject of HRH, at the same time I willingly participate in a global footballing democracy.

I have no grudge with the foreign talent – both on and off the field, and off it as well – which floods the game. No grudge at all.

I shake Aram Shishakli's hand and then he does a little arm waft which means I should sit. And I do. I take a chair. There's some tissues, and a box of Marc Demarquette bespoke English Collection chocolates on his little table. And there's two mobiles. One of them is a Continental LG Secret in 24k gold with tempered glass and 3d-design carbon fibre casing. And so's the other one.

Two lines, the Syrian. Nice touch. No, wait, those phones will have three lines each, at least. So actually, he's got a minimum of six lines, the Syrian. On two phones. And two phones sporting ambient light detection facilities at that. Promising.

'So, Mr King,' he says, 'I don't have much time.' He glances at the Omega Cosmic. 'I'm due in the Salle Privée with Adnan Khasoggi in seven minutes. So,' he leans forward, 'this is your situation. Your agent is a convicted fraudster who your club will rightly not deal with. You are contracted with them until the end of the season, at which time you will become a free agent. What I propose is that I buy you then for a nominal fee, then I rent your player registration back to the club, for a higher wage next season, retaining your economic rights, which we share, and splitting any subsequent transfer fee fifty-fifty between the club and myself, then handing you fifty per cent of my fifty per cent.'

What? 'I only get the twenty-fives?'

'Yes.' He pauses. 'Mr King?'

Indeed, Mr Shishakli. It's not good. He's put me in a toughie here, has the Syrian. Because one hand, intention was to sign up, so getting Bahta onside. But then cracking me with the hard sell, as Shishakli here has done, has raised the King hackles, because I'm a fucking informed consumer, fully advised of my customer human rights and I can look after myself, negot-wise.

I will not be bullied. I can't let it go. I rise up with a King haggle.

'Firstly, for the time being and until I say otherwise, Colly is my agent. Secondly, why would Bahta want to just hand you fifties of my transfer fee? And thirdly, why would I want to hand *any* of my transfer fee to you? You're offering me twenty-fives of my own fee, when I can buy myself, rent myself out to the club, then sell myself later, giving myself fifties of the hundred, which is double your offer of the twenty-fives.'

Nice, Kev. Nice.

I'm expecting a wobble, expecting the Syrian Svengali to wilt beneath my wised-up contractual broadside. But the boy just checks the Omega.

'Firstly, I can do nothing if you wish to be represented by a fraudster who is unsuited to maximizing your global endorsement revenues. Secondly, Mr Bahta lost rather heavily to me at cards and you are his payment to me.'

I am his *what*? Bahta's what? Christ. I am no one's payment to no one. I am Kev. One hundred and fifteen per cent pure Kev King. Still, still, calm it. We are both adults here in Les A, we are men, and we are in dealings and – to be honest and fair – I am enjoying the brusque style in which the Syrian conducts the business. He does not fuck about.

Keep a lid on it, Kev, talk to the man.

'Why doesn't Bahta just pay off the card debt?'

'Well, it may surprise you to learn that Mr Bahta is currently having a little issue with funds.'

Fucking Moses. Right. The credit crunch nibbling even at the Chairman. Well I never. And after he gave me that 'money means nothing talk' down at Mr Chips as well. No wonder I'm being paid a sub par sixty-three by the club. And no wonder – and it hurts me to think this – they went for me on a free to cover the Duke's ball fuck, rather than an expensive, in-contract continental import. And maybe that's why Colly was barred from the club, nothing to do with a dodgy past, but just so that his players could be handed over to Shishakli, to cover Bahta's card debts. A thought which means I need to know about Colly's two other ex-clients at our club.

'Have Anselmo and Whelan signed with you?'

'Of course,' the Shish says and smiles. 'And to answer your third point. Believe me, a player cannot own his own registration...I have to go. Phone me when you decide to accept.'

He stands and I watch him gather his phones and chocolates and waddle round the table, out of the bar, and towards the casino rooms. And I am angry, confused. Because one hand, signing'll gain me Bahta's favour. But then again, the Syrian's take-it-or-leave-it is anti-consumer, anti-competition. The Shish is trying to establish an unfair monopoly on your Kevin Kings, and, having just redoubled my unswerving faith in vigilantism, it would be criminal – in the non-criminal sense of the word – to cave in and sign.

I am confused. I stride out of Les A and they bring up the Bents and I'm in it and driving up the Park Lane, and do you know what? I am neglecting my duties, I am neglecting to uphold customer rights.

All day I have been playing magnificent humpty in front of a global TV audience, or negotiating at the very highest levels with the Syrian. Or else, and I admit this, shitting my whack because the cops are now on my tail. It has been a whirlwind. But in this hustle and bustle I have neglected my core duties, I really have.

The rudeness shown to me – a visiting dignitary – by a member of the ManU staff was disgusting. The way that the bibby Herbert stood in the tunnel, where perhaps he even had no right to be, was an all-out affront to public standards. The rogue way in which he insulted me was an attack on my rights. And what with them being current Premiership champions and such a solid global brand as well, you would imagine that the powerful ManU franchise would not allow such match-day infringements.

The bibbed insulter from Old Trafford needs a clampdown. He needs hunting and confronting. He does. But then, he is not to hand. And I could not very well have done him there, could I? So he wriggled away. But there is always a way to send out a clear warning to those who would compromise consumer culture, to those who would con and cajole the customer away from his righteous destiny.

And as with the two dead Lampards, who offered themselves as a deterrent sacrifice, so the sweary tunnel Herbert will find his own stand-in.

His demeaning actions cannot go unpunished.

I pull off Park Lane into Stanhope Gardens and still the Bents. I pop on the new Lemar album. They say that one in twenty people is a ManU fan.

A young couple wander by. That's two people.

Another couple, that makes four.

I count the civilians that pass. When I get to twenty – a youngish Herbert, wearing a West Ham beanie hat as it later turns out – the Case Trapper pocket knife with mother-of-pearl handle and grooved nickel silver bolsters is out of the Duckie Brown jacket, and I'm on the street and tracking him.

One in twenty, Herbert. One in twenty.

He disappears round a corner and when I catch up with him he has stopped his little stroll and is pissing on to some kind of bush.

Christ!

A public piss, in the West End, so very near to one of HRH's gaffs. He is virtually pissing in dear Liz's face, stinging her actual eyes with his rogue civvy slash. I am incensed. I Kev forwards, like an urban lynx, the Case Trapper out and abundantly ready.

I've got no plan really. I'll just improvise, and I chop him one into the lower back, right side of his spineless spine, angled upwards so that I just sort of tickle through the bottom of his lung, as well as also no doubt bursting a few useful other body-type things that he keeps stashed in that part of his back.

And the funny thing is, he keeps on pissing, a decent enough stream as well. I mean, he must know he's been done. He must be able to feel it, and he is sort of groaning. But also he just carries on with the slash, as though it's more important to keep his strides dry than it is to deal with the excruciating knife wound. And to be honest, I admire that.

But, you know, busy boy and all that, so I get all symmetrical then.

I do him left side of the spine, so as to tickle up into his other lung, and then the vigilante sap is rising a little, must be, because I get into it a bit more and dart in a slender couple, one up under each shoulder blade, so that if you joined the wounds with a line they would form a kind of rudimentary oblong, the shape of a badly-marked football pitch, say, that a tottery groundsman might fudge for some spastic cub team.

Anyway, as I'm withdrawing the Trapper and musing on the

puncture pattern I've just created, there's a scuttling sound, I'm sure of it, behind me, and I look round but see nothing, though I do trust the King ears. And so I finish the lad with a harsh sawing sort of one to the neck and then shove him forward into the bushes and then I'm away following the sound and I'm back on to the side road, and stood there – next to, as it happens, a shit Hyundai – is some tall scruffy cunt, and I'm sure I've seen him before. And he's wheezing all excitedly into his phone.

'Honestly. Definitely Kev King. Saw him. With a knife. Got to go. Christ.'

He ends the call. But that's not right, is it? Talking about me behind my back. And so I shimmy all Kev-wise towards the scruffy Hyundai-driving piss drinker, and – I really am not arsing about – I plunge a wild one deep into the side of his neck, and then drag it backwards, as though I were a drunken Boxing Day uncle, badly carving a stringy gammon. And then I jimmy the Trapper all around, making the hole much bigger, at the skin end of things.

And this Hyundai twat's head would easily come off now, with a little bit of attention, but that's not my game. Never has been. The old decap routine. Never had a taste for it. Not in the consumer's interest. Because what I want now is his phone, what I need is to see who this tall cunt was calling.

And I look away from his neck, which is slashing a geyser of blood, and there, still cradled in his left hand, is his phone – and it's a fucking Arte 8800, which surely the low rent should have upgraded by now – and I'm holding the lad now with my left arm and trying to reach his phone with my right, but I just can't make it, I just can't reach.

So I let him go, drop the lad backwards, so that he crunks heavily against the kerb and does a little bounce, which is a surprise because you expect a cheery bounce like that when a fat guy goes down, but not from such a skinny lad as this, and anyway, as he lands again – after his perplexingly bouncy skinny-guy bounce – his arm sort of flips and clatters and the phone shoots out and spins in the air for a moment before landing on a kerbside grate and then tilting, tilting forwards, so that it falls from the grille and through the grate and into the sewers beneath. And I Kev quickly over to see the phone's – the Arte's – once startlingly innovative screen display float slowly away to swim through London's shite.

Moments later, I'm on the Vertu.

'Got yourself a client, Mr Shishakli,' I say. Because if the Hyundai Herbert was tailing me for Bahta, then the Parsi Chairman'll be yelling when he turns up dead. So best to play nice.

But then again, maybe the tailing had nothing to do with the Chairman. So, 'Yeah,' I'm saying into the Vertu, but this time to Billy Four Chins, Mr Location himself. 'Got you a job, Billy. Grand a day, then ten more when you get it. You've got to find me a phone.'

'Sounds easy.'

'It's in the sewers.'

'Uuuuufff,' I hear Billy wince. 'Thanks, Kev. Jesus. You know how big the London sewers are?'

'Course I fucking don't.'

'I do. Saw this documentary on the History Chan…'

'Billy!'

'OK. OK. Tough one. Fifteens a day and a twenty lump.'

'Done.'

221

major transport hubs

Kevmas time, mistletoe and wine.

Not really, but it is. Sort of, anyway.

The Vertu rings. Nan.

'Why are you having Christmas today, Kevin? It's the eighteenth.'

'I've told you, Nan.' And I have told her. 'They're doing our "at home" lifestyle shoot today, so it can go in their Xmas edition. The mag are trimming up for us, bringing the grub. Everything... It's Christmas. Just get in the cab and come over.'

Busy time for the Premiership superstar, the Yuletide period. Three league games in a week, plus a Carling Cup first leg semi and an FA Cup third round following hard on the heels of that little bundle of football. Toss in Bahta paranoia, the police looking into the gaffer, and now the missing phone, and it's a testing time of year, Kev-wise, the festive period.

I end the call to Nan and stride – with seeming excellence, despite the free kicks of fear which are rattling my mental crossbar – into the galleried reception hall, which is sunlit – even now, in this bleakest and middest of bleak midwinters – by a curved, south-west facing window offering uninterrupted views.

There's an absolutely fuck-off Christmas tree in the hall. Some mag employee, who you wouldn't, is decking the boughs with quality baubleage. No sign of Sas, probably still up the solid oak stairs, preparing herself in the genuinely self-indulgent opulence of the master suite. I check the Panerai Radiomir Black Seal timepiece. Nearly time for my little meeting, my seasonal gift to Kev.

I check the Vertu, leave the front door and walk over to the quadruple garage suite, each of its electronic doors modified, size-wise, to accommodate even the largest of 4x4s. Not that we have a 4x4, that would be crass. Instead, I dink the little hand-held dinker and a door buzzes open. I hop in the Bents and back her out, tootling down the brick driveway towards the ornate gates of this, my outstanding new modern country house.

I buzz the gates open, drive through, and turn left, parking the Bents to one side of the slender country lane. I wait, checking the Vertu. Moments later – very good, nice and punctual – a black cab pulls up outside the gates and its door opens. The Mexican steps out, and as the cab waits to ferry the obliging hooker back into town, she walks over to the Bents, climbs in, sees to me in a calm but disgusting way, then makes back towards the cab, clutching not only her large fee – Christmas bonus, unsociable hours allowance – but also the cab fare.

I'm nothing if not generous.

The cab turns and disappears and I spin the Bents round, opening the gates and driving back towards my sensational modern house, with exceptional quality and stature, set in an unarguably secluded position, despite its superb closeness to major transport hubs.

Shitting my whack, killings-wise, I may be, but these days I am a gent and I take the time to be impressed by the topiary avenue which leads up to my home, each bush expertly pruned into the shape of a football, the Premiership trophy, or the Bentley symbol.

I am also impressed by the simple clean lines of my mansion, the iconic architectural cues it takes from the Arts and Crafts movement, and by its elevated position, towering as it does above the open vista landscape. But most of all I am impressed with myself. I am wearing a Dsquared2 grey, two-button suit, a white Number (N)ine shirt and Tod's Gommini musk-coloured suede loafers.

I am absolutely the absolute shit. But Billy should have got it by now. Bloke like Billy. I mean, I realize that it's just a fucking phone, bobbing now in a gigantic metropolitan sewer, but Billy's a pro.

The snapper arrives, and you would, and she's got two assistants with her, one who you wouldn't and some huge buff model-type geezer. He is wearing an Artist Proof appliqué T-shirt, Supra Ns Cuban trainers and LRG el Vampiro straight root fit jeans. It's a good look, it's OK I mean, but it's inappropriately casual for the festive season, chez King. And what's more, the buff casual assistant makes no effort to help with setting up the equipment. He looks, truth be told, as if he wouldn't know the left-hand side of the camera from its top.

They set up lights and shit and the cameras and shit in the galleried reception hall and then Sas comes down in a Pinko white sequin embroidered fringe dress and grey Chie Mihara Serpan heels. You absolutely would. In fact it's a treat, having two such doable ladies – the partner and the snapper – in the love nest mansion, and all this so soon after such an invigorating quickie with the Mexican. Testing times these may well be, other fronts-wise, but it really is all coming together for Kev, gaff-wise, as we have seen, and ladies-wise as is now unfolding, and I wonder, as the undoable assistant dabs the King nose with some apparently necessary make-up, if the snapper would assent to a little de luxe tour of the King ranch, so to say, at some point during this wonderful Yuletide shoot which is now getting underway as she – the snapper – positions both Kev and Sas in front of the now-fully-dressed tree.

Snap snap snap. In front of the trimmings.

'Mr King,' says the snapper. 'Do you mind not checking your phone for a few seconds.'

'I need to.'

'It's got a ring tone though, hasn't it? You'll hear it if it goes off.'

'I need to check it.'

'How about you hand it to my assistant and she can check it for you?'

I compromise. I hand it over.

The snapper clicks away. We are providing some genuine Xmas glamour to cheer the beleaguered rank and file consumer.

Sas tosses the mane. She drops the hip. She works it.

'Any messages?' I ask the undoable assistant.

She shakes her shit head.

'Mr King,' the snapper asks, 'can you try and look less angry please?'

'I'm not angry, I'm more stern.'

And it's true, I am stern. Because I do not want to give *all* the secrets of the Kev face away to the civilian readership of this downmarket but frankly deep-pocketed magazine. I want to retain some mystique, some unvolunteered depths, so as to both bedazzle the civilian consumer with my stoic dignity, but also lure them on towards further shoots.

'Well, if you can't stop looking angry, Mr King, we'll have to move on. What's next?'

The snapper peers over to the undoable assistant who is studying a piece of paper, presumably a shot list.

'Security chic,' says the assistant.

'What?' I ask.

'You and Sas, with your state of the art home security system.'

And it's true, we've got that. Sas had some major paranoia technology fitted.

'Why do we need that?' I ask the snapper.

'To exclusively reveal how seriously the football community is taking the football killings.'

'But *they're not* football killings. They're clearly the work of a committed consumer vigilante.'

Everybody frowns or looks at their feet. Sas does both.

'OK, Mr King. We'll leave that shot until you're feeling a little more...Amenable. What else is there?' the snapper asks.

'Threesome,' says the assistant.

What?

'Into position please, Marco,' the snapper says and the buff geezer in the insolently casual attire steps forward and stands with me and Sas in front of the tree. Well, he actually stands *between* me and Sas in front of the tree.

Why is he in these shots? Wearing that overtly casual clobber? What is happening? I can't handle it. My mind is melting. My brain is trickling from my ears.

'Mr King,' says the photographer who you would, 'please, just try and look a little less savage. This shoot is about your cosy home with Sas, but also about your open relationship. You need to look comfortable with this.'

'Can I have my phone?'

'No.'

I restrain the King face. The snapper clicks away.

'That'll have to do.' She sighs heavily. 'What's next?'

The undoable assistant checks the shot list.

'Bedroom.'

'Right, Mr King, if you wouldn't mind waiting here while we do some shots with Sas and Marco together in the master suite?'

Together in the master suite?

'Give. Me. My. Phone.'

They hand it over.

The snapper, her assistant, Sas and this Marco walk off upstairs and I wander dazed into the kitchen where the trimming-up civvy, who you wouldn't, is now preparing the food for the Xmas dinner section of the 'at home' shoot. There's no smell, though, in the kitchen, the food doesn't smell of anything, and the TurboChef double wall Speedcook oven doesn't seem to be on. Is it fake or something, the food? Are they going to serve us wax food? Plastic food?

What's happening? I can't tell the Champs League places from the play-off spots; La Liga from the Conference North.

Do I eat wax food? Is that what I do?

I retire to the individually air-conditioned home cinema with 7.1 surround-sound system infrastructure.

Bridge On The River Kwai? The Great Escape?

Not interested.

Who was he calling? Who was the Hyundai Herbert calling?

a quarter of eu gas reserves

Second half, Champs League knock-out stages, first leg, away to Zenit St Petersburg. We're two down. The pitch is my refuge. I'm not having this.

I nick it off the toe of diminutive Zenit midfield playmaker Andre Arshavin, who did ever so well in the 2008 Euros, despite looking like a sun-drunk farm boy, and I impose forward. Their versatile Czech midfielder Radek Šírl is on me, but I merely lay a slide ruler off to Ali el-Masri on our right wing and find space. Which is not that hard to do, admittedly, or so it seems, in this massive open bowl of a stadium, surrounded by a running track.

There's a terrific sense of space about the night and when it comes to it, when el-Masri has skinned their number nineteen, Venezuelan-born Portuguese international Danny Alves, and cut it back, I am in acres just outside their D.

My life may be chaos off-field, but this I can handle. This can be controlled. I am not going out of the Champs. I am not going home, so early in the knock-out stages. I see myself, see Kev, reaching the final at the Stadio Olimpico in Rome, I really do.

Professional strength balancer John Evans rested a 159.6 kg car on top of his head for thirty-three seconds in 1999.

I am not going home.

I absolutely fuck the ball, right-footed, and it bananas in the air, as these new balls are prone to do, while moving to the left, dipping improbably so that it just nips beneath the outstretched flapping hand of their keeper and Vice Captain Vyacheslav Malafeer, and into the actual net itself.

Two one. If you will. Not pretty, but they all count. Just appearances and goals, the history books list, and they will not mention that I got lucky with a swirly ball and a wrong-footed keeper. The books don't list that.

I'm not going home yet. I'm going to Rome.

Back to our half for the restart and I look at Zenit in their blue and white Puma kit. I look particularly at the two lads sharing the kick-off, lank-haired Ukrainian international Anatoliy Tymoshchuk with his disturbing Alice band, and the rangy Pogrebnyak, joint top scorer in Zenit's successful 07-08 UEFA Cup campaign. I look at them and feel no fear. I feel no challenge. These two – *all* the Zenit team – are just pieces of meat between me and silverware, little human-shaped meats, feebly trying to divert me from my destiny. They're just nothing. Nothing players.

And they're dispossessed early by our ball-playing Turkish German centre half Baki Ozan, recovered now from his alarming case of double vision, and he feeds our Dutch winger Wally de Groot out wide. And really, let's just get this done now, let's just go up their end and score again right now, that way we won't have to get all sweaty and desperate, late doors, resorting to the long ball to nick a late one. No. Let's not do that, leave it for a panicky late equalizer. Let's get it sorted now.

I shift from centre mid and pelt, chalk on boots, outside de Groot, bombing on for the overlap, and drawing the man but managing to keep half a yard from him as well, and de Groot makes to cut inside, but then threads one through to me and I'm coming up to the by-line, their left back Alves sliding in to me, our striker Leon Bédard imploring me to find him in the centre, which I do, chipping in an unexpected one to the *front* stick, before absolutely barrelling, along with Alves, into the hoardings, but also looking up at the same time somehow, to see Bédard nod in the simplest of goals at the near post.

At the *near* post, keeper? My oh my.

Don't you read the coaching manuals?

At three and a half metres, strongman Dariusz Slowik holds the world record for the furthest throw of a washing machine, beating Australian Bill Lindon's previous record by twenty-two centimetres.

Two all. That's how it ends; with us taking two precious away goals back for the home leg. I had a blinder, a game so good it would have sent the blind blind.

Changing up and I check the Vertu. Nothing. Bahta doesn't come into the changing rooms to congratulate the team and engage Kev in some chat about the HP sauce, or what have you. Which creeps me out.

Strange and scary. Scary and strange. Because Bahta would normally be in here, wearing a cardy made from the cheek bumf of pre-pubic elves, or what have you, shaking my hand. The hand which cost him nothing, the hand that came on a free, and the hand I just used to drag us back from the brink. Not that I used my hand. Because this is football. And you play it with your feet. And a ball. Though you can use your head. And your hands as well, if you're a keeper. But I'm not a keeper.

Flight back in the morning so I'm at the hotel.

Sumptuously appointed room. Excellent views on to Nevsky Prospekt. But the views do not move me. Having been exiled now from the sanctuary of the pitch, I am flung back into waiting. Call me, Billy Four Chins.

The room's only a Classic. Not the Exec suite, as with Neeskins. And not the keeping-up-appearances Presidential, as with Bahta. But an OK room, except I'm sharing it with Simmy, our fourth choice, bean-pole striker who's got so many splinters in his arse that if you tweezered them all out you'd have enough wood to make a perfectly serviceable child's desk.

Simmy, who really should have been moved on in the transfer window, is in bed, still in the club Hermès, knocking one out to the adult channel under the pastel duvet. I am in the bathroom, changing into a grey Armand Bassi two-button suit, a mauve Junya Watanabe shirt and smart, grey Vael Borg lo trainers.

'You going out like that, Simmy? You going out in the club suit?'

'We're supposed to when we're on club business.'

'Fuck's sake, Simmy, wear what you like.'

The hotel phone rings. I snatch it up.

'Kevin.' It's Bahta. 'Come and join me in the hotel restaurant.'

Aye aye. Here we fucking are then. Defcon 1.

Colliding with destiny, I am.

Shaking, I take off the Armand Bassi two-button, the Junya Watanabe shirt and the Vael Borg lo trainers, and shaking I pop on the club Hermès.

'See you in a bit, Simmy,' I say, trying to sound all chirpy and everyday. 'You still on for it, yeah?'

'I'm really trying to finish, it's just I haven't been feeling very well lately, very, you know, sexy.'

'I don't mean the wank, Sim. I mean for going out.'

'I'll be here, Kev.'

Corridor. Shitting it. Lift.

Lobby. Shitting it. Restaurant.

Very nice actually.

Art-nouveau stained-glass picture window. Lovingly restored parquet floors. Live harp music. Some kind of belle époque gastro cathedral, if you will.

There's Bahta, the man, friend or foe, sat with some Slavic-headed geezer, bang in the centre of the restaurant, receiving speciality breads from a white-gloved waiter. I make over, feigning Kevish confidence. Is this the moment? Am I to be compelled from my Eden?

'Ah, Kevin. You have some catching up to do. We have already ordered. This is my friend, Vasily Zyrakov. Sit.'

I do sit.

'Very well played, Mr King,' says Zyrakov, being all fake fucking civil, because he's got to be pissed off, really, being as I single-handedly fucked his team over. One-man army, I am.

'Did you know, Kevin,' says Bahta, handing me a menu, 'that Mr Zyrakov controls a quarter of the entire EU gas reserves.'

Zyrakov nods and does a 'please don't flatter me' sort of grimace-smile, but what he really means is, 'Yes I do, and I could put out all the lights, turn off the gas tap any time I wanted. On Champs League finals night in Rome, say, thereby plunging the entire continent into darkness and hurtling Europe backwards, if you will, into a new medieval-lite period of energy austerity.'

That's what he really means.

'Right,' I say, seeming all chipper chipper.

As I order, there's some small talk between the current and the ex billionaires. Yada yada, cash cash. I take the scallop creviche with blood orange and Sevruga caviar, the whole baked quail stuffed with duck liver and salsify, and a 2002 Riesling tradition Hugel AOC.

Zyrakov delivers a swingeingly polite little head bow, saying, 'If you will excuse me for two minutes, gentlemen.'

The Russian stands and walks from the table, leaving it unclear if he's off to decimate the energy supply of Denmark or merely siphon out a swift, mid-meal slash. I look down at the tablecloth. Why has Bahta called me here? What does he want? Will he crumple Kev's dream? My heart thrashes like a fondued bullock.

'You saw my friend Mr Shishakli, Kevin?'

'Yes, Mr Bahta.'

'And you took my advice and signed with him, I hear.'

'Very much so.'

I look at him now, his small face shining and clear with status and cash, but there, bagged beneath his liquidly brown eyes, dark circles of recent troubles beginning to swirl.

'So. Kevin...'

Come on, Bahta. Spit. It. Out.

'The police now know that on the night of the Chelsea match, between the game ending and you eating with Sas, you were...'

What? What do the police know? What was I fucking doing?

'The police know you were…having a drink with me in my
Mercedes.'

'What?'

'And they also know that more recently, directly after leaving
Les A, where you met my friend Mr Shishakli, you were, once
more, very much in my company.'

What does this mean? I'm trying to speak but it's hard. My
tongue is made from some mutinous jelly. But, 'Alibi,' I manage
to say.

'Yes, Kevin, alibi.'

'…Why?' seems to be the word I'm saying.

'Because you did what I asked. You signed with Shishakli.
Which was polite. But more importantly, Kevin, because you are
surely the best player in my team right now, and if you are
arrested then the treble disappears with you.'

'Can I…'

'Ask me a question? Of course.'

'You been following me?'

'I knew what you were doing.'

'So who was that Herbert in the Hyundai?'

'Your last victim?'

I just stare at him.

'I have no idea, Kevin.'

'Nothing to do with you?'

'Nothing at all.'

'You sure? Skinny cunt, I mean bloke. Scruffy.'

'I can promise you, Kevin, I do not know him.'

I glance up then to see Zyrakov returning to the table.

Later, I'm back in the room. Right. Shit. OK. The cops are off my
back and Bahta's onside, which is tasty. But if it wasn't the Parsi who
had me tailed, then who was it? Who hired the Hyundai Herbert?

'I managed it, Kev,' says Simmy, proudly doing little wank
motions while stepping out of the bathroom in his club Hermès,
which he's teamed with a deplorably unimaginative Prada shoe/
Armani shirt combo.

I can't stay here in the room and stew. Got to do something. Got to keep the lifestyle moving, crack on to some Rusky muffski, if you will.

I take off the Hermès and change back into the grey Armand Bassi two-button suit, mauve Junya Watanabe shirt and smart, grey Vael Borg lo trainers. Ready. A call to recep for a taxi.

The corridor, the lift, the lobby, the cab.

Yeah, town, nice. Lights and shit and buildings and that, and out the cab and down a small staircase to basement level and a shimmy through the face control and we're in.

The Onegin restaurant-bar.

There's some who you would and there's a whimsical juxtaposition of antique and plastic furniture. Modern variation on the theme of Imperial Petersburg.

Fashionista clientele. Velvet and chandeliers.

Yeah, yeah. Good good. Good enough, anyway. I check the Vertu and head to the bar. And Simmy takes a beer. A fucking beer. I'm on the 2004 Beringer Fume Blanc. Which they don't actually serve. So I take a beer as well and we look around. And this is like shooting fish from a baby. Because, already, the fittest eyes in the room are on us. Very fit eyes, your St Petersburg resident. And already, before we can even say 'Premiership footballing superstars' – well, superstar anyway, in the singular, because Simmy has not exactly pulled up a lot of trees since his big cash move from West Ham – before we can say 'Premiership footballing superstar', two of them, including the one with the v. fit eyes, are over to us, in the bar zone, and she – The Eyes, as I will call her – is wearing a Supertrash leather zip biker dress with L.A.M.B. heeled Gladiator sandals, and a Marc by Marc Jacobs logo print bangle timepiece. She is holding a Patrizia Pepe contrast trim underarm bag.

You really would.

Finn Juha Rasanen holds the world person-throwing record, hurling a 60kg man 5.40 metres on to a pre-marked safety mattress in Madrid, June 2006.

'So,' I say to The Eyes, but she sort of edges by me to stand next to Simmy, and her mate – in a burgundy Marchesa dress with Gaspard Yurkievich peep-toe trim front pin-heel sandals – is sort of standing at me, all expectant for the chat, while just behind me, and slightly to my left, it has to be said, where she leans now on the bar, The Eyes is moving right in on Simmy.

Her mate's all right.

Nice dress. Nice tits. You would.

But not if you also had the option of The Eyes. Which I do. Or which I should do, as I glance all cornerly from my left eye and see her asking Simmy something, firing the opening salvo in the fuck chase that is developing.

And I cannot see why she is into Simmy. When I am stood here. A consumer goes to market, and that consumer – almost wilfully, it seems – passes on better merchandise, while taking a frankly eccentric liking to inferior goods. The inferior goods that are Simmy. In his club Hermès, which he couldn't even be arsed to change. The inferior goods of Simmy, who did not even make it on to the turf of the Petrovsky stadium tonight, the stadium in which I, Kev, both scored and assisted.

What she needs, what The Eyes needs, is to be taken under the wing of a consumer expert, a knowledgeable guide who can educate her regarding the worth of items in the marketplace. Her barbaric consumer ignorance needs taming. It really does.

I reach into the Armand Bassi jacket and pull out the Case Trapper pocket knife with mother-of-pearl handle and grooved nickel silver bolsters. Except I don't.

Fucking customs. I left the Case Trapper at home.

Instead I turn to The Eyes' mate. 'Very nice Lara Bohinic bracelet,' I say. 'You into the football, yeah?'

b&w nautilus loudspeaker

Corlham Wood changing rooms after training.

'His orchid's doing well,' says our dim-but-gifted centre back, Ash Hughes. 'And his balls are much better.'

Do I care about Dukey, the nut-knacked Scottish midfielder that Ash has been to visit on a number of occasions? Naturally I do not. I care about the Prem, yes; about fanny and customer service, certainly; and I care deeply about sourcing the last call made by the dead Hyundai Herbert. But the Duke is off the King radar, if you'll allow.

Still, 'Nice,' I say, before glancing across the changing rooms to see our Brazilian left back Alvar pointing something out in a glossy to Leon Bédard. And what is the magazine they're scanning, the two internationals? Never seen it before.

I hate to ask, but I am curious.

'What's that mag?' I say, all whisperish, to Hughes, so that the rest of the lads will not notice the lifestyle ignorance I'm currently feeling.

I point my eyes towards Alvar and Bédard, and Hughes follows them and spies the mag.

'Oh. That's *Icon* magazine.'

Icon. Nice.

'Oh yeah,' I say, all casual like. 'What's that then?'

'It's Jamie Redknapp's lifestyle magazine,' says Ash.

Redknapp, ex-Liverpool and England midfielder, has his own magazine? His own lifestyle magazine? I am crushed by the news.

'What?' I manage.

'Yeah, it's an invitation-only lifestyle bible, aimed squarely at the Premiership footballer.'

'Invitation only?'

'Yeah. You can't buy it. They contact you.'

For fuck's sake. *They* contact *you*.

'Do you get it?' I ask.

'Yeah.'

'What about Simmy?'

'Simmy gets sent it, yeah.'

Even Simmy gets it. Even ninth fucking choice Simmy.

But why not me? Why no invitation from Redknapp? Some kind of mistake on behalf of the *Icon* staff. Some terrible, terrible mistake.

Alvar's all changed up and he heads off, leaving the mag on the changing-room bench right next to Bédard. I want to walk over and snatch the fucker up, have a good old look at *Icon* mag, but I can't. Do that and the lads'll know I've missed the invitation.

Instead I change up all slowly. One by one the lads leave the room and then I'm alone. I don't like the solos, not these days. Too much on my mind. But I need to see the lifestyle mag. I walk over and scoop it up.

I have a flick. Gadget reviews: Sennheiser PMX sports headphones; the XT series speaker; the Denon 3930 DVD. Quality, high-end gear. Kevish appliances.

But no invite.

I continue to flick. Timepiece trends, including the Zenith Defy Extreme Open El Primero. Property features: Dubai, Vegas, Palm Springs.

Boutique hotels. Bespoke furniture. Wine investments.

Top, top designers.

It's all very Kev. It's all so very, very Kev. But no invite.

Why have I been forsaken, bruised by the lifestyle gods? I can't work it out. Why has this Premiership lifestyle bible, this high-end publication, which so carefully matches advertising and features to the aspirations of its affluent readership, not put in a call? After all, these days, I'm the first name Neeskins writes on the team sheet. In fact he probably doesn't even *write* my name on it any more. Neeskins has probably got a load of pre-printed sheets done, with my name already typed on to them by his secretary – who you would – so he doesn't have to trouble himself with wielding the biro to add the King moniker.

I am scoring. Assisting. I am biting into the tackle.

I am obviously, so obviously, the absolute fucking bollocks.

And yet no call.

If Redknappy (as I will call him) was here I'd. I'd. I'd definitely and irreversibly fuck him right over for his customer awareness negligence. I would find some way to use his lifestyle bible as a murderous appliance against him. Perhaps I would suffocate Redknappy by feeding carefully selected articles on jewellery designers into his mouth. Or maybe I'd diligently open up an enormous paper cut right across his throat. But he isn't here.

I just don't get it. What do I have to do?

Maybe he's ill or something, maybe Redknappy is lying there in his sickbed with his little to-do list in his mind, thinking, 'First thing I'll do when I recover is call the unplayable Kev King and offer him a free subscription.'

Yeah, that's it.

Or maybe the boy Redknappy has wronged his dialling finger somehow. In a freakish golfing accident, potentially. Or else lost his memory, temporarily at least, after a badly wall-mounted B&W Nautilus loudspeaker fell and dashed into his hairstyle, forcing a trip to the specialist hospital, where he sits right now, thinking, 'I'm sure I was about to call someone just before the deeply unlikely hi-fi accident.'

That'll be it. He can't have just not bothered, Redknappy. He can't have not heard of me. Watched me on the Sky. It is unfeasible that he hasn't witnessed – along with the rest of the footballing fraternity – the rise and rise of the likes of your Kings. It is impossible.

I fold up Alvar's copy of *Icon* magazine and pop it into my Andrew Marc Marshall sports bag. Then it rings. The Vertu does its nifty little trill and I whip it from the Balenciaga jacket. Billy at last? No. Unknown number. Not Billy then. Redknappy maybe? I take the call.

'That Kev King?'

'Who is this?'

'It's Stuart Pearce.'

What? Hard man ex-international left back Stuart Pearce. England Under 21 manager Stuart Pearce. The only senior Englishman in Fabio Capello's national coaching set-up.

'That Stuart Pearce?' I say.

'I'm Stuart Pearce,' says Stuart Pearce.

'How do I know you're Stuart Pearce?'

'I don't give a fuck if you know or not.'

It's a very Stuart Pearce answer. It's him all right.

'Look, Kev, Mr Capello wants a look at you training with the England squad.'

'What? Shit. What?'

'Christ, Kev, I hope you're better on the field than you are on phone. Look, I'll fax through the details to the club. All right? Just come along.'

He ends the call.

Bleeding fuck. My oh never. Did your phone just ring, Kev?

It did, Kev.

And what type of call was it, Kev?

Well, Kev, I'll tell you. It was the England call.

Which is nice. Though overdue. Because it really was only a matter of time, given my eye-gouging recent form, the national squad call-up. That said, even knowing that my ballistic humpty prowess was so unignorably good, I remain elated to have received the international nod. And from

Pearce as well. Hard man international Stuart Pearce.

A man of such footballing integrity, a colossus of such application – both on and off the field, and off it as well – that I actually believe I would never kill him. Keegan I would never kill. And Costner, clearly. And without question, top broadcaster and consumer rights overlord Nicky Campbell would always be given the benefit of any doubt, killing-wise. I mean, just look at that man's track record. And now Pearce has just catapulted himself up there with these untouchables.

I sit down and nod slowly.

'Kev, Kev, Kev,' I say.

I've made it.

Gerrard and Lampard, I'll be up against, looking to unseat them from their attacking central midfield thrones. Not that they have thrones. That would be unwieldy. But they do have thrones as well, in a way. If you like. Yes, it is Gerrard and Lampard who I'm up against now, national squad-wise.

I pick up the Vertu Ascent Racetrack Legends to spread the good news – as Jesus was keen to spread his own good news, through the medium of sermons and parables, and returning from the dead and the like.

I call Nan. No answer. I eye the Franck Muller Long Island timepiece. She'll be having her nap. I call Boves. Straight to message. I call Gravesy. Again, the machine. Then it rings. The Vertu rings. Billy Four Chins.

Finally. I was beginning to doubt him. I snatch the line open.

'You found the phone?'

'Yeah, I found it, Kev. Some sewage works near a golf course in South London. Very difficult job actually, I had to…'

'Billy! The phone!'

'Well, it weren't working, all that piss it'd been soaked in.'

'Fuck.'

'But I've got a mate who's got a mate who can fix this type of thing, Kev.'

'And?'

'The last number dialled from that phone was…'

And Billy tells me the number. And before he's done I recognize it, know the digits very well. I know who hired the Hyundai Herbert.

I end the call to Billy and dial the number he just gave me. No answer.

I pelt out of the changing rooms, dive in the Bents and gun out of Corlham Wood towards Maidenhead, nailing the A4130 towards Henley, dialling dialling dialling all the time. But there's no answer.

Passing excellent local amenities. I don't get it. Passing exceptionally secluded plots. It can't be right. Arrive at the house. Five receptions. Show-home condition. Ironwork gates.

I buzz down the Bents' window and ring the intercom. The gates stay shut. I jab again at the intercom…Still no answer.

I leave the Bents and run towards and jump up at the gates, hands over the top, arms dragging me over and I'm in, prowling the grounds of the exec ranch.

The lights are on, the front door's open. I run inside and Kev quickly from room to room, shouting out as I pelt around. The kitchen smells of pizza still. The TV's on, and there's a still-warm arse dent in the brown leather Cerak modular sofa. Not long gone. Must have legged it when I started calling, or when I pulled up at the gate.

I stand in the hallway and pant. My phone rings.

'Shut the fuck up, Kev, and listen to me…'

'Colly, I…'

'Kev, shut up, or I hang up. I had you followed, Kev, to see if you were bullshitting about wages, or about to bin me. And when Taffy called me and said you were the killer, I didn't believe him. Thought he was scheming, or just wrong. But after this little performance, well…'

'Colly…'

'Seriously, Kev. One. More. Word…It was a shock, Kev. And we've been good mates, so I could just shut up. If you'd kept with me, that is, like Boves and Gravesy. But you had to meet with Shishakli, didn't you? You had to play the big man.

'Still, it's all worked out. Because I need cash. And you've got cash. You've got my bank details…I'll keep schtum for, let's say…What you earning, Kev? Careful now, no bullshit.'

'Sixty-threes.'

'Yeah, that's what I heard. Bit lowish, Kev, for a man of your talent. Maybe if you'd stuck with your agent, you might have got more…So, let's see…Oooh, seventy-five grand a week should keep me schtum.'

'Seventy fucking fives!'

'Shush shush now, Kev. First payment tomorrow. We won't speak again, and every time you try and call me, I'll stick another grand on the fee.'

Colly hangs up and I stand limp in his lounge, staring at the place where the wall-mounted sixty-inch Pioneer Kuro plasma used to hang, before, presumably, the bailiffs clunked off with it.

Now before, as we know, I have said that I am fucked. I have said it quite often. But never, until now, did I know – really – what it meant. But I do now. Because now I am properly, properly fucked. Royally so.

I slump to my knees. It's over. Nearly.

But I've got one move left. I pull out the Vertu and make a call.

'Nice,' says Four Chins. 'Manhunt. Falling off a log, mate.'

Part Three

the mystical ruins of atlantis

Thing is, I'm ensconced in a dazzling world of imagination, high-end leisure and effervescent luxury at the Atlantis Hotel on Palm Jumeirah Island in Dubai. You know, which is good. But at the same time, I'm finding it very hard to shit, which, while it does not completely neutralize the exclusive glamour of my surroundings, does make it hard to appreciate them as much as I'd like.

And the reason I'm finding it so hard to drop the kids off into this particular bespoke shitter is because at the moment I'm being eyeballed by some kind of manta ray. Which is very off-putting, dump-wise.

The bog on one hand? An unusual marine creature on the other?

I know. A confusing mix. Difficult to imagine how they might co-exist, so to say. And even I, Premiership Kev, would have – well, *might* have – felt confusion about the not-everyday mixture of undersea life and constipation. Had I not been booked into one of the hotel's Lost Chambers Suites, a gaff involving floor-to-ceiling windows looking out into the mesmerising undersea world of the Ambassador Lagoon. Yes. A hotel room – and a hotel bog – peering out directly into a vast aquarium, containing a cornucopia of swimmish animals.

Hence the manta ray, just the other side of the glass, peering in at me – or so it seems – and providing a challenging environment in which to shit.

And I wonder if they tested this, if when they were installing these jaw-dropping marine habitats, so very close to the guest's shitter, they stopped and thought for a moment how the gimlet gaze of the manta ray – or the stare of a scalloped hammerhead shark, even – might affect the shit-ability of the guest. I wonder if they tested it. Sat a local Herbert down and cajoled him towards delivery – in a professional way – so as to ascertain the possible detrimental effects of the marine gaze on the body's natural movements.

It is my guess that they did not.

It is my hunch that Kerzner International Holdings, the originators of the Atlantis flagship brand, did not run such a test, did not anticipate the constipatory effects of this fish nearness. And that to me is an oversight. At least. What is the point constructing a brain-crushingly opulent landmark hotel on the crescent of this manmade island in Dubai if your guests – not all of them, admittedly, but the better ones, the ones residing in the Lost Chambers Suites – are waddling around with eight pounds of unfired torpedoes in their guts?

It is my feeling that the designers of this suite did not subject it to international dump standards, did not run the mandatory shit tests on this otherwise supreme guest environment.

So yeah. OK. Fine. Build a revolutionary manmade island, if you like. Do it. Construct the first wonder of this, the Kevish era. Then add the ultimate resort destination hotel to that island. Stuff that hotel with multi-faceted dining options, a boutique boulevard, the mystical ruins of Atlantis, and an eleven million litre lagoon. Jet in some bottle-nosed dolphins to not only thrill guests in your aqua park but also demonstrate a strong commitment to conservation.

Fine. Do all that. It is decent enough stuff. You will not find me opposing your plans to design a masterpiece of luxury and elegance. But at least let your guests take a fucking dump while they're here.

I give up. I really do.

I stand and yank up my Alessandrini classic cigarette trousers and ensure they drape correctly over my smart, Schmoore leather high-topped trainers, then I wander to the mirror and eye the Frankie Morello charcoal-grey cotton shirt.

I walk from the bathroom to the bedroom and there's Sas in a Pinko white lace yoke and sleeve jersey bodycon dress with Terra Plana black Capricorn ankle boots. She's sitting on one of the twin beds, gazing into the exotic undersea kingdom.

'Kev, it's so …' she says.

And she's right. Having-a-shit-wise, the bathroom may not be up to much, but the bedroom is lit with an otherworldly, subaquatic hue which makes Sas look, somehow, even fitter than she is.

I am looking forward to a bit of the old squeaky with Sas a bit later. I really am hoping to sort her out this time. It's fine – and actually quite addictive – doing the Mexican, and the other little things that come my way – and I have to say that I really am amassing a nice little fan base, or fanny base, which might be a better phrase – courtesy of my staggering profile and consistent on-field heroics.

So, yes, it's all fine. Doing them. Doing that. Doing that to them.

All that stuff is a profitable sideline. But it would be nice for once for me to enter my upmarket model sleb partner Sas. After all, she is the one who's brought me here. Well, I paid. Obviously. A financial layout decided upon before Colly's crushingly heavy blackmail demands, I might add; and one I couldn't then cancel, in case Sas got wind of my cash ructions. But it was her idea for a little trip and she did choose and book the destination. But how did I manage to shoehorn this little break in, considering my unprecedented on-field commitments?

Well.

Neeskins has given me a few days off, which might have been a major cuss, seeing as we are still mid-season. But then the enigmatic Dutch manager explained his desire to keep me fresh for the business end of the season. And since the only game I'm missing is a home contest with West Brom – which will be a walkover, considering the Baggies are all ears up worse than us, and are also managed by a bloke who has a shovel for a head – I am not too put out by the gaffer's decision. It does make sense.

Keep Kev box fresh for the home banker with West Brom?

Or keep Kev fresh for the Champions League and the away Prem game against title rivals Liverpool? Put it that way and you can see how the Dutchman did his maths, added up the equations and arrived at the numbers he did, Kev-wise.

I walk over to Sas, all seductive, and seeing as I know – really know – how to play the ladies, I ask her the question dearest to her heart.

'How many times do you think you've been on TV, Sas?'

She laughs, she's flattered.

'I don't know, Kev. A lot.'

She's right. It will be a lot. Not as many as me, obviously, but quite a few nonetheless, what with the sleb jungle show and the many, many follows-ups that resulted from the public's extreme affection for her astonishing G cups.

I sit down next to her on the bed, my hand spidering up her back towards the tie of her dress. She's not looking at me, though, she's staring at the manta ray that has flapped over now from the bathroom window to peer into the bedroom. Right then, fucking manta, you may have stopped me delivering the post, so to say, but now you're going to watch me get my nuts in. And jealous as hell you'll be, fish boy, with your spindly little underwater cock, when you see me going at this delectable model sleb.

I continue the seduction.

'And how many snaps of you do you think have been in the papers?'

She laughs again. And again it will be a lot. Not a Kevish amount. But a lot. Because very photogenic tits, Sas has. My hand begins to loosen her dress.

'Kev,' she says, 'we've got a table booked at Ossiano.'

And indeed we have reserved a table at the new restaurant of three-star Michelin chef Santi Santamaria, or the architect of food, as he is known in chefing circles.

'Come on, Kev,' Sas says. 'We can't be late.'

Though it is beyond me why timing matters so much that I can't bend a quick strike around the three-man wall of her Ayten Gasson lingerie. Still. Mysterious beasts, the ladies.

She stands and walks to the door and I follow. We take the elegant sweeping staircase out from the Lost Chambers Suites and make the sumptuous corridors. If you will. Turquoise and yellow carpetage. Mythical murals depicting mythical scenes of myth and legend.

We make the Ossiano entrance and are met by a greeting Herbert who is polite enough, if shit. He takes us to our table.

Elegant and mysterious space. Mutedly decadent decor. Pearl and silver colour scheme. Highly visible caviar bar.

I do like a restaurant with a high minimum spend. Or I fucking did, before Colly started milking me for more than I actually earn, a state of affairs which can't roll on, truth be told, for too long before the fabric of the actual lifestyle is tested. But then Four Chins – with his unnerving connections to every squint-eyed pub villain in sceptred Blighty – can save me. Four Chins'll spot Colly. He will. Given that the Chins turned up Taff's phone amongst the shit of ten million, he'll surely finesse the Colly needle from the Blighty haystack.

Anyway. Our restaurant table stands right next to the aquarium, in which lay the mythical ruins of Atlantis itself. The sommelier comes over and we chat about the booze, which he brings, and then there's a waiter who's over and he wibbles on about contemporary Catalan cuisine and the culinary journey we are now undertaking.

I kick off with the light apple and whitefish mince with caviar. Sas plumps for the cuttlefish cooked in its own ink, which is a bit like marinating something in its own piss, as far as I can see. But

I don't say anything. Tonight is not a night for chat about fish piss. It is a night for glamour and elegance. And later on, quite a lot of the old in out.

Sas is lit by a soft blue glow from the surrounding aquatic ambience. She really is fit, an appropriate partner for a Premiership legend such as Kevin King, who is sitting here, watching her as she gazes into the water, eyeing the rune-marked masonry which litters the floor of the underwater world.

'Kev?'

'Sas.'

'Are you sure that these boulders and stuff are from the mythical civilization of Atlantis?'

'They must be, Sas.'

She looks relieved. But I'm not relieved. The mail delivery I failed to make is playing havoc. Here I am, supposed to be enjoying an intimate dining experience in a restaurant plunged into the very heart of Atlantis itself, and I'm getting all this fucking grief from my bowels.

I try to forget about my arse, but it's rowdier than the Shed End in the 1970s and I can't cope. Especially now, when I look into the table-side aquatic world and see that fucking manta ray again. Must have swum round or something. Stopped me shitting. Gloated towards me when I couldn't beat Sas' defensive muff shield. And now he's here again, laughing his little subaquatic tits off at my imploding guts. Right, I've had enough. I'm going to drop these fucking kids off one way or another, and drop them off where I can't be persecuted by a disrespectful, leering manta.

'Excuse me, Sas.'

There are bogs in the restaurant, I know. But they'll probably have a fucking mermaid in the bowl or something, ready to peer up into my arsehole as I go, so I leave the eatery and march down a corridor looking for a shitter that will not open on to Davy Jones' locker, so to say.

These guts are killing me, they are assaulting Premiership legend Kevin King. And here's a little Herbert marching up the corridor towards me, all fucking chuffed and smart in his little hotel uniform and there's some kind of lower belch – like the bursting of the South Sea bubble, it is – and I fear for the Alessandrini classic cigarette trousers, and I am furious that my schmutter might be spoiled, ruined, by the lax toilet research of this epic, mythical hotel.

And I'm nearly level with the hotel Herbert when I spot a toilet door and I kick that door open a little and have a quick look in and it's all quiet, so I reach out and collar the passing Herbert, yanking him hard and chucking him backwards into the bog – which is nicely kitted out, actually – then striking out with the Schmoore high-top trainer as he falls, so booting him all promptly in the head.

And one thing I learned in St Petersburg – apart from how to rip through pony Russian defensive formations, that is – was if you can't bring a knife through customs, then pick one up at duty free.

Which I did.

Although it's only a Victorinox Voyager Lite, as used by the Swiss Army, apparently. Still. I whip the Voyager Lite from the Alessandrini strides and make towards the Herbert who's all bleeding now on to the tiles. I do him just a quick one, towards the liver area, I would guess, then I step all Kevly back.

'Why didn't you check it?' I ask. 'It would have saved all this… bother.'

But he just does a little gurgle, which I take to mean, 'What?'

'Your hotel lot should have checked. How can a man shit properly when he's being eyed by a manta? How can he?' I ask, being all informative and helpful about things. But he just doesn't seem to know what I mean.

It's infuriating. But I will not lose my temper and lash out. Because I'm a pro, and if the question's not getting through to the lad, let's give him a practical demonstration. I at least owe him that.

I drag the Herbert into a cubicle and I plonk him down on to the seat and stand there in the cubicle doorway, all Premiershiply above him.

'Right. Right. I'm a manta ray, yeah? Or any other fish thing, come to think of it. And you're me, trying to shit, yeah?'

But I don't know if he's got it. Even though I sort of scrunch my face into a fishy kind of pout. 'I'm a fish,' I repeat. 'And you're me, shitting. Go on! Shit! See if you can.'

He just sits there, bleeding and crying, crying and bleeding. I mean, is he even trying? It's annoying, but I will not lose – or even misplace – the King rag.

Then eureka! Binfuckinggo! Of course. It'll be the trousers.

Because it's hard to shit your own trousers. Spoiling the strides directly is undoing the conditioning of a lifetime, violating the ingrained potty training, so to say. So again, I will be fair.

I lean forward and slit his belt with the Voyager Lite, then pull the Herbert forward, slightly off the seat, and yank down his mincey little hotel strides and – much as it pains me, but the lad deserves a fair go – I pop down his flimsy kecks so that he's bare-arsed on the bog. Which is fine. Which is good. Because now we have optimum testing conditions.

'I'm a fish and you're me, OK. You must get it now…Do. A. Shit.'

I give him a bit of time. But there's not even the opening blasts of a movement, despite all the chances I've given him.

'See. See,' I say. 'You can't go, can you? You're not able to drop the kids off in these conditions, are you?'

He doesn't answer. He's not the brightest. But there's a light now in his eye, which other people might interpret as terror, but which I know is the penny finally dropping. At fucking last. Finally he understands that his hotel's failure to meet international dump standards has inconvenienced a prize guest.

The lad gorps forward then, all dribbling and demisey, and I Kev cheetahishly into the cubicle, lock it from the inside and dish out a few strokes – but tenderly, tenderly – then lithely slide over the top of the bog door.

Okay dokay.

I pluck a few hand towels – very luxuriant – from the dispenser and mop the blood off the floor, then I retire to the cubicle adjacent to the dead Herbert and set about my own business. And it's so easy now. Without the aquatic audience, getting this dump out is like taking candy from a barrel.

'How you getting on?' I shout to the Herbert in the cubicle next door, giving the separating wall a friendly little bang. Which I shouldn't, I know. It's a bit naughty, me disturbing him like that in his private, dead little moments, but, you know, I've finally delivered the post and I'm elated.

I leave the toilet and wander down the corridor towards the Ossiano. I check the Vertu for Billy's call, but there's nothing. Still, keep the faith, Kev, the Chins will get your man. But the truth is – despite my excellent customer protection work – that as I now step back into the eerie blue light of the restaurant, with the lost civilization of Atlantis all tumbled around me on the floor inside the aquarium, I am visited by a strange sense of peakiness.

'Where've you been?' snaps Sas as I sit down. But my throat's all dry and weird somehow and I don't reply.

'Kev?' says Sas, now glancing at her watch, all strangely nervous.

'Yeah, Sas,' I manage.

'I've been thinking about something,' she says, all serious, but not looking at me, instead kind of peering over my shoulder towards the entrance of the restaurant.

'What's that, Sas?' I ask, feeling now as weird as she's acting.

'Well,' she says, still looking beyond me and appearing all oddly tense, 'I've been thinking about something.'

'Yeah, you just said.'

But still she doesn't explain, just carries on staring beyond me.

And what is happening? What's she doing? This weird underwater light and this nervous girl. And my brain feels weird too, like it's made of gas, or like it wasn't really there, wasn't really anything, but then a hard little sleb smile sneaks quickly up on to the corner of Sas' mouth, and she leans forward and reaches into her green leather Carla Beeby Lozzie handbag and pulls out a silver-edged ebony ring box.

'Ask me to marry you,' she says, and hands the box over to me, and even though I don't mean to, don't want to even, I find that I take the box and slowly push the lid open, and inside see a Fabienne Trilogy platinum engagement ring with a flawless six-carat central diamond.

'Go on then, Kev, ask me,' she says. 'Give me the ring.'

And the gas thing, or the nothing thing that is my brain, or my mind, or what have you, is kind of stuck and broke and crashing, and although it is Kev that asks, 'Now, Sas?' and then watches her nod, it's not really actually me at all.

And then, 'Here, Sas?' I hear this gassy me thing say.

She nods and says, 'Get on one knee.'

Then this Kev thing pushes my chair, or his chair, or the chair, backwards and I feel him step towards her side of the table and everything is sort of underwatery in this weird blue light, and then the Kev-but-not-Kev person takes the ring out of the box and sort of half falls down on to one of his or my knees.

And, 'Will you marry me?' asks a voice like Kev's, and then there's some pulse of light from behind, some flash of white light, which then happens again and again. And there's a photographer stood there, snapping away. And next to the photographer is Min, Sas' publicist, and she's whispering to the photographer, giving him directions about the photos he's taking.

Then, 'That's great, Kev,' says Min. 'But look at Sas a bit more. Look lovingly towards her.'

And Kev does look at Sas, and the ring sort of slips over Sas' finger, and there are more white flashes, and Min says, 'You can get up now, Kev.'

And Kev finds that I am standing.

Then, 'In you go, Marco,' Min says. 'Let's get a shot of the couple with the best man.'

The best what? And then there's the buff, modelish bloke from the Xmas shoot now standing there as well, and he's wearing… But I don't know what they are. I don't know what his clothes are…And this buff Marco bloke steps towards the table and Sas gets up and steps forward and the three of us are stood there – Sas in the middle, flashing her rocks at the snapper, and this Marco and this Kev bloke on either side.

And then over there, inside the aquarium, the manta ray is hovering, all boggle-eyed and tripey, and just sort of laughing.

genuinely intolerable cords

Caxton's got the Hush Puppies up on his coffee-stained desk. He's got a pencil in his gob. He's got a sloshy cuppa in his left hand. We're doing a session on the autobiog.

'What we've got to remember, Kev, is that this is not a straight footballing autobiography, it's a hybrid football-lifestyle book…'

Hybrid football-lifestyle book? Have I died or something? Am I flirting with the seraphim upstairs in the old heaven? A hybrid book about Kevin King? My oh me oh my. Seem unrealistic?

Maybe. A while ago I would not have credited it. But then that is what's happening. That is what my enormous book deal requires. Granted, the advance for that deal has already been spunked by Sas – on silk cutlery and spangled fucking lamps or what have you for the King love nest mansion – and granted further, my ex-mate is blackmailing me for unsupportable wedge to keep buttoned about the large number of shall we say killings that I've been involved with, but here, right now, I'm consoled – untouched by the harsh complications of Kev's life – because this is a moment of pure lifestyle.

'And what that means, Kev, is…'

'Don, before we go any further on in this working relationship, which no doubt we will both come to treasure, might I say something?'

'Of course, Kev.'

256

'Can we call it *The L*?'

'Call it what?'

'*The L.*'

'Call what *The L*, Kev?'

'The lifestyle. Whenever in these meetings we have call to use the word lifestyle, can we instead call it *The L*?'

'Fine, Kev. We can do that. So, this book is as much about football as it is about…*your L*?'

'No. Not *your L*, Don. Instead, "Your *The L*". That'd be better. Not *my L*, but my *The L*.'

'OK, Kev.'

'And I want to write it like that in the book itself as well. Refer to it as *The L* in the book throughout.'

'I'll make a note of that for the publisher.'

'And I want a chapter called that, called *The L*, Don.'

'Another note for the publisher.'

Was there a tone there in Caxton's voice? A weary kind of tone? Because there shouldn't have been. He is spending QT discussing *The L* with one of the country's topmost footballers. That is a rare op for the hack. And by the looks of it, sitting there as he does, wearing genuinely intolerable cords, he could do with some chat about *The L*. He could do with a lifestyle ambulance.

He really needs some help.

This office, or whatever he bills it as, is a fucking disgrace. At least. At the very least it's a fucking disgrace. It's probably a lot worse than that. If he'd open those fucking curtains, those what-type-of-curtains-they-are-I-don't-know type curtains, then we'd see the dingy corners of Caxton's fucking rat trap. The dusty fuzz. The dirty walls. The Artexed ceiling. Yes, Caxton has an Artexed ceiling. And is that a carpet? Is that thing down there on the 'floor' really a carpet? Not worth the name, in my book. Which we are currently writing.

Anyway. Caxton's got me sat on some kind of chair that's longer than normal chairs. A chaise longue. He says. I am sitting

257

here, casual in MHI by Maharishi Motor Cargo pants, LRG Driven Snow pullover hoody and Cipher Shoes Seditionary trainers. I am looking at those what-the-fuck curtains and he is at the desk. He's recording all we say. So that he can traduce it later. But. And it's a big but. He is recording it on a Panasonic RQ-A170.

Nice, some might think. Except that it is a cassette player. I'm not pissing about. He is actually using a *cassette player*. Later, he may boast – and he seems well capable of it – of its auto reverse and sound level equalizing functions. He may do that in the future. But what that boasting, should it come, will never do is remove the grievous fact of the actual use of tape.

Now. Of all times. In your two thousand and nine.

Even actually now the cunt remains in thrall to the cassette.

This is worse than that shit with the Ericcson T28.

Actually, know what, I'm going to walk out. I'm going to walk out.

'So, Kev, what in your *The L* is the most important thing? Apart from Sas, and the fulfilling open relationship you have with her. We'll be coming on to Sas in detail later. She's definitely a big part of the book. But what I'm trying to do today, Kev, is get a broad feel for *The L*.'

'Nan.'

'We've spoken about Nan, Kev.'

'Keegan then. Keegan's a bit part of *The L*.'

'Yes, Kev. I've got loads of notes about Keegan already. Anything else?'

'*The L*-wise, you mean, Don?'

'I do.'

'Consumer champion and top broadcaster Nicky Campbell.'

'You've mentioned Campbell already and we'll come back to him later. But for now, Kev, anything else?'

'Costner and Coe are a big part of *The L*, Don.'

'OK,' he says, nodding over to my long chair from his desk. 'You mean Kevin Costner, the actor?'

'Naturally. And producer. And Oscar-winning director. The greatest sports film actor of all time.'

'With *Bull Durham* and *Field of Dreams*?'

'No. *Tin Cup*. The 'ninety-six golfing romcom with Rene Russo and Don Johnson, in which Costner plays frat boy golfer Roy "Tin Cup" – hence the tile – Roy "Tin Cup" McAvoy, unambitious wise-guy golf coach who falls for Russo's clinical psychologist Dr Molly Griswold.'

'Right. Is *Tin Cup* your favourite film, Kev?'

'*The L*-wise, yes. Although there was the blistering 90-91-92 sequence of *Dances With Wolves, Robin Hood: Prince of Thieves*, and *The Bodyguard,* with Houston.'

'Whitney?'

'Whitney Houston, Don. And of course Costner crafted *Waterworld* and *The Postman* either side of *Tin Cup*, but yeah, the golfing romcom *is* my favourite film, Don. In which Costner's Roy "Tin Cup" McAvoy romances Russo's Dr Molly Griswold, her seeing through his laidback cynicism and inspiring him to enter the US Open.'

'OK, Kev. Fine. That's Costner. What about Coe?'

'*Sebastian* Coe?'

'Yes. Isn't that who you said? Didn't you say that Coe was also a big part of *The L*?'

'I did. So Costner, he actually trained properly for the golf and many of the golf shots you see in the actual film are actual Costner golf shots. He trained exclusively with a top golfing pro. He developed a swing. He worked out his pre-shot routine. Costner's...'

'And what about Sebastian Coe?'

'You mean *Lord* Coe, KBE?'

'Yes.'

'So. Costner's depiction of a wasteful-but-gifted athlete being emotionally galvanized is important to me as a professional sportsman. His...'

'Isn't Lord Coe...?'

'*Baron* Coe, of Ranmore, you mean?'

'Yes.'

'What is perhaps too little known about Costner is that he has a long-standing interest in playing live music. An interest recently revived with the release of *Untold Truths*, his debut album, recorded under the moniker Kevin Costner and the Modern West. This move into – back into, we should say – this move *back* into music was a way for Costner to connect to people, to his fans, in a more intimate way than just signing an autograph.'

'And what about Coe?'

'Look, Don, we can get to Sebastian. I am happy to talk about Lord Coe at length. But please, please let's first do justice to Costner.'

much-needed nutrients

We've all got sides that most people don't know about. You'd never have believed, until you'd clocked it with your own, that Gravesy loves the opera. And Nan's an absolute demon for the podcasts. We've all got our little things, our unsuspected side interests.

One of mine's gardening. Well, digging, really. Surprising, I know. But I made sure Nan had a big secluded patch when I bought her this house. For her benefit, yes, but also so I could indulge my own hobby.

I walk over to the Bents and jab my spade into the ground. I open the boot, take dirty Dr Roger Hartwell out and sling him on the grass. I take him out of his plastic wrapping and have a look at him…He let me down, he let himself down, and he let customer advocate Nicky Campbell down. He just should have washed his hands. But he did put up quite a fight. Which got me quite excited.

Hence his lack of arms. And eyes.

He does not look at his best. Wouldn't want his wife to see him like this. He's really let himself go. Terrible state really, the once dashing doctor. I hate to see people going to seed like this.

The doctor's going in right next to John Wallace, who delivered the gear from the Harrods splurge. Wallace who was insolent, who butted into the client's private phone conversation. I was surprised at the time.

Still, I tracked Wallace down and corrected his degrading ways and now he's here, in Nan's garden, all nice and dead, and buried right next to Vince Burton, the doorman from Bungalow 8. The one who wouldn't give me his name. The one whose name I had to find out. The one who I did over terrifically well some weeks ago. And the one who lies now, not so punchy as he once was, rotting away in Nan's patch, adding much-needed nutrients to her soil.

Anyway. I start to dig the doctor a nice little hole, I get quite far with it, but then the Vertu trills. Quality. Nice. Billy. End of the manhunt.

But no, text from Colly: *Top of the league. Quarter finals of the Champs. Still in the Carling and the FA Cup. You must be on some win bonuses eh? Unless you forgot to negotiate for that. Let's up it to ninety.*

What? Ninety. Fuck.

I go to call Colly, but then I stop. Moment of weakness that'll be, costing me a grand a week. Nothing money really, usually I mean, but under my current circs even a grand a week's fair wedge.

Calm it, Kev. Think.

I can't keep shelling this out. I'm holding on by my fingertips as is, but with this increase, already I can feel my lifestyle crumbling, and if I don't sort this, if Billy doesn't call me, then soon I'll be living in zone fucking nineteen, wearing a cider-stained shell suit, and listening to retard civvies talk about Aldi offers and botched hysterectomies. If I'm lucky.

And where can I turn? I can't sell Nan's gaff and donk her in a home. That'd only cover me for a few weeks, and besides, the new owners aren't going to take too well to my little vigilante cemetery, are they? And I can't go to the bank: 'And Mr King, why do you need this money? And while we're here, why is ninety grand a week disappearing from your account?'

And not to Bahta either. Neither. Because he's got funding probs himself, and even if he could find the money, I'm not all that keen about spilling these particular beans to the Parsi.

Because it doesn't sound too good. I mean: 'Chairman, you know you fibbed the Bill to save me? Thanks and all. But turns out I'm being blackmailed and you're in line for perjury.'

No, not going to say that, am I? Not going to scare those fucking horses. Do that, and Bahta may well turn on me, cut me loose, tell the cops he lied because I threatened him. Because one thing's a little white one to save your star player, and quite another's landing your own self in the brown.

Then there's Gravesy. But he's skint, even if I could go to him. Which I can't. Never show a fellow pro you're needy, and never land yourself, situ-wise, where testing questions can be asked. That's why I can't ask Boves either. Because he cares he'd want to know the trouble I was in.

I am marooned then, cash-wise, until the Chins can deliver.

I call him.

'Weird, Kev,' Billy says, his many necks rubbing against his phone mic and so sounding, my end, like some kind of wind turbulence. 'Not a sniff of him. Usually we've had at least a visual by now.'

Not good. I'd been quite calm until now, Colly-wise, because of Billy's excellent manhunt record, but that's just shat me right up. But I carry on, I need to think, and later, when I've done the grave, and I'm dumping the doctor into his nice new hole, Shishakli just pops into the King mind. Because maybe the super-agent can maximize my short-term income and keep the Colly furnace fed until Four Chins lands him.

Got to be careful, though. Can't let Shish know I'm short. I dial the Syrian.

'Look, Aram, I'm really keen to get going in our, er, working relationship. Aren't there any Mega Bowls, or Laser Quest-type things I can open?'

'Kevin. I appreciate your eagerness, but to land the big fish we need to go slowly. I've got you a charity photo shoot. It's not as high profile as we might like, but it is the type of work you need to be seen to be getting into.'

This is Shishakli's Kev King brand strategy: put in the charity hours in front of the camera. Build up the genuinely nice guy thing. That way you get the biggest product endorsements coming your way, because you've already done the groundwork of ramming yourself into/under the public's eye/nose.

'Oh yeah, what's it?' I ask, now chucking the first spadeful on to the recently deceased medic's face.

'Visit to a children's hospital.'

'Nice. How much do I get for that?'

'It's for charity, Kevin. You'll be expected to make a contribution yourself.'

Shit.

I end the call. Christ. It's coming at me from all angles. The temple of Kev is being everyway mullered...But relax. Got to think, got to relax. Be calm, Kev. And methodical. PMA, Kev.

I gather myself together and return to composting Nan's garden with the doctor, and soon he's done. Interred, to use the jargon. I return the spade to the shed, and glance over to the house. Nan's bedroom curtains are still closed, and I don't want to disturb her, so I step into the shed to get changed.

Minutes later and I'm sat in the Bents, wearing Alejandro Ingelmo Toby snakeskin trainers, Haversack Lodencross trousers and an Ute Ploier funnel-neck jumper with epaulettes.

I check the Franck Muller Long Island timepiece. Meeting Gravesy in town in a couple of hours. Make good time and I'll just manage to fit in a couple of rounds with the Mexican. Nice. That'll perk me up. Takes my mind off things, does the Central American pro. Oils the cogs, if you will.

I pull out on to the road. The sticks, out here, it is. Weird little horse-and-carty villages, full of retired cunts and cunts who have not as yet retired but may as well, really, given the feeble contribution they make to the GDP. But Nan likes it out here and Nan can have what she likes.

I drive through the villages, looking at the houses and cheering Kev with a little game. 'One hundred and four,' I say as I pass a large detached, set back from the road.

'Two hundred and ten,' I say as I pass a shitty little semi.

The rules of the game are simple. Guess how many times more you earn than these civvy 'homeowners'. It's not an exact science, I admit, these rough calculations, and obviously there's this bitter-sweet thing about Colly now snaffling more than all of my wedge, but you know, you have to stay on the front foot, you have to pass the time.

'One hundred and eighty!' I say, in my best Lakeside voice, to a thatched cottage.

I am feeling a little more relaxed. There must be a way out for Kev. Chad Kruger, Nickleback's singer and muse, is filling the Bents with quality sounds and I am heading towards zone one, for a bunk-up. And, you know, sometimes you have to just put money worries aside and concentrate on the higher things in life, like love, and I am in love with Kev. I really am.

I unzip the Haversack Lodencross trousers and whip out the King cock. It really is an excellent cock. And as I stare at my world-class manhood, it enlarges. I buzz the Bents seat upwards and rest the King member against the steering wheel, then lift the King hands from the Bents wheel and begin to steer the Continental GT – with torque-sensing central differential and 552 horsepower – actually with my actual cock. The King cock itself is steering the twin super-charged coupé its very self. Brilliant.

I am determined to enjoy myself. I am such a great bloke.

Some shit kind of Ford-type car is coming towards me on the opposite side of the road – though, given the stingy breadth of these country tracks it is virtually the same side – and I tense my left buttock, so tilting the King cock across the steering wheel of the Bents and moving the coupé into the path of the Ford-type object.

Not a lot of tilt. But just enough so that the zone seven thousander driving the oncoming piece of shit swerves, pinging his Ford, all crumply, into a verge.

I relax the buttock and resume a straight course, glancing into the rear-view to see the shit-awful crashed motor fade into the distance behind me. It really is an excellent turn-up. I have just crashed someone's car. With my cock. What an athlete! That's one up on *Thunderbirds* lookalike and F1 maestro Lewis Hamilton. Nice. But then I check the Franck Muller.

Shit. Having all this fun has put me behind sched. If I'm going to see to the Mexican before dinner I'd better get my finger out. Not that my finger is in. But I had better get it out.

I accelerate, pop my left hand on the steering wheel, and proceed to knock one out with my right. The Westway. The arch of Wembley stadium over to my left. Edgware. Marylebone. All that. Nearing Soho. Feeling good. I park the Bents and step out, dinking it shut and striding towards the lair of the Mexican.

I *knew* I was looking good today, but this is ridiculous. Everybody is staring at me. *Everybody.* Those you would. Those you wouldn't. Those you wouldn't but would anyway. Those you have. Everybody is gawping at his Kevcellency. I really, really must be the bollocks today.

It's the clobber maybe, giving me the edge?

I glance down towards the Alejandro Ingelmo Toby snakeskin trainers and notice that my cock is still out, flapping excellently from the fly of the Lodencross strides. I re-throne the champion and stride on, Kevishly, towards Wardour Street. Left into Broadwick and then here we are, the temple of the Central American professional.

Up the stairs and up the stairs again and then I knock – a gent, see – and enter and there she is, sitting in a little velvet chair by the window, painting her toenails.

She says nothing. Nor do I. Don't speak a word of the Spango, and she doesn't do the English too well. But we share a common tongue: the international language of sex trafficking.

I approach the Mexican and she nods towards her toes and then towards the bed, indicating I should wait for her to finish coating the tootsies. I walk across the room and sit down. I'm not used to hanging around for services, but what the Mexican offers is truly bespoke, so I will be patient.

There's a pile of magazines by the side of the bed and I eye them, spotting a copy of *Icon*. Fucking *Icon*. Redknappy's magazine. Redknappy's lifestyle mag, for which I have still not received my invite. How did this get here?

Gravesy? No. He's never set foot in the Premiership.

There must be another top player frequenting the Mexican. Which does not surprise me. Best hand job in zone one, she's won, three years running. Or she would have done if such a prestigious and competitive award existed. Which it should. I pick up the copy of *Icon* and have a browse. There's a snap of Michael Owen on the cover.

Poor ickle Mickey.

Must be hard to know that you peaked at the age of eighteen. All downhill for Michael from there on in. Not that he's got a hill. But he could have. If he wanted. He could afford a hill, that lad, despite having only played one-seventh of a Premiership game in the last twenty-six seasons. Due to injury.

Injury prone, your Owen. Very much so.

Anyway, I eye the snap of Owen on the cover, but then the Mexican is over and she's already reached into her wardrobe and donned the Kev King team shirt and slipped off her kecks and she pushes me back on the bed and makes to give me the full English breakfast, but I glance at the Franck Muller Long Island and realize I don't have time for all the trimmings, so I give her the international 'wank me off' sign, and she nods and pulls the champ from the Haversack Lodencross strides and starts doing the thing that she does, that little trick, handed down from father to son in the backwaters of Mexico, which has made her such an in-demand wank professional across all HNWI sectors in this, the greatest city in the world.

And yes, it's good, and despite jacking off in the Bents on the way I can already feel the sap rising, due to the smooth yet filthy skill that she brings to bear on the King helmet.

And yep, yep.

I check the Franck Muller and all is going swimmingly,

time-wise. And wank-wise as well. But then there's a noise outside the door and it opens suddenly and there's a face peeping into the Mexican's boudoir and I recognize the face, the little Aussie nose and the shocked Aussie mouth and the Antipodean eyes, looking all furious all of a sudden, as though they've just spotted that the billabong's run dry.

'Gravesy,' I say, and sit up, just as the King sap rises fully and I shoot my load forward on to the floor, my gism slapping across the photo of Owen's face on the cover of *Icon* magazine. Then the Mexican is off me and Gravesy is over and he just stands there, right in front of me, where I sit on the Mexican's bed.

'Kev-o,' he says, all aghast, as though he's caught me going at his mum. Or his dad, even. And not merely receiving inventive hand relief from a respectable pro.

'Kev-o,' he says again.

And he looks so sad and floppy for a moment, which really does upset me, him actually being my actual mate, but then he swings and absolutely mugs me right across the chops and I feel one of the King teeth sort of jump from its socket, and so I do a sort of little spit thing. And there it is – my fucking molar – on the floor next to the man muck-coated copy of *Icon* magazine.

And then all of a sudden the pain starts, mouth-wise, and I'm wondering what hit me. Not that I need to wonder, because it was Gravesy that hit me. I know that. And then the little Aussie striker turns on his black leather Regain buckle shoe-clad heel and marches out of the Mexican's door.

And fuck, there goes my friendship with Gravesy, which I do not need to happen. Not ever, but particularly not at this moment of high financial strain, not at this time when I need all Kevish wagons to round into a protective – and excellent – circle.

But then I look down at the magazine and see that the spunk stain on Owen's cheek appears – from the angle at which I view it, at least – like a very accomplished map of the Outer Hebrides. And so, despite the Gravesy upset, I can't help thinking about the Turner Prize, and the possibility of entering this Hebridean map gism-faced art into that competition. Because, you know, I'm skint, and there's a lot of cash in the old fucking art.

But before these thoughts can percolate fully and cement themselves into the King brand strategy, I look over to the Mexican and she slips on a skirt and – quite sensibly – takes off her Kev King top and replaces it with a neutral T-shirt, and runs out the door, in pursuit of the offended Australian marksman, leaving me to receive the acclaim of the British art establishment alone.

And so I'm sitting there, looking down at my tooth, where it now lies, all bloody, next to the gism photo map, and I'm wondering about Gravesy, but wondering too if the addition of this blood-soaked dentistry to the Owen-based conceptual art might just be one step too far, for the Turner Prize judges, that is.

I mean, I'm wondering if this extra detail of the claret-coated gnasher might suggest artistic overkill to the judging committee. If perhaps they might interpret the addition of the tooth as a little too try-hardish. And not as a profound comment on the excruciatingly visceral trials that ex-England strike dwarf Owen has put his body through during his illustrious if truncated career. A meaning that was naturally intended by me – Kev – the artist.

It's very difficult to judge.

I'll need a consultant.

journey to the centre of the earth

'No, Sas, it's got to be Boves.'

'But the magazine, Kev...'

'Has the magazine won the World Cup?'

'Might have.'

'It hasn't, Sas.'

'So?'

'Boves has won it. The actual World Cup. I can't get married and not have a World Cup winner as my best man.'

But more than that, having so recently lost the matemanship of Colly and now Gravesy – not that Sas is privvy to these ructions – what I actually need most of all, on my increasingly spooky and expensive wedding day, is a good old-fashioned mate.

But, 'The magazine said it had to be Marco,' Sas says. 'To show, you know, that our open relationship is not a media scam.'

'No, Sas.'

'But it's already gone out, announcing it.'

'Can't Marco give you away or something instead, Sas? That would be a truer indication of the lack of jealousy in our uniquely modern, trust-based love.'

'My dad's giving me away, Kev.'

'Look, Sas, it's got to be Boves. It would be the icing on the cherry for Premiership legend Kevin King to be so intimately associated with World Cup winner Florent Bovary.'

'Kev, no.'

I decide to hit her with the P word. 'It'd be better for both of our profiles, Sas. How many people actually know this Marco? But having Boves there would make the wedding snaps more marketable across the French-speaking world.'

She goes quiet. I've got her.

'OK, Kev. I'll talk to Min about it.'

'And talk to Min about getting more cash out of the magazine as well. You've already spent twice what they're paying us.'

And she has. And no doubt, by the time this higher than high-maintenance sleb has finished with her crazed princess specs, it'll be four times what the snaps are landing us. And the rest. And where oh where oh where am I going to get that fucking money from? Because Four Chins hasn't called yet. Four Chins is leadless. And things are turning to shit in my hands. The lifestyle is falling falling falling...

I leave the den of my sensational modern manor house with breathtaking rural views and stride into the galleried reception hall, with its curved, south-west-facing window and I text the housekeeper for a garage meet. Because nuts in, these days, is the only way I can relax – excluding, naturally, the refuge of the pitch, and the solace I gain from talking about *The L* with custard-headed Caxton, though even that, I admit, is beginning to pall, as what we celebrate turns to turd before my eyes.

I take the solid oak stairs, pausing for a moment to enjoy the uninterrupted country vistas. Actually, scrap that. Truth is, I don't enjoy the vistas at all. Because the countryside is shit. It's just dirt with grass on it, and a few retards with guns, and a few uncooked meals walking around, in the form of cows and sheep and shit like that.

The fields are only here because they've failed to attract cut-throat property developers. They're shit. Really. I mean, you can't drive fields, you can't wear them and you can't fuck them. They're pointless. That's the truth of it.

But there is another side. Because when a man reaches a

certain income – as I have done, many times over, not that I see any of it these days – tradition dictates that he acquires a country house of exceptional quality and stature. And I am nothing if not a traditionalist.

I am doing this, living here, in order to keep the lifestyle of the aristocratic country gentleman alive. And not for my own pleasure. It is a sacrifice I am prepared to make. For the Queen. For England. And for the memory of Princess Di, the actual Queen of Hearts.

Anyway.

I enter the genuinely self-indulgent opulence of the master suite, vainly check the Racetrack Legends for a Four Chins call, then pick up the already-packed Andrew Marc Marshall sports bag. I return down the solid oak stairs, walk through the galleried reception hall, and head out the front door on to the brick driveway. One of the garage doors is open already and I stride towards the quadruple parking lodge, step inside, and spot the housekeeper, leaning already, skirt up, knickers down, over the bonnet of the Bents.

I pop the bag in the boot, walk towards the bonnet, unzip the Satyenkumar Airtex trousers and take the housekeeper from behind as I check the Panerai Radiomir Black Seal timepiece. Don't want to be late. It's a big day for Kev, meeting up with the senior England squad for a spot of training. A training session which will decide who takes the field in the upcoming away friendly with Argentina.

I withdraw, wipe myself down aristocratically on the housekeeper's skirt, and step towards the driver's door.

'Don't forget to buy the venison,' I say to the housekeeper and she nods. Not that I like venison. In fact I fucking hate it. But it's this whole country gentleman responsibility issue again. Sometimes we have to do what is right, and not what we want. Sometimes our life is not our own. You learn that as you get older. Wiser. Kever.

I fire up the Bents. Right. Big, big day. I motor down the

brickwork drive towards the confusingly ornate ironwork gates which I buzz open, then I drive through and park to one side of the slim, country lane which fronts the King manor.

I spot the black cab parked up beneath some kind of tree, so I toot the horn and moments later the Mexican steps out, walks towards the Bents, climbs in, furnishes me with a skilfully mangling hand job, takes her cash and the cash for the knowledger, and returns to the cab. Nuts in, as I say, is keeping me going. All set. Off I drive.

Villages. Villages. Villages.

I'm heading towards London Colney, the Arsenal's Hertfordshire-based training centre. No idea why, but thrust-chinned Italian disciplinarian Fabio Capello has selected the Gunners' training base for this England get-together.

Still. I drive into some village or other and outside its cruddy little pub – which, let's be honest, will be shutting down in a week or so – there's some kind of troll-man standing there, wearing some kind of shit-awful Cotton Traders-type fleece or something. Looks like he's escaped from the Middle Ages, this fleecy bloke. Looks like he's probably got the plague.

And. Crucially. This suspiciously hideous troll-man is holding hands with a kid, some kind of girl or something, and looking at her as I do, seeing her actually quite good hair, and excellent boots – for a civilian, I mean – I can't imagine for a minute that they share the same gene pool.

I mean, how could *he* give rise to *her*? How can someone wearing unforgivable rags like that have fathered a well-dressed girl like the one he's holding hands with? It's really very suspicious.

Fuck. Christ. Right under the King nose, so to say.

I pluck the Vertu Ascent Racetrack Legends limited edition with laser-etched Silverstone circuit map, bezel-nosed radiator grille inset, and liquidmetal chassis from the Camoshita wool pea coat and dink in the old 999s.

'Which service to you require?'

'Paedophile.'

'Ambulance, Police or Fire, sir?'

'He's a fucking paedophile.'

'Calm down, sir.'

'There's a fucking paedo standing outside the pub. He's swiping some child.'

'Can you give me more information, sir?'

'He's a kiddy fucker. Clear as day. Holding hands with some sweet kid, outside the pub.'

'Which pub?'

'Dunno. Some shit pub.'

'What makes you think he's a paedophile, sir? Do you know him?'

'Know him? You saying I hang around with kiddy fiddlers?'

'No, sir, I'm trying to get more details of this suspected child abduction case.'

'No you weren't, you were suggesting that I'm part of some kind of paedo ring. You were implying that I'm a key member of some international child sex racket.'

'I can assure you, sir, I wasn't. Can you tell me why you think this man has abducted this child? And can you please tell me where you are?'

'There you go again. I am not, nor have I ever been, a member of a fiddlers' cartel. You can check my computer.'

'That won't be necessary. Now. Do you know this man?'

'Look, you've gone too far this time. Put me through to your superior.'

'That won't be possible, sir. We need to keep these lines open for emergencies.'

'Fucking typical.'

'Language, sir. And unless you answer my questions, I'm going to have to cut you off.'

'What's this, some kind of interrogation?'

'Where are you, sir?'

'What's your name? I'm going to make a complaint.'

'Of course, sir, that's your right, and this call has been recorded for just such an eventuality.'

'Well?'

'My name's Jane Cook. Now, sir, can you please tell me why you believe you have encountered a case of child abduction?'

For fuck's sake.

I end the call.

What is the matter with this country? With broken Britain? A citizen – and one of extremely high standing, I might add, a citizen footballer on his way to train with the national squad, no less – tries to help, tries to do his bit for the vibrant local community by reporting a grievous and obvious case of child molestation, and what happens? As we have seen, the very light of suspicion falls on to the very face of that helpful – and excellent – citizen-athlete himself.

It's all wrong.

Who is this country run for, anyway? For bad fleece-wearing, turnip-nosed paedos? Or for gentleman footballers? For the decent, common, hard-working – if shit and poor – man, or for your actual fiddlers?

It is beyond belief. No. It's worse than that. It is beyond beyond belief. I accel and punish the Bents forward through these paedophilic villages, imagining the child sex horrors happening behind each front door. This country has gone downhill to the dogs.

I reach London Colney, and there's all kinds of gates and shit and then I'm in and it's only when I see the startling array of wildly upmarket motors parked on the Colney tarmac that I actually detox out the remaining paedo-inspired fury, and focus. Better. Got to be on my game today, in order to cement the King self into the Capello thoughts.

I open the Bents door, but for some reason I don't climb out.

No. Instead I sit there for a moment and think how far I've come this season. From foot-fuck and physio with cheese-head Jimbo and a place in a muppety Championship side, to the

Prem, to the top of the Prem, and now this, the England call-up.

It has been a high sky high rise for Kevin King. And as I sit amongst the exquisitely high-grade upholst of the Continental GT with twin elliptical exhausts, there come – to be honest and fair – a number of nerves jangling through the athletic King physique. And I want to talk to someone, hear a soothing voice.

Not Nan, no, because much as she is wise in many fields, she is not, bless her, my go-to girl, humpty-wise; compared, I mean, to the professionals with whom I daily mix.

No, I need a pro – a mate and a pro – to big me up, to tell me I'm international material. I call Boves but there's no answer. And in fact there's rarely any answer from Boves these days. Not since the Colly stuff, and the 'You fuck Sas?' question I foolishly levelled at him, and now this Gravesy stuff.

And I want to call Gravesy. I want to hear his voice, but the Mexican lies between us now, her tits like some impenetrable mountain range, separating the King tribe from the Gravesy peoples, if you will, the distance breeding supernatural suspicions and loathing between the two otherwise v. similar communities, with neither realizing that though the vast girth of the Mexican's fun bags separates them, still, on clear nights, both tribes are united in longing gaze at the same nippled summits.

Gravesy's lost to me, and I look again at the London Colney training pavilion, knowing that the gods of the Premiership will be in there.

The likes of your Rooneys, with his receding barnet. Your Gerrards with his somehow *acceding* hairline. And soon Kev'll be in there as well. Donning the Three Lions, so to say. Standing amongst the giants of the modern game. Playing at the very highest level. And it's what I've always wanted. No. It's what I've always *deserved*.

And isn't there something like destiny at work here? Something like fate? Because I have long known that I am worthy of the Three Lions, and now those actual lions are in reach, snarling and felling antelopes on the Serengeti of the training pitch; the actual Three Lions themselves, copulating with their harem and flatulating wildly and eating the odd honeymooning tourist from Nottingham, who has ventured too close to the pride.

Yes. Three Lions are a pride of lions. And that is, I admit, intimidating. But isn't a single Kev a pride of Kevs as well? And am I not worth this? I can show baldy Rooney and foreheadless Gerrard who's got the most lionish right boot, who can chase down the Land Rover of the ball in the parched grasslands of Wembley.

I'm on it now. No problems can reach me here. Humpty is my refuge.

I step from the Bents and walk towards the entrance of the s-o-t-a training complex, hearing a satisfyingly efficient swish as the doors part for Kev. There's some Janice or Doris-type woman who you wouldn't on the old recep and I swagger – yes, swagger – by her and open the changing room door, which is actually a cupboard. So I swagger back to the desk and she points me towards the changing-rooms, and I Kev over and push the door open all gunslingerishly, expecting to see the crème de la elite of the Premiership world arrayed all change-upishly in front of me. But there's no one there. Well, there is. There's hard man ex-international and Capello confidant Stuart Pearce stood there, tapping his timepiece.

'You're late, Kev,' he says, all fucked off. 'We're upstairs, come on,' and he turns and walks through a side door and I follow. Corridors and stairs and shit, and then we come out into some kind of cafe set up with a relaxation area at its far end. And we walk towards that area, a massive TV at its centre, sofas arranged around it and I begin to make out the players sat on these sofas.

Goal-scoring Everton centre back Joleon Lescott. Pasty Middlesborough wideman Stuart Downing. Reliable Villa distributor Gareth Barry. Wild-haired engine room Jimmy Bullard.

They're all there.

277

And odd-voiced Chelsea hard man John Terry's there and Rooney and Gerrard themselves, with their widely variant barnets, they're there. And the squad, the Lions, are staring – to a man – at the TV, which – and this fucks me off – is more massive than the one which looms within the King lounge. And next to this more-massive-than-Kev's TV is Capello himself. Straight-backed, curly-haired. And there's a space on one of the sofas next to veteran Portsmouth netminder David James, which I take. And I look at the TV. Which I can't actually see. Well, I can see the sides of the screen, but not the middle, because I'm sat right behind the basketball player-esque figure of underrated strikeman Peter Crouch.

And what *is* this? What are they watching?

I don't know.

But then I begin to make out the screen beyond the lanky figure of Crouch. It's a recording of the last England game, the 2-1 away victory to Germany. A satisfying score line, if not a completely satisfying performance, if I remember. Which I do. And now I know what's happening. Capello's debriefing them, stopping the DVD, playing it back, pointing out some flaw in someone's play. Passing on a compliment, some positional advice, a comment on the quality of a pass.

And the lads – the pinnacle of the Prem – are sitting there, nodding, looking thoughtful. Some of them are even taking notes. Actually writing actual things down with actual pens and paper.

And it's not right, this use of the paper. These lads, sat here, are probably, between them, on a hundred mil a year, a hundred and twenty mil, even. And yet some of them are actually using paper, which is just bog roll with lines on it as far as I can see. And which could be used by any old zone twenty-sevener writing out their Lidl shopping list: eighty Lambert and Butler, fourteen packets of microchips, fifteen family bags of crisps, an apple. That kind of shit.

Or this paper could be used by some ancient fucking Egyptian bloke even, sitting by the banks of the Nile, nine hundred thousand years ago – well, before the invention of the football at least – sketching the blueprint for some kind of pointless pyramid thing, some pointed building shit that you can't even have a kick-about inside because the rooms are all so small and gloomy, rooms which do not have south-facing picture windows peering on to manicured private grounds.

It's not right that these athletes are using paper. It seems an affront to the lifestyle dignity of these top, top players to be sat here in front of the schoolmasterish Italian coach, jotting things down.

And what's more, where are the bibs? Where are the cones and bollards, around which I, Kev, was expecting to jink and swerve? I'll fucking tell you. Not here. Nowhere to be seen.

No cones, no bibs, Mr Capello, do you really know what you're doing?

Criminal, it is. Tolerating this rustly paper shit and yet not even supplying these top players with the requisite cones and bibs, the crucial infrastructure of training. What is an England get-together without different-coloured illuminous bibs, without orange plastic bollards, around which to chicane in football excellence? I'll tell you, Mr Capello. Nothing. That's what it is.

This training session is shit, Capello.

You have really gone down in my estimation.

Really. Down. A long way. Perhaps even to the very centre of the earth itself, you have fallen, where you are languishing now in a bath of molten lava without even a protective suit on. In fact, as you swim through the scalding lava at the centre of the actual earth itself, Capello, do you know what you're wearing? Nothing but a pair of ratty old Speedos. That's it. No foily, heat-repelling suit or lava-resistant helmet type set-up.

No. Not at all. Nothing like that.

You've just got the Speedos on, mate. And they are an unforgivable lurid yellow colour which does not harmonize with your Mediterranean skin tones. In fact, these Speedos clash all violently with your natural colours. That's how far you have fallen,

Capello, with your jut jaw and your bewildering toleration of the use of paper, and your total and complete lack of bib or bollard.

And – because while we're here, talking about this, let's get all of the brass tacks out into the open – when I Keved into the room – late, I admit, but that was the fault of the Central American pro – did you stop your DVD-based debriefing and introduce me, a new Lion, a recent addition to the national squad, to the other players?

No, you did not.

You did not stop this tactical wibble that you are indulging in and welcome me – Kev – a new recruit to the set-up. It is frankly nothing short of disgusting. And your hair is shit.

Shit hair, you have, Capello. Really.

But then he stops and seems to look my way, though how he can see me with the totem pole of Peter Crouch between us is anyone's guess.

'Ah, Mr King,' Capello says. 'Welcome…Everybody, you have met Kevin King. He's here for his first England session.'

The lads turn round to eye me, their faces all football playerish.

'Right, that's enough analysis,' says Capello. 'Let's get changed up and get on to the training ground. Stuart, if you'll bring the bibs and cones out.'

fungicide-impregnated sofa

Caxton takes out the Panasonic and starts the tape.

'Capello is a master tactician, Don. Really. Genuinely inspired use of the bibs. A demon with the cones. Very handy with the DVD as well, I have to admit. You can see why he's got so many pots and pans in the cabinet, or whatever they call it in Italian. The Cabineto.'

'But what is he like as a man, Kev?'

'As a man, Don? Manly. At least.'

'Right.'

I'm casual in Know1edge Lui Araki trousers, a Caked Out Paid In Full T and Alfie Everybody mid-canvas trainers. He is wearing. Actually, fuck that. Don't want to get into it. What Caxton's wearing demonstrates a serious lack of self-respect. I am angry about Caxton's clobber and his minging fucking office. But I am here to tell my story and I will be professional. I lean back in the long chair and relax.

Funny, really, me lying back all psychiatrically in this chair. Him at the desk, taking the notes, plying me with the questions. And know what? A civilian happening to peer in through the window – which they can't, being as Caxton's tragic curtains are tugged right shut, so masking the full seediness of his den from your actual daylight – might feasibly mistake this scene for therapy, as I believe they call it.

C.M. TAYLOR

Yes. Truthfully. A civvy, seeing me reclining, may not realize that what he spied was, reality-wise, an outstanding athlete dictating his lifestyle autobiog to a chubby, custard-headed hack. Rather, I can see how this peeping Tom zone eighter – who cannot, as we've established, actually see into Caxton's grubby lair at this juncture, even should he exist – might construe this couch and desk set-up as a head-to-head, so to say, between a shrink and his client.

Anyway.

It's a bitter-sweet day for Kev. Even as I scale towards the Prem crown, even as I make the Lions' shirt my own, even now Four Chins fails me, and my cash-fucked lifestyle is imploding. So, let's record the epic glory of *The L*, before the end, as, say, the artists of ancient Rome sketched hard to capture that city's final magnificence, even as the barbarians wiped their arses on the gates.

'We're doing Nicky Campbell today, Don, right?'

'Actually, Kevin, there was something I wanted us to talk about. The publishers have said…'

'Good. Let's start then…Bogus holiday clubs. Bloated hospital parking charges. Fake airline insurance. Unscrupulous conservatory salesmen. These are the sorts of things, Don, that top broadcaster and consumer affairs giant Nicky Campbell has to deal with on an everyday basis.

'Take the case of Vance Miller, otherwise known as the Kitchen Gangster, who repeatedly supplied products which differed wildly to those advertised. Operating in the Oldham area under a variety of company names – Kitchens, for example, Kitchens Direct, but also the seemingly innocuous Maple Industries – Miller was hunted and confronted by Nicky Campbell's *Watchdog* team, and was robustly and fairly challenged about the quality of the kitchens he was offering. It was a blisteringly brilliant piece of investigative journalism.

'That's just one example. There are many others. And there are few people – truly – on this earth who are up to the job. Because Campbell helms BBC1's consumer affairs flagship show

282

with an easy demeanour which belies his underlying forensic intelligence, displaying the mixture of strong views, curiosity and assertion which have made the Campbell name a watchword for customer protection, across the world. Across the nation, even.'

'Kev, the publishers are very disappointed...'

'Raising consumer awareness regarding purchasing rights. Challenging unfair customer policies. Shutting down rogue and dangerous businesses. Fighting for changes in the law. These are just a few of the things Campbell has on his plate. What Campbell *knows* is that fake, dangerous or illegal goods have no place, either on the old-fashioned High Street, or more latterly in the emerging online environment.

'Amazon, for example, a trusted name in the online marketplace, recently fell under the irresistible Campbell scrutiny when the *Watchdog* team uncovered that its offshoot Amazon Marketplace was offering genuinely dangerous goods.

'Pepper spray, banned in this country, was available on Amazon Marketplace. For example. As was CS gas. *CS Gas*, Don. Horrifying. Unbelievable. That's officially classed as an offensive weapon. Imagine if those dangerous goods fell into the wrong hands? Imagine it. The havoc that might have erupted had Campbell not stepped in.

'But that's not all. Frightening letters sent to customers. Dangerous chip pans. Filthy doorstep tactics. Unreasonable hikes in energy bills. Copyright infringements. Irresponsible locksmiths. Capricious electricians. Cable customers experiencing viewing difficulties. Irresponsible gas fitters. Difficult-to-cancel gym memberships. Skin injuries from fungicide-impregnated sofas. Cowboy chocolatiers. Mercenary funeral parlours. These are all part of Campbell's everyday world. He deals with the situations that we don't want to. He gets his hands dirty. And what does he get out of it?'

'Well, Kev, a few hundred thousand quid a year and nationwide fame, I suspect. But anyway, we shouldn't even be talking about this. The plans have changed...'

'But what does Campbell *really* get out if it, Don? It's a lonely job. Imagine the threats he faces, the aggravation. But he has stepped up to the mantle, donned the plate. Campbell has said, "Not one single person, even if they are a zone nineteen ring piece, enjoys being conned or scammed or sold dodgy goods. And I – Campbell – will take responsibility and try to make the customer world a better, brighter, safer place." That's what Campbell has said. And achievement-wise, he's set out to achieve just that.

'Campbell is a terrier fighting on behalf of the lowly customer. To be honest and frank – and that's what top broadcaster Nicky Campbell is all about – his pro-consumer work is not going to get us – well, them, the civilians – out of this debit munch that we – well, they – are in, but he can stem the tide off at the pass by fighting and fighting for customer rights, Don.

'Take the case of Eloise Burke. Campbell highlighted her plight. She was sold – again via Amazon Marketplace – some H2D hair straighteners, which broke just six months later. Only *six months* of use, Don! And her hair wasn't even that curly to start with. Now, when she returned these goods to the manufacturer, she was told – and she was as shocked about this as you or I would be, Don – that the hair straighteners were counterfeit.

'Incredible! Counterfeit! Horrifying! Imagine if that had happened to you, Don. Imagine if it had happened to Nan. It doesn't bear thinking about.'

'Look, for fuck's sake, Kevin. This is total shit. All of it. The Costner stuff. The Keegan stuff. And this Campbell bollocks as well. The publishers have listened to the tapes. They hate it.'

'They what, Don?'

'They think it's crap. There's been a change of plan. Apart from Sas and the open relationship, they're cutting out the lifestyle angle on the book.'

'But they can't! We signed a contract.'

'They can, Kevin. You should read the things you sign. They can change anything they want. You don't agree and they can even take their advance back.'

Got him there though, because, 'Already spent it, Don.'

'Not their problem. You'll just have to find it.'

Christ. What. Fuck. No.

'They think the only way to salvage this dog's breakfast is by concentrating on the football murders.'

'But *they're not* football murders…'

'What?'

'Nothing.'

'No. That wasn't nothing. What did you mean by that, that they aren't football murders?'

'Slip of the tongue, Don.'

He looks at me then, his somehow-fat eyeballs resting on the King visage. 'Kevin, the publishers are insisting. The police now know that your old manager from the Championship was murdered. You were at the Newcastle game when that waiter was killed. You played against Chelsea the night that those two fans were knifed and strangled. That radio host was even talking about you just before *he* was killed.'

'How do you know all this?'

'I *am* writing a book about you, Kevin. I have done some research. You're very near to the action, Kevin. The publishers think if you give the changing-room view on the murders, then sales will be boosted.'

'Right.'

'I mean, Kev, there was another murder the other day, right after the England training session at London Colney. A man was found suffocated with a bib. The papers think the football murderer is progressing from simple knife killings to more elaborate and brutal murders.'

'Do they, Don?'

'They do. It's the natural path of the serial killer, to begin to commit more ornate and gruesome murders.'

'The further into their career they get, you mean, Don?'

'In a way, Kev, yes.'

'The more skilled they become at their profession, you mean?'

'Yeah. If you like.'

'Don't know about that, Don. Some killers, you know, may experiment a bit, but they'll still have a favoured method in their locker.'

The Caxton glare.

'I've heard that, Don, I've read it.'

'What's the feeling in the dressing room, Kev? Is the football community running scared?'

I'm being mullered out here. I need a diversion.

'The football community *is* running, Don. But that's to be expected, I mean they're athletes. Some more gifted than others, naturally, but they're all capable of running.'

'Kev, I really *am* going to push you on this. What did you feel that day, for example, knowing that a young waiter had been murdered while you sat not one hundred metres away in the Jackie Milburn Stand of St James' Park?'

'You find that out from your research, Don, where I was sat?'

'Police source.'

Shit. 'What else did the police say, Don?'

'Lots of things. You must know that. They must have interviewed you.'

'No, why would we have spoken? We haven't spoken.'

'Really? They've spoken to everyone else at the club. Why everyone else but not you, Kevin? That's an interesting angle.'

'Was with the Chairman, wasn't I, at the time of the other killings.'

'Right…I see…'

Those lingering eyes, the Caxton brain thinking, thinking, thinking…

'But how did you feel, Kev, when those two Chelsea fans were killed?'

'I felt, you know, that some days you win, and some days you lose. I mean, Chelsea have bagged a couple of titles recently. Which was a winning day. And then the day those boys were killed, that was a day they lost.'

Caxton's getting irate now, his eyeballs are getting all ping-pongy within his padded face. '*Right?* Is that it? You don't feel, for example, in danger, because there's a crazed psychopath stalking the modern game?'

'But there isn't.'

'What?'

'I said, I don't feel in danger.'

'OK. Fine. Then what about your teammates? What do they think?'

'Don, the modern game is jam-packed with foreign players – or flat-packed, if you will, in the case of the Swedes – and most of them can't string ten words of the Queen's together. Do you think they're wheeling out their intimate thoughts about danger to me when they can't even order a haddock?'

'So you didn't feel anything really? You didn't think about these murders too much and you didn't talk about it with your teammates?'

'That's about right.'

'Don't you think that's a bit weird, Kev?'

'A bit *what*, Don?'

I have a good look at Caxton now, as he blubbers over his tea-stained office chair and then later on – when I'm alone in the Bents, staring at the Vertu, wanting to call much-missed Gravesy, or waiting forlornly for Billy to call, or screening a call from Sas, a call asking, no doubt, for more cash for the wedding dwarves or the dancing bears, or some other wild princess fuckerness like that – I wonder about Caxton. I wonder if he knows.

Knows, I mean, that beneath the sleek Premiership lifestyle of Kev – a lifestyle which, I might add, despite its current chronic predicaments Caxton is still earning his living from – there lurks a customer service vigilante, ready at any moment to pounce and uphold consumer virtues and rights.

As a select few confidants of billionaire industrialist Bruce Wayne knew that beneath his urbane exterior there lurked a pure and crusading bat heart, I wonder if Caxton – despite his unforgivable clobber and cretinous head hair – is aware of the other side of Kev. The inner side of Kev. The crusading side which is a disciple of consumer watchgod Nicky Campbell.

I really do wonder.

Does he know that I am prepared to go as far as it takes – further, even – to withstand the erosion of consumer quality in this country?

I drum on the dash. I finger the silent phone.

He's far too close.

franchise-o?

Nothing can touch me here.

Colly or not, Caxton or not, cash or not, cross that white line and it's all so simple. Love it, the humpty, I do.

And I love these Argentinians.

Harder and less flouncy than your Brazilian; exhibiting more flair and attacking ambition than your Italian. They are Kev's kind of people.

Traditionally, I know that the Albicelestes v. Three Lions fixture is a heavyweight grudge match. But I don't feel that. I mean I might, but we're fucking them. Away. In front of a capacity 65,000 crowd in the Monumental stadium. A stadium in which the Argies clinched the 1978 World Cup.

Know my history, I do. Football-wise, at least. Professor of football, really, I am. And thrust-chinned England coach Capello must agree with me, having stuck me in for this match.

The ball's with our keeper Jame-o, and he's winding up for a goal kick, so I've got all eyes on Maradona, the current Argentina manager as he stands in the technical area, urging his team on with movements of his pudgy arms. He's a diminutive footballing colossus, Diego, so very big and so surprisingly small at the same time. A contradiction which was his main strength – or one of them at least – during his career. A playing career which took him from the slums of somewhere to a massive house somewhere else, stopping only for a short spell at Barça; a long one at Napoli; a World Cup winner's medal and a World Cup ephedrine ban; a fifteen-month suspension for failing an Italian dope test; a stomach bolt fitting, and, of course, the Hand of God goal.

Yes. The Hand of God goal, punched in against England in the quarter finals of the 1986 World Cup, in Mexico City. I look at Maradona's left hand, where it falls beyond the plasticated cuff of his team jacket, and I think about the Hand of God. Except I don't because our keeper hoofs it and it's on we go.

I'm partnering Gerrard in the heart of the team, and doing – even considering that my commentary, I admit, may occasionally display a pro-Kev/anti-everyone else bias – very well. I didn't exactly make our goal – stuck away by the spud-headed dynamo Rooney – but I was pivotal to the flow of the sumptuous passing move which built to it, laying on, as I did, a tidy, inch-perfect pass to Villa's Carlton Cole.

One nil, it is. And jumping up and down, the crowd are, shouting some shit with the word 'Ingles' at the end. No doubt we are not receiving the greatest of compliments from the Buenos Aires crowd.

No matter.

We came here to play football, and to win. Not to ingratiate ourselves with the South American footballing cognoscenti.

Real Madrid defender Gabriel Heinze receives the ball from their keeper Juan Carrizo and mazys forward, bringing it out from the back and for some reason – his hair probably, I have never liked his hair – I just sort of wig out and pelt towards him, with no obvious footballing logic, catching him hard and unfairly on the shin, way after he's released the ball into the path of Maxi Rodriguez, their jinky Atlético midfielder.

I go down with Heinze, collapsing bolt-to-the-headly on to the lush pampas of the Monumental pitch, and as I lie there, Heinze rolling around, clutching his well-paid shin and managing to spit unmentionables at me as he does so, I toss a sly little glance towards the Ukrainian ref who now has his back to me, running up the pitch to keep tabs on the play.

Rodriguez is chalky-booting it on the right and he makes a half from our cheetahish left back Ashley Cole, and pounds up almost to the by-line before chopping one back into the path of their Barça striker Lionel Messi who uncharacteristically flubs it, drilling what he must think is a shot well wide and so failing to test our veteran keeper Jame-o, who mercifully is not wearing one of his pony haircuts on this evening of top-class international football.

Another goal kick to us.

But before it's taken, the man in black makes over, popping his hand in his pocket and brandishing a yellow towards me, a card which without question would be available in any reputable stationers – not in that exact size, possibly, but card like it, in a larger format perhaps. Easily available to the layman, this type of card may be, but in the context of this match, the flaunting of the yellow is a profound action. Twenty-eight minutes in and I'm in the book.

Not happy.

The ref does his little swirly finger motion, indicating I should turn so he can see the back of my shirt, and so jot my name and number down. But I interrupt this little piece of footballing theatre by making towards him.

'It's a friendly,' I say to the Ukrainian official. 'You don't card in a friendly. You gonna put that in your book as well? Friendly. Shall I spell it for you? F. R. End. Lee.'

'Move away,' he says, as though I'm some kind of unruly labrador.

But, 'The Captain is allowed to seek clarification from the officials,' I say, not that he is, and not that I am the Captain, but you know, worth a try.

And, 'Move away,' he says again.

Which I don't. Instead, I fix him with a Kevish glare and, 'Four hundred and eight,' I say, to which he looks all brow-rumpled.

'Four hundred and eight times, I reckon,' I say.

But he doesn't seem to get it.

I clear up the confusion. 'The amount more than you I earn a year.'

Not that I see any of it, these days.

But the boy does not like that. He's feeling the tension now and so he reaches into his pocket again and it's red. It's actually a red.

The man in black is sending me. Propelling me towards an early bath with one simple brandish of his card. Incomprehensible.

'For fuck's sake,' I say, getting all close up to him so that he can smell my anger. 'Can't take a bit of banter. I mean, you just yellowed me. You dished it out. But you can't take it. Fucking officials.'

He just stands there, looking away from me, looking up into the stands somewhere, refusing to make contact with the King eye. Impassive, he is, despite having wrecked the King full international debut, despite having exiled me from my true refuge. Despite that, he just stands there. So I stand there too. I stand *at* him, in fact. Refusing, via the medium of body language, to accept the man in the middle's decision.

But Gerrard's over and he's got his arms round me in some kind of bearish hug and he's seeking to remove me from the ref's vicinity, so to say, and I yield to the Liverpool midfielder and allow myself to be pulled away, though I do twist the excellent King head so that I continue to stare at the ref. And then I'm walking towards the dugouts, in front of which Capello now stands, looking vexed by the recent turn of events. And next to him is Stuart Pearce, glaring at me, and the crowd all around the Monumental are going ballistic, they are ballisticating right across the stadium, lifting the stadium roof off. Not that it has a roof.

But if it did, it would be off.

Like me.

And these changing rooms are shit, and I Kev quickly into my clobber, the Kato One Wash trousers, the Kling by Kling Fragment of Dreams T and the Shofolk Alaric Kid Robot shoes. Then I walk out of the changing rooms, not turning right and taking the degrading walk back down the tunnel, to sit all shame-faced on the bench, but instead I turn left and walk away from the pitch, heading towards the players' entrance, out of it, into the staff car park, and beyond, on to the deserted walkways leading up to the Argentinian national stadium.

Outside and the Ascent Racetrack Legends rings and – finally! – it's the Chins.

'Not too bright of you, Kev, the early bath. Watching it on the TV. Things are getting to you, mate.'

'Can it, Billy. Any news?'

'No news at all, Kev. Can't find the prick anywheres. He has properly gone to ground. Want me to keep looking?'

'Any point, Billy?'

'Honestly? No fucking point, mate. Tried everything.'

I close the call and it all just hits me.

I feel shattered and wretched; boneless as a ball bag.

Dismissed on full England debut; exiled from the sanctum. And what am I to do? I can't keep shelling out Colly's fucking Danegeld. I can't. I don't have the rent for it. And Caxton's on me now. Caxton knows, I'm sure of it. Old custard head has done his little custardy sums. And what's he going to do? Go to the red-tops? Blackmail me too? Go to the filth?

The dreams of silverware and lifestyle glory, and proper fucking customer protection, they're almost over. I wanted too much. I pushed too hard.

The challenge, the match, the cup's nearly lost.

The gaff, the Bents, the Wag slip away.

I trudge slowly forward. I have nothing left but my consumer idealism. It is the only pure thing that remains. I spot a food vendor standing all lonely on the stadium walkway, touting some grub from his little wheelie cart. Burgers or something. Or chicken, perhaps: el cockadoodledoo, as they no doubt call it in the primitive Argentinian language.

Wearily I make towards him and wearily I smile, seeming to

order some grub off him, not using Argentinian words as such, but instead using the international language of waving my cash and pointing. And while he's delving into the cart to put the snack together, I slowly pull out the Victorinox Voyager Lite pocket knife – obtained, once more, at customs – and stretch going-through-the-motionsly over his cart to prick a neat if lacklustre little hole directly into his windpipe, just below his Appleio Adamso, to use the local phrase.

At which he looks all shocked.

'With onions,' I say, in a deflated, gentle voice, nodding towards the food in his cart.

But to be honest and frank about it, not even the service is so good now. He's staggering about, not even looking at the food, instead eyeing me in a sort of shocked manner, which is rude. And if he's doing this now, with only one customer waiting, how is he going to cope when the fixture is over and the 65,000 capacity crowd is on him, demanding el burgero with relisha, or what have you?

'You need an assistant,' I say, helpfully.

But he's just sort of wheezing and rasping now.

So, 'Assistanto?' I clarify, wanting, all of a sudden, his business not to fail, because despite the poor service, I do actually see something in him. He could make something of himself, if he sorted things out. I mean, his cart is clean and tidy, he has a well-pressed – if shit – uniform on. He has consumer satisfaction potential. I believe that, I really do.

I mean, if I hadn't been unfairly sent off, and so compelled to set an example to this peasantish food vendor about the need for justice on the pitch, I might even have invested in this little snack cart. After all, it is quite nifty.

I pick up the little wooden handles of the cart. Nice. Not too heavy. I push the cart forward and go on a little mazy along the empty walkway, returning it promptly to the now-collapsed proprietor, to assure him I have no designs on stealing his pride and joy.

'Very manoeuvrable,' I say to him. And I mean it. I am not just buttering him up, ensuring good relations between our two top-tier footballing nations. Not at all. It is a sincere compliment. It *is* a well-designed food stall. Really.

Shame really, that the Ukrainian official made me seek retribution from this up-and-coming food retailer, who could, you would be inclined to predict, have made it all the way in *Dragon's Den*, or some other entrepreneurial finance forum – be that televised or not – had he not just taken a blade to el throatio.

'You thought of franchizing this?' I ask, though again I am forced to clarify to the now prone and bleating chef.

'Franchise-o?' I ask.

But to no avail. Whatsoever. And do you know what? I have lost my appetite. Well, not exactly lost it. I know where my appetite is, it's just that it's shrunk. Probably all that twitching he's doing.

I turn and sigh and walk forlornly away, the weakening gasps of the dying vendor forming an appropriately mournful soundtrack for my lonely trudge.

The Vertu trills. A text from Sas: *The zoo have agreed thirty thousand each for hire of the wedding tigers.*

I throw up and stagger down the last of the walkway, through the car park and back into the stadium. I make the changing rooms just as the boys are coming in for the half time pep talk.

'Ten men, you dozy cunt, King.'

'What the fuck were you thinking? You fucking cat's cock.'

And they hate me, all other ten – it *seems* – of the three lions hate me.

Capello doesn't even look at me.

humpty donty

'Why won't you talk about the football murders, Kev?'

'Because, Don, they're not what everyone says they are.'

We're on the extensive terracing surrounding my infinity pool, sitting on two of the many artfully placed, anodized aluminium Luma contemporary chairs. Well, I'm sitting on one. Don's sort of *oozing* across his chair, rather than actually sitting on it, him being such a weighty knacker and everything. Between us, on the Gaze Burvill triangular oak Cloister Collection table with rotating slate centre, is Caxton's Panasonic RQ-A170 dictaphone, its rubbish little tape heads spinning round, its red recording light feebly illuminated.

I am wearing Atelier La Durance Royston broken twill 12.5oz Selvedge slim jeans, a Yohjiyamamoto check shirt with attached scarf and Raf Simons Half Blocked Military trainers. Don is wearing…Well, he's not exactly *wearing* anything, he's more just covered-up by his clobber, rather than actually wearing it, as such. And while it's a relief that his I Can't Believe It's Not Butter-type physique is not in view, the things he's covered it with – clothes you might call them, at a stretch, anyway – are not exactly Premiership quality.

I wanted Don to be firmly in my clutches. Hence I suggested that we exit his dirty cave and have this interview session at my sensational – if, since this morning, officially repossessable – modern manor house.

'Look, Kev, the publishers have made it pretty simple. Talk about the football murders or hand back the advance.'

'I...'

'What's the block, Kev?'

'I...'

So why don't I fake it, talk to Don about these football murders, that are not even football murders? Why not just remove the role of customer idealism from these vigilante strikes? But I can't. Because that idealism is my bedrock and I cannot betray my Kevest part.

But Caxton's still trying. 'Release yourself,' he says – which seems a bit ridiculous – leaning forward, his face all coaxish and eager and 'confide in me'.

And though I cannot lie about the football murders, perhaps I – being so very, very tired – might instead take the opposite path and disclose the full, frank truth: tell Caxton all. And as I think this, I feel the shackles and harnesses that have tied Kev in, held Kev up, begin to loosen and inside I stumble, stumble, stumble; and what fine relief it would be to share, to unburden myself of these lonely vows. And as Boswell documented Dr Johnson's invention of baby oil, the dictionary, and cotton buds, so perhaps Caxton may be my witness.

'Release yourself, Kev,' Caxton lullingly repeats, and I am swooning.

And there's a tempting, terrible silence. And I look at Caxton now, out of the corner of Kev's eye, and he is staring straight forward, unmoving, silent, thinking perhaps that he has done enough, and that one more word or gesture will spook me, and that I am about to reveal to him my vigilante side. And I think that I am.

And I stare straight forward too, looking far away, beyond even the needlessly extensive terracing, to all those trees and shit that clump here and there within my breathtaking rural views, and each leaf or newt or lice or whatever seems to be beckoning Kev on to confession. And it all rises up towards my throat in a truthy sort of burp...

'Don, I...'

'What, Kev?'

'I...I...'

But the words won't come. I cannot confess.

So what then should I do? I feel so tired, but perhaps I might lift one of the many Luma contemporary chairs in anodized aluminium – one, perhaps, with nutmeg-coloured seat cushion – and make towards old custard head.

And perhaps then, if the energy came, I should lash the heavy chair across Caxton's Caesar-like hairstyle, poinging his head with erstwhile King athleticism, so that a section of the rubbish Caxton skull cracked open suddenly, all Humpty Dumptyishly, as he performed some shit little groan and fell sideways from his chair, to hit a section of the terracing.

And maybe then, if the King verve was somehow renewed, I could lean down – as of old, as in my pomp – and peer in though the new gap in Caxton's skull, thinking for a moment about dipping a few soldiers into the boiled egg of his brain, before realizing that that was madness, and instead flipping him over, so that he faced upwards.

And 'Did you know it was me?' I might then ask, if I had the gusto, as I stared at his clammy face, greying quickly like an overboiled meat shank.

Then 'Cus...' Don would perhaps say, all trail-offishly, so that I had to bend right down towards the gawping zero of his mouth, before, 'Cus...tomer...ser...vice, Kev,' he might weakly but ecstatically conclude.

And then perhaps I might smile at him, thinking that although he was my adversary, my yellow-haired nemesis, still he was the only one who truly understood me. And I might then summon the power to lift the Luma chair once more, and finish Caxton off with a few affectionate if clinical donks to his head, before constructing a raft – using, perhaps, the Hekman Maison de Provence leather cocktail ottoman from the King lounge – placing the Caxton corpse on that raft and floating it out into the infinity pool, arcing burning arrows...

'Kev…'

Hang on. What's that?

'Kev,' a voice now says, and I come to and look at Don, but it's not actually Caxton that's speaking, that's saying my name as such, because the voice instead seems to emanate from the King mind.

'Kev…Kev,' it says in my inner ear, if you will, and whose is that voice? Because I know it, but somehow can't place it. It's the voice that advised me to do the Lampards, to re-commit to my pure vigilante life. The voice is visiting me again…And is it Nicky Campbell maybe? But no. I know Campbell's burr too well, and this direct and passionate voice lacks his joshing subtlety.

Is it Lord Coe then, whispering to me in the simple, emotional manner he used during his critical presentation to the International Olympic Committee in Singapore, July 2005, a presentation which secured the very Olympics for London?

But no. Too untutored, too raw for Baron Coe.

Then, 'Don't do Caxton,' this unidentified, charismatic inner voice intones.

And I think, 'Fuck off,' but something is happening in my brain, some odd slackening somehow, as knots unknot, and ravels unravel. And there's a Kevish sense of calm suddenly all around me. And everything unclear is now clear. And the voice is right. It's as fresh as the daisy on your face.

Caxton *is* more use living, he's better off alive.

And there's a way out for Kev. I can see it.

I've been on the back foot far too long, absorbing the pressure, pinned in my own half, but it's time to run the channels and press; through the middle of the park as well as down the flanks. Because, that's it. I'm not taking this any longer, I'm on the fucking offensive. I've spotted the perfect pass and it's on.

I turn and look at Caxton, an irresistible smile on my face.

'Nice session, Don. Really good. The book's going to be brilliant.'

Caxton turns to me, he crumples his forehead and narrows his eyes in 'what the fuck?' He opens and closes his mouth. But I don't care about that. I batter on, all chipper.

'But best be going now, though. See you next week, yeah?'

And before he can speak, I stand and saunter quickly away, across my extensive poolside terracing and over towards the Bents.

the world of steak

I can feel the lifestyle coming back, seething into every gland and orifice.

I know just what I'm doing.

I check the Panerai Radiomir Black Seal timepiece then reach for the red card which I've placed on the bedside table for just this moment.

'You're off,' I say to the Mexican, turning towards her and showing her the card. She shrugs but climbs from the Hypnos bed, walking to the corner of the room, where she slips from her King team shirt and dons the muck she normally wears.

After the incident with Gravesy, it seemed prudent to liaise with the Central American professional in hotel suites, and no longer in her boudoir. Because of course, despite the aggrieved toothing that I came by via the Gravesy fist, I do still care for the boy, I do not want him to spot me once more grappling his sweetmeats. Hence this little session at the Athenaeum, a *Travel and Leisure* magazine-listed top 500 world hotel, on London's famous Piccadilly.

The Mexican picks up the cash she's owed from the bedside table, then walks towards the door and leaves, not pausing for a moment, not even casting me a glance as she goes. Many might see that as rude. But not me.

No complaints. No looking back. That is dignity.

I climb from the Egyptian cotton sheets, enjoying the

combination of English elegance and twenty-first-century technology that the suite provides as I step towards the bathroom to wash my cock off. I'm expecting another visitor, and this little touch of cock wash etiquette is what separates the gentlemen from the beasts.

Back in bed and I look around, enjoying the discreet glamour of the suite.

Unfold Kev's excellent plan now?

No. I will savour. I will wait a little longer.

The phone rings. Receptionist.

'Send her up,' I say and then lie there waiting for my second match of the day to arrive. Not a professional this time, but a layman. Or laywoman, if you will. Because a man of taste and refinement should not always fuck hookers. He should seek to enter civilians as well at times, so as not to lose sight of the fact that some women are not meat, and they cannot always be ordered out for, as a civilian might call up for a Chinese takeaway, or a Kazakhi home delivery meal even, in these increasingly cosmopolitan times. Yes, a gent should not pay for all his shagging, but should also stay in touch with the more sensitive side of the feminine experience, by fucking amateur birds as well.

There's a little knock on the door.

'Come in,' I say.

'Hi,' she says, this girl who's always hanging around the training ground, waiting for exit autographs, and more as well, it seems. She looks OK. She's tried to dress well, and considering the fact she's on a civilian's wages, she's done all right. She's got great big tits. Not as big as Sas', but very big nonetheless.

'Come over here,' I say to this eager member of the football fanny base.

'Show me your studs,' I say and she looks a little puzzled, but I beckon her over and she stands, her back to me by the side of the bed, and lifts her foot up so that I can see the sole of her shoe.

'Fine,' I say. 'Let's have a look at your hands.'

She pushes her hands towards me, fingers spread, and I point at the two gold rings on her left hand.

'Tape them up, or take them off,' I say, and she eases them off her fingers and puts them on the bedside.

'Any other jewellery?' I ask, and she reaches inside her top and pulls out a necklace, which she slips over her head and places next to her rings.

'Right. Fine. You're ready to come on.'

She nods and starts to strip.

I check the Panerai Radiomir Black Seal.

'Twenty minutes left. You're an impact sub. Try and make an impression on the game.'

Again she nods and I lift the Egyptian cotton sheet. 'Get amongst them.'

Twenty minutes later and I'm stood in the bathroom, changing up into my Balenciaga pin dot suit, Kolar pleated Chambray shirt and Alden Cordovan lace boots. The girl, who was an eager if unspectacular substitution, is in the suite behind me. I've already red-carded her, but she won't leave the field. She's just sort of hanging about in there in the bed, although play has clearly moved up to the other end of the pitch.

Why won't she go when she's carded? As the Mexican did. That's the problem with screwing civilians. It keeps the romance alive, I admit, and that is a good thing, but they don't have the same dignity as hookers. The same stoic calm. When a hooker gets carded, a hooker walks. But straight red a zone fifteen wannabe Wag and they just hang about, protesting. Not good for the image of the game.

Anyway. I'm dressed and I walk by the wannabe and out the door.

I stroll down the corridor to the lift, which I take, then emerge into the sumptuous decor of the reception area.

I walk over to the receptionist and pay.

'Have the Bentley brought round,' I say.

'Very good, sir.'

You would.

'And oh,' I add, all calm like. 'There's an intruder in my room.'

I walk from the hotel and give it a bit of the old foot tap on the pavement. The Bents arrives. I nod to the motor monkey in the camelish rag, but his hair is shit so I don't tip him. I slide into the Bents, pop on the Stereophonics *Greatest Hits,* and fire up the engine.

Right. I glance at the Panerai. Plenty of time to make the reception. Unroll the old plan now? And actually, yeah, OK. Why not? I feel pretty relaxed as it goes.

Okay dokay.

I pick up the Vertu and call, cancelling the weekly ninety grand payment to Colly's account, then I text Colly's phone: *Fuck you,* I write, straightforwardly.

Next, I call Billy Four Chins.

'Billy. Got another little job for you. First of all, I want you to call this bloke Don Caxton. Here's what I want you to say...'

In five mins flat the plan's on the go and I am feeling better than for weeks. I'm erect with pure Kevness. I check the timepiece. I knock one out. I wang the Bents up Piccadilly, bend it on to Shafts Ave, then hang it left. I park the motor then Kev excellently over to Soho Square.

The coach is already there, outside the FA HQ. I deplore – yes, deplore – this persistent use of coach, resent that it is so intrinsic a part of the humpty lifestyle. But what can you do? It's a team sport and we all need to travel together, apparently. Though I can't see why a stretch limo wouldn't tick the boxes, as opposed to this cereal-box-like transport, which is the favoured choice of management, across all levels of the game.

I excel towards the coach, and there's Stuart Pearce stood on the door, hustling the players onboard for the short trip to Downing Street.

'Stuart,' I say.

'Fuck off, Kev,' he replies as I get on the coach.

He's a master of the banter, Pearce. And since coming up with my little plan, I'm feeling better about everything, including my England debut, inauspicious though my sending-off was. I'll get back on the good foot, England-wise. Starting with the avalanche of silverware that'll undoubtedly come Kev's way in the next few weeks. That should twist Capello's jutting jaw in the King direction.

Anyway. A load of the England squad are already on the coach. There's Man City wideman Shaun Wright-Philips. There's Terry, and Ferdinand and Rooney and Gerrard. Yep. There's little Joey Cole up at the back, and Gary Neville, trying to look all serious despite his sub-Musketeer facial hair. I stride down the coach aisle and sit down next to Jermain Defoe and he nods at me and then looks out the window. A couple more of the boys arrive and then Capello gets on and we're off.

Out on to the Charing Cross Road, shimmy it round Trafalgar on to Whitehall, then right on to Downing Street, just before the Cenotaph. Colly calls but I do not take it. I listen to his message though. Not happy, that lad. Seems a bit cross about something. The tit.

Off the coach, tra la la, and we're through the famous black door of Number Ten, into some kind of entrance hall with pinkish carpets and black and white checked tiles. Up some staircase and we file into a big reception room, with pillars and some fussy coving and a Persian rug spread out across the parquet floor.

Anyway, there's a chandelier as well, in here, and there's a load of cameras lined up on the far wall and behind these cameras are a load of blokes dressed in dark-coloured outdoor jackets, which appears to be the favoured wardrobe staple of your lensman but which seems inappropriate in the elegant grandeur of the PM's crib.

Still. We – the national squad – stand around for a bit on the Persian, having a few snaps taken, getting a bit of filming done, and waiting for the arrival of the tubby Scotsman.

And here he is. Gordon Brown. Wandering in through the door, the economic wonderman and glowering square face. The actual Prime Minister himself, which means he's like a normal minister, but primer, which is how they do it in the world of steak also, where you have normal steak, and prime steak.

Not that he is a steak. No. He's the leader of this country, the hand on the tiller of the Queen's ship, and for this he should be accorded respect, even if he is a miserable, short-tempered Jock twat.

Anyway, this PM makes to the centre of the room and the England squad sort of parts around him and then he waves Capello over towards him and they shake. Brown does the, 'Pleased to meet you,' bollocks. And then he faces the cameras, Brown does, with Capello stood next to him.

'I'd like to thank everyone for coming today, both the press and England national squad,' Brown says. 'We're here to send a message out to the young people of this country, to use the positive power of these players, as role models, to show what can be achieved by young men.'

Very much so, PM.

'There can be nobody unaware of the spate of knife attacks plaguing the country, especially in the world of football...'

Jesus Christ. Even the PM's fallen into the trap.

But, 'They're not football murders,' I do not shout. Because this is not the place for it. Button it, Kev. Enjoy your special day.

'We are here today,' the PM continues, 'to discuss with these players some ways out of the trap of violent crime.'

He wibbles on like that for a while, bigging up this Knife Crime Crisis Summit, as it has been billed. He lists some stats about knife attacks on the city streets, and it does get a bit Pro-Zoney at times, what with all the figures being bandied, but nonetheless I am impressed with the PM's vision which is in marked contrast to his lard-arsed, volcanic image.

I am fully behind the PM on this. I deplore – that word again, and again used correctly, used from the heart – the use of violence against others, unless, naturally, that violence is harnessed to a particular and socially useful end. The protection of consumer standards, for example, is a legitimate reason to wield the knife against those who would drag the customer experience into the gutter, those who would seek to defile our very lifestyle.

But the kind of post-pub carve-up that the PM here outlines is not the way forward for the youth of this country, no matter how many pots of Artois they have skulled in the preceding hours. He is absolutely right on this one and I am fully behind him.

He finishes his little speech and there's some photo ops with the PM and some of the senior members of the squad, myself not included, which is noted. And then there's a kind of mingley free-for-all, with some political advisers or something now in the room and wandering about, chatting here and there with the England boys.

But guess what? Soon as the PM finishes his little chat with thrust-chinned Italian disciplinarian Fabio Capello, he seems to be heading over to me, towards his Kevcellency. But then, *of course* he's over to me. He can spot the talent, straight off, this boy.

Brown's got his hand out to me, which I shake.

'Kevin King,' he says. 'Pleased to meet you.'

'Likewise, PM. Or is it The PM?'

'Gordon's fine. I saw the game the other night,' he says. And is that a little smile on his dour yet chubby lips? I think it is.

My phone starts to ring. Colly. I turn it off.

'You weren't on the pitch very long,' Brown says, now smiling fully. And a lot of people in my position – not that there are a lot, or even any, because I am a truly bespoke and Kevish individual – might take this smile of the PM's as an example of your Scotsman's traditional gloating at English sporting fuck-ups.

But of course it's not.

dented casserole dish

Boggle-eyed TV pundit and ex-Tottenham marksman Garth Crooks makes towards me in the tunnel at Goodison Park, mic in his hand.

'A quick word for the cameras, Kev?' he asks, all politely.

'Why not, Garth.'

He's got some camera-wielding henchman waiting by the advertising boards, and I step over, positioning myself excellently in front of the logos.

'Right, Kevin,' he says. 'We're on air in three seconds.'

He does a little countdown for me, then, 'Well, Kevin,' he says, 'your first major domestic honour. With this away draw to Everton, I can confirm that you are the Premier League Champions.'

'What?'

'I can confirm that you're the Premiership Champions.'

'Garth?'

'Yes?'

'We've just been running up and down the pitch with the trophy for the last ten minutes.'

'Yes?'

'I'm the one who's been sweating them off out there. I've been doing that all season. I mean, I do look at the table. I do know what's going on. Do you really think I need you to confirm we've won the league?'

'It's just a figure of speech, Kev. How do you feel?'

'Well, I was feeling pretty good, you know, clinching it here at Everton, a great club, with a great pedigree. The sort of club which could enter Crufts. If it was a dog. Which it isn't. I mean, I *was* feeling good, elated even.'

'Right? OK?'

'But then I come in here. Into this tunnel. And you stand there with your weird goldfish eyes and tell me I've won the league, when I obviously know that. And to be honest, Garth, it's taken the edge off things really.'

'Kevin, I…'

'Where do you get off, Garth? Shepherds in Uzbekistan know we've won the league. Submariners know it by now, and you're stood there, in your frankly mince clobber, stating the obvious, and being paid good money for it. I mean, not loads, not as much as me, obviously, nowhere near what I'm on, but still more wedge than your average civvy, and looking at you, I can't help feeling that the standards of punditry in this country have gone to the dogs.'

'Kev.'

'Not to the aforementioned Crufts, obviously, because they wouldn't be let in. More to Battersea, really, to the dogs' home there. That's where punditry standards have gone, Garth, to Battersea dogs' home. And you've taken them there. On a lead, Garth. And I just think you need to sort yourself out, before, you know, you have some kind of accident.'

'*What!*?'

I shake my head.

'You've wrecked this title for me, Garth, squeezed all the joy out of it with your dismal punditry. You've tarnished the silverware, dented football's casserole dish, so to say. The people of Britain deserve better than you, Garth.'

I walk off.

Fucking Crooks.

the unforgiving bracknell track

I check the Ascent. Seven missed calls from angry old Colly, today alone. Give a fuck. I pop the Vertu in the Andrew Mark Marshall and tune in to the changing room.

You might have thought that Neeskins would be giving it the blood and thunder at this juncture, might have thought he'd be involved in some puce-faced rant about passion and the need for unwavering commitment. But not a bit of it. Neeskins instead is sitting down – wearing, it seems, some carpet slippers, and drinking a cup of the old herbal tea – looking almost like he couldn't give one.

Instead, our eccentric Dutch manager has left it to his head coach, the Spaniard Morales, who won the Champs himself with Real in the not-so-distant past, to give it the pep talk. Which is, you know, quite hard for him, considering his English is, in a word, absolutely fucking shit.

I tune out again, I really do, catching the occasional use of the word 'footballistically' and the word 'footballization' from the Spanish coach, but otherwise looking at the floor: the floor of the changing rooms in the Stadio Olimpico in Rome, a floor which is five minutes away from facing Bayern Munich in the Champions League final.

Not that the floor has made the side.

You can't pick a floor. UEFA wouldn't allow that. And, to be fair and honest, they'd be right. Football is a game played by men. Not floors.

I have my own pre-game prep and I focus on it now. I think of the gaff and the Bents – now almost safe – of all the cash I've ever spunked, and all the clobber I've ever bought. Then I think of my wonderful fiancée Sas, and her absolutely massive tits. Which are not all her own work, admittedly, but who doesn't need a hand in the midst of this recession? Apart from Kev, obviously. Kev who will soon be righted again – Colly-wise, cash-wise and everyways-wise – just as soon as Four Chins calls to tell me the bait has been taken. Which he will. Soon enough. Because irresistible. My plan is.

Anyway. I think about the coming game. Then for some reason I drop the eyelids – which is not part of the usual Kevish prep – and something not everyday seems afoot because I somehow find myself compelled – yes, compelled, almost by forces unseen, you might say – to think about football and marketing genius Kevin Keegan. And then suddenly – kabam! – Keegan stands before the Kevish mind's eye in his bubble-permed pomp, with all his pots and pans and gongs and whisks and what have you around his neck, wearing one of those rubbish 1970s tracksuits with the little strap that goes under the foot.

He's wearing all that. And Keegan is standing in a deserted football ground somewhere, its grass supernaturally green, which you can see, even though it is the dead of night, because of the four flaming suns of the floodlights, which seem to float almost, at each corner of this empty pitch. And around Keegan is a halo, a smelly halo, if you will, a halo comprised of Brut 33 aftershave, a fragrance and brand, remember, which he took enormously downmarket, while still retaining its essentially masculine appeal.

And Keegan is standing there, permeated with the great smell of Brut, and clanking slightly – in a musical and subtle way – beneath the weight of all his silverware, which as I say is strewn across him, some of it even encaptured by his tenaciously curled hair, and he seems to be leaning forward; leaning forward to speak to me.

'Kev,' Kev says, and it's him! I recognize that now. It's the voice that advised me before, that told me not to do Caxton, that re-swore me to the way of the vigilante.

And, 'Yes, Kev,' I eagerly say. But not out loud. I say this word instead with my mind's mouth.

'Kev,' he says, again.

'Yes, mate,' I say and I look at Keegan and I know he's about to tell me, impart the ultimate wisdom of football to me, decant it into my mind's ear, so to say. And the Brut is billowing around Keegan now, in a great mystical cloud, and he's leaning closer towards me, and I know that he's about to tell me how to pull the footballing sword from the Champions League stone, if you will.

But then I hear Wally de Groot, our Captain for the night, who, it seems, has followed Morales in the team talk stakes, shout, 'Let'sh fuck them up the arsh!'

Which is pithy. And helpful. And rousing.

But it is not the advice of charismatic football and brand endorsement leviathan Kevin Keegan. And now Keegan has turned and is walking up the deserted floodlit pitch, the Brut halo enlarging and swirling and becoming a curtain almost, a curtain which falls between me and Keegan's footballing wisdom. And he's gone. And the football wisdom is gone with him. Like Merlin, he is vanished into the mists of footballing time.

And when we're out on the pitch, after all the fanfare and the other cobblers, with the game underway, and with the 82,000 capacity Stadio Olimpico crowd baying like wounded lobsters and the global TV audience nudging one billion, I feel *not* enraptured with this, the biggest night of my footballing life so far, but more bereft, abandoned sort of, as though I am a deformed, tabby kitten which Keegan has stuffed into a seldom-used haversack, weighed down with soggy grass cuttings and lobbed into a trench.

That's how I feel.

Not that I think Keegan meant to abandon me. His vision did, I believe with all my eyes, want to impart the wisdom of football to me, it was just that we were interrupted, Keegan's message to me was scrambled by Wally de Groot's incautious but rousing urge to sporting sodomy.

And so weirdly, I'm not up for it. I, Kev King, seem to have lost my footballing mojo. Which is proved when Bayern's charismatic French wingman and current German Footballer of the Year Frank Ribéry pings it off my toe in the central third and cuts inside, feeding the Bayern hitman Miroslav Klose on the edge of the area.

And do you know what? I don't track back.

Inconceivable.

I feel all jelly-legged and instead I peer around the ground, staring up towards the exec boxes of this Roman amphitheatre-type Roman amphitheatre, and seeing our Chairman Abtum Bahta looking down at me from on high, seeming all puzzled. And next to him sits der Kaiser, footballing legend and Bayern president Franz Beckenbauer, a World Cup winner as both player and coach, and a man who has hoisted the Champions League trophy – not that he needed a hoist, his arms being strong enough to do the job alone – on three separate occasions. And Beckenbauer seems to have a little smile on his lips, and is he looking at me?

No, in fact he's looking towards our goal where our Uruguayan keeper Anselmo now lies sprawled on the turf, the ball behind him in the onion bag, as Klose and his Munich teammates wheel away, leaping on each other in acceptable sporting molestation, to celebrate the opening goal of the Champions League final.

That was my fault. It was.

Lost the ball cheaply. And made no attempt to win it back. More precious than gold, the ball is, and I threw it away. Not that I threw it. Because this is football and you play it with your feet. Though outfield players can handle the ball, for throw-ins. But still, this is football, and I tossed possession away. And they've scored. A goal.

Disconsolately we trudge back up the field for the restart, but I'm not right. I know that. In fact I begin to walk towards our bench, attracting the gaze of Henk Neeskins as I do, and as I near the touchline Neeskins emerges to the very edge of his technical area.

'You've got to bring me off, gaffer,' I say.

Which may sound like I'm asking Neeskins for a hand job. But I'm not. I am admitting my own error, I am letting him know that the King footballing mechanism is somehow strangely knacked on this crucial night of European football. A night when history will be made. Or at least written. Not that we have pens. Because this is football and you play it with a ball. Not a pen.

Neeskins looks at me all disgustedly, and then turns his head and looks behind him to the bench, spotting dainty Croatian midfield playmaker Janko Lasich. He gives Lasich the 'get warmed up' eyes. But what can Lasich do out here? Bayern are a big side, and they are big with it, and Lasich will be brushed off the ball as though he were a rogue piece of twill on the knee of a pair of Comme Des Garçons Homme Plus tartan appliquéd trousers.

That much I know. I can't let this happen.

Confused, I turn away from the technical area and make towards the centre circle, where our boys are waiting for me, hugely fucked off expressions on their faces, and the ref has the whistle to his lips and he blows and on we go.

And, 'Kev,' I hear a voice say, and look around.

'Kev,' again it comes. But it's not my teammates.

I recognize the voice, its quivering passion. It is Keegan, it must be, talking to me directly, as though he were the fourth official communicating to the man in the middle, via the means of a high-tech earpiece.

But then Keegan is not around.

Still, 'Kev,' the voice continues, disobeying various physical laws. 'Remember *Superstars*.'

And I think, 'What the fuck?'

But, 'Remember *Superstars*,' the mystical disembodied voice of Keegan insists once more.

And I do remember *Superstars*, the long-running TV sports show in which athletes from a variety of disciplines competed in a variety of sporting contests. The famously arduous gym tests, for example. And the four hundred metre run, on occasion. Weightlifting. The obstacle course. Tennis. They were all thrown in.

I *do* remember *Superstars*. TV sporting gold, it was, rewarding the most physically versatile athlete from across the entire pantheon of sporting endeavour. But what can Keegan – or rather this ethereal, Keeganesque voice which is whispering to me amidst the din of the Stadio Olimpico – mean?

And then it hits me. Smacks me Keeganly across the King footballing chops.

Nineteen seventy-six, it was, surely we all know that, the year Keegan himself appeared on *The Stars*, as I will call it. Not that I saw the famous episode when it was first broadcast. No. I am too young for that. But as a serious admirer of Keegan I have sought out the clip and studied it.

And I can see him now, picture Keegan in his skimpy blue Adidas vest, the *Superstars* logo ironed across it in a proud, gregarious font. He is on the starting line of a cinder running track in Bracknell, Berkshire, but – and this is the beauty of *The Stars* – it is not a running race in which he is about to compete.

No. Keegan is next to Dutch footballer Rudi Kroll on the starting line. But they are on *bikes*. Drop-handlebarred racing bikes, no less.

Because this is *The Stars* and this is the bike test.

The starting pistol cracks and, employing the astonishingly concentrated force which marked every stage of his career, Keegan crunches down on the pedals, the bike itself juddering under the power of the bubble-permed twice European Footballer of the Year's exertion. But this is not only about Keegan. This is a race. Between men. And Rudi Kroll is an amateur cyclist of some repute. He must be, because by the time the bikes make the first bend, Kroll has somehow edged out Keegan, has gained both the lead and the inside lane. To which Keegan massively responds, levering even more force on to the pedals.

He gains on Kroll, but midway round the opening bend, Keegan clips the Dutchman's rear wheel. The bike angles and falls. Keegan himself falls, skidding across the cinder track in a cloud of orange dust. Kroll stops. The bike test stops.

Severe skin abrasions, that's what Keegan suffers. To the back, and knees and elbows. Swathes of his Brut-saturated skin have been ripped off and lie amongst the cinders like a desiccated tea towel.

Then what?

Easy. An astonishing demonstration of sporting courage.

I can see it now. The camera on him, the *Superstars* officials crowding around as he picks himself off the track and tries to look at the damage. Which is hard, looking at your own back, I mean. Without a mirror anyway, and there are no mirrors – or any other appropriately reflective surfaces, like a highly polished kettle, for example – on the unforgiving Bracknell track. Meaning Keegan can't see the extent of the skin rip. But surely he can feel it.

But, 'I'm fine, I'm fine,' Keegan says as he stands up, waving away the fuss in a manner which might not have entirely convinced the vast TV audience. Then, entranced viewers from Mali to Macclesfield witnessed something rare and beautiful. Yes, beautiful, I am not afraid to admit that. Keegan dusted the cinders from his wife-beater vest and insisted on restarting the test. Despite the catastrophic abrasions assailing his priceless well being, he got back on the bike. He did.

And answer me this. Would Beckham have got back on the bike?

Would the likes of your Ronaldos or your Drogbas or your van Persies have returned to the saddle with such titanic courage? I think not. And that's what Keegan – the disembodied voice of

Keegan at least – is telling me, whispering to me as he is in his lilting Yorkshire voice, urging me to remember *Superstars*.

He is telling me to get back on the bike. Dust the cinders of the opening goal from the marred shoulder of the current scoreline, so to say, and return to the saddle of the match. It is a simple message. It is also genius.

I come to.

Bayern Captain and midfield enforcer Mark van Bommel is in possession. Or at least he was, because Kevin King tracks back, and as the Dutch international checks his run so as to evade our left back Ilias Pappas, who is coming terrific towards him, van Bommel unshields the ball, if you will, allowing Kev to Kev in and help himself. Because this is football and this is about the ball. And about feet. In fact, given that every player Kev knows has two feet, and not one foot, perhaps the game should be called feetball and not football. Just a thought.

Anyway.

Because the likes of your Kevin Kings has the feetball itself and he is motoring brilliant forward now, propelled not only by his own innate athleticism but also by the mystical power of Keegan.

Into the circle, still our side of the pitch, and German international Bastian Schweinsteiger makes towards Kev, who merely drops the shoulder and floats away towards their gangly number twenty-four, Tim Borowski, who is simply undone by coruscating acceleration. And then Kev looks up, eyeing the runners, assessing the channels, our Egyptian winger Ali el-Masri on the left, our Gambian striker Boro Danzo dropping off their Brazilian centre back, Lucio. And King clips the easy one into the feet of Danzo, motoring on excellently – Kevcellently – towards the edge of the Bayern box where he receives the one-two nice from the intelligent Gambian and glances up, spotting Michael Rensing, the Bayern keeper, off his line.

The chip is on, but their Belgian centre back Daniel van Buyten spots it too and back-pedals furiously to protect the net.

Not that he has pedals. But there *is* a net.

That is not a figure of speech. The net is actually there. Itself. And van Buyten is making back towards it. But is he quick enough?

King shapes up for the chip, but then, remember, feetball is a simple game, if you play it simply, which you should, and so trusting in the quality of his teammates, instead Kev squares the simplest of blind balls into the space vacated by the Belgian defender, and coming on to meet it is French marksman Leon Bédard, who catches it all sweet on his laces and absolutely fucks it – high and rising – into the top left side netting, which, as I say, is actually actual netting.

Gooooooooooooooooooooaaaaaaal!!!!

Get in. One all.

Kev wheels towards the fans in the Curva Nord behind the Bayern goal, jumping the hoardings, making across the cinder running track, pelting towards the fencing and slipping his fingers through the mesh, clambering up it and bouncing his chest off the metal, the faces of the fans close and ecstatic, the smell of their spittle all on him.

'Remember *Superstars*!' Kevin King shouts to them in a meltdown of concentrated feetballing exhilaration.

'Remember *Superstars*!'

the sacred pact of matemanship

'I don't see a problem with that, Mr King.'

'Good.'

'We should easily be able to find a way for you to parachute into the ceremony.'

Nice. I like Sophie, our new wedding planner.

Very efficient, she is, and a good multi-tasker as well, the evidence for which should be obvious, as while we discuss the upcoming King splicing, she is also bending over a La Porta Isottina oval glass desk, her Fifi Chachinil chiffon thong and 18th Amendment Colbert Two Flare jeans pooled on the floor around her Rupert Sanderson patent peep-toe pumps, as I take her from behind.

'Can I ask you a question, Mr King?'

'Naturally, Sophie.'

'What was it like scoring the winner in the Champions League final?'

'You mean that exceptional individual goal that secured us the double?'

'Yes.'

'Well…'

But there's a trilling and I reach into the back pocket of my Ann Demeulemeester floral wool trousers and whip out the Ascent Racetrack Legends limited edition with laser-etched

Silverstone circuit map, bezel-nosed radiator grille inset, and liquidmetal chassis.

Is this the hundredth call from not-got-the-message-in-any-way Colly? No. Which is good, because how many threatening phone messages can you listen to before they all bleed into one? And how many variants on 'don't pay and I'll go to the cops' can he produce? It's tiring.

Maybe the call's from Le Chins then? Because, to be honest and fair, not that I'm shitting bricks about it, but I thought Billy would have called by now.

Still. It'll happen. Soon enough.

But no, the call's from Nan.

'I'd better take this,' I say to Sophie and withdraw. 'Hello, Nan.'

'Have you seen the papers this morning, Kevin?'

'No.'

'I think you'd better look.'

'OK, Nan, I will. I'll come round and see you later.'

I end the call.

'Get a red-top up on the MacBook, Soph.'

Which she does, and there I am, front page. Or top of the screen to use the parlance more appropriate to this technology.

Kevtus Interruptus, runs the headline.

'Click on that, will you?' I ask the planner and she does so, getting the story up on to the MacBook screen. And there's a shot of me and Denise in the buff, going right at it. A shot taken just before I left to go to the Kingly, the night I first met big custardy Don Caxton. And taken, as I remember, on an RIM Blackberry Storm, by none other than Australian striker Gravesy. Gravesy with his gambling debts and his lack of contract, now that my old club has gone tits up; Gravesy with his possessive fondness for the Mexican.

I am furious.

Gravesy must have sold these pics on to the tabs. Must have. There's no other explanation. And he's an Aussie as well, heralding from a country where the institution of matemanship is held as sacred.

What has he done?

Because while he did hit me, I was prepared to let that go. Because I missed him, because he's Gravesy, and because, after all, it was a blow forged in the heat of passion, and a blow which produced interesting results, art-wise I mean, dislodging as it did the tooth that added the extra quality to my Michael Owen gism face sculpture.

Yes, I was prepared to let Gravesy's assault go. But this, well, despite it being another excellent notch on the King profile, it is also a cold-blooded attack on the standards of friendship in this country; to say nothing of the grief I'll get from Sas for not running this relationship story through Min first. Because we had a contract, me and Gravesy, an informal one, sure, but a contract nonetheless, written in endeavour on the pitch, scribed in shopping off it.

Athlete to athlete, man to man, consumer to consumer, we had a deal.

And he has torn up that contract, tossed it to the very actual winds themselves. He has annihilated the sacred pact of matemanship.

Again the Vertu trills.

Christ, it's all go. Angry Colly? Billy Four Chins?

Nope, it's neither. It's the Syrian sports Svengali. I take the call.

'Mr Shishakli.'

'Kevin, good news. Unicef want you to open an eye hospital in the Sudan.'

'What? War-torn Sudan? Saharan death zone Sudan? That Sudan?'

'I'm afraid so. But it'll be very good for your profile.'

'Maybe, but what about my health? Not so good for that, is it?'

'Football's huge over there, Kevin.'

'It's huge in France as well. Isn't there some hospital in St Tropez I can open?'

'No. Unicef work in developing countries. What about Indonesia, Kevin? That's developing. Huge emerging football country. Some very nice beaches as well.'

'Bali, you mean, round there?'

'Maybe, Kevin.'

'I'd definitely open some shit in Bali. If the hotel was right.'

chimpanzee waiter

'It's on, Kev.'

'Where are they?'

Billy tells me. Some sort of beauty spot, out in Berks, he says. Dogging spot more like. Crashed in a few housewives' back doors there myself, as it goes. I know the place. I know it well.

'Stay there, Billy.'

I close the call and re-route the Bents, flinging her west.

I send Neeskins a cheeky text, letting him know I'll be late meeting up with the team. Will he not like that, but right, we're off, the twelve-cylinder Continental GT with twin elliptical exhaust throats out of London, and do you know what? Could do without this today. Glad that Le Chins has called and that, but you know, it's cup final day, time is tight, and this might take a while.

Still, the early bird is worth two in the bush and I will seize this chance to iron things out. Not that I have an iron. Because naturally I pay some 'pino bird to uncrease the King schmutter. Anyway. Out we go. The Westway. The sun Keving all brightly down and the Wembley arch to my right, high and smooth above the chunky London skyline.

Nice. Because within that stadium, a man could shit in a different bog every day for more than seven years – including the extra leap year days which would naturally fall within that time period – without having to repeat himself, dump-wise.

The new Wembley is that good.

Thirty-five miles of power cables. Twenty-three thousand tons of steel. A four hundred and ninety-five foot circular section lattice arch.

And one football pitch. And although this footballing cathedral was delivered late and over budget, I ask myself this: was Notre Dame, for example, opened on time by the medieval masons that crafted it? Did the Parisian bishops in charge of commissioning and overseeing the gargantuan stone edifice receive a thorough pasting in the Gallic press because work on the buttressing, and gargoyles and so forth, stretched on beyond the arbitrary due date?

No, they did not.

They were given some elbow room, these priests from the Dark Ages, because of the enormity of their task. And so it is – or should be – with Wembley. You can't make a twenty-first-century footballing Mecca without cracking a few eggs together, can you?

No. Simply not. Anyway, driving. On and straight and straight and then the fields start popping up, and the old trees, and muck like that, either side, and we're getting near. I'm nearing them. And right and left and left again and I know just where they are.

I stop the Bents in a lay-by, two hundredish away, and I still it and get out, the Olukai Maoli sandals with pigskin and neoprene strap lining stepping quick now across the rutted zone zillion tarmac with the gnarly old trees shitly tenting over, and the birds or what have you giving it all the tweet as I spot Billy.

His motor – a Lancia, Christ, still, after all the fucking rubs I've handed over – is tucked right close to the bushes and he's got his back to me, looking down the road to the dogging area, the so-called beauty spot.

And I'm up close to him, my hand on his back, his head spinning round quick, his eponymous chins whiplashing softly into his burly shoulder.

'Kev, you gave me a fright.'

'They still there?'

He nods. He smiles. He points.

I look down the slender country road towards a small car park. There are two wildly variant motors stilled there and I know the both of them.

'You got a ticket for today, Billy?'

He shakes his head and I pull a spare from my Kokon To Zai embroidered track pants and hand it over.

'See you later. I'll be the one scoring the winner.'

'Thanks,' Billy says, but then just stands there.

'Off you go,' I say.

'Don't you need some muscle, Kev?'

I look him up and down. Well, actually, round and round would be more appropriate, given that the girth probably equals the height.

'You got any?'

'Any what, Kev?'

'Muscle, Billy. Go on. Chip off. See you later.'

The Chins nods then and moseys over towards the Lancia, sways in, turns her over and drives off.

And so it's eyes on the game, it's right you are then. It's chimchimaroo.

Because Caxton knew about me, right? But maybe he wasn't one tens, and certainly he was lacking the proof. And so he'd be looking for more evidence, in order to sell his hunches to the red-tops, or whatever his game was now that the biog was kiboshed. So I got Billy to call Caxton, anonymous like, and tell him about someone who really did know. Namely Colly.

And making Billy hand Colly's number to Caxton ensured that they'd meet, that Caxton would flush Colly out for Kev. Because – Kev having snipped his cash flow – Colly'd be looking for another way to earn. And yeah, OK, Colly threatened me with the Bill, but I knew that was bluff, because where's the coin for him in that?

So, with Caxton's journo connections, and with disgraced Colly's own network dried up, Colly'd be seeing pound signs over custard's head. Meaning it wouldn't take long before the special new chums were meeting up at a KFC – or a local beauty spot, it seems – and haggling over 60/40s or 50/50s. So all Chins had to do was keep tabs on Caxton, which would inevitably take us to Colly.

And, you know, the cash they'd make from this story would be huge. It would. The so-called football murderer, on course for the treble. Exposed by his ex-agent and his ghost writer. Exposed as being weirdly obsessed – how fucking dare they – with Campbell and Costner and Coe and Keegan; with customer service.

And why these two will be meeting on FA Cup day is because if I win the treble, then the asking price for the story – when King is replete with silverware, when his retinas even are endangered by the pot dazzle – will be stratospheric. Or higher.

I am getting a lob on.

I look right. I look left. Nothing coming. We're on.

I stealth all Kevly forwards, because, you know, I've got to get close, unspotted, in case Don fires up the Toyota and flees, or else Colly wakes the Jag and does one: a Jag, incidentally, which Colly must have bought back from hock once my funds kicked in for him. Because they do that, they sight me and evade the King clutches, and it's all over Kev-wise, they'll never meet up again, they'll cook up their dirty anti-consumer business all incog, hiding from Kev in their manky lairs; hanging me out to dry, wrecking my humpty and vigilante worlds with a treacherous glee.

These two get away and all will come to nothing, and what time is it actually? I check the Panerai Radiomir Black Seal timepiece. Living fuck, it's getting on. Got to do these two before kick-off and time time time is slipping through my hands.

I speed Kev up. I'm getting close. I can see that they're in the same car, that they're chatting – or however they will style this little head-to-head – inside Don's pony cart. Which is a bit weird, because given the choice, you know, you'd naturally rather chat in the Jag. But then people are weird, aren't they?

And I'm very close now. And the birds are swaying and the

trees are singing, and Colly's my side, passenger seat, window open, while the old custard head is in the driver's seat, other side, and I'm so close that I can see Colly's butcher's fingers as he scratches the back of his neck.

And I can see his fingernails, the red marks even that his scratching leaves as he chats away to Don, haggling away all Judasly about their King-centage split, and I can see Colly's eyes, the whites of them even, because – fuck! – Colly's spotted Kev, and he's turned towards me and is staring madly at me now as I dash the last few feet, the Case Trapper pocket knife with mother-of-pearl handle and grooved nickel silver bolsters already in my hand.

And Colly scrabbles for the door handle, to release it and flee from the unfamiliar Toyota, to run to the safety of the Jag and bomb away from the likes of your Kev Kings. But too late. I'm on him, thrusting the Trapper blade into the earhole of the huge Colly head; jabbing it in right firm, and so crunking it through the skull bone and then pushing, pushing on again, so that it squidges deep inside, up to the very handle, and is turned then and twisted all sharpish, and then yanked quickly out with a slurpy little pop.

'Fucking no!' Caxton shouts and I look at the knife, and there are small flecks of brain all on it, like flecks of a very grey Stilton, it has to be said. And at this point, if I had the time, if I wasn't so foisted deep in the thick of it, then I might think about having done Colly. You know, I might think about that, grieve on it, muse on how I arrived in a situ where my crusader's duty forced me to scuttle an ex-mate. And I might look at Colly, lolling already dead and heavy in the Toyota as he is, some warm grey foam emerging slowly from his ear, and mournfully hugged by the black sash of seat belt; and I might feel all bad that despite the many top items we have bought together, still, the very last thing Colly felt on this earth was fear of me, was pain at my hand.

I might think about that and I might regret it.

But I don't because, shit, the Toyota's waking up as Don's panicky hand twists the keys, and Kev does a nifty sort of break-roll across the bonnet of the Caxton car to find himself face to face with the hack, driver's side window. Except the window and door's all shut. So I draw back the King fist, I make to smash through the glass, but I can't, can I? Do that and yes certainly I may bag old custard head, I may well get my hands on the tubby journo, but the ref's not going to let me on the pitch, is he, claret oozing down the King forearm to crimson up the Wembley turf? Not going to bag the trebs that way, am I?

So I pivot sideways to raise the foot and boot the window in, but then I stop, because leather-wrapped midsole with fish-scale laser etching these Olukai sandals may have, but sturdy they are not, and I don't want to risk the hooves either, don't want to fuck my dainty metatarsals smashing through the Caxton glass, do I? Not with kick-off so very fucking close. So I scan round the car park for a rock or a branch to slam through the glass, but there's nothing here.

Fucking council. Fucking busybodies. Tidying up the beauty spot. Because where is an impromptu weapon when Kev needs one?

But right. OK. PMA. I break-roll back across the bonnet, to make for Colly's open window, but find Don's had the same thought, and he's leaning now across the Colly corpse, clicking the button locked, nervy hand twiddling the window winder round and round, sealing the motor, shutting me out.

The car's ticking over. Don's popping her into gear. He's clicking off the handbrake. He's going to drive off with dead Colly, leaving my humpty dreams tattered and broken.

I jump on the bonnet. I stand up, adopting a kind of surfboard-type balance style as Caxton begins to back the Toyota out of the car park and on to the road. I stare down at the journo through the windscreen, his movements all swift and jagged. He darts me a hot glance, his terrified, chubby eyes about to pop. Heel down through the windscreen? But no, with these stylish yet slight sandals I'll slice the feet right up.

Fuck. Deadlock. Fuck.

There's nothing for it.

Diplomacy. It's the only way.

I pluck the Ascent Racetrack Legends limited edition with laser-etched Silverstone circuit map from the Kokon To Zai embroidered track pants, flip to Caxton's number and call.

'Answer it, Don mate,' I shout at the glass, raising my eyebrows all imploringly, using Kev's unmatched athleticism to balance still on the bonnet of the reversing car.

'Answer the phone, Don,' I shout, staring at his pony Ericcson where it sits on the moulded dash shelf.

He doesn't answer. The car's in the middle of the road now, he's popping her into first, the seconds till kick-off ticking themselves away.

'We can work something out, Don, me and you,' I bellow.

Confusion now rumples the padded Caxton forehead. He glances at his ringing mobile. He could accel the Toyota and flick me off the bonnet right now, he could be away. It's all about the choices. But the hack is indecisive. It'll be the terror, muddying the functions.

He looks over to Colly, all quietly dead as such in the passenger seat, and now Don's staring at the mobile, his ears and mind and heart all full and pumped with fear of Kev.

Caxton reaches forward. He makes his choice. He picks up the phone.

Good. Right. Nice.

Close, close. But got to get this right.

'Hi, Don,' I say.

Shallow breath comes in reply. Not so great under pressure, is he, your Caxton?

'Look, Don,' I whisper all amenably, 'you drive off now and I will find you and I will kill you. Simple. As. That. You may sell the story and fuck me over, but one day, one way, I will find you and I will hurt you.'

I look down at Don. He gulps, he sweats. He gulps his sweat. Probably. And still he could pump the pedal and be away. But he points his somehow chubby peepers up at me, Don does, and, 'Don't…hurt…me…,' he manages.

'No intention, Donly mate. Need one little favour and then you're free.'

'Anything.'

Down the line I tell him my plan, and in a mo I'm off the bonnet and standing by the now open driver's side window, looking at wheezy Caxton who's got his fucking criminal Ericcson T28 in his shaking hand as he dials the good old 9s.

'Which service do you require?'

'God, get here quickly!' Caxton says, well, shouts really, staring at me as he does, and seeking, I assume, my approval, which I am in fact happy to give, because he's doing well, performance-wise.

'Colly's going to kill me,' Don continues. 'He killed them all.'

That'll do. Because I don't want Caxton telling them where we are, just yet. Because despite the looming kick-off, I need a bit of time still.

I chuck Don the 'end the call' eyes, and he does and then I let him go.

Not really.

And because I liked the feeling, because it was so very efficient, because I really am hurried by now – I crash the Case Trapper blade, handle deep, through the Caxton lug and into the brain section of the journalistic inner head. And he really does die then. Ever so. But then withdrawing the Trapper, the flecks from Don's brain are not so Stiltonly as with Colly, and if I was forced to compare Don's brain – cheese-wise, because we are cheese-speaking now – then it would be more of a dolcelatte. Or perhaps a very dry – a fibrously rustic – cottage type of cheese.

But now's not the time to think about that, about the variance in brain texture between adult males, because it's still very much business hours, and I really am pushing it for kick-off. So I shove the Toyota back into the car park, next to the Jag, and turn and pelt excellently down the road, careful not to fuck over the King

330

feet in the flimsy Olukai Maolis. Then I hop into the Bents, tonking her up to the beauty spot.

I climb out, walk to the Toyota, open the passenger door, fireman Colly out, checking there's none of his Stilton splurged on Caxton's car. Then I carry Colly to the Bents, pluck his car keys from his Triumvir Castor Raw Selvedge jeans, and chuck him in my boot.

I return to the Jag, open its boot, spotting – as I had hoped, Colly being a creature of habit – his laptop, before lifting it out and stashing it in the Bents. Finally, I return to the Toyota, wipe the Jag keys on Caxton's pony jacket, then lob them under Caxton's seat.

Fuck. Right. All done.

Back in the Bents I smooth down the Salvage Schizo Scolex T and look in the rear-view, spotting the serial killer's locked Jag, abandoned in panic presumably after he dropped and lost his car keys while killing Caxton in the journo's own car. So forcing Colly to flee on foot and provoking, no doubt, over the coming hours and days, a huge – if ultimately unsuccessful – manhunt across the fields and what have you of royal Berks.

I check my Panerai Radiomir Black Seal timepiece. Very, very tight, Kev.

Now is the time of the Bents.

I engage the twelve-cylinder Continental GT with twin elliptical exhausts and monster off, barrelling recklessly down the country lane. The Vertu rings. Neeskins. Wondering, no doubt, where his star player is. I don't take the call, I don't listen to his message, but I do reply, driving one-handed, texting other-handed: *I will be fucking there.*

All of which is proof, once more, if any were needed, of my innate quality. And I drive like a fucker, like a fucker I drive, and fields and fields and shit and I'm moving into town and soon, far off, I see the sun-coated Wembley arch, the very temple of football beneath, and I'm jumping lights and mounting kerbs and closer, ever closer, I am Keving.

I approach and find the players' parking and dash from the Bents, shouting, 'Kev fucking King,' to the security who might stop me. But the club must've told them to expect Kev and I'm inside, in the actual Wembley now, and I'm mazing through the tunnels and I'm finding the changing rooms, and I Kev in through the door and all the lads are there, and they all stare at me with rabid fucked-offness, and Neeskins is there and he shakes his weird Dutch head at me.

But industrialist Abtum Bahta's in there too, flanked by his Wii goons, which is unusual for the Parsi, this pre-game visit. Normally, he pops his little head in after a game. But still, this is his club, so I suppose he's entitled to waft in when he likes.

And he looks at me, cool as you like, Bahta does, as though I hadn't missed the pre-match lunch, and the drive-in by team coach, and the stroll about the Wembley pitch, and the pre-match gibberish from Morales, or Wally de Groot, or what have you.

'Gentlemen,' Bahta now announces to the Wembley changing room, addressing us, the cup final favourites, en masse, 'quarter of a million win bonus each.' To which there are grunts of affirmation, the sort you might hear outside Halford's if a civvy spotted a nugget on the pavement.

But it's good news. It means, surely, that the Parsi's funds are back on track, that some company, or some country or something, has been bought or sold or something, and the Parsi has come back to the liquid. And, 'Kevin,' he then says, coming straight over to the best player in the country, a player taken on a free, no less, from a struggling and now defunct Championship side, and a player, let's not forget, with whom he shares a special secret.

'Mr Bahta,' I say, winching out my right hand. A hand which he takes and shakes and then drops, peering queerly at his own palm as I spot a bit of Colly's brain, or Caxton's, on Bahta's hand, which I must have unwittingly palmed over to the Parsi.

'Stilton,' I say. 'Had a sandwich.'

'Excellent.' Bahta smiles. 'The king of cheeses. Did you get the gift I sent you, Kevin?'

'The Harry Ramsden's mushy peas, Mr Bahta?'

'Yes. The other players in the squad received a case of nineteen-eighty-nine Pommery Grand Cru Methuselah, but you, Kevin. You are special, a connoisseur of authentic working-class English culture, like myself.'

'Very much so.'

'And, Kevin?'

'What?'

'How were they?'

'The peas?'

'Yes.'

'Mushy, yeah, good.'

'I hear you're getting married, Kevin.'

'Very much so, Mr Bahta.'

'Feel free to use my yacht for your honeymoon.'

'Yeah, thanks. Very decent of you.'

He leans in all close then, giving me the 'our little joke' eyes, and whispering, 'But please don't kill my crew.'

'Right you are, Mr Bahta,' I say.

'Win today, Kevin.'

And, 'Course,' I reply as Bahta walks off.

Right. OK. The treble. The final hurdle. Concentrate.

Because having flourished through the squeaky bum time of the Premiership home straight, having seen off an array of continental footballing superpowers in the Champs League, we are now faced with this, the FA Cup final.

The treble is on. Really. And do you know what? The King footballing sap is still rising. There's still some room for improvement, football-wise, Kev-wise, I admit that. But my deep footballing sense is that today will be the day of days for me.

The Vertu rings. Boves. Excellent. I take it.

'Just been fitted out for my wedding wear, Kevin.'

'Oh yeah, how is it?'

'Not sure, Kevin, it seems a bit…'

'A bit what?'

'Humiliating. Why do I have to wear it?'

'*All* the guests will be wearing shell suits Boves. Sas doesn't want to be upstaged.'

'And what about you? You want your best man dressed like a fool?'

'I...'

'Look, you're losing it. Your head's been turned. You spoken to Gravesy?'

'No.'

'You should. I know what he did, but you hurt him. Call him. I don't want to take sides, Kevin.'

Boves hangs up and I stare at the phone. Can I really call Gravesy, after he sold those snaps? Can I really do that? And what's that stuff from Boves about taking sides? But there's no time to think because we're out on the field, and for once mule-headed Spanish super coach Rafael Benitez has put out his best Liverpool team. Doll-faced European Championship winner Fernando Torres is out here. As is Gerrard, and I swear his hair has climbed further down his forehead since I saw him at the Argentina game. Is that his secret, the key to his game?

No matter.

We kick off and the crowd is giving it the big one, or at least I think it is, because I can't hear them too well. The architects must have done that deliberately, made sure the crowd noise and atmosphere dissipated within the huge, soulless bowl of Wembley. And it's professional of them, it's appreciated, because you don't want all these zone thirteen million cunts, who've parked their Fiestas in Hillingdon then cattle-trucked it in on the tube, being too close to you, do you? You don't want the stench of civilian all over you while you're engaging in high-level football science. Which I am, as I rob their monstrous Argentinian midfield enforcer Javier Mascherano and slide-rule it across to our rangy Togolese water-carrier, Gilchrist Eyodema.

Using the esoteric art of Tibetan Tumo meditation, tantric master Wim Hof stood encased in one thousand five hundred

334

and fifty pounds of ice, for seventy-two minutes.

Gilchrist Eyodema feeds Wally de Groot on our left and he makes good ground towards their by-line as I, myself, Kev, hurtle towards their box, receiving it nice on the edge of the D and making time for myself before curling one wide of their left post.

Shit, Kev. Wasteful.

Needed my shooting head on for that one.

Still. With his bare hands, Luxembourger George Christian bent three hundred and sixty-eight nails of a seven-millimetre diameter in the space of one hour.

They come at us through flame-haired Dutch international Dirk Kuyt, who powers through the middle, before being dispossessed by our dozy-but-gifted centre back Ash Hughes, who feeds Ali el-Masri in the middle third.

Ashvita Furman holds the world record for underwater rope jumps, achieving a near-impossible total of seven hundred and thirty-eight in one hour. Big lungs, that boy. Big engine.

As have I, but despite this game being end-to-end, there's a distinct lack of penetration, shots-on-target-wise. Clear-cut chances are not emerging, being blocked as they are by the defensive buses parked at both ends of the ground. And not even legendary Kev, who so recently was guided by the Jedi powers of Keegan, can seem to find a way around – or indeed under – their defence. This one's got penalties written all over it.

In big black marker pen.

And so it is. The 128th FA Cup will be decided by spot kicks. The competition billed as the most romantic in the world by TV channels too skint to afford the rights for better competitions has come to this.

The ball. The spot. The keeper.

One man. One shot. One Kev.

The treble is hingeing on this. By its hinges.

It's three all, each side having missed just the one, and I take the ball from the ref and Kev towards the area. I place the ball of glory on the spot of destiny. Then I piss about with it, twiddling it around a bit for absolutely no reason. As is the custom on these occasions. The crowd are going ape shit, their passionate cries totally neutralized by the hollow, muted atmosphere of this world class s-o-t-a stadium. The most expensive stadium in the world. And in Europe.

I look at their keeper, egg-headed spot kick specialist Pepe Reina. I give him the eyes, the 'you've got absolutely no idea where this is going' look, which I have perfected, over the years, in the bevelled Rocco Verre mirror which hangs now in my galleried reception hall.

But which way shall I put this potentially treble-cementing kick?

On his third attempt at the task, Georgian strength specialist Lasha Pataraia pulled a seven thousand seven hundred and thirty-four kilo military helicopter over a twenty-six metre course in Tblisi. Using only his ear. His *left* ear.

That's it. It's decided. I'm shooting left.

Reina will never guess that. The chances of the Iberian shot-stopper diving the correct way because he knows the world ear-pulling record was achieved using the left ear are minuscule. But then again, he is the consummate professional, and maybe he does know. Maybe Reina is well up on his knowledge of extreme feats of ear strength. You wouldn't put it past the man who is known as a goalkeeper in his home town of Spain. Maybe he does know. Or maybe he can smell it in my feet, that I'll go left I mean, because of Lasha Pataraia's record-fucking use of the left ear.

Shit.

Shit.

But didn't the Georgian ex-wrestling champ and extreme strongman – after declaring himself happy and satisfied with his left ear strength – state that he intended to repeat the feat later?

But with double the weight. And using both ears. Yes, both ears.

Neither the left, nor the right.

It's decided then. I'm going down the middle.

Second-guess that, Pepe Reina.

Right. I show the keeper the ink, then I Kev slowly forwards, throwing mini body shimmies this way and that, so as to upset the Spaniard's shot stop radar. I absolutely foot shag the ball forward, straight down the throat of the goal. Not that it has a throat. Because it's a goal.

And it *is* a goal.

It's in. And where's Reina? He's gone left.

I guessed correctly. The keeper *was* up to speed on his ear strength record knowledge. But he's been outfoxed. By Kev.

I want to run to the crowd, spunk Kevish footballism all over them, but there is an etiquette in these shoot-outs and Liverpool have one kick left. A kick which if made will level things up. A kick which if missed will hand us the treble. On a plate. With mash and gravy all around it. Carried into a Tudor-period dining hall by a chimpanzee waiter in a wetsuit.

I control myself, and return to the centre circle, receiving plaudits from my teammates, and then joining them in the traditional chorus-line formation of the penalty-taking side.

Their helium-voiced central defender Jamie Carragher strides out of the centre circle to take their last kick.

Chuck Wilson of Mildenhall, Texas, survived for three hours and seventeen minutes with a live cobra clamped to his nose, the deadly snake dangling from his right nostril for the duration of this pointless act of daring.

The *right* nostril. The right. It's got to be.

I lift my arms from the shoulders of our Turkish central defender Baki Ozan on one side, and Brazilian World Cup winner Alvar on the other. I wave my arms in the air, trying to catch the eye of our Uruguayan netsman Anselmo. Which I do. I point to the right.

'Carragher's going right,' I mouth to our keeper, not that he can hear me above the morgue-like din of the wonderfully soulless new Wembley.

I jump up. I point right. I am going a bit mental.

Anselmo seems to get it. He gives me a little nod.

Carragher places the ball, and the Liverpool-born, ex-Everton fan walks back and then takes his run-up, weakly and un-Kevishly hitting the ball to the right, to which Anselmo responds, easily palming the ball round the stick.

Oh Kev. The treble.

Our footballing chorus line moves forward as one man, high-kicking down-field, as in the thrilling dance routines of *Chicago* the musical, currently playing at the Cambridge Theatre, London, and featuring Tiffany Graves in the role of Velma Kelly.

We rush to Anselmo and engulf him in a multimillion-pound footballing group fuck.

The treble, Kev. The treble.

The pots. The pans. The silverware.

The treble. Which is like the double. Only there's one more.

After the leaping, and the inelegant and juddery chest slides, we take the cup. The FA Cup. We take it romantically and then we give our interviews to the channel which could not afford the TV rights for the Premiership or the Champions League, and we wibble sentimentally about the joy of the competition and what it means to us, without, of course, referring to our monumental win bonuses.

We're in the changing rooms now and the lads are spraying around the case of 1989 Troillard Brut Grande Reserve, which Bahta left for them. And I'm staring at the bottle of Ben Shaw's dandelion and burdock which he left for me.

The boys are changing up, they're all heading on to the Funky Buddha Lounge in Mayfair for a mash-up, but – weirdly – I'm not into it. I feel tired. More than tired, actually. I feel lost.

I change slowly into my beige, two-button Claiborne by John Bartlett suit, my Alejandro Ingelmo metallic leather trainers and my pink, Junya Wantanabe shirt with tartan trim.

After the boys have all headed off, Neeskins comes into the changing room. 'Kevin, you played very well today.'

'Course.'

'OK, Kevin. I was young once too. How do you feel?'

'I feel nothing.'

'Good. You could be a great player, you know?'

'Yeah.'

'Kevin, do you want to go for a drink?'

'I don't know what I want to do, to be honest, Mr Neeskins.'

'OK, I understand.'

Neeskins nods and walks towards the changing-room door and opens it, but before he leaves, he stops in the doorway and turns. 'I haven't told the squad yet, but Mr Bahta's just fired me.'

'What?'

'His nephew will be managing the team next season.'

'Fuck's sake.'

'And you'll be his Captain.'

Later on, I'm in the Bents, looking at the Wembley arch in the rear-view and heading into town. Edgware. Marylebone. Marble Arch. I do all that.

I still the Bents off Park Lane and slip *Legacy*, Boyz II Men's greatest hits collection, into the Acura ELS surround sound.

Sas texts but I do not reply. Nan calls but I do not take her.

There's no congrats from Boves, though.

I sit in the Bents with Boyz II Men on repeat. I feel so...I don't know what I feel. And surprisingly, it's not the Colly thing that's getting to me, the whole friend-slaughter aspect of the day; nor is it the Gravesy or the all new Boves shit, even. No. I do not even dwell on Boves' hard words. Not at all. Because now that I've bagged the treble, those are the concerns of the little man, they are yesterday's woes, and it's the humpty, the career, that's what's doing my cake; it's acclimatizing to my astonishing new football level, coming to terms with being a Kev-sized footballing colossus, that's what's spinning my head. Because what now? I'm the Captain of the Prem champs. And after the treble, then what? Another treble?

I don't know. I feel lost somehow, desolate. Like I'm in need of guidance.

When it's dark I leave the Bents and walk down to Hyde Park

Corner, up Knightsbridge and on to the Brompton Road. I walk slowly towards Harrods and then stand outside the main doors, which are now closed. I stare at my reflection in the plate glass of the retail cathedral.

Thousands and thousands of exclusive products in there, in one building. Enough high-end consumer items for many lifetimes, for many lifestyles.

Enough for the Premiership. And the Champions League.

Enough for the FA Cup.

There's enough consumer satisfaction in there for the treble.

For a treble of trebles. Even.

I look beyond my reflection into the retail paradise within, which seems, at that very moment, like the centre of the world itself.

'Three of everything,' I say to Harrods. 'I'll take three of fucking everything.'

Better. Much, much better.

three and in

Just sent an email from Colly's laptop. To the red-tops. And the filth.

A full confession: You'll never catch me. I am the killer. Shit like that.

Gave them enough unreleased details of the killings so they'd have to believe. That'll do it. Especially as Bahta's pulling a few levers here and there to make sure the blame sticks to Colly.

Enjoyed it actually, the old scribing. Good writer, I am. Way with the words. And I set the record straight as well. Told them that they aren't football murders, that all of the killing was pure vigilante work, in the service of consumer protection, and that I – in this mail meaning Colly, but really, you know, actually me – will continue to stand guard, to shield the rank and file civvy from consumer exploitation.

That ought to stop all this football murder talk, so next time, when again I am forced to crusade, people will get it, they'll see it as the work of a service industry saviour, a sort of darkly righteous twin of Nicky Campbell.

Anyway. All done now.

Been some season actually, the 08-09, if you think about it. Squeezed a few things in. Has it changed me? Football-wise, I am of course a living god, which naturally helps fanny-wise. And cash-wise as well things are different, under the Syrian's guidance, and now with Bahta more than doubling the King basic.

So yeah, yeah, there's been changes. But really, deep down in my vigilante heart, I'm still the same old Kev. Got a few less living mates, got a few million more fans, but that's here nor there. I remain fundamentally Kev.

And you know, now I need to relax, unwind. Because next season I'll be playing straight through, from Prem kick-off in August 09, right the way through, no doubt, to captaining the World Cup-winning Three Lions in July 2010. Long season, that is. In fact, mother nature-wise, it's actually four of the fuckers.

But, yep, I need to relax. And I am, actually. Because this is the life. It really is. Having a kick-about on my own back lawn. Not a care in the world. No pressure. No pots and pans on the line. Just like the old days in the park, when you were kids and you played for fun.

Stag night, see. Could have gone anywhere: Barbados, Vegas, Míkonos. You name it. But no. I wanted the King stag at my sensational modern manor house with breathtaking rural views. The boys hadn't seen the gaff yet and I wanted to show off a bit.

Sas is staying the night before our nuptials at a hotel, as is traditional.

Nan's asleep upstairs. I knew she wouldn't last the distance, but I wanted her on the stag anyway. So right now it's just me, Four Chins, and Gravesy.

Gravesy who I admit may seem a surprise stag invite, given a few recent things that may have happened, and Gravesy, truth be told, who I had to drive over and fetch. But he's here in the end, give him that.

Le Chins is in goal. Not that he's taking the task too seriously. And why should he? This game's just for fun. He's slumped in the anodized aluminium Luma contemporary chair that I carried from the pool terrace and placed on the goal line. Not that there is a line. Just a pair of Copa Mundial boots we're using for posts.

Gravesy's out in the field with me. We're playing three and in.

Not that Gravesy's got much chance of beating me. Even if I hadn't cut his head off.

Which may sound a bit funny, but you know, the human head is quite footballish, shape-wise, if not weight-wise, and I wanted to see how it would stand up to actual play.

I peer down at Gravesy's head, his dead fishy eyes glassing up towards me, and I feel so sad that he betrayed me, a treble winner. I place my toes on his forehead and roll him back towards me, flip him upwards on my instep, dink him up to my knee, juggle him once, let him fall and then leather his pasty Aussie head, right-footed, towards the goal.

Gravesy's bonce swerves in the air. Which is to be expected. I mean, the human head is not completely spherical. And it is actually much heavier towards the skull area than it is towards the grizzled neck zone, and so does not have a true flight.

The shot easily beats Billy. Who just sits there. Which is not entirely his fault, I mean him being so dead and everything. And even if he wasn't he'd be hard pressed to stop it. Since I cut his hands off I mean. Hard to get a pair of keeper's gloves to fit those stumps, I expect. Shame really, but then Billy knew way too much. Anyway, that's my third goal, which means I'm in.

'Come on, Chins,' I shout over to him. 'It's my turn in nets.'

But he doesn't reply. Which is a bit off, this being my stag night. And what is also off is that I'm the wanker who's always got to go and fetch the ball.

I'm getting a bit bored. I've had enough now.

One of the great things about this house is that with its spacious, elegant garden, I can pursue my hobby without driving over to Nan's every time I get the urge. I walk over to Gravesy and Billy, drag them over, and start to bury them, but when I'm nearly finished, I spot something, something in the corner of Kev's eye. Was that a twitch of Nan's curtain? She up already? No. She'll not be nosing. Anyway. I go inside.

Big day tomorrow, and while I'm angry that Boves has pulled out, meaning fucking buff Marco will end up as best man, it's certainly still on course to be the wedding of the century. Early night then, I think, because even the likes of your Kevin Kings need to kip early doors sometimes.

Still. I check the Franck Muller Long Island timepiece. Not too late. Got a bit of time left to spend with Nan. I go up to her room to see if she wants a quick spin on the Wii.

I stop outside the door and wait. She's talking to someone, but I can't hear what she's saying. I step inside her room. Nan's stood up in the en-suite's doorway. Maybe it was her I saw, twitching at the curtain while I buried the boys. She's got a mobile in her hand, the Gresso Lady Diamond with scarlet titanium alloy that I bought her for Mother's Day.

'...I think there's been a murder...' she says, all hushed and petrified, into the phone.

'Nan,' I say, and step towards her, my hand outstretched to relieve her of the mobes. 'That's enough now.'